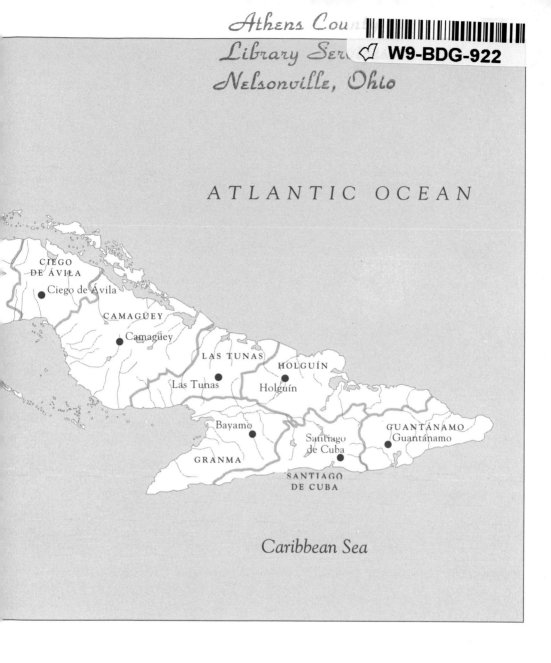

ATLANTIC OCEAN

CIEGO
DE ÁVILA
Ciego de Ávila

CAMAGÜEY
Camagüey

LAS TUNAS
Las Tunas

HOLGUÍN
Holguín

Bayamo

GUANTÁNAMO
Guantánamo

Santiago
de Cuba

GRANMA

SANTIAGO
DE CUBA

Caribbean Sea

CUBA
(with inset detail of Havana)

SINS
OF THE
FATHERS

SINS
OF THE
FATHERS

A NOVEL

John Blackthorn

WILLIAM MORROW AND COMPANY, INC.
NEW YORK

Copyright © 1999 by Art Tarmon, Inc.

Grateful acknowledgment is made for material from
The Kennedy Tapes: Inside the White House During the Cuban Missile Crisis,
edited by Ernest R. May and Philip D. Zelikow (Cambridge, MA: Belknap Press, Harvard University Press, 1997), used on pp. 111–113, 150–152, 177–179.

It is the policy of William Morrow and Company, and its imprints and affiliates, recognizing the importance of preserving what has been written, to print the books we publish on acid-free paper, and we exert our best efforts to that end.

Library of Congress Cataloging-in-Publication Data
Blackthorn, John.
Sins of the fathers : a novel / John Blackthorn.—1st ed.
p.   cm.
ISBN 0–688–16191–X (acid-free paper)
I. Title.
PS3552.L34286S56   1999
813'.54—dc21   98-24575
CIP

Printed in the United States of America

First Edition

1 2 3 4 5 6 7 8 9 10

BOOK DESIGN BY OKSANA KUSHNIR

www.williammorrow.com

We are children of our age,
it's a political age.

—WISLAWA SZYMBORSKA

SINS
OF THE
FATHERS

PROLOGUE

There was a knock as ephemeral as a dream on the decrepit door, a door that admitted almost as much light and air as it kept out. Then it came again, and the lone occupant of the narrow, spartan room struggled to escape the cocoon of sleep. He imagined at first that he was back in Salinas and tried to remember if this was Sunday. Fuddled, he wondered vaguely if his sermon was prepared and groaned at the impression that he might have to wing it yet again.

Then the knock again and the urgent whispered voice, "Señor, señor. Por favor. For God's sake. Let me in. Quickly!"

Now shocked awake by the desperate voice, the man shuffled to the door, remembering where he was and thinking, oddly, how relieved he was that today there would be no sermon. He peered through the widest of several cracks in the door, saw an eye wide with fear a few inches from his own, and heard a voice softly hiss, "Quick, please!" There was sufficient predawn light to see a stark pale face outside.

The mysterious visitor was through the door as fast as it was opened. Gasping, he leaned forward, hands on knees, searching for breath. He waved one hand behind him, unnecessarily, for the door to be closed.

Down the street a car squealed angrily through a turn. Headlights flashed and running feet approached. More lights, handheld, swung back and forth, searching out dark corners. The prey took a few quick steps toward the rumpled cot in the corner of the room. He pulled the thin blanket so that it hung almost to the floor. Then, putting a finger to his lips, he nodded, lay down, and slid himself across the rough floor planks until he was completely under the cot.

"Get back in bed," he whispered.

The tall thin occupant of the room ran both hands through his bushy hair, then gradually stretched his lanky frame the length of the cot. He felt a lump in the middle of his back. It was the intruder's hands, folded at belt level. The hidden figure whispered, "Sorry."

"You're him, aren't you?" the host said. He spoke softly. "We met at the rally last week. You're Yankee, too."

They were in a two-room flat in a row of houses given to foreigners committed to supporting the revolution. Some taught school, some worked in clinics, and some cut sugarcane. Only the hardiest were still there. By now, the glamour had vanished like air from a burst balloon. Only the most committed stayed on.

Outside the heavy footsteps receded. There were probably six or eight searchers. But fear made it seem like more to the hidden men. Beneath the cot, the only response was a grunt and the still heavy breathing of the prey.

"How did you know where to find me?" the lean man asked.

Beneath the cot the voice said, "I followed you. After the rally." For a while he was silent. "I thought I might have to find you sometime." Then he added, with a husky chuckle, "Besides, you wrote down your street and number . . . remember? . . . on my hand."

"You mean, have to find me sometime—like now."

"Yes."

"You didn't want to find me. You thought you'd need a place to hide . . . with a sympathetic Yankee."

"Yes." There was silence. "Prescott, right?" He heard a murmur. "Thanks."

"What did you do?" Prescott said. "Why did you think you'd need to hide?"

The only sound beneath the cot was breathing. After a while, the intruder said, "You're a priest. That's good. You can probably help me."

Prescott muttered, "Why do I think you are not speaking spiritually?"

"Do you have a collar?"

"Yes. Of course."

"Do you wear it?"

"No. Los comandantes don't like it. They did in the early days. It showed Catholic solidarity with the revolution. Now only if there are foreign journalists at some demonstration against imperialism, then they want to see it. Rome against capitalism. Sort of a joke against the Pope, don't you think?"

Prescott got up and moved silently to the door. He peered through each of several cracks, then listened. Beyond the thin curtain across the single window the sky was lightening perceptibly. "Stay where you are," Prescott said. "They're not done yet." Outside, the doors of vehicles could be heard opening and closing. "You're not one of the originals. If you'd come down with the rest of us . . . in '60 or '61 . . . I'd know you." He returned to sit on the cot and noticed his guest's pungent odor. Fear, and he hadn't bathed in days. On the run. Suddenly, Prescott was deadened by a thought . . . more precisely, a revelation. "You're a spy."

"Shhh," the intruder whispered.

"You're CIA," Prescott muttered woefully. "If you're CIA, then we're both dead."

The prey said, "Even if I were, it will do you no good to know it. So, let's say I'm not."

"It's about the missiles, isn't it? Of course. You're down here to find out about the missiles."

"You don't know anything," the man hissed threateningly. "Do you hear me?"

"I know you're in this room. That's enough to put me away for a long time. What I know or don't know doesn't matter now, does it? You might as well be Allen Dulles."

"When traffic starts outside, I'll be gone. Just give me a few more minutes."

Prescott said, "Where do you go?"

The man sighed. "Father, you don't listen well, do you? The less you know, the better for you." After a silence he said, "My job's done. I can't do any more. My ride's coming for me ton—"

Prescott said, "Shhhh," then moved quickly toward the door. Outside there were shouts of anger followed by pleas and protests. "They're still around. They're taking someone away. Maybe now they'll leave." Then he said, "Did you have anyone with you?"

Prescott took the man's silence for a denial. A car pulled away.

The man said, "Wait," as if he knew danger still stood watch outside the door. As if sensing doom, he uttered a desperate message to be delivered in a future lifetime, sought a blessing, and then lay still in silence. Then there came an explosive pounding on a door that could withstand the assault only brief seconds. The door flew off its rusty hinges and hit the plank floor like a cannon shot. What seemed like a full platoon of men, some in uniform, some in the street clothes of the security forces, were in the room faster than Prescott could come off the cot. He had only half-risen when the burly man first in the door shoved him backward with both hands. Prescott's thin frame sailed back five feet and hit the wall with a crack that sounded like a broken back, but it was instead a thin plank on the interior wall.

The burly man signaled toward the cot, and three uniformed young soldiers heaved it up and onto Prescott, still lying stunned against the wall. The figure under the cot came up swinging and caught one of the young soldiers with a quick right cross before a rifle butt knocked him to the floor. He struggled to get up, but the burly security officer kicked him in the ribs. He went down with an explosive grunt. The security man kicked him again and again. Struggling to emerge from behind the cot and the thin blanket, Prescott could hear his visitor's ribs give way as they cracked audibly under the barrage of kicks. The fugitive groaned but made no other sound.

Suddenly, Prescott felt strong hands lifting him up, and he was being carried out of his tiny flat into the street. His semiconscious visitor, groaning again with the rough movement, was dragged out ahead of him. Police and security officials filled the narrow street outside as a surreal dawn lit the tableau. Though his neighbors dared not appear, he knew they were watching, terrified, behind imperceptibly parted curtains.

Still trying to get air into lungs almost collapsed by his impact with the wall, Prescott was thrown headfirst into the back of a black government sedan. As the burly man pulled him up into the seat, Prescott had a moment's glance out the back window of the car. He saw the open back door of a long black hearselike vehicle. And he saw four plainclothes security men, one on each arm and leg, throw his visitor headfirst into the back. The door was slammed shut.

Prescott spent almost three years in hard labor, and he never saw or heard from the man again. But, of course, he hadn't expected to.

PART ONE

September 1998

1 The oppressive heat and dust had a kind of fabulous quality to it, swirling about the weaving antique car and transforming the passing countryside—part decaying suburb, part primitive farm-scape—into a kind of impressionist vision. To a visitor unfamiliar with the area, the experience was dreamlike. Here was an earlier place preserved like a run-down museum with none of the plastic sparkle of his own country.

McLemore edged forward slightly in the front passenger seat, letting the faint breeze created by the car's lurching motion lift the back of his sweat-soaked shirt. Next to him, the mute driver watched the road with one eye and, occasionally, his passenger with the other. The car swerved awkwardly to avoid a spindly pony cart driven by a child that suddenly appeared in the outbound lane. In the back, the only other passenger, a disdainfully attractive woman, stared furiously out the window.

The American, tongue-tied by an unfamiliar language, tried to think of something appropriate to say but, after rejecting a series of clichés, chose to maintain the tense silence. He cursed himself for his parochialism. Wickedly, the car gained speed even as the highway became a road and the slow-moving traffic increased in density. The challenge of maneuvering seemed to be the driver's only motivation.

The more McLemore thought about it, confronted now with the blunt reality of his circumstance, the more he believed himself to be on a fool's errand. Desperate to resuscitate a floundering academic career and lacking any other goal or purpose, he had greedily latched onto a meager foundation grant and set about to plow old ground. The grant appeared like driftwood in a fast-moving stream, and he miraculously negotiated a sabbatical from his cold-eyed, tyrannical dean eager anyway to be rid of him.

It had all happened so fast that he was having difficulty remembering how he got here.

He was doomed to fail, again, he thought. There were now a torrent of books, monographs, and articles flooding both the academic and popular marketplaces on the Cold War's startling disappearance. And the Cuban missile crisis, its most dramatic moment, seemed a magnet to the countless political historians picking and sorting like lethargic vultures through the rubble of the Cold War's collapse. What he expected to learn and write about the missile crisis, McLemore hadn't a clue. As with the rest of his life, he would worry about that when the time came. In the meantime, he had brought himself to Cuba, ground zero of the missile crisis, and in many ways the fulcrum of the Cold War itself, in search of—what?

Between honks of the antique Chevy's horn, McLemore cleared his throat and ventured, to the silent woman in the backseat, "Are we out of the rainy season now?"

"More or less," she said presently. Then silence. Then, "It will end soon. But of course, *los huracanes*—some hurricanes—will come." After a while she added, "But it doesn't matter much to us. The seasons. It is all pretty much the same here."

McLemore turned sideways in the front seat and, hunching his shoulders apologetically, said: "I'm really sorry, but I didn't understand your name when we met at the hotel. I'm afraid I'm terrible at names . . . Ms. . . . ?"

"It is Santiago . . . like the city. But you should call me 'Trinidad' . . . also like the city. It is my first name. We like first names here."

"It must be difficult to be two cities at once," McLemore observed. He sounded more ironic than he intended.

The result was briefly achieved. A reluctant smile momentarily brushed across her disdainful features.

"Do you do this, ah, *have* to do this much? I mean accompany people like me around?" McLemore asked.

"It's my job," she offered. Her tone was officious. She looked at her watch. "We should be there soon," she said, as if to relieve her own boredom. McLemore continued to look pleasantly into the hostile space in the backseat, inviting more. Then she said, "You will probably not be able to see everything . . . everything you have asked to see. It's the military. These are military places. There are lots of rules." Answering an unasked question, she said: "You can take pictures, but only of the not-military places."

Señora (or should it be Señorita?) Santiago had been McLemore's first pleasant surprise in Cuba. As she moved to the backseat of the government car at the hotel, to give him the front-seat view of the countryside, he had glimpsed—too briefly—a tall, lithe figure clad in a simple, lightweight beige pantsuit. He presumed haute couture to be beyond the reach of government employees in poor countries. But his shepherdess, he quickly decided, was the kind of woman who improved the look of any clothes she chose to wear. Her brusque self-confidence made him assume that she calculated the success the beige had in setting off her flawless light skin, itself punctuated by very dark, almost black, brunette hair, eyebrows, and lashes. Her shoulder-length hair was pulled straight back and tied with a matching beige bow. Her brightly painted mouth was wide. He imagined her teeth would be very white against that backdrop—that is, if she ever chose to smile. Her nose was prominent but thin. And then, there were those eyes.

Swiveling more often than he needed to, as he pretended to survey the passing urban, then suburban, then rural scenery, he stole sideways glances at those gleaming dark brown eyes, themselves promising . . . treachery? . . . or . . . who could know? Much too soon to be thinking those thoughts, McLemore mused. Abstractly, he decided to make Señorita Trinidad Santiago's humanization a side project. Anyway, he thought, he was better at that than at researching modern history. Then he mused, isn't "modern history" an oxymoron and, if so, didn't that make him a walking oxymoron?

Like a burst of machine-gun fire, Trinidad rattled some Spanish at the driver. Fueled by a spurt of machismo, the car briefly retaliated by speeding up, then began to slow down as it approached a ragged queue of people strung along the road seeking any means of transport. As the day progressed, the temperature and humidity elevated, leaving McLemore, a stranger to the climate, feeling increasingly soggy and slightly cross. He wished he had followed Trinidad's advice at the hotel that morning and brought a liter of *gaseoso*.

After they left Havana well behind, the vegetation became more verdant and lush, tamed only by irregularly shaped cultivated fields. The landscape rolled in swells, as if a giant ocean heaved beneath it. He pointed, but before he could ask she said, "Cane fields." Her preoccupation precluded any effort he might make to stimulate a seminar on the Cuban sugar industry. Most of the uncultivated areas were slopes too steep to plant and were covered with thick, rich green shrubs and bushes with an occasional royal palm resembling a tall natural umbrella. Despite the old car's jerks, jolts, and unpredictable bursts of speed, McLemore thought he could glimpse the occasional bright colors of what seemed to be a vast natural aviary of exotic birds. The birds are free, but the people are not, he thought.

Before launching himself on this venture, McLemore had given little thought to Cuba as a place. He had seen the *National Geographic* pictures, picked up some brochures, recalled a mad week in St. Bart's after college. But he had no real sense of Cuba. Now, suddenly immersed, he was slightly stunned by its careless beauty, the immediacy of life without a comfortable commercial facade, its primitive and earthy context. It seemed to him a kind of Caribbean Brigadoon. And though a long way from the type of idealized paradise most of his countrymen sought, Cuba seemed to have a simple ease he thought he could adapt to without much training.

They were nearing their destination of Bejucal, a small town no more than thirty or forty kilometers south of Havana but more than an hour traveling time because of the chaotic traffic on the climb into the hills. It was approaching midday. The car, with Trinidad Santiago, had arrived almost an hour late at the hotel. There had been no explanation. McLemore would soon learn that this was part of a cultural pattern. It would take the length of his stay before he began to shed his Yankee obsessiveness and actually begin to enjoy this liberation from punctuality and his introduction to abstract time.

"Do you know Bejucal?" McLemore asked his guide.

"Yes, I know it. Of course. It is close to Havana."

"No, I mean what happened there in '62 . . . during the missile . . . the crisis time." McLemore suddenly felt awkward, as if raising a delicate personal subject. Never mention rope in the house of a man who has just been hanged.

"Yes, of course. It was a critical place. But secret . . . highly protected." McLemore thought, Do I sound like this when I'm beginning a lecture? She continued in the formal, guided-tour tone. "We know this is where many critical materials, weapons, were kept. There were many Russian military around this place. We always knew from that when a place was important. The more Russians, the more *importante*."

The car bumped and clanked off the main road onto a narrower but equally congested road headed slightly east and climbing now into the hills south of Havana. The driver furtively checked McLemore's reaction, already calculating the possibility of a clandestine tip.

"The Russians protected us then. They stopped another invasion by the CIA and the *batistianas*. The whole plan worked, you see. Even though they took the missiles out, Khrushchev forced Kennedy to promise to leave us alone. That was all we wanted anyway." McLemore thought he saw a slight triumphant smile. "They . . . how do you say . . . guarantee us our liberty from the Yanquis."

This is going to be a long day, McLemore thought. Then he remembered . . . it would be a whole week. Maybe, eventually, more. He had to find out if Señorita Trinidad, herself clearly from some central ministry of propaganda, would be along the whole while, providing the official party line. Ah well, he should have expected as much. You take the bitter with the bitter. The side project of humanization had rudely taken on a lot of heavy political baggage.

"Let me guess," he said. "In 1962, you would have been . . ." Then, applying mathematics to diplomacy with lightning speed, he said, "You would not have even been born yet." He looked squarely at her. "Tell me how old you are. You aren't more than thirty-two or thirty-three. Right?"

Momentarily thrown off balance by his bluntness, Trinidad proudly replied, "I was born in April 1961." Her smile was ferocious. My God, McLemore thought, during the Bay of Pigs invasion.

"And you, Professor McLemore," she asked, "what is your age?"

"A few more *años* than you," he said. "Maybe *seis* or *siete más*." His feeble attempts at pidgin Spanish clearly were not impressive to her.

As the car weaved from side to side up the winding road to Bejucal, Trinidad consulted some written directions and fired off a burst of Spanish commands to the seemingly heedless driver.

McLemore said, "According to documents released last year by the Russians, Bejucal was a little more than just a weapons storage depot *muy importante*. This is the place the Russians stored *all* their nuclear warheads during that October. They brought their cargo ship into Mariel and transported enough warheads to Bejucal to wage a pretty good nuclear war.

They apparently had already constructed some heavy-duty bunkers to store something important. Whether they had nuclear weapons in mind at the time remains to be seen." He was suddenly aware that he had, unconsciously, adopted the professional lecture tone used only moments ago by Trinidad and used by him routinely in his college classroom.

"Anyway," he concluded lightheartedly, "it's a starting point on the magical military tour of Cuba in 1962."

She said, "Is that what you are doing here? What kind of magic do you think you will find here?"

Sensing the sudden flare of her fury, McLemore backed off. "Sorry, Trinidad—you said I may call you 'Trinidad,' didn't you?—I didn't mean to be frivolous. I am here on serious business. I hope to find out what happened here thirty-six years ago . . . why every side almost blundered into disaster. How could it all have happened? What mistakes were made? Who made the mistakes? Why did they make such serious mistakes? Is there anything to learn from it?" After a pause, "I'm a teacher. I'm supposed to be in the learning business."

Trinidad said, "Do you people *del norte* believe everything is a business . . . even learning?"

"Sorry again. It's a figure of speech. I don't mean business, I mean profession."

"Are you good at it, this professoring?"

"No," he said before thinking. "I mean, I don't consider myself a particularly good teacher. It's an art, not a science. I'm not an artist. The best teachers are the best learners, and I don't know very much. The older I get, the less I really know."

"But this is wisdom itself, *Profesor* McLemore. To know you do not know."

The driver, abruptly extricating himself from monitoring this conversation, pointed up ahead and tossed a soft-spoken Spanish query over his shoulder. *"Sí, señor,"* Trinidad replied, then ordered the driver to proceed forward around the hillside, then to the right, then farther ahead to the left. They were entering the Bejucal military compound containing the bunkers that formerly housed the warheads meant for the United States.

In the oppressive heat, McLemore felt a slight chill. When he saw what he had come to see, then what would he know that he had not known before? Would there be some magic of history in that empty concrete tomb? What were the Soviets thinking when they unloaded the lorries from Mariel? They had to know their cargo. Even more interestingly, what did they think when, ninety days later, they loaded the same cargo on the same lorries and sent it back home? Suddenly, for the first time, he gave a blessing to his dean and the foundation director. This might be interesting after all.

What McLemore guessed, more by his age than his meager decorations, to be a junior military officer waited for them in the shade of a lonely tree. McLemore found himself remarking the patience of these people. On the other hand, where else did they have to go? They unloaded from the steaming car, and the officer gave Trinidad a vague salute, a polite *"Buenos dias, señora,"* and motioned them into an enclosure surrounded by a heavily rusted barbed fence and, inside the enclosure, toward a reinforced steel door. Immediately through the door a dozen steps led down into a cavernous, thick concrete bunker. Over its top was an irregular covering of cracked earth to a depth of two to three feet. Some desultory weeds held most of the dirt in place, but much had already blown eastward toward Guantánamo years ago. The officer had a flashlight, which appeared to be the same vintage as the Chevy that brought them. Following its beam, McLemore could barely discern a series of chambers, most empty but some with large dilapidated crates and metal frames.

As they walked down the ominously dark, low-ceilinged corridor fronting these chambers, McLemore could make out Trinidad and the young officer conducting a rapid-fire but hushed conversation. The officer kept his light away from the crates as, after walking the length of the corridor, he turned to lead them back to the sunlight. McLemore was in no hurry. Despite the scampering of large, noisy rodents behind the crates and just beyond the circumference of the light's beam, this was the coolest place he had found in Cuba. He tried briefly to imagine what might have happened if the power struggle had taken a worse turn three and a half decades before, if some commander had gotten jumpy, if some message had been misunderstood. As he stood where all that hostile energy had been concentrated closer to the United States than at any time in history, his imagination quavered.

"Could you ask him what is stored here now?" McLemore said to Trinidad.

"*Nada.* Nothing, he says," she replied without asking. "There is some old military equipment left here, but it is too rustic for use."

Rusty or rustic? McLemore wondered. Or both?

"There is some military equipment in this compound. That is why we cannot go farther beyond this place," she said. "But this is the storage place for the warheads in 1962." She sounded mildly proud of that fact. "It is interesting to me also," she volunteered. "I have never been here. It must be a historical place . . . *uno puesto histórico.*"

McLemore felt glad the day was not entirely wasted for her. He had shown her something new in her own country. "Is this the whole thing then?" he asked.

"*Completamente,*" responded the young officer, clearly needing no translator.

McLemore felt disappointed and discouraged. He was standing, in a symbolic way, at the epicenter of his study, the place where the nuclear explosives that could have launched World War III were stored, and there seemed to be less here than met the eye. He felt like a child given a cheap toy for Christmas who knew it to be cheap.

"*Muchas gracias, señor . . . ah, capitán?*"

"No, he is a lieutenant," said Trinidad without checking.

He led them back to their Chevy baking in the sun and proffered the same limp salute as the driver reluctantly relinquished the lieutenant's small spot of shade under the lonely tree. He had seen all he came to see, and all he could see, in less than half an hour.

They started back down from the hills north toward Havana, Trinidad now with some of the morning's fury baked out of her, and McLemore wondering what there was to do now. There were the R-12 missile sites near San Cristóbal and Los Palacios to visit, perhaps tomorrow. He could try to go six hundred kilometers to the east to visit the R-12 missile sites planned for Calabazar de Sagua north of Santa Clara. He had been granted permission to research some Foreign Ministry files on the period, presumably containing records very carefully edited and culled. All in all he had allocated a week for this visit and, depending on the outcome of the research and his impressions at the end of the week, had registered an open-ended request with the Cuban government for one or two future visits.

He had never had a research grant before. He had never even taken a real sabbatical. He didn't quite know what was expected of him when he had to make some kind of report to the foundation and to the college at the end of the term period. He knew he had promised to produce a publishable paper in consideration of his grant. But the prospect that he might turn up a startling revelation on the epic confrontation of the age was virtually nil. This was heavily plowed ground. The real secrets were in Washington and Moscow. To the Cubans' fury, the superpowers had mounted their most dangerous confrontation on Cuban soil without consulting the inhabitants themselves. Indeed, in the most critical life-and-death hours of '62, Cuba itself had become almost irrelevant—simply one superpower's convenient launching pad against the other. He would have to see what he could get from his own government. But even there the family jewels were reserved for members of the family, favored academics with high-level friendships and access to old-boy networks within the power elite. Like valuable military contracts, even political secrets of recent history were parceled out to friends of the powerful at powerful universities sure to cast the most favorable light on the powerful decision makers. For a lot of reasons, McLemore had never made it into these overlapping political and academic circles.

Besides, he reflected, as Trinidad drifted in and out of sleep in the stifling backseat, if he did discover some well-concealed secret of the Cold War, there were those who would question his motives, who might ask themselves what he was doing in Cuba after all these years. Was he truly there on some half-baked research project, or was he really searching for a ghost from the old Cold War days? This was a question he would deal with later . . . maybe when the project was finished, or maybe when he had a couple of cold rum drinks later that night.

As the Chevy weaved, creaked, and honked its way back down from the hills and along the still-congested roads and highways, McLemore himself dozed, weary from the damp heat. Blustering Russians and shy Cuban soldiers drifted in and out of his dreams.

Even as McLemore succumbed to a hazy, almost drugged, torpor, Trinidad, now fully awake, took the occasion to size him up. With his mouth slightly ajar and his light brown hair tousled by travel and breeze, he resembled an adult version of a small boy. He was of average size, not as large as many Yanqui men she now saw on the streets of Havana and at Varadero's beaches. He wasn't any taller than she was, but he also wasn't as fat as most of the others were either. He wore a light blue dress shirt with the collar open and sleeves rolled to the elbows and light gray wool pants. She would have to encourage him to do better for the Cuban climate. Lighter cotton stuff, or he'd be sweating all the time. He had nice green eyes. Pale, almost icy. He smiled naturally when they met, and she had noticed the slightly crooked front tooth. Nice touch, almost as if he had calculated it. Most interesting was his voice—soft, and a little husky.

As they swept to a halt in front of the Hotel Deauville, he awoke, startled, unsure where he was. Trinidad had given his shoulder a gentle tap.

"*Caramba!*" he mumbled in his confusion, involuntarily reaching for one of the few Spanish clichés he knew.

Trinidad laughed lightly, the first friendly gesture of the day. "See, you are now Cuban. You are speaking perfect Spanish on your first day."

"*Mañana?*" McLemore asked as he struggled from the car, now fully in the spirit.

"*Mañana*, you will go to the Foreign Ministry. One of our young translators, Carlos, will wait for you there at ten o'clock in the morning. They have some records prepared for you. Then we will see about the other trips you have requested . . . to San Cristóbal and elsewhere."

"Will I see you tomorrow, or sometime?" McLemore asked, more plaintively than intended. He was suddenly feeling alone in a strange place.

"Of course, *Profesor* McLemore. But, if you will excuse me, I have some other work to do. Then I will probably accompany you to San Cristóbal and perhaps interpret some of your interviews with our officials."

Trinidad shook hands briskly, took McLemore's front seat in the Chevy, and as he bent and waved good-bye, the car lurched away from the hotel in a burst of honking horns on all sides.

As he turned to enter the low-budget Deauville, McLemore noticed a lean, bearded figure across the street. The man, framed against the cracked, dusty pink stucco wall, with the stick figure profile of an elongated puppet, seemed to have paused in a square of shade on the narrow street. He looked as if he were studying McLemore. McLemore wondered if it could be an American he might know and, if so, whether he should wave a greeting, seek a handshake. Soon, the lanky, slightly stooped figure moved away, but slowly, as if reluctant to surrender a post.

2 The humid breeze, the jumpy salsa music, and the exotic spicy food were a bit of heaven to Viktor Isakov. Little Havana was a long way from Ekaterinburg in the Urals, where he had grown up. But he was a long way from home in more ways than that. Viktor Isakov was a new breed of man, a new-Russian entrepreneur, one of that unique, fast-moving capitalist caste set loose upon the world by the collapse of a hollowed-out political faith. Viktor Isakov was here in Miami to do some serious business, and he was loving every minute of it. If this deal came off—not if, when—*when* this deal came off, Viktor Isakov would soar overnight into the big leagues of international business.

But now he was not Viktor Isakov, he was Victor Isaacs. And that is how he was addressed by the two men who stood before the dark corner table at La Casa Blanca restaurant in the heart of Little Havana. The men sized one another up quickly. All were very well tailored in fine tropical suits. Languid silk handkerchiefs adorned breast coat pockets with the studied casualness of the newly rich. Matching silk neckwear was, in each case, carefully tied. Custom-made shoes were professionally polished. The significant difference was that Viktor weighed thirty pounds more than either of his new acquaintances and his shirt bulged dangerously at the central buttons. Viktor could not help but dedicate some of his new wealth to the kind of rich food they did not have in Ekaterinburg when he was growing up, indeed which they did not have in Ekaterinburg today. But, *when* this deal went through, he would make sure to take care of his mother, who still lived there.

"Let me introduce myself, Mr. Isaacs," said one of the new men. "I am Manuel Lechuga. Please call me Manny. And this," he said, patting his friend's arm, "is Antonio Varona."

"Tony, I bet," said Viktor with a stiff Slavic lilt. They all chuckled and shook hands. Viktor quickly measured them out. Manny was the clear leader. Tall, impressive bearing. He was big enough to play American football, Viktor thought. He was dark with styled wavy hair. Strong hands. Manicured nails. Takes care of himself. Self-confident. Kind of guy you noticed when he walked into any room. Self-consciously, Viktor felt his protruding stomach. If he was going to be a successful American businessman, he had to look like Manny. People waited for Manny to tell them what to do. That kind of guy. Viktor sighed; Manny was also the kind of guy who pushed desserts away. Most of all, Viktor noticed, he had black eyes that stared at you and didn't blink. I bet he's got some beautiful ladies, Viktor thought. That idea made him very jealous.

Now, Tony was more his kind of guy. Shorter, little heavier. Suit was expensive, but didn't fit as well as Manny's. Manny pinned you to the wall with those eyes. Tony looked amused all the time, like he knew a funny secret. Tony was the guy who made sure the beautiful ladies got home all right after the party. If Tony walked in the room, nobody would notice. Like me, Viktor thought. If I get in trouble with this deal, Tony will help me out, he hoped to himself.

"Well, it is now making me heppy to see both," he continued, nodding his head. "Biliv me, was hell to find you. Cannot tell you twists and turns."

Twists and turns, indeed, Viktor had been thinking. Here we are in 1998, thirty-six years later, a capitalist Russian making some business with Cuban Americans. Who would have thought it possible? Forty years ago, these bastards would have killed me with their own hands. Forty years ago? Ten years ago! Now here I sit in my expensive suit. A slick arms dealer. What has this world come to? Cubans talking to a Russian about buying some kind of hammer to use on other Cubans. Forty years ago, these guys were trying to throw the Russians out of Cuba so they could go back in. Now they're buying guns from the Russians for the same purpose. What kind of sense does that make? Viktor wasn't sure the post–Cold War years made any more sense than the Cold War years. First the Yankees were pushing guns into Cuban-Americans' hands, pushing them onto boats, pushing them off the boats onto a Cuban beach, and pushing them into the muzzles of Castro's Russian-made guns. Then, the next thing you know, Kennedy is negotiating a deal with Khrushchev to lay off Castro if the Russians pulled out the goddamn missiles. Now here these Cubans are, negotiating with a Russian *biznizmin* for Russian weapons to kill their fellow Cubans with. The whole thing doesn't make any sense.

They ordered drinks: sparkling water for Manny, white wine for Tony, and a Cuba libre for Viktor. They all laughed at that. "It's okay, Vic. It's okay if I call you Vic?" Manny said. "We had to do some checking about you . . . you understand. We had to make sure who we were talking to. The CIA and FBI are all over us down here, you understand. They let us go about our business down here, probably even hope we succeed. But they always are trying to find out what we're up to."

They talked some more, mostly chitchat, then ordered lunch. Manny got a salad, Tony a grilled *langosta*, and Viktor ordered *empanadas, arroz moro*, and *plátanos fritos*. They all laughed about that too. Leaning forward as the waiter turned away, Manny said, "We understand you have something to offer us . . . perhaps something big."

Viktor considered that opener momentarily. He had tried to teach himself not to seem too eager. How should he say this? "What I here discuss, is safe to say, perhaps bigger than big. Is . . . *very* big." He spoke slowly and paused dramatically for effect. His effort to appear nonchalant and sophisticated failed early. "You understand my business, yes?" They nodded. "It is business about military equipment, yes?" They nodded again. "As I more successful become, is about *big* military equipment. Yes?" Only Tony nodded this time. After a moment, "What is biggest military equipment for you to imagine?"

"Vic, I don't know," Manny said. "Ships? Planes? Tanks? If that is what you're talking about, we can't really use those right now. Maybe later. But it isn't what we need now."

The food came, and the two Cuban Americans watched with concealed amazement as Viktor tackled the *empanadas*.

Viktor smiled at them with his mouth full. It was not a pleasant sight, and Manny studied his salad. "Try just one guess more," Viktor spluttered, immensely amused with himself.

Manny looked at Tony. Involuntarily his eyes widened, and he suddenly looked undertaker serious. "Vic, there is only one thing bigger than ships and planes." He looked over his shoulder. "You're not talking nuclear here. Are you?"

Viktor smiled.

"Vic, *Madre de Dios*," Manny hissed, all suave facade now flown. "Are you talking nuclear here?"

Viktor continued to smile. Like a small boy with a great secret, he seemed incapable of speech. Then he casually nodded his head.

"My God," Tony said softly, pushing the half-eaten *langosta* back.

Viktor chewed thoughtfully, considering his bargaining position.

Manny said, "Look, we intend to get our country back. That's our main purpose. But what do we have if we blow it up in the process? You probably are talking to the wrong customers here, Vic." He checked his watch, hoping his voice wasn't shaking.

Viktor held up his hand and swallowed a mouthful. "Moment, my friends. There are nukes and there are nukes. We talk not about World War III here. Is not megatons, what I have . . . although," he said thoughtfully, "is not impossible. We discuss here 'tac nukes' . . . tactical weapons. Low yield, local use. 'Discrit,' they say. Battlefield weapons. Not blowing up city. Blowing up maybe division." He held up his hands, perhaps a yard apart.

Manny and Tony looked at each other, suddenly desperate for some privacy to discuss this. "Vic," Manny said, "how in hell are you going to get your hands on tactical nuclear weapons? And, if you got them, how in hell do you get them into Cub . . . ?" Even though his voice was low, he looked over his shoulder again and hissed, "You know, into where we could use them."

Viktor's smug smile suggested someone who had thought of everything. "What if already I have them practically in my hands? What if is not have to get them into . . . into where wanting to use them?"

Manny sat back in his chair, now totally without appetite. "I don't get it," he said, suddenly suspicious, as if he realized he was being fleeced. "What if you already have them and you don't have to deliver them?" Then, looking at Tony, "How can that be? What's he talking about, Tony?"

Tony adopted the logical course. He shrugged with his hands out, palms up. "The only way they don't have to be gotten in is to have them there . . . already. *Already?*"

Manny leaned threateningly across the table. Viktor picked up a napkin for protection. The black eyes bored in. "You can't possibly have nuclear weapons already in Cuba, you Russian son of a bitch!" Manny had the look of a man both confused and furious, but furious mostly because he was confused.

"We did, one time," Viktor said for protection.

Manny briefly considered this. "Yes, but that was thirty or forty years ago. And, as I remember," he added bitterly, "we made you take them all out." The pronoun clearly cast Manny as Yankee, not Cuban.

"Maybe."

"Maybe what, you bastard. You took them all out. I remember." Then Manny realized he couldn't exactly remember because he had been five years old. What he remembered was his embittered father, a senior official in the Batista government of the 1950s, cursing the Soviets and even more their lackey, lickspittle, son-of-a-bitch puppet Castro.

"Maybe," Viktor parroted.

"Let's get out of here," Manny blurted.

He left Tony to pick up the bill and put a firm hand under Viktor's arm, practically lifting him from the table. Viktor glanced longingly at the remaining food scraps. They exited La Casa Blanca, Manny's fake smile a mask of camaraderie and goodwill. Past the closely packed shops and chattering shoppers crowding the hectic sidewalks of Little Havana, they strolled slowly enough to allow Tony to catch up. Then they headed for a tiny, dusty neighborhood park sheltered by a few scruffy trees. Tony surged ahead and cornered a shaded bench away from the nodding domino players.

Manny sat Viktor down like a naughty child. Manny said, "Look, we are serious businessmen doing serious business in a serious cause. Don't mess with us. I want to know what you're talking about and what the deal is. Right now. No more dancing around." His silken voice was low, but his words—each one followed by its own punctuation—issued from behind clenched teeth. His black eyes riveted Viktor to the peeling park bench.

Not to mess around with *this* guy, Viktor thought. He means serious business. Viktor had the distinct impression that he had fallen in with a band of tough true believers. He will kill me quicker than it takes my heart to beat, he thought. And right now it was beating very fast.

Deflated by the rough stuff and the heat coming out of those eyes, Viktor said, "In Cuba can be deliver to you, one . . . maybe two . . . tactical nuclear warheads, preserved with care, ready to go. You interested or not?" He was eager to regain the initiative. Always take the initiative. Never get on the defensive. The business books had taught him that.

"Vic, these are either new or they are old. If they are new, you can't get them into Cuba. If they are old, they won't work. Which are they?"

"Since you must know, they are old. But close friends to me, Russian nuclear experts, say to me they still work. Maybe some wires restoring. Is all that could go wrong. I know people can do such work. They are having little to do these days, and they are looking for work. Particularly if work is in sunny place. Have they been properly stored, is most important thing."

"Vic, nuclear warheads could not have been stored in Cuba for almost forty years without somebody knowing about it. That's crazy. And, even if they were stored, how do you know they were properly stored?"

"Are stored with great secrecy and properly done, biliv me. I know."

"How do you know, Vic?"

"Because, my own father was he who store them."

■　■　■

Before dawn on September 17, 1962, the Soviet ship Indigirka, *a freighter of some 19,500 tons used virtually exclusively by the Ministry of Defense to transport military equipment to Soviet military installations and Communist insurgencies around the world, weighed anchor at the Barents Sea military port of Severomorsk. Very few people outside the highest levels of the Ministry knew its destination and fewer still knew its cargo.*

The official destination of the Indigirka *was an obscure West African port, and its manifest listed a variety of kinds of farm equipment.*

In truth the Indigirka *was headed for the port of Mariel just down the Cuban coastline west of Havana. And its real cargo was nuclear warheads.*

The ship's authentic manifest, kept in the captain's secure safe, read as follows:

1. *One-megaton warheads fitted for R-12 rockets: quantity—forty-five;*
2. *Twelve-kiloton bombs for Ilyushin-28 bombers: quantity—six;*
3. *Twelve-kiloton warheads for FKR (cruise) missiles: quantity—thirty-six;*
4. *Two-kiloton warheads for Luna (tactical) missiles: quantity—twelve.*

The total destructive power of the Indigirka's *cargo equaled 45,500 megatons or roughly twenty times the yield of all the Allied bombs dropped on Germany throughout World War II. By comparison, the Hiroshima atomic bomb yield was fourteen kilotons.*

Despite growing tensions between the United States and Cuba, and through Cuba the United States and the Soviet Union, during the historic fall of 1962, the Indigirka's *seventeen-day passage was uneventful. Within days, Soviet cargo ships carrying even more lethal nuclear weapons would be stopped by the United States naval embargo of Cuba and would be turned back.*

The nuclear-rich freighter Indigirka made port at Mariel on the fourth day of October 1962. Within the next thirty days, its cargo would play a central role in the greatest drama of the Cold War.

The unloading of the ship began promptly under the supervision of Colonel Georgi Prokov. The entire port area was secured as dockside cranes lifted heavily protected crates directly from the ship's hold onto waiting Soviet lorries. The heavy trucks were escorted from the darkened port by specially trained KGB security forces three at a time. Throughout the night the transport caravans rolled forth and back from Mariel to the Soviet's especially prepared main nuclear depot, centered around heavily reinforced bunkers, in the hills south of Havana at the Cuban military base outside Bejucal. Bejucal offered proximity to the command authority, rural security, and rough equidistance between the missile sites already under construction near San Cristóbal and Los Palacios in the west and an area near Santa Clara in the east.

■ ■ ■

3

The small group of men in the center of the Plaza de la Revolución, some in civilian, some in military dress, all carried their hats, a sure sign it was very hot. To put on a hat, especially the green military hat, was to bake your brain entirely. At the center of the group of perhaps a dozen, Lazaro Suarez carried a sheaf of notes in a worn folder. He consulted them occasionally as the group talked. Suarez looked up momentarily directly into the four-story-high face of Che Guevara, complete with the black beret and red star, dominating the facade of the Ministry of the Interior on the Plaza's north side. To the right of the group was the Ministry of Defense and the National Library. Fifty meters behind them to the south was the giant grotesque obelisk designed as a monument to José Martí, and behind Martí the Palacio de la Revolución, the seat of the Cuban government and headquarters of the Cuban Communist Party. Thick traffic swirled up and down the wide avenues on both sides of the huge plaza.

Lazaro Suarez was the nominal leader of this ad hoc band of officials tasked by *el Commandante* himself with planning the security for the monster rally to take place in the Plaza less than four months hence on the occasion of the fortieth anniversary of the revolution. The celebration date was January 1, 1999. During the days following January 1, 1959, *los barbudos*, the bearded ones, had stormed into Havana after years of guerrilla warfare, largely carried out in the mountains and villages of Oriente province, to claim power on behalf of the people, *los campesinos*, the poor ones, the workers, everybody—except the hated *batistianas* and their Mafia friends. The event had electrified the Western Hemisphere and much of the rest of the world. The revolution's themes seemed egalitarian and democratic. Its complex, evolving economic and political content would be filled in shortly.

The third son of an impoverished *campesino* from the tiny village of Cruces near Santa Clara, Suarez was a small child during this time. Though he was mild mannered in his youth and early adult years, his quiet studiousness and earnest commitment to the revolution's goals carried him through a degree at the Universidad de la Habana and a planning job in the security services. He kept his head low, carried out his functions— largely planning trips for *el Commandante*—and moved up the ranks on the high tide of his superiors' trust. A stocky man with prematurely white hair topping his square head, he was good at what he did. He took care of his family. Suarez had a wide smile and broad likable countenance. At first glance, he seemed too quiet, too shy to be in his line of work. But he had proven, even to the tyrant Nuñez, his immediate superior, to be dependable and conscientious, and his subordinates would follow him into an inferno.

But like many, perhaps even most, Cubans, Suarez had long abandoned his illusions about the revolution. Whatever good it was going to do had been done long ago. Now the people in power were just aging and hanging on, refusing to bring up a new generation, Suarez's generation, of modern leaders, maybe even leaders who would reform and open up the system. Of course the people were better off today than before. His father and mother and the older ones constantly confirmed that. They had basic food, medicine, and shelter. It wasn't the best in the world, but it was a lot better than under the corrupt, oligarchical *batistianas*. The old ones remembered the past. The younger ones didn't. And the younger ones were the restless ones. They didn't like the outdated doctrinaire speeches about ideas in which they had no stake. They didn't like the isolation from much of the world, particularly from fabulous rock music, MTV, and movies. Most of all, they didn't like the monotonous lifestyle. Some nights were fun, but life to a young person in late-twentieth-century Cuba was the worst thing it could be—boring.

In between the young and the old, Suarez felt this. His younger sister was in that crowd, and he took its temperature through her. Something had to change. Fidel would not last forever. Then what? Fidel's brother Raul maybe, but he wasn't getting any younger. More likely some jumped-up small-caliber version of Fidel from the Revolutionary Council. One of the old doctrinaire Commies from the revolution times. But without Castro's mystique, personal charm, warmth with people. They would get the worst of Castro without the best of Castro. This recurring thought depressed Suarez and made him cross.

Colonel Nuñez showed up at just the wrong time.

"Lazaro, what are you all doing? Taking a siesta? Get on with it. What have you got here?"

The men, all outranked, turned awkwardly in Nuñez's direction without exactly coming to attention. "Very well, Colonel, *buenos dias*, we are allocating some responsibilities here. As usual the Havana traffic police will be in charge of rerouting traffic and setting up the necessary detours. This will anyway be a big holiday, and in the middle of the day we will not have regular traffic to and from work. So that will not be so bad. Captain Ortega's men will also have the primary responsibility for overall crowd control . . . making sure everyone behaves properly."

"Lazaro," his boss interrupted, "this isn't just another political event. The party intends to have well over a million people here. They want to fill up the side street as far as the eye can see. We're inviting in a lot of international press. It's a very big show. This isn't just another political rally. This is the biggest one of all. It's also, by the way, a great chance—*una opportunidad grande*—for somebody to make some trouble."

Suarez said, "Understood, Colonel, we're all aware here. The captain's going to have every policeman out that day. It will be the full force. Plus, of course, as I was going to say, the military police will be in charge of all the security details, clearing and securing the area beforehand, and helping the city police with crowd surveillance. And then our department will have the responsibility for all VIP security."

"Amigos, excuse us," Nuñez blustered, taking Suarez by the arm and turning to stroll back to the Martí monument. "Lazaro, that's just horseshit you're talking, and you know it. Let me tell you something you are not to tell the others. Our sources in Miami have confirmed in several reports that those *batistiana* bastard relatives of ours over there are planning something big for this anniversary. They thought they were going to be back here almost forty years ago and they still haven't made it, and the old ones think this is their last chance. They would do anything . . . anything . . . to bring our revolutionary government down. Do you hear what I'm saying?"

Suarez said, "Of course, Colonel, I understand, but—"

"But nothing, Lazaro. You don't understand or you wouldn't have simply dusted off all the old security plans for an occasion like this. There is nothing new here . . . no sense of emergency." Nuñez stepped back, now in the shade of the Martí tower, and studied Suarez. "You don't care much about these things, do you, Lazaro? The party, the revolution, this celebration. It's all just a job for you, isn't it? You've become like all the other apparatchiks of your generation. Come to work. Pick up your pay. Live your life. And screw the revolution. It doesn't matter to you, does it? The only difference between you and those greedy Yanqui bastards *del norte* is that they make more money."

Suarez flushed, less from his anger than from the truth of Nuñez's remarks. "Colonel, let's go up the tower. I can explain our plan better from there."

They entered the large glass doors leading into the museum at the base of the granite obelisk dedicated to Martí's late-nineteenth-century revolution against the Spanish. The air-conditioned space was a great relief. The museum's security chief led them toward the elevator. The three men boarded the elevator and quickly rose the 140-plus meters to the top.

Havana and its harbor lay before them. They had a commanding view of a city that, from this height, looked gleaming, clean, and vital. It almost could be any of the great capitals of the world, not the decaying urban center of a slowly collapsing social experiment. The large compass etched into the marble floor of the tower's observation level showed *Habana vieja* off to the northeast a mile away, straight north the more modern Vedado section of the city with the shops and hotels left over from Batista's heyday, and to the northwest, farther away, looking past the Cementerio Cristóbal Colón, the magnificent city of the dead, the most famous cemetery in all of Latin America, there was the Miramar section of the city, where late-colonial mansions once housed the oligarchy, the families of consequence in the last regime. Although Nuñez took no notice, Suarez was struck once again by the magnificence of the city he had come to cherish. As Nuñez raved on, he thought to himself, Why didn't I become an architect instead of a cop, after all? That had been his dream. To rebuild and restore the great city, not to chase terrorists. But he had needed the income for his new family. So now he was stuck with the treacherous Nuñez—probably for the rest of his life. Now before him lay the brilliant city, its poverty dimmed behind the walls of the gleaming buildings. As with a lovely but aging woman, distance preserved her beauty.

Suarez turned to his superior. "Colonel, maybe I have become a soul-less little apparatchik. But if so it is in part because of the daily grind of living in this revolution. Of course my parents are better off than in the old days. They tell me this constantly. But that isn't good enough anymore. My kids want to live like other kids. They want what other kids have. I would not want them to live under the old regime. But that isn't the only choice. There are more than two kinds of politics. Why can't we experiment with some of those—without giving up the achievements of the revolution. We're in danger of becoming a kind of insect in amber, frozen in time like our old friends the Russians. Look what happened to them."

Nuñez studied the younger man crowded close to him in the narrow peak of the Martí monument. "That's not healthy talk, Suarez," he said with icy carefulness. "It's your soft generation that would sell us out in a very quick heartbeat. You're ready to surrender after all these years to the gringos who will load up their *batistiana* friends on ocean liners and troop ships and they'll all be back down here overnight, shooting all the socialists—me among them—taking over the government, and giving the casinos back to the mob." His battered face had twisted into a hateful snarl. "Then your kids will be happy, of course. They can watch Michael Jackson kiss little boys, Madonna take off her clothes, and all the perversion that has made the States so great." He spat. "But when they get their well-paid jobs working for the goddamn mob in their goddamn casinos, tell your kids not to even think about a political protest, or real justice, or crossing the people in power. They'll find themselves shot in an alley."

"Colonel, *con mucho respeto*, they can't think about those things now," Suarez said quietly.

■ ■ ■

As the lorries arrived at the military base outside Bejucal before dawn on the morning of October 5, 1962, Soviet troops moved the crated warheads quickly into the reinforced bunkers. Carefully segregating the R-12 warheads from the Luna warheads and the Lunas from the FKRs, the troops were driven to complete the job before light and the possibility of overflight detection or even the possible presence of local spies with telephoto lenses in the surrounding hills.

Commanding the Bejucal depot and supervising the unloading of the warheads was Colonel Leonid Isakov. Colonel Isakov was chosen for this critical assignment because of his special training in the handling of nuclear weapons and, particularly, battlefield-ready warheads. Within the Soviet Army, he was one of a handful of recognized experts in the handling, storage, and arming of nuclear warheads, all drawn from the Twelfth Main Directorate of the Ministry of Defense. Anticipating Chairman Khrushchev's decision to sign the order to deploy nuclear weapons to Cuba, Minister of Defense Rodion Malinovsky had assembled the special team of nuclear experts—all loyal party members—trained to manage all aspects of nuclear weaponry from their construction to their firing. Colonel Isakov was a member of that team. The team had been flown to Havana by special military aircraft even as the Indigirka made its passage.

As the last crate was unloaded from the last lorry, dawn was creeping over the hilltops surrounding Bejucal. Colonel Isakov swore as he consulted a clipboard with his second in command, Lieutenant Colonel Dankevich.

"Count again, Dankevich. Goddammit, it doesn't add up."

"Colonel, this is exactly the cargo from the Indigirka. Every crate."

Furiously, Isakov lit a Cuban cigar. That, with the rum and the ladies, made life bearable. And, of course, there were the nice beaches on days off. Shouldn't forget those. Come to think of it, why hurry to leave Cuba. If the goddamn balloon doesn't go up, this might not be a bad place to serve some time. But now, goddammit, he had too many weapons. The last thing he needed. "We got to sort this out, Dankevich, or you and I are cleaning up Siberian shithouses."

"Colonel, the only way this makes sense is that they sent us too many."

"How in God's name could those idiots in Moscow do a thing like this?" Isakov fumed from behind a fog of cigar smoke.

Dankevich folded over a sheet on the clipboard, dampened a pencil stub on his tongue, and murmured as he added the numbers again. "Look, you have thirty-six FKRs on this load and forty-four coming, that's eighty total. Then you have six Il-28 bombs and you have twelve Lunas. Together that's eighteen. Add the two together and you get ninety-eight." Smiling at the thought, he said, "It's clear what they did. Some screwup in the Ministry or an even bigger screwup in the storage depot rounded it off. I can hear them now. 'Ninety-eight's a shitty number for a load of tactical nukes. They must mean a hundred. Give the Luna boys a couple of extras.' That's what we have. Two extra Lunas."

■ ■ ■

 The file room of the Foreign Ministry of the Republic of Cuba had the charm of a morgue. These files did not want research, they wanted dusting. McLemore sat at a plain long table in the back of the room. Light came into the room from a small window high up behind his head. In its narrow beam floated all the microscopic dust particles in the world. The medieval atmospherics caused McLemore to sneeze with a kind of hiccup regularity every time one of the voluminous stacks of files was moved.

Despite years of academic research occupying virtually his entire mature lifetime, McLemore never ceased to amaze himself at his patience in searching old documents. But this was his first experience at research based almost exclusively on foreign-language documents. So at his side sat Carlos, a very young file clerk in the Ministry whose beatific features made him seem much younger than his nineteen years. According to their agreed routine, Carlos read the file title and heading and McLemore would say yes or no. Or he would simply nod his head. Carlos's earnest, high-pitched voice droned on, and McLemore disciplined himself to listen for key words. He was under no illusion that top secret documents, never before seen by the Great Gringo of the North, would make their way before him. On the other hand, the head of the U.S. section of the Foreign Ministry seemed genuinely interested in his project and, according to Carlos, had been specific in his instructions to the head of the files office to cooperate fully. For himself, Carlos seemed thrilled at the opportunity to practice his English.

Mostly Carlos was reading from memoranda and bureaucratic filler various high officials had placed in the files to cover their political backsides. They were heavy on rhetoric, lashing the perfidious Yankees, and light on fact. McLemore was rejecting these, with a sideways nod, as quickly as Carlos could start them. There were extensive exchanges between the Cuban and Soviet high commands during the late summer and early fall of 1962, some of which were interesting, but almost all of which had previously been digested and written about.

Just as McLemore was prepared, for the third time, to urge Carlos to read faster, he heard him say, "Here is a copy to the Foreign Ministry of a Defense Ministry memorandum to *el Commandante* entitled Operation Anadyr: Special Weapons. It is dated the thirteenth of September 1962."

"Read that one, Carlos."

"*Por favor, señor*, what is 'Anadyr,' 'Operation Anadyr'?"

"It was the code name of the Soviet project to bring nuclear weapons to Cuba. It's the name of some Russian river. They used it to throw off the U.S. code breakers, to make them think it was about something in Siberia."

"*Señor*, here is what it says:

"According to Operation Anadyr, the Soviets propose the following deployments:

"1. R-12 Rockets. Three nuclear missile regiments will be deployed: the 79th near San Cristóbal; the 181st north of Los Palacios; the 664th near Calabazar de Sagua. Each missile regiment will have two launch sites. Each launch site will have four launchers distributed over a geographic area of not less than one and not more than two point five miles. The R-12 is a medium-range ballistic missile (MRBM) with a range of 1,100 nautical miles (1,050 miles). This target area will cover most of the southeastern area of the United States from Dallas, Texas, to Washington, D.C. The R-12 carries a one-megaton payload. The missile is seventy-four feet long, including a seven-foot nose cone, and is transported on special sixty-seven-foot trailers. Total deployment: thirty-six R-12 missiles and forty-five one-megaton warheads.

"2. R-14 Rockets. Two nuclear missile regiments will be deployed at sites yet to be selected and cleared. Each regiment will have twelve missiles with an appropriate number of warheads. The R-14 is an intermediate-range ballistic missile (IRBM) with a range greater than two thousand miles. This target area will cover most midwestern U.S. intercontinental ballistic missile (ICBM) sites. The R-14 carries a one-megaton payload. The R-14 missiles will be deployed after the R-12 missiles are in place and prepared for launch. Total deployment: twenty-four R-14 missiles and thirty-two one-megaton warheads.

"3. Ilyushin-28 bombers. One squadron of six Il-28 bombers will be shipped in crates to be assembled on site at military airfields selected in cooperation with the (Cuban) Ministry of Defense. This medium-range bomber carries a gravity bomb whose yield is twelve kilotons. Total deployment (subject to increase): Six bombers and six twelve-kiloton bombs.

"4. FKR missiles. At least thirty-six FKR missiles are proposed. The FKR missile is the newest Soviet cruise missile. The FKR is capable of being launched from both land- and sea-based platforms. It has a range of approximately two hundred miles. The FKR carries a warhead with a twelve-kiloton yield. It is anticipated most of the FKR missiles will be deployed on Cuban soil. Total deployment: thirty-six FKR missiles and thirty-six twelve-kiloton warheads.

"5. Luna missiles. Three divisions of Luna missiles with two launchers each and two warheads per launcher, for a total of twelve warheads, will be deployed. Each division is manned by 102 personnel. The Luna is a tactical weapon designed for battlefield deployment. The Luna's range is approximately twenty-five miles. It carries a warhead of two kilotons. The Luna warhead is programmed to detonate at an altitude of approximately six hundred feet directly over the battlefield target. [Note: Defensive forces must take special precautions. The Luna detonation creates 100 mph winds at the epicenter and creates a crater approximately 130 feet deep and 130 feet wide. All life within one thousand yards will be destroyed immediately and secondary casualties from nuclear radiation will be widespread beyond this immediate area.] Total deployment: Six launchers and twelve warheads."

Carlos stopped reading. "That is all, *señor*. Shall we go to the next file?"

McLemore had lapsed into a reverie as Carlos read. It all sounded so long ago and far away. But there it was—missiles, warheads, epicenters. What were the Soviets thinking about? What had Khrushchev been up to? Was he pushed by some hard-line military faction, or an even harder-line, anti-American Politburo faction, or a combination of both? What was the conventional wisdom inside the Kremlin at the time? Was this wacky adventure—nuclear weapons in Cuba—a result of aggression or paranoia? Clearly, the Cubans, and the Soviets, had been waiting for the other shoe to drop after the Bay of Pigs. Efforts to assassinate Castro and subversive plots had intensified. U.S. military training exercises increased. The region was alive with rumors of another invasion, this time with the Eighty-second Airborne, a division or two of Marines, squadrons of bombers and combat aircraft, the entire first team. So the Soviet missiles and the combat troop buildup could have been simply a deterrent against that move. Or maybe the crafty peasant Khrushchev saw a chance to play high-level chess with Kennedy. Tie him down in the Caribbean, right on his doorstep, and then make a move to seal up Berlin. Or work a trade. Give us Berlin and we'll give you Cuba.

The Cold War hadn't been about ideology—democracy versus communism—that was just a system for identifying the sides. The Cold War was just a more civilized form of a game called power, McLemore thought. But what a game to play with the stakes in the millions of lives. From Genghis Khan to the idiotic World War I generals, human life had been cheap. Hadn't we advanced beyond that? Obviously not, he thought. The missiles and warheads were nothing more than technology's improvement on trench warfare. Quicker, and much more efficient. Was there a lesson

of the Cold War, he wondered, and was anyone anywhere studying it? Or
was it all just an exercise in folly with little meaning and no relevance?

"*Señor?*" a puzzled Carlos said.

McLemore looked at his watch. "*No mas*, amigo. We need fresh air,
and besides it is time for *comida*. Will you join me?"

Carlos smiled at McLemore's primitive Spanish. "*Si, señor, muchas gracias.*"

Carlos led the way out onto the street, waved a taxi to the curb, and
had the driver take them to the old city, *Habana vieja*. After several hours
in the tombs, McLemore welcomed the hot sun and worshiped the fresh
breeze blowing in from the bay.

As the quickest way from the Ministry to the old city, the taxi headed
down the Malecón, the corniche that, in its prime, had been among
the most striking in the world. Built over a number of years, the Malecón
was begun by Americans in 1898, after the Spanish-American War,
McLemore learned later. It extended almost four miles, linking the fashionable Miramar district of west Havana, residential area of the rich *habaneros* of former days, with *Habana vieja*. High seas crashed against the
wall, sending spray across McLemore's taxi and spread even across the six-
lane avenue to dot the decaying pastel walls of the colonial row houses
on the other side. Carlos explained that when the sea was high like this,
men and boys who normally cast off from the rocks below the seawall in
heavily patched, inflated inner tubes to fish were prohibited from doing
so. Regardless of its condition, the famous avenue remained for Havana's
lovers, youngsters, and families the place to watch the sun drop spec-
tacularly in the west, to promenade, romance, and hustle, and to gaze
northward and wonder when *Tio Sam* might show up again and whether,
when he inevitably would show up, he would have a sword or an olive
branch.

In prosperous times, McLemore thought, the Malecón's three- and four-
story row houses and shops must have been magnificent. Now the flaking
facades appeared propped up by the random scaffolding placed against
them years ago—with some long-forgotten socialist promise of restoration—
and since left to rust against the decaying buildings. These turn-of-the-
century structures had once housed wealthy landowners, entrepreneurs,
foreign yachtsmen, movie stars, gamblers, and corrupt politicians. Now all
gone, on to the next resort, the newest international hideout, the latest
fashionable neighborhood in Piraeus, Bonifacio, or Aqaba. Inside the gap-

ing windows and open doors, McLemore imagined for a moment lights and laughing people at dusk, a sparkling glass, a languid glance, dinner jackets and shimmering dresses, daiquiris passing in anticipation of an elegant dinner on the yacht, then an erotic floor show at the Tropicana, and a nightcap at El Floridita bar for a *Papa Especial*, Hemingway's own daiquiri.

Instead—reality restored in the bat of the eyelid—he saw crumbling shelters for the rural restless now crowding Havana, like most other cities in the world, in search of . . . what? Better lives. More income. Something more interesting to do than the *zafra*, the annual harvest of sugarcane. Nightlife, excitement, television, contact with foreigners, something. Anything but the monotonous rural village life. Cubans, particularly younger Cubans, were driven by the universal restlessness and energy rush spreading throughout the world. They headed for Havana. Fidel's government tried to head them off. Nothing—threats, deportation back to the village, promises—nothing seemed to work. On they came and they seeped, then flooded, into any vacant space, whether on the Malecón or any side street. Tiny flats were jammed with relatives, friends of relatives, and friends of friends. As the taxi sputtered down the six-lane boulevard, the faded pinks, blues, and grays fled back into a past buried so deep by the *revolución* that it might never return.

Presently they unloaded on the open-air doorstep of a *paladar*, a family café, midway down one of the maze of narrow streets. The hostess-mother-cook rushed from the kitchen to embrace Carlos and his Yanqui friend. *"Bueno, bueno, bueno, Carlito,"* she repeated endlessly as she thrust them toward the table just inside the sidewalk edge, only a long meter from the passing traffic. Julia, Carlos's aunt, was all thick waist, ample hips, and blossoming black hair.

"It's my mother's sister. She speaks little English," Carlos explained. "They feed me as I try to graduate from the university. Do you mind this kind of humble . . . *humilde* . . . place, *señor profesor?*"

"It's a perfect place, Carlos. I'm happy to be here. *Por favor*, order for me what you are having."

Carlos had an innocence not usually identified with turbulent cultures. Perhaps it is only that kind of indomitable innocence, McLemore thought, the kind that survives the chaos of the ages, that is truly worth knowing. "Do you want to go to the States, Carlos?" he asked.

"Sometime." McLemore would later realize this was the only answer that could be given to a predictable question posed by an insensitive Yanqui tourist. "Well, I hope you get a chance someday," he replied limply.

Carlos expressed puzzlement. "Maybe a million Cubans have gone to the States to live—a hundred and twenty thousand or something from Mariel alone last time," he mused. "Now we have all kinds of people coming here . . . even a lot from the States . . . and they all say how wonderful it is. So warm, so beautiful, so good music." Big plates of spiced rice and beans with some pork, the traditional Cuban dish *congri*, the Cuban french fries *papas fritas*, and *cervezas* came from the kitchen borne on the plump arms of the beaming Julia. "I don't understand. Why do all Cubans leave and everyone else want to come?"

"Politics, don't you think, Carlos? People have more freedom in other countries. And they can own property. That's the big difference. Wouldn't you like to choose your leaders and own your own house and land?"

"I don't know, *señor profesor*. I think about this. I come from a poor family. We work . . . at least as hard as most Cubans . . . but we have very little. So in the States, could I go to the university . . . even if I have no money? Could my father, who is very sick, get his medicine? We are told you have no chance without a lot of money in the States. We are told many people are without shelter or medicine in the States. Is it true, *señor*? I don't know. Sometime I would like to go see—for myself."

McLemore chewed and thought. "No question it is better in the States. Better than almost anywhere. But we have our problems. To tell you the truth, even though many people are rich and have nice homes and cars and clothes, there are still too many people left out. We haven't solved all our problems yet. We have figured out a system that enables a lot of people to do very well. But we haven't figured out a system that helps everybody."

Carlos studied McLemore shyly. "Why do you come here, *profesor*, if you don't mind. I know you are studying our struggles with the United States and Fidel's—*el Commandante's*—*alianza* with the Russians. But I don't exactly know your project." Then he became awkward, embarrassed by his directness. "I am sorry, *señor*. It may be improper to ask. Forgive me."

"It's okay, Carlos. I am doing a research project focusing on the crisis of 1962 caused by the Russians bringing nuclear weapons and missiles here. I'm a historian. My field is modern history. The events of the twentieth century. Mostly political events, which means mostly the Cold War. The struggle between democracy and communism. That's certainly the story of the second half of the century. And what happened here in the fall of '62 was the most critical moment of that struggle. But it was very dangerous." Then, "Did you study it in school or did your family talk about it?" For Carlos, he reflected, this was all ancient history, of little more relevance than the sack of Rome.

"Some, *señor*. Mostly the story is that the Russians . . . the Soviet Union . . . came to our defense against Uncle Sam. By bringing their most powerful weapons they prevented a certain invasion by the U.S. Army. Another Bay of Pigs." Again Carlos hesitated. "*Es verdad, señor?* It is true?"

Julia brought thick Cuban coffee, took away the plates, and with a volley of harsh Spanish threats, chased an encroaching claque of *jineteros* away from the front of her tiny restaurant.

"I guess from your point of view, that story makes sense. From the U.S. point of view, our leaders said that the Soviet missiles were aimed at us, that, for the first time, the Soviets had brought . . . sneaked, ah, how do you say *sneak* . . ."

"*Furtivo.*"

"*Furtivo*, they brought the missiles in with the intention of threatening or perhaps blackmailing . . . do you know *blackmail?*"

"*Chantaje.*"

"*Chantaje*, then. You know, to threaten us. That is what we saw . . . what President Kennedy said."

Carlos said, "Even, how do you say, in spite of, in spite of the Bay of Pigs, Kennedy my parents liked. For me, he seems like some distant god. Did the Mafia . . . the ones we had here with the *batistianas* . . . did they not kill him?"

McLemore stared down the street, suddenly preoccupied. "What? Oh, yes, sure." He collected his thoughts and abruptly reached for his wallet.

Julia came from one side and Carlos the other. "No, *señor*. No, no. It is for us to be hosts for you. For Julia, it would be a very big insult if you try to pay her. Do not consider it, *por favor*."

McLemore thanked his hostess over and over. "*Muchas gracias, señora, muchas gracias.*"

"*De nada, de nada*," she repeated each time.

"She asks that you please come back while you are in Havana," Carlos said. "It is your only way to repay her."

Distracted, McLemore started down the narrow sidewalk toward a small sunlit square, *una plazuela*, slightly ahead. Overhead, the narrow wrought-iron balconies from the colonial era were draped with drying laundry. He seemed not to notice anything about him. Carlos embraced his aunt, then trotted to catch up. "Did you say the Mafia had killed Kennedy?" he asked breathlessly.

"What? No. I mean, yes, some people think they did. Why do you ask?"

"Because we were discussing it a moment ago, *profesor*. You seemed to agree."

"We will discuss it more later perhaps, Carlos."

"Do you wish to return to our work in the Ministry, *señor*?"

"*Momento*, Carlos. There is someone . . . something I wanted to see down here." They walked toward the square, alternating between the street and the sidewalk, as pedestrian and car traffic dictated. They came to the edge of the square. At the end of the narrow, shaded street, McLemore squinted against the stunning sunlight. Across the small square a figure sat facing them. He was an older man with a white beard and wore a traditional *guayabera* shirt and thin, much-laundered trousers. He had on a traditional *campesino* straw hat against the sunlight.

McLemore stepped back momentarily into the narrow shade of a balcony. Carlos looked confused. *"Profesor?"* he said.

"Nothing, Carlos. It's okay. See that old man? It's just that I think I must know him. I believe he was outside my hotel last evening. I'm not quite sure. Is he Cuban, Carlos? Or could he be an American?" Dummy, McLemore thought. We're all Americans. "You know, Yankee."

"It is impossible to know. It is appropriate in this country simply to greet people. Do you wish to do so? We can greet him. I'm sure he wouldn't mind."

"I don't think so. It doesn't seem right. It's just my imagination. There are a lot of old men everywhere who look like him." The two men turned to hail a passing taxi to return to the Ministry and their tedious odyssey through the dusty records of a confrontation fading quickly from memory. As they did so, McLemore believed he saw the old man touch his hat in salute.

■ ■ ■

MEMORANDUM
Republic of Cuba

From: Ministry of Defense
To: Ministry of Foreign Affairs
Date: 15/9/62
Subject: Operation Anadyr/USSR Order of Battle

According to the order signed by N. S. Khrushchev on 7/9/62 pursuant to a unanimous decision of the Politburo, the USSR has deployed or will shortly deploy to Cuba the following conventional forces:

Approximately 42,000 Soviet military personnel in the form of four (4) motorized rifle regiments of 2,500 troops each and two (2) tank battalions with new T-55 battle tanks. Of this total of ground forces, 10,000 will be Soviet ground combat forces.

The Soviet forces will be principally deployed in and around the following Cuban military sites: Bahía Honda and Artemisa; San Antonio, San Julian, Isabel Rubio.

These conventional forces are separate from but in support of the "special weapons" in the process of being deployed as described to you in the Memorandum dated: 13/9/62.

It is estimated that implementation of this order will require at least eighty-five ships from the Soviet merchant fleet, transporting personnel and matériel, making at least 150 dockings at one of several Cuban ports.

■ ■ ■

5 In ones and twos a group of a dozen or so men drifted casually toward the private dining room behind the kitchen of La Casa Blanca in Little Havana. Each appeared to be, and indeed was, a well-dressed businessman. They were elegant without ostentation. Their average age was in the early forties, and several of the men appeared to take physical conditioning seriously. Their demeanor was casual and their personal greetings to one another were of the sort seen at any monthly meeting of any service club. They could easily have been planning a charity event for the local zoo or a hospital fund drive.

In fact, they were the board of directors of Bravo 99, the most militant of several Cuban-American groups. The principal aim of Bravo 99, which was headquartered in Miami, was the overthrow of the Castro government and the restoration of a prerevolutionary regime in Havana. This meeting in Little Havana was to plan a reunion in big Havana.

If a believer is devout, a fanatic is obsessively devout. All the men collecting for this monthly meeting were devout in their dedication to the liberation of Cuba. It was the cause that united them. Their purpose in forming Bravo 99 was to crystallize devotion and direct it to action. These were serious men, upstanding citizens, generally good husbands and fathers, community leaders. Given their otherwise conventional behavior and intelligence, it would have been difficult to marginalize them. But for a few, their passion had become an obsession, their devotion excessive, and their monomania would cause them to marginalize themselves. And it is, after all, men on the margins of civilization who are usually the most interesting—and the most dangerous.

These men were the principal heirs to the leadership that fled Cuba on New Year's Day, 1959. Their fathers had each been wealthy landowners, businessmen, or Batista ministers in Cuba-before-Castro. Their hatred of Castro, their common legacy from earliest years, had no boundary. Unable to speak the name of the enemy who united them, they simply referred to him as "that Commie son of a bitch." They were here, as they were at some different meeting place on an irregular date each month, to plan Castro's death.

After coffee had replaced dinner plates, Juan "Johnny" Aragones cleared his throat. "We've got to talk some serious business here tonight, and so I want everyone to listen carefully and keep the talking down. Manny and Tony are going to tell us about a meeting they had right here, in this restaurant, a few days ago." He got up nervously and tested that the only door opening into the room was securely closed. "Manny, why don't you tell us what happened."

Nervousness was not a characteristic Manny recognized. It was unclear whether the silence of the men occasioned by Manny's dark gaze was the result of respect or fear. Manny said, "We were contacted a few weeks ago by some friends of ours, people we trust, about a Russian businessman named Isaacs. His real name is Isakov, and he's peddling Russian weapons. Like about a thousand other guys. Those people have some state-of-the-art hardware—at least they scared the hell out of us for a while—so we decided to talk to this guy. First, we checked him out. Usual channels. Even some friends in the Bureau. He comes up legitimate every time. Got a green card and a house in Westchester County. Knows the bad boys in Brighton Beach but stays away from them. He's done business mostly in the Middle East, some in Africa, some in Asia. The stuff he sells, he never touches. The way it works is, he takes the order, the equipment is delivered. He collects the payment once delivery has been made and settles with the suppliers in Moscow. Mostly, he just wires the money to some accounts in Cyprus. His partners in Russia have the contacts in the military, and he's the international rep."

"Do the Feds know what he's up to?" one of the men asked.

"Basically, yes. So far he hasn't broken any laws. He's got some smart U.S. trade and immigration lawyers, and they keep him clean." Manny barked a laugh. "A couple of deals he did, the Feds even approved. Clever bastard got word to them who he was selling to and they said, 'Go ahead, they're on our side.' "

There was low laughter around the table. Several men reached for their drinks and leaned in. They were eager for the deal.

"Here it is," said Manny. "No, before I tell you, we have to have an understanding. Nothing that is said here tonight goes anywhere else. Anywhere! No wives, girlfriends, pals, other guys in the organization or the movement. Not Alpha 66. Nowhere!" He paused. "Yes?"

The men nodded soberly, sensing something big.

"If this gets beyond this group . . . ever . . . we'll find out who did it and take care of them. Permanently. Do we have an understanding on this?"

The men nodded again, shifting restlessly. Despite the melodrama, no one even smiled.

Johnny said, "Go ahead, Manny, it's okay. If this group can't trust one another, we can't trust anybody. Go ahead. Tell us what you've got."

"All right. Tony and I met with this guy . . . Isakov . . . Isaacs . . . whatever. He can get us some *very* powerful explosives." He paused.

"Yeah, so what," one of the men said. "We can get powerful explosives in this country."

"Yes, and how do you get them into Cuba? You know the trouble it takes for us to get a stick or two of dynamite or a little C4 for the hotel jobs in there. The difference here is this . . . the Russian already has the stuff down there."

The room erupted into murmurs and side discussions, and then, under Manny's sable gaze, quieted. "Now, listen to me. This is as serious as cancer. He has substantial explosive power already there. Don't ask me how, I can't tell you. I have an idea. But we're not supposed to know. If this gets out, the Feds come down on him. He's out of business and out of the country." He paused. "And then, we're out of our best potential supplier."

"All right, Manny, so we buy his stuff, then what?" a man called Pete asked.

"All right," Manny said, "let me ask you a question, and you think about it just for a minute. Who's going to be at the fortieth anniversary celebration. All of them. Fidel, Raul, Alarcon, Lega, all of them. The whole goddamn Revolutionary Council. Everybody in the party. Every important Communist in a couple of thousand miles will be there. And what about the million people who'll be there. Anybody think these are the ordinary *campesinos*? Every party member on the island is going to be there. Everybody who's ruined Cuba and who *continues* to ruin Cuba is going to be there. One time, one big time, they're all going to be there—in the goddamn 'Plaza de la Revolución.'" He said the phrase as if it had a foul taste.

They were listening.

"The idea is that we plant this stuff in the Plaza and sometime during this celebration we get rid of all of them, all at once."

There was the kind of silence that results from mass stupefaction. "How much stuff is there, for God's sake?" someone finally asked.

Manny said, "A lot. Very big boom. Enough to wipe them all out."

"You mean everybody?"

"All the leaders for sure and most of the party structure."

"How many people is that?"

"Depends on how much stuff we plant." Manny rubbed his forehead, as if calculating, then produced a foxlike smile. "Couple of hundred thousand at least."

Two or three of the men pushed their chairs back. One loosened his tie. Several men exhaled audibly. "Johnny, it's one thing to plant a little device to light up a disco or strafe a hotel to scare off tourists," one of them finally said, addressing the group chairman. "Killing a couple of thousand people is something else."

Another one said, "Not a couple of thousand, dummy—a couple of *hundred* thousand! Maybe more." Several men shook their heads. One man said, "Count me out, Johnny. I'm for drastic action, a lot more even than Alpha 66. But a couple of hundred *thousand* people?"

"They're Communists," Johnny said, producing the most persuasive argument he could think of.

"No way," said another. "It's crazy. How are you going to do it, first? So the stuff is there. A big load of explosives. C4, whatever. You just going out into the Plaza some night and bury the stuff under the VIP stand? But, let's say you get that done and somehow . . . by some miracle . . . you blow up all the Commies. Think of the press! Think of the reaction! We got the Feds on us. Somebody will figure out who is involved and we'll all end up in some prison somewhere."

The last two men to speak stood up and were joined by three others. One said, "Nobody here wants back in more than me. Nobody. I'm ready to give my life for it . . . so my kids can know their grandparents' home. Cuba belongs to them as much as me." He shook his head, as if to clear away a bad dream. "But this'll never work. It sounds like Larry, Moe, and Curly." This half of the group headed for the door.

Johnny said, "Wait a minute, you guys. Think of what we're doing for the United States here. Suppose in a year or two we decide to bring some pressure on the White House and Congress to overthrow the bastard. What if we heat things up like in 1960 and '61. So he sends in the Marines and a lot more than a couple of hundred thousand are killed. Then you got everybody involved and a lot of women and children are killed when the U.S. Army fights its way across Cuba to Havana. Think about it. A long war and a lot of people killed. No picnic. This way, we do brain surgery and the body is still alive."

The others continued out and one said, "Johnny, can it. Don't even think about it. I think the Russian is lying. And even if he isn't, we'd never pull it off. Let's stick with the original plan. Low-level sabotage. Ruin the crops. Ruin the tourism. Scare people away. Dry up the food. Dry up the sugar exports. It'll work. Just takes more time." He and the others waved over their shoulders. "See you next month."

This left six men in the room. Johnny, Manny, Tony, and three others. Two, Pete and Joe, were among the fitness crowd, and one, Orlando, was plump and quiet. He was the only one of the group not to have entered the discussion. Pete went out to see that the others had left and to bring in more coffee. The men sat silently. Then Tony said, "I told you, Manny. I told you right off they wouldn't buy it."

Johnny said, "Did you see them? Scared to death." After a minute he continued. "A couple of hundred thousand. I knew we shouldn't tell them the truth. What if you'd told them the truth? You'd be sweeping up the floor under each one of them." They all chuckled hesitantly.

Manny looked at the three men who, with himself, Tony, and Johnny, remained. "What do you think?"

After looking at the other two, one of them, José whom they called Joe, said, "I want to blow them all up. I'm here for one reason. My father was in the brigade. A captain in the 2506. Castro tortured him to death before Kennedy got them out. I intend to kill the Commie son of a bitch with my own hands. Blowing him up's too good for him."

The two other younger men nodded. They were also heirs of the brigade, weaned on vengeance with the single-minded goal of stringing Castro up to a lamppost. "We're with Joe," one said. "I think we ought to blow up the whole million."

Manny looked at Johnny. "Gentlemen, you may get your chance." He went to the door again to check its security, then poured himself another thick coffee. "I didn't tell our friends the whole story. I needed to find out first who was who—who was up for something big and who wasn't. From now on the six of us are the *only* ones to know what I am about to say. Tony and I know about the Russian's real product. Johnny knows a little, but not all. So here goes."

By now the six men had formed their chairs into a small circle at the end of the room. They leaned toward one another, and Manny dropped his voice to just above a whisper.

"The Russian has one or possibly two nuclear weapons." He looked at the others. Johnny's face slackened. Two of the younger men gave each other high fives. "They are small warheads. The Russians . . . Soviets . . . produced them for the battlefield. We . . . the U.S. . . . had the same thing. They're used on short-range rockets . . . twenty-five maybe thirty miles . . . to stop an attack from the other side. Wipe out some tank battalions, a division or two. That kind of thing. They kill a hell of a lot of people. But it's nothing like the big nukes . . . you know, the long-range missiles that destroy whole cities."

One of the athletic-looking men, Joe, interrupted. "Manny, what are you talking about? Are you serious? What the hell can we do with nuclear weapons—even tiny ones? Look, I thought we came here to discuss doing something big on New Year's Day." Looking around the room, he said, "Does anybody here have a clue how to use a nuclear weapon? It's a joke."

Pete, the bodybuilder, said, "Any chance we could put it in that Commie son of a bitch's pocket?"

They laughed again until Johnny said, "Listen, you guys, this isn't so crazy. Listen up to what he says."

"So, what if we get one of these things . . . warheads . . . and we put it right in the middle of the place. And when the Commie son of a bitch gets up to talk and they're all yelling their heads off, we let the thing go. Boom. All gone. All of them. Like that," he said, snapping his fingers.

There was stunned silence.

"Manny," the quiet Orlando said. "Manny. Do you mean a million people?"

"I mean all of them. Every goddamn Communist in the Western Hemisphere. Gone. Like that." He snapped his fingers loudly under the table.

"Wait a minute," Joe said. "You're going to launch this thing from thirty miles away? Does the Russian sell rockets to go with it?" He grinned. "Even if he does, I don't think any of us could light the thing, let alone drop it into the Plaza."

Manny said, "Nope. The Russian says you can blow the thing up just like a bomb. He's got friends who can fix the wiring and set it on a timer."

"Where is this thing now?" Orlando asked softly.

Tony said, "It's already down there. It has to be surplus from the missile crisis in '62. That's all we can figure out. How the thing got left there, we don't know."

Johnny said, trying to put the pieces together, "Let's see. We buy the nuke from the Russian, then . . . wait a minute," he said. "We haven't even discussed price. How much does he want for this thing?"

Manny hesitated, then said, "One million. For one. One million five for both."

The room was silent. The clock over the door showed eleven-forty-five. Joe exhaled, as if to whistle, but no sound came. No one talked.

Tony asked, "How much we got, Johnny?"

"Not a million five. Not even a million." He paused. "But I think I can get a million. There are a few people who would put that much up personally to get rid of Fidel. I know some people who would put up a lot more than that if they could get back to Havana and start up in the casinos where they left off. They'll pay if they are sure it will work."

"Nothing's for sure absolutely," Manny said. "But I'll tell you this, if we nuke him you can bet he'll stay dead."

Joe said, "How did you leave it with the Russian?"

"He's given us two weeks to get back to him with the money . . . in cash. Otherwise, he says he can sell this thing easy to about a dozen Moslem countries."

Pete stretched out thick, muscular arms, yawned, and said, "I'm in. Where are we going to put this thing?"

Manny's unblinking black eyes took in each man one at a time. Then he said, "Ground zero. At the very top of the Martí tower."

6 McLemore was now conditioned to look for the omnipresent old wraith everywhere he went. And when his car pulled up at the Deauville in the late afternoon, after a day-long trip into the Pinar del Río province, he absently looked across the street to the spot of shade where he had first seen the old man. There he was. McLemore couldn't believe his eyes. He started across the street as the silent figure began to move off, but Trinidad clutched his elbow.

"*Profesor*, if it is agreeable with you, I will return at nine o'clock. Unless you wish some other arrangement. I need now to return to my department to finish some papers and then wash some of the dust away." Before arriving back in Havana after a day on the road, McLemore had suggested dinner and was surprised at her ready acceptance.

They had spent the day traveling to San Cristóbal and Los Palacios to visit the two western R-12 Soviet missile sites. Trinidad and the car, as before, arrived at the Deauville almost an hour late. No explanation. The silent driver headed the antiquated Chevy out the Malecón westward toward Pinar del Río province by way of the Carretera Central, the rough two-lane road weaving its way down the center of the western Cuban peninsula. There were very few cars but a host of bicycles—brought to Cuba by Castro from China as an offset to oil shortages—and, as they reached the countryside, an increasing number of primitive oxcarts, the kind tourists found colorful. San Cristóbal was eighty kilometers southwest and Los Palacios another twenty or so beyond that.

Eventually they passed through the crumbling, colorful village of San Cristóbal on the edge of the lush, steep Sierra del Rosario hills. Trinidad's hand swept across the Sierra skyline and said, "It is our *orquideria*. It is the thirty-five-thousand-acre botanical garden set aside as a biosphere reserve by the United Nations. It has three hundred and three varieties of native orchids." Then, pointing south, she said, "Down the Pinar are the *vegas*, the tobacco farms. Small fields, not so large as the sugarcane fields in the east."

Hitchhikers dotted the roadsides, headed both north and south. McLemore saw occasional small fields ploughed by desultory *guajiros* wearing straw hats, smoking cigars, and switching equally desultory oxen. Short trees and full island shrubbery were punctuated by random royal palms whose great green elephant-ear leaves seemed to explode from the tops of the gracefully curving, tapered, tall trunks.

McLemore found himself becoming entranced with these parts of Cuba as they unfolded—the lush foliage, exotic birds, tropical languor. He tried to imagine this pre-Columbian paradise inhabited only by indigenous peoples at home in nature, wanting little . . . primitive people unfamiliar with conquest. Then came the Spanish, then the Anglo-Saxons, the British, and the *Norte Americanos,* all bringing "civilization" and "progress," enslaving their bodies, then their minds, then their spirits. Finally, predictably, came the Soviets. In addition to the glories of the nuclear age, the Soviets introduced the addiction of petroleum. Sugar for oil. It was a wonderful contribution to Cuban modernity. Except that when the Soviet cousins left, they took their oil with them. Thus a modern country on bicycles. Which is all right, thought McLemore. But in the distance men were chopping down beautiful trees and surrounding brush for firewood. The stunning countryside was being cleared for fuel.

A few kilometers outside San Cristóbal and well into the countryside had been the home of the Soviet's Seventy-ninth Missile Brigade for a few brief weeks in the fall of 1962. Having no stake in preserving the nuclear age, nature had reclaimed much of its own. It was still vaguely possible to tell where the Soviet bulldozers had cleared and flattened the sites, knocking down trees and uprooting crops and vegetation. The concrete blockhouses used as command posts and launch centers were now inhabited by multitudinous farm families or left to jungle overgrowth. The remains of hastily constructed concrete launch pads, freighted all the way from cold Soviet seaports halfway around the world to reduce construction time, were now badly fractured by neglect and nature. Down the road, a portion of the Los Palacios site had been converted into a regular army post and depot by the Cubans. McLemore had been permitted to take photographs of everything but this. Overall he had a sense that some large-scale but frantic construction carried out by feverish children with great toys had taken place here decades ago, but that little of historical interest remained. As at Bejucal, there was less here than met the eye.

He, Trinidad, and the silent driver had lunch at a small *paladar* of four tables, one of a thousand or so unlicensed family restaurants in a starkly simple home in Los Palacios. They had a straightforward but tasty *ajiaco*, a stew common to *el campo*, the countryside. They had discussed the events of almost forty years ago. How the local people knew something big was going on with the influx of civilian-clad Soviet military personnel, the rapid arrival of great earthmovers, giant crates, enormous long trucks and trailers. Security forces, Cuban and Soviet, were all over the place. Great spotlights were set up to illuminate the countryside so that work could continue throughout the night.

"What do you think the local people understood about all this?" he asked.

She said, "I am sure they accepted the information they were given that the Soviet people had sent their forces to prevent the U.S. from bringing another invasion. The victory at Playa Girón—what you call the 'Bay of Pigs'—was still in people's minds, and there were many rumors that the Yanquis would return, this time in full force."

"Were the Cuban people afraid that this might be the battleground for World War III?"

She said, "I only know what my parents and family have talked about. But I believe our people thought that the U.S. would not attack at all if the Soviet forces were here." She paused, then said, "But I am not a military person, *profesor*. I just tell you what I was told. For me and my friends, people my age, we look at this period as one of great struggle, of life and death for the *revolución*. For us, looking back, it was the turning point. We knew after that, after the missiles were taken away and Kennedy promised not to invade, that the *revolución* would survive. That the *batistianas* were not coming back to reclaim their power over us."

Trinidad had a discussion with the hostess, chef, and mistress of the house, a woman well on in years. Presently Trinidad reported, "She says everyone here knew what was going on. It was hard for the Russians to hide the giant objects they were bringing in. She said everyone assumed they were missiles to be aimed at the U.S. She said they all assumed there would be a big war and that the Uncle Sam would blow up everyone here with nuclear missiles. The Yanquis would get the Russians, but all the people here would be killed in the process. There was nothing they could do about it, so they went on about their lives . . . farming, eating, sleeping."

"Ask her what she would like to happen now."

After further discussion, Trinidad laughed, amused at the folk wisdom. "She says she assumes when *el Commandante* goes to the Communist heaven, the Yanquis will come back and there will be some new Batista in power. Either way, it doesn't matter much to her, she says. There is nothing she can do about that either."

After lunch, they again walked around the remaining artifacts of the Los Palacios missile site. It might as well have been the archaeological remains of a previous civilization. McLemore wasn't sure what he had believed would be here or what he had hoped to find. But it was a kind of pilgrimage. He wondered momentarily what his father would think about him being there.

"What did *your* parents tell you about this time?" she asked.

He stopped and scraped dirt from some covered concrete with his shoe. "For us, it all happened very fast. First, we knew there was some crisis. Kennedy came on television to tell us. Then for several days I heard family discussions about war. People were afraid. My mother and her friends talked about taking their children away from Washington. No one knew what to do. Some families actually moved in with relatives far outside the city. Then in a few days it was over. Everyone was very happy and relieved. I was almost six years old at the time. But I remember people were afraid. Kids like me talked about it."

"And your father, what did he say to you?"

McLemore stopped to kick dust from his shoes on a concrete support. He looked into the distance. "He wasn't around at the time. He told me some stories that fall, thirty-six years ago this month. I now understand what they were. He was telling me kid stories to help explain this. But then he was gone." He glanced at her. "Actually, he was involved somehow in all this."

The sun in the clear area was blinding. They started back for the car.

"How was he involved? Was he in the military?"

"Not exactly. I think he was involved in some kind of intelligence work. He didn't talk about it. We never knew exactly."

"Has he ever talked about it since then?" she asked.

"No," McLemore said as they reached the car under a shade tree. "No, I haven't talked to him about it since then."

Then they turned back to Havana. The driver took the *autopista*, the six-lane highway built by the Castro revolution to bring the tobacco-rich but economically lagging Pinar region along with the rest of the country. When it was built, he had the Soviets to supply oil. Now there were no Soviets and there were no cars. Except for a few military vehicles and an occasional relaxed policeman, they had the highway to themselves. They were back in Havana by late afternoon in half the time the old road had taken.

Momentarily distracted by Trinidad's question about their plan for the evening, McLemore saw the wraith's back as he disappeared slowly into the narrow side street.

Trinidad returned to the Deauville only a few minutes after nine; they met in the lobby and set out. During the day she had worn a plain white cotton blouse, with a colorful flowered scarf tied loosely across her chest, and a full denim skirt. Unlike their first meeting, on this day she had worn no lipstick, and she had let her thick brunette hair fall free. She had looked much younger, almost like a graduate student. But tonight, she was a different creature altogether from the first two. She wore a simple dark blue fitted dress, the rich red lipstick as before, and her dark hair was swept across her forehead, almost covering her right eye. Confronted with striking beauty, McLemore routinely found himself tongue-tied. Tonight was no exception. As he stared at her, then glanced around to see if passersby were similarly awestruck, he tried and failed to think of something conversational.

She stopped a passing taxi and they drove a few minutes away to the Plaza de la Catedral in *Habana vieja.* Trinidad led the way around the corner to La Bodeguita del Medio.

"You must come here once," she said, "so you should get it over with."

He said, "You don't like it? We can go someplace else."

"No, it is very nice, very famous. Every visitor must come here. Many years ago our most famous artists and writers came here, then everyone followed. It is touristic, I am afraid, but also historic."

She had arranged a table up the stairs in the back and away from the door. McLemore briefly considered that she had some influence, which meant that she was something more than an interpreter or rank-and-file Foreign Ministry guide for itinerant academic archaeologists of Cuba's Cold War history. He wondered if she might have a connection with some security service. Most likely. Watch your step, he cautioned himself.

She seemed oblivious to the male eyes throughout the restaurant following her up the stairs. She ordered *mojitos* and said, "Please forgive me, but I will try to introduce you to all our famous national treasures in one evening." She sounded ironic. "Perhaps the *mojito* is the most famous, our national drink. It is rum, sugar, mint, and some other things. My friends look down on me, but I actually like it a lot."

The drinks came and McLemore said, "May I offer a small toast to you and say thanks for your very valuable help on this trip. You've made it possible for me to accomplish a lot in a short time. You've been very helpful. And so, thanks and *salud.*"

They drank. McLemore said, "Bravo. I am now a *mojito aficionado.*"

The waiter came, and she briskly ordered a second round of drinks and dinner for later. She told him they would have *palomilla,* a pork steak, and *tostones,* twice-fried plantains, and asked McLemore if he approved.

"Sounds great," he offered enthusiastically. "Do you mind if I ask about food shortages? I don't mean to be rude, but we've had plenty of very good food this week, and I have been told that there may not be very much food down here."

She drank the *mojito*. "Actually, everyone has enough. But there is not plenty. For our guests, of course we make special effort." She laughed. "Do not worry. You will not starve here. No one starves here. There is enough." Then her stern countenance returned. "Your embargo will not stop us. We will get by." The sword of her bitterness was tempered by pride.

"You don't like Uncle Sam very much, do you," he said.

"In my place would you? We have had three governments really. For centuries the Spanish colonists. Very brutal, how do you say, oligarchies. Then, after our independence from Spain, a series of local governments, some good, some bad, but always with heavy U.S. influence. Ending up with Batista." She spat the name. "He was as brutal as the worst of the Spanish, but even more corrupt. He was a puppet for the Mafia. They gave him millions, a lot of which he kept for himself and a lot of which he used to keep down any threat to his power or any demand from the people for justice. He was a torturer and a sadist. There was no justice. No democracy. This is the regime supported by the U.S. government. So, why should anyone be surprised that a revolution came. You yourselves had a revolution against much less than this. It took Fidel almost ten years. Including time in prison. But he kicked out Batista and his Mafia friends. So here we are. We have almost forty years of revolution, our support from the Soviet Union and everyone else is gone, the Mafia and our 'cousins' in Miami want to come back, the U.S. once again is trying to dictate to us and is trying to starve us out. We are a relic of the Cold War. But we survive. And because we are human beings, as your writer Faulkner said, we will prevail."

The food had meanwhile arrived, and McLemore was eating as he listened. "Do you think Castro has brought justice? Are people here any more free?"

She also began to eat, though without great enthusiasm. "I support the *revolución*. Which means that I understand its faults. I believe you will understand when I say that we are much better off today than we were forty years ago. Fidel is no god. He has made mistakes. But at least he is Cuban. And he is controlled by no one else. We do not have everything you have. We are not so lucky. Most of the world is not so lucky. If we enjoyed your abundance, perhaps we would be more liberal. Right now, we are struggling to survive. There were times when you thought you were struggling to survive—including as recently as the Cold War—when you were also not so liberal. It is human nature to restrict freedoms when survival is at stake. Now we feel our survival, our independence, is at stake. We do not know what will happen tomorrow."

McLemore forked his food around the plate. "You're not afraid the U.S. might try something, are you?"

"Not so much the U.S. itself as our other enemies. Our 'cousins' up north. They hate Fidel so much, they might try anything. I will be honest, since you read this in a few of your newspapers, we are having more attacks all the time now. It is like the days of the CIA and Operation Mongoose in the early 1960s. Bombs are planted in hotels. Fast boats are shooting from offshore at our hotels. Chemicals are sprayed on our crops. We are being sabotage—*sabotaje*—by someone. Who do you think it could be? Maybe the Norwegians?"

McLemore laughed in spite of himself, and Trinidad smiled at her own joke.

Around them the place was alive with *touristas* and a few locals with dollars. The noise level rose as rounds of *mojitos* multiplied. Several sun-burned men, *touristas* off deep-sea fishing boats and flush with excess testosterone, ogled Trinidad in her low-cut dress. McLemore looked at the walls darkened by decades of signatures of the famous, not-so-famous, never famous, and forgers of the famous.

"Why don't you ask me what happens after Fidel," she said. "You see, I can already read your mind, *Profesor* McLemore." She added mockingly, "If I were a man, you see, I would be a Santeria priest, a *babalao*."

McLemore laughed. "How did you know? You did read my mind."

She leaned toward him, touching his hand, as she sought both to escape the ogling tourists now crowding quite close and to overcome the rising noise. "No one knows what we will do. There is no one else like Fidel. *El es unico*. He survives for forty years despite the best efforts of the CIA to make him a martyr. There was no one else like Kennedy or Martin Luther King also. Nevertheless, the *revolución* will continue. We cannot go back. Someone will arise. Some new leader."

McLemore was thinking how complex Señora Santiago was, part stern revolutionary, part passionate woman, when she said, "*Profesor* McLemore, somehow I do not think you are like many in the States. I don't know, you seem more interested in learning, not so much orthodox and dogmatic in your views. You do not give speeches. You ask questions. It is not so common for U.S. people."

He shrugged self-consciously. "You asked me about my family today," he said. "Do you mind if I ask about yours?"

She smiled. "It is not so complicated. My father was a teacher. He died"—she looked into the noisy space of the bar—"many years ago. My mother and I live together here, in the Vedado section nearby." She pointed vaguely outside. "I have only one sister. She is in the United States."

McLemore looked confused. "If you don't mind, did she defect? Does it mean you have no contact with her?"

Trinidad smiled again. "It is acceptable to us, *profesor*. She left many years ago. We are still friendly. We remain very close." Her tone and smile suggested mystery, one McLemore did not have standing to explore.

"And your work," McLemore asked. "You are with the Foreign Ministry, or Tourism Bureau?"

"*Sí, profesor.* My diploma is from the Universidad de la Habana in diplomatic history, and I am occasionally assigned to accompany visitors because of my languages." Dark hair fell across dark eye. "But, of course, only visitors *muy importante.*" Momentarily tongue-tied once again by the performance, McLemore could only grin and blush. This in turn brought an appreciative smile from Trinidad, acutely aware of the game she was playing. The seductive arts had come naturally to her since the age of fifteen, but she rarely found a use for them in recent times.

McLemore swallowed and stuttered, "No . . . ah, ah . . . let's see, husband, I mean, family, you know, family. Husband, children. Family?" His face burned.

She shook the long brunette tress back as she nodded a no. "I find romance . . . interesting. But, so far, not so interesting as to . . . change my life. My job is *muy importante.*" She hesitated, then smiled and started to say something McLemore thought could be even more important when a driver from outside came up the stairs to their table and spoke quickly and confidentially to her in Spanish. She nodded and turned to McLemore. "*Señor*, I am very sorry. But it seems my superior at the Ministry is waiting for me outside. There is something about my duties tomorrow. Will you forgive me? I must go speak to him. I will try to arrange a car for you to the hotel."

McLemore rose with her and said, "Please, don't worry. I understand. There is no need for a car. The hotel is not far away and I will walk or find a taxi. *Mañana?*"

"*Mañana*, you should return to the Ministry file room. Carlos will wait for you. I think you wished to see more documents, *sí?* Then I will contact you the following day. *Acuerdo?*"

"*Muy bien, señorita.*"

She laughed. "*Señora, por favor. No señorita*, anymore. *Hasta mañana, profesor.*" The driver lead her down the stairs and through the press before the bar, as she adroitly avoided the drunks trying to slow her progress.

Outside Lazaro Suarez waited in the backseat of a plain black government car, she joined him, and they quickly drove away.

When the waiter eventually came, McLemore paid the bill in dollars and rose to leave. He glanced around the noisy crowd, confused, when a loud voice from behind him familiarly said, "You look like a Yankee to me. Possibly CIA. Let me buy you a drink." McLemore turned directly into a red, beaming face topped by a shock of blondish white hair. "Ramsay. Los Angeles. And you're . . . ?"

"McLemore. Madison, Wisconsin."

"Well, Mac, the *mojito*'s on me. Tonight, that is." Ramsay laughed brightly. "What brings you down this way?" he said as he shoved through the raucous crowd. "You can't be selling anything. It's illegal. You're not selling anything are you, Mac? If you are, being a Yank, it's got to be guns, Bibles, or whiskey." His laugh boomed like a football cheer.

That's it, McLemore thought. He was a college cheerleader. "No, I'm buying," he shouted back.

"What're you buying, Mac?"

"Whatever they're selling." McLemore grinned provocatively. Might as well play along. Who is this guy? he asked himself.

Ramsay grabbed two *mojitos* in one large hand and McLemore in the other and headed for an only slightly quieter corner out of the flow. "Here's to Sam. Long may he wave . . . and all that stuff." They rang glasses. "I hope you're not buying shares in Fidel's *revolución*, Mac. That stock went down some time ago. About the time Gorbachev shorted it, I think." Ramsay beamed with good humor.

McLemore ignored the question and asked in turn, "And yourself, Mr. Ramsay, what brings you here?"

"Sam, like our Uncle, Mac. See, I offered myself a toast a minute ago.

Ha, ha, ha." Then he leaned in and said, "Sam's the name, good government's the game. Ha, ha, ha. I'm actually, in all probability, the only American in this room legally. I mean, we can come down here so long as we don't spend any money. You knew that, didn't you, Mac? I mean, you're not spending any money here, I hope. Otherwise, you're in deep doo-doo. Ha, ha, ha." His face became artificially sober and he formally stuck out his hand. "Ramsay, of the 'U.S. Interest office.' We're here to serve."

"Interest office?" McLemore asked.

"Yeah, you know, it's a half-assed substitute for an embassy. We don't recognize Fidel, so we can't have an embassy. So we have something called an interest office. Actually, I imagine Crown Prince Lucifer has a better chance at diplomatic recognition by the U.S. than Castro does. Hell, we recognized Joseph 'By God' Stalin and Mao Tse-tung." He wagged a hot-dog-size finger back and forth. "But no Fidel. No way, José. Ha, ha, ha."

"So, what does an interest office do actually?" McLemore shouted.

"We watch out for our interests. Like you, Mac. You're one of our interests." Ramsay smiled evenly, but this time did not laugh. "We're interested in you, Mac. See, Sam's watching out for you. We can't lose track of our interests."

"What if I don't want to be 'watched out for'?"

Like an experienced fraternity man, Ramsay snatched two *mojitos* off a passing tray. "Can't help it, Mac. It's our duty. We got to do our duty. Besides, as a taxpayer, you're entitled to our services, including being watched out for."

"Thanks so much. But let's just say I'll call when I need help. Okay?"

Ramsay shook his surfer mop. "Don't work that way, Mac. Sometimes when you need help, it's too late." He looked at McLemore, his pale blue eyes unblinking. "We can't wait for that to happen. The bogeyman grabs one of our folks, we want to know about it right away." He looked around the room. "Take that lovely *señorita* you were with tonight, Mac. I bet she says she's from the U.S. section of the Foreign Ministry. Right? Well, I'll bet you this *mojito* against Fidel's beard that she's a spook."

"A spook?"

"Come on, Mac. You know. An agent. A spy. Intelligence. The People's Republic of Cuba fucking State Security Department." Ramsay pushed a sausage finger into McLemore's shirt between the buttons and pulled him closer. "Now let's say you're some kind of academic, a professor, down here on some grant doing some kind of research. Let's say you're doing a study of the Cuban missile crisis. Right? Well, strange as it may seem, they're interested in that. They want to know about you . . . follow you around . . . make sure you don't try to see something you shouldn't. That kind of thing. Do you think they're going to send some ditsy secretary along to translate for you. No way!" Ramsay checked the room, smiling a professional smile. "For all they know, the study is your cover. Maybe you're a spook. You look like a professor and you sound like a professor. But you're not really a professor. Maybe you're a professor of central intelligence." Ramsay smiled largely at that. "So, let's say they pull you into some bushes . . . clearly by mistake, of course . . . and they whack you. We're *interested* in that. Understand?"

McLemore nodded, not sure if there was a correct response. "I don't feel exactly threatened actually. They've been extremely cooperative and polite. I think they figured out pretty quickly that I was not exactly spy material." Then he said, "But I am interested to know that, on my third day here, *you* seem to know who I am and what I'm doing. How does that happen? Did you take an 'interest' in me before I came?" His voice tightened. "In fact, it seems to me you knew I was coming here tonight. You don't have a tall old guy in a straw hat working for you, do you?"

Ramsay shook his head soberly. "No, Mac. I don't know anything about any tall old man in a straw hat. There are probably only about three hundred forty-nine thousand of those in this town. But let's just say I happened by and we bumped into each other and I let you know you have a friend in town in case you need one. Okay? No big deal. Nothing more than that."

"Fine, thanks, Sam." McLemore held up his glass. "I'll return the favor sometime. *Buenas noches.*"

As McLemore turned to leave, Ramsay took a firm grip on his elbow. "I tell you what, Mac. Why don't you drop around to see us while you're in town. I'll introduce you to some of our folks. You never know when our 'interest' might be helpful." He resumed his businessman's smile as he handed McLemore his card. "We're officially connected to the Swiss Embassy. But we actually have a little place of our own, don't you know. Right on the lovely Malecón. So drop around. Say, tomorrow about ten?"

"Is that an invitation or a command?"

"Old pal, please! A command? No way. It's simply a friendly invitation. An invitation that, if you are smart, you will accept." Ramsay beamed full wattage.

7 Twelve days after his first meeting with Manny and Tony, Viktor Isakov finally saw the classified ad, in English, in *El Diario*, one of several Spanish-language newspapers in Miami.

Victor.
We wish to sign a contract.
Help us prepare for a victory.
Victoria.

Viktor had thought the message too cute from the beginning but had registered no objection when Manny suggested it as they parted after their first lunch. It was the agreed signal to return to the obscure neighborhood park and negotiate a deal.

He watched the two men, jackets over their shoulders, approach the corner bench where he sat in the shade. The same domino players were there, nodding in and out of sleep. Viktor wondered if they had actually moved in the twelve days.

"Do we have a deal?" he asked, almost before the two men sat down.

Manny looked daggers, at close hand. "Keep your voice down, will you? Who knows who these old rummies are? The Bureau and the Agency have people all over the place down here. I'd be surprised if they haven't already pinned a tail on you."

Viktor said, "Nothing to worry. I am using other name on plane ticket and at hotel. And I am paying cash for everything. No computer trail."

Manny said, "Vic, here's what we think. We want to do business with you. We can find a use for your 'product.' But, on the price, we have a counter to your proposal. Instead of the whole bundle up front, we pay you half up front and the second half when we find the thing and place it under our control. That's only fair. Otherwise, what if we pay you the bundle and then find out that the 'product' isn't where it's supposed to be. Or there's a barn on top of it or a highway. A lot has changed since those days. Anything could have happened. This is fair. Don't you think?"

Viktor looked troubled. "Maybe you get product and Vic don't hear from you again. You got valuable product for half price."

"Can I say something to you, Vic?" Manny said. "That happens, then you dial 911 and you say, 'FBI, *pazhalista*. Mr. FBI, for a reward I will tell you a story about some crazy Cubans running around with an unstable nuclear weapon. For that, *they'll* pay you the other half."

Viktor nodded slowly. "Okay, I guess you got point, as I know." Vic was still a little shy of qualifying for the Harvard Business School. But he was, if anything, a quick study. Manny had just taught him an invaluable lesson in the byzantine bazaar he had selected. The lesson was blackmail, and he was briefly transfixed by its elegant simplicity. It was so crystal clear he almost laughed . . . if you sell something you shouldn't be selling to people who shouldn't be buying it, and if they then don't pay up, you simply call the cops. At moments like this, Viktor Isakov loved capitalism. It made so much sense. It was so practical. How stupid the Commies had been—his father and grandfather—not to appreciate its subtlety, its symmetry, its beauty. It was a system measured like a bespoke suit to his natural contours—cunning, guile, and linear deduction.

"So, how to do this?" He looked around the two men. There were no briefcases or bags. "Vic don't take checks."

Manny and Tony laughed like crazy, enough to wake up the domino players nearby. "Right, Vic. No checks. Now what we want from you is three things. We want a map to the product that's as clear as glass. No *maybes*, *somewhats*, or *possiblys*. Precise to the inch. You understand? Second, we want a wiring diagram, a blueprint, for this thing. So we know exactly how it works. Third, we want an electrician who can check the wires and hook up a timer. Somebody who knows something about these things. Somebody who worked on them before. So he's going to be a pretty old guy. Maybe somebody who worked with your old man."

"That can be done," Viktor said. "Who pays him? You or me? He must be paid."

"How much?"

"I think maybe ten thousand dollars, cash."

"Okay, Vic. We'll take care of it. That's extra. He does the job, we pay. But you have to get him down there and link him up with us. Okay?"

Viktor said, "Do you want one or two? I'm sure there are two."

"It works this way," Manny said. "We pay for one. We follow your map and we find it. Your wiring wizard takes a look at it, kicks the tires . . ."

"Kicks the tires? There are no tires."

"Figure of speech, Vic. It means he drives it around the block. You know, sees that it's wound up properly. If it's okay, then that's that. We pay for one. If it's not okay, if he says it can't be fixed, then we find the other one and try to make it work. So we're only going to pay for one, but we got the rights to two in case the first one doesn't work. If the first one does work, if it's ready to go, then you've got the spare one to peddle in the Middle East or wherever, after the dust settles, so to speak."

Viktor said ruefully, "Only after dust settles. If you light one of these up, it'll be very long time before I get other copy out of there."

"Can I tell you something, Vic? Something about business? You're going to be a businessman, you have to think this way. Sell the second copy to the Arabs—Gaddafi or Saddam Hussein or Hamas or whatever—and let *them* get it out. You got a unique product there. It should draw a big price. Sell it as is. Shipment is *their* problem. Look at us. We don't have any COD here. We have to go find it. Dig it up. Whatever. Then get it to where we want to use it. Same deal with the Arabs."

Viktor smiled, enlightened. "You're right. Not my problem, getting it out. Their problem."

Manny said, "So do we have a deal? The terms I've just said?"

Viktor stuck out his hand. "*Khurosho. Ochin khurosho.* Very good. Okay. Let's deal."

They all stood up and shook hands, businessmen on a lunch break. Manny said, "Next week same time, come to the same restaurant where we first had lunch. Bring the two documents and a plan to put us together with the wire man, and we'll have the first installment. Cash."

He looked at Tony. "No checks." They laughed.

■ ■ ■

As the last rays of light faded, a string of thirty-two-foot Soviet military lorries, especially equipped to transport nuclear warheads, pulled out from the cover of a line of trees along the road and entered the Bejucal military compound. A Soviet Army major in civvies—the gray pants and checkered shirt worn by all Soviet military personnel as a laughable deterrent to detection—directed them one by one as they backed up to the bunker. With a small portable derrick, hand trucks, and the plentiful manpower of Soviet enlisted men, large crates were extracted from the bowels of the bunker and loaded one to a lorry. As each crate was securely lashed down, the major thumped the metal shell of the lorry roof and the driver started his engine and eased out of the compound bound for the R-12 missile regiment sites a slow hour and a half away. Each was escorted again by KGB security forces trained in the protection of nuclear materials.

Lieutenant Colonel Dankevich supervised the loading. His superior, Colonel Leonid Isakov, met the lorries at the sites and supervised the careful unloading of the precious crates. Each one contained enough atomizing power to reduce Washington to very fine rubble. Dankevich rode the last lorry out to the site near Artemisa to join his boss.

"Dankevich, did you find out any more about the Lunas?" he asked.

"No, Colonel. I've recounted a dozen times. It comes out the same. We've got fourteen instead of twelve. Two extra. Do you want me to cable the Ministry through the embassy to find out what happened?"

"Hell, no. The Ministry bureaucrats would go crazy, and we might get some general in trouble and then he comes after us for pointing out his stupidity. So we keep it to ourselves . . . for now. Besides, if this thing heats up we may need two extras. Let's just wait to see what happens."

They watched a group of men struggle with a crate, almost tipping it over. "Careful, you stupid bastards!" Isakov roared. "You bruise that thing, you've enjoyed your last señorita! I guarantee it!" He said, "Dankevich, get that dumb-ass corporal's name and make sure he doesn't see the local nightlife for a month. Stupid bastard!"

Dankevich made a note on his clipboard. He said, "What do you think is going to happen?" He sounded nervous. "What do you think the Americans are going to do?"

"You mean when they see these fireworks set up?" Isakov asked. "Well, first they'll mess their pants. And then they'll be in a great hurry to negotiate. That's what I think's going to happen." He lit a cigar and puffed madly. A great cloud drifted upward. "See that? That's what they'll be thinking about. Big, thick column of smoke rising up from Washington."

"Colonel," Dankevich stuttered slightly, "what if, on the other hand, they decide to test us . . . to see how far we'll go? Then what happens?"

"Then we'll see who's the toughest, won't we." Isakov stuck his face almost nose-to-nose with Dankevich. "Don't be a sissy, Dmitri Dmitrivich.

This is what the Union of Soviet Socialist Republics pays us so much for. Now we got a chance to earn our huge salary, and you're shaking like a goddamn leaf. Get a spine, you quaking birch." He puffed three times and laughed delightedly. "*We're about to have some fun.*"

▪ ▪ ▪

 8 The only decoration on the wall of Lazaro Suarez's office in the State Security Department of the Ministry of the Interior was a simply framed letter of commendation from *el Commandante* for his work in organizing the security for a highly successful trip to the former Soviet Union a decade before. Occasionally Suarez would look at it and wonder why he kept it there. It was scarcely unique; hundreds of similar letters adorned walls throughout the ministries of the Cuban government. He didn't feel that it provided him any special personal protection or immunity from purge. It served no real purpose, but there it stayed, perhaps as some sort of validation.

"Trini, what do you think? Is he up to something?" he asked Trinidad as they shared a morning coffee.

"I have no reason to believe so, Lazaro. He is what he seems to be. He researches the files, Carlos says, and he visits the sites. But he seems kind of confused, maybe not totally enthusiastic about his project. He asks a lot of questions . . . how do people feel now about the revolution? . . . do we have enough food? . . . what's going to happen after Fidel? Pretty ordinary questions. Maybe he's working for the CIA. But I don't think so. If he is, they're not really getting their money's worth." She sipped the hot coffee and gazed at Suarez thoughtfully, as if distracted. "It's almost like something else is going on in his mind . . . that he is thinking about something else always."

"He's a professor, Trini. They all act that way. It's what distinguishes them."

Trinidad said, "One interesting thing did come up yesterday. We were walking around the old missile site near Los Palacios and he said his father was in U.S. intelligence. He thought. He wasn't sure because he was a little kid at the time. He didn't say CIA, but I assume that's what he thinks. Then he got very quiet and wouldn't talk about it anymore. I tried to ask him, but he wouldn't say any more."

Suarez made a note in a thin file on his desk. "Do you need some help with him? After hours? Is he chasing the *jineteras*? Do we need some pictures?" Suarez was surprised to see Trinidad blush.

"I have no idea what he's doing at night. As you know, we had dinner last night. But then I left to come here . . . with you."

A thin elderly man slipped into the room quietly and handed Suarez a note. "Ramsay got him last night. One of our guys at La Bodeguita, just working the room and patting down the drunk fishermen, says Ramsay got him. Talked to him for half an hour or more. They didn't leave together. He says your man more or less bolted. He says Ramsay was smiling and doing his good-old-boy routine, but that McLemore didn't seem amused. Walked right through the *jineteras* around the door and back to the Deauville. Says he got there about eleven-twenty. No diversions." Trinidad blushed again.

Right then three other men entered Suarez's small office, one carrying an extra chair. They were colleagues who had been at the first security briefing at the Plaza a few days earlier. Suarez put the note in the file and closed it.

"All right," he said, "let's go over the event last night and see what's up. Estevan, tell everyone what you told Trini and me last night."

Estevan said, "Like I told you, we had a small explosion again at the Capri, just outside the restaurant. Probably a small quantity of C4, on a timer like the others. This is the fourth 'incident' in the last two months. All the same. Same explosives, timers, hotel locations."

Someone said, "Any injuries?"

"Not this time," Estevan said. "A lot of dust and smoke. People panicked and screaming, running around. No injuries, but it killed the evening. The hotel manager said about thirty or forty people checked out early this morning. Like the other hotels, he says his revenues are way down from the last couple of years. All of them are down."

Suarez rubbed his forehead with both hands. "We have more traffic from Miami. Our people at the telephone exchange said they had a call about twenty minutes after the explosion. Same kind of question." He picked up another note on his desk. "Let's see . . . a man says: 'Anything big happening there tonight?' A woman answers: 'Yeah, we had a little dust storm. But no one was hurt.' The man says something we couldn't figure out . . . a noise, maybe a curse, like he's upset. Then he hangs up. That's it. Pretty much the same as the other times."

One of the other men said, "Where did the call go to?"

Suarez shook his head. "One of the public phones in the lobby of the Cohiba. Just like before." Then he said, "We also had another drive-by at Varadero. Same pattern. Almost exactly when the bomb went off at the Nacional, a fast boat came in to about two or three hundred yards off the beach, no lights, and let loose at the Sol Palmeras. Probably a couple of hundred rounds and then takes off at top speed. No one was hurt and only a few tourists out for a late walk on the beach even knew what was going on. Hotel security told them it was a coast guard training exercise, but the hotel manager says they had a bunch of people check out early this morning. The gossip was all over the breakfast buffet."

Trinidad quietly said, "Goddamn it."

Suarez shuffled through some papers, then said, "That makes about a dozen and a half 'incidents' in the last three months. Let's see. The numbers keep going up. Colonel Nuñez has been all over the Coastal Patrol and the Customs police to tighten things up. But the more tourists we bring in, the more chance we have for trouble. The patrol says it has souped up its boats to the maximum. They just can't keep up with the *batistianas'* hot rods."

Suarez asked Trinidad to close his office door. Then he said, "We've got more bad news on top of this. This is the most serious. One of our best sources in Miami says there are rumors of some very bad stuff being planned for the anniversary celebration. One or two radical groups have spun off from Alpha and are trying to figure out how to do some real damage down here. She says that Little Havana is alive with rumors. Some of the old-timers who've been quiet are coming alive again and, apparently, their kids, guys now around forty or so, are becoming militant and activated."

One of the men said, "Is it just the anniversary? Or is something else going on?"

"She says it's the anniversary mostly, and some phony patriotism on the part of a bunch of guys who don't even have a memory of Cuba. But, there is also some talk about the Mafia stirring things up. Pumping in some money and encouraging all kinds of crazy plots. That's the dangerous part. You get a lot of money floating around . . . then you start seeing sophisticated weapons. Then suddenly we're dealing with a lot more than a fistful of C4 in a hotel disco."

The room was silent. Suarez got up and walked around the spartan office. He opened his single window wider to let in more breeze against the rising heat of the morning. "I've reported all this to Colonel Nuñez of course, and he has reported it to the senior government officials. The *jefes* take it seriously, and of course they expect us to solve this problem. We're increasing collection in Miami. A couple of recent 'defectors' are now in place and trying to work their way into these new radical groups. But so far nothing from them. We may send one or two more. We picked up a rumor about some hard-line 'Bravo' group. We're monitoring everything on the phones that we can, but when someone is talking about the sugar crops or some rum drink or disco music it's hard to know whether they're actually talking in some code. We're going to have enough of our hardware in and around the Plaza at the celebration to equip a large army. But, somehow, I don't think any of this is enough. I have to be very honest. I'm very worried. I'm worried about something big."

Trinidad said, "Lazaro, if it will help increase our intelligence, I will make the sacrifice and go myself to Miami." There was a silent moment, and then they all broke into loud laughter. Suarez grinned broadly. The chuckling continued, and the tension was broken.

"Only as a last resort, Trini. You are too valuable to us to sacrifice you to the *capitalismo norte americano*." Then Suarez said, "All right, everyone give this some thought. See if we can come up with something new for the Revolutionary Council. I'm sure there is a big promotion for the one who turns out to be the security genius of the ages. See you here next week."

He motioned Trinidad to stay behind when the others had dispersed. Suarez had been Trinidad's superior almost from the day she transferred from the U.S. section of the Foreign Ministry to the State Security Department ten years before. They had both become increasingly active in the counterterrorism unit that had grown larger in response to the new wave of bombings and strafings in recent months. Beyond their office assignments, their friendship had grown also when Trinidad made Suarez her life raft to escape a destructive romance. Suarez, in turn involved in a separation from his wife of many years, welcomed the relationship of mutual consolation, which quickly turned to affection, then to intimacy, and then to romance. Despite Nuñez's harsh disapproval, this relationship intensified until suddenly Suarez's wife developed cancer, and he returned to support her through the ordeal.

Suarez said, "How long is your *profesor* staying?"

"His plane ticket is for the weekend," she said, darting a dark look sideways. "But, Lazaro, I can't baby-sit him night and day. Give him to someone else . . . let me do something worthwhile. I'm wasting my time. We've got some real problems here to deal with." Then she added with considerable heat, "And besides, he is not *my profesor*."

"I would take you off him except for what you told me he said about his father. That's something important. If he still has some connection with U.S. intelligence, it is important to know."

Disappointed, she said with some heat, "It isn't clear to me why."

Suarez said, "Because, if our 'cousins' up north are cooking some treachery, the question is whether somebody in the U.S. government is behind it. And even if they are getting some help from some 'rogue elephants' inside the CIA, we have to find out if that's official U.S. policy or a bunch of cowboys off on their own again."

He paced up and down the office, rubbing his chin. "If we find out that the Cuban Americans are off on their own or that they're getting help from some loose cannons inside the CIA, Fidel might be able to stop it by making a private appeal to the U.S. president or, if that doesn't work, by even calling in the international press and blowing the whistle very publicly. So you see, it could be very important if McLemore has some connections. We need to keep the contact with him in case we can use him to carry some messages for us."

Trinidad sighed. "I doubt it, Lazaro. I can't imagine he has any contacts. He is such an . . . an *academic*. And not a particularly impressive one at that."

"Is he planning to come back?" Suarez asked.

"It's unclear. We talked about it returning from San Cristóbal, and he suggested that he would probably try to come back in October if it's agreeable to us. He said he didn't want to become a burden. He does have a general request with the Foreign Ministry for one or two more visits."

Suarez sat on the edge of his desk and touched her hand. "*Por favor*, Trini, try to get close to him. Find out if he still has any connections. Or maybe if he could make some through his father's old friends if necessary.

It might become important to us. And, before he leaves, tell him that his return visa has been granted."

Furious, Trinidad got up and positioned herself behind Suarez's desk. "So, Lazaro, you, the professional security man, are not above using a recent lover to seduce a gringo. Very nice. Anything for the *revolución*! Good motto. It should get you far. Nuñez will approve. I'm sure you will report all the details to him. Shall I take the pictures myself? That might be a nice touch. Maybe an added bonus for me also." She stormed past Suarez. "I'll see what I can do, Lazaro . . . maybe even tonight."

The wake of fury created by her retreating figure drowned out his protest.

 McLemore met Carlos at the Foreign Ministry file room promptly at 9 A.M., as they had agreed. The archivist, a retiree from the faculty of the Universidad de Habana, had not arrived yet, so they got coffee at a nearby shop. Over the coffee McLemore gave Carlos a list of topics to look for in the mass of interministry memoranda and paperwork. All materials were filed chronologically, so any topic index was useless. McLemore instructed Carlos to focus particular attention on the crisis period of October 15 through 28 in 1962, but not to overlook significant documents leading up to that. He explained that he would be away for an hour or so but would like to have the documents organized by topic when he returned later in the morning, and they would then go through them one at a time as before.

McLemore got a taxi and had Carlos direct the driver to the U.S. Interest office on the Malecón. Overnight he had decided to call Ramsay's bluff and possibly get some information from him. When he arrived at the Interest office, he identified himself and asked for Mr. Ramsay.

"Mr. . . . Ramsay?" said the confused receptionist. "Oh, yes, Mr. *Ramsay*. Is he expecting you?"

McLemore said, "Yes and no. He 'invited' me to visit him this morning. But we didn't have an actual appointment."

Presently, after what seemed to be some confusion behind the scenes, the jovial face atop the large man appeared. "Hey, Mac, what a surprise! Didn't expect to see you quite so soon."

McLemore said, "The way we left it last night, I wasn't sure I had a choice." He followed Ramsay down a narrow hallway crowded with temporary files and busy staff people pushing their way up and down as they bustled in and out of tiny jammed offices. "On the other hand, I said to myself, what can he do to me if I don't show up? Have me thrown out of the country? Or maybe demand my passport and strand me here."

"Mac, please. Remember our motto . . . we're here to serve."

They went up an elevator, then squeezed themselves down the hallway into a room set entirely within another windowless room. It was a glassed-in conference room set on riserlike legs and covered all around with thick drapes. "Easier to talk in here, Mac. Here's our coffee. Make yourself at home." McLemore was in "the bubble," a special secured room common to U.S. intelligence stations throughout the world.

"What is your name when it isn't Ramsay?" McLemore asked.

Ramsay said, "To our hosts I'm Ramsay, and that's all that matters, Mac. But my friends call me Sam . . . and so should you." He downed half a cup of bad-tasting lukewarm coffee and said largely, "How's the research? You found out why that dumb peasant Khrushchev thought he could blackmail us? Or what about how Castro felt when the Soviets pulled out within a couple of weeks and left him standing there with his ass hanging out?"

McLemore said evenly, "It seems to me a little more complicated than that. Clearly Khrushchev miscalculated the U.S. response. No one knows quite why. We made plenty of miscalculations of our own during the Cold War. There were plenty of miscalculations to go around. But he was playing poker with Kennedy, a leader he came to judge at the Paris summit— wrongly, history shows—as young, naive, and indecisive. He was threatening to sign a separate peace treaty with the East Germans at the time and create a huge mess for us in Berlin. He was trying to figure out a way to get us off Castro's case . . . assassination attempts, invasions, et cetera.

And his generals kept complaining about the intermediate-range missiles we had pointing at them on their Turkish border. So Khrushchev just upped the ante."

"You make it sound like the Soviets had a case, Mac."

"I didn't say that. But there are always two sides to the story."

Ramsay said, without his amused veneer, "Are there now. Well, I always thought the Cold War was pretty cut-and-dried. Good guys, bad guys. Moral democrats and immoral Commies. That sort of thing. You don't see it that way?"

McLemore said, "I guess I see more grays and plaids, but I didn't come here to defend a thesis."

"Exactly why did you come here then?"

"To try to find out why you were trying to push me around last night, Mr. Ramsay . . . or whatever your name is."

The beam returned. "Listen, Mac, we're feeling around in a big dark room here. We're trying to serve our government and the American people under very difficult circumstances. We need all the help we can get. I was just trying to tell you to watch your six and maybe see if you could provide a little information on the side."

"What kind of information?"

Ramsay said, "Mood of the people. Morale of the troops. Gossip about Fidelito. That sort of thing. Grist for the mill, don't you know. Now, for example, take that *señorita* you were squiring last night—"

"I wasn't 'squiring' anyone, Mr. Ramsay. She has helped me a lot on this project, and I hope will help me more, and so I wanted to say thanks. That's all. What about her?"

"Sorry, Mac, no offense. Okay . . . having dinner with. As I told you, we're pretty sure she's well in with the State Security Department. The Cuban CIA if you will . . . part of the team. She's got to have interesting information stacked right up to those lovely dark eyelashes. Just drain a little off the top, if you get my drift. Big help to us. Anything you got." He leaned forward, a hurt look on his big face. "It's really tough here, Mac. These people don't like us."

McLemore said, "I'm not sure I would like us either if I lived here. We dominated their politics for a century. Virtually replaced the Spanish colonials. Our companies owned the oil refineries, the sugar companies, the tobacco companies, everything worth a damn. We supported a corrupt tyrant who neither of us . . . or maybe I should speak for myself . . . would have dinner with. He sold out his country to the Mafia and tortured any-one who objected. Predictably, they had a revolution and we responded by hiring the same Mafia to kill the new leader and, presumably, permit the old crowd . . . our friends . . . to come back. That sound to you like a formula for making Uncle Sam popular?"

Ramsay's red face suddenly turned angry and his voice flared. "Listen, Prof, you want to preach that liberal horseshit, take it someplace else. I've got a job to do here. You either want to help or you don't. You want a love affair with Fidel, that's your business. But I don't have time to listen to some puffed-up academic carrying around a big bag of liberal guilt lec-ture me about my country's presumed perfidies. Can we count on you or not?"

"Mr. Ramsay, or whoever you are, I didn't sign on to spy on my hosts. Puffed up or not, I'm also trying to do my job. My job is to try to understand just a little bit of history and share *that* information so that maybe someday an American leader will come along who understands the folly of sending people like you to hang out on the street corners and back alleys of the world looking for trouble. Call it horseshit if you want to, Mr. Ramsay, but most people call it history. And occasionally, not often, but occasion-ally, somebody intelligent enough comes along in American politics who understands it." McLemore stood up and said evenly, "Now I will thank you to let me out of this claustrophobic little fishbowl of yours."

Ramsay also stood up and opened the door. "Be my guest, Mac. But I must say, you disappoint me. I would have thought your father's sacrifice might have produced a son with a slightly stiffer spine."

McLemore froze and stared at him. "What do you know about my father, you son of a bitch? You don't know a thing about my father. And you're way off base in trying to drag him into this. My father is none of your business. And I would seriously advise you never to mention him again . . . not to me, not to anyone. You understand? Do you understand?"

Ramsay shrugged and waved his hand, as if to dismiss a pesky fly. Ges-turing to the open door, he said, "Thank you for your time, Professor. Best of luck on your 'historical' research. And do enjoy your stay in this workers' paradise."

Shaking, McLemore rudely shoved his way past clerks, secretaries, and bureaucrats filing up and down the corridor. They stared after him as at a madman. He reached the secured door and pushed through it without looking at the guards. As he reached the street and started back to the

Ministry, he was sure he had heard Ramsay's mocking voice following him down the hall. . . . "Just remember, we're here to serve."

After several attempts McLemore finally found a taxi driver who understood "Ministerio Exteriores" well enough to get him there. He was still shaking with anger as he entered the file room.

"*Señor*," Carlos said, "are you all right? You look as if something might have happened to you."

"It's fine, Carlos. It's fine. *No problema.* It's just that I had the misfortune to encounter one of my fellow countrymen down here and we were not pleasant with each other. As you may know, it's part of our character to debate everything and oftentimes violently disagree."

"Is this the reason why everyone must have guns in your country, for these debates? Or is it because one has a gun that one wins the debate?"

McLemore smiled, momentarily relaxed by Carlos's simple colloquy. "The only guns we must worry about today are Soviet ones well before you were born. ¡*Adalante!* Read some files to me, *por favor.*"

The earnest young man started his cadenced monotone, reading document after document relating almost exclusively to speculation, both within the Cuban government and between the Cubans and the Soviets, about U.S. intentions in the tense days of late September and early October 1962. Many of the memoranda documented the large-scale movement of Soviet merchant ships carrying troops and matériel from Soviet military ports to Cuba. After a time Carlos began a document entitled "Intelligence Report: Estimate of Movement of U.S. Military Forces." It was a copy to the Foreign Ministry of a document originally directed from the head of Cuban intelligence to the Ministry of Defense and was dated in late September 1962. "Read that one, Carlos, *por favor.*"

"*Señor*, it says:

"Various sources in south Florida have reported the following information in recent days. There is evidence of the arrival of a large number of C-130 U.S. Air Force transport planes into local military airports. Numbers are uncertain but clearly somewhere between fifty and a hundred. There is also information that U.S. Marine combat units are being redeployed from West Coast bases to military bases in south Florida. Further, there is an unusual number of U.S. Navy transport ships maneuvering off the Florida coast and in the northern Caribbean. Several squadrons of U.S. Air Force combat aircraft have also been redeployed from other bases to south Florida. Finally, the national press has reported, as previously noted, that President Kennedy has called up 150,000 U.S. military reservists to active duty. Conclusion: taken together, all this information confirms our continuing estimate that the U.S. is preparing for a major invasion of Cuba, possibly as early as the next thirty days."

A lot was going on on both sides, McLemore mused, trying to re-create in his mind what the U.S., Cuban, and Soviet leaders were thinking as tensions increased and threatened to boil over. He wondered even more what individual U.S. Marines, Cuban militia, Soviet privates were thinking, how they felt as they contemplated combat, whether they shared that sense of immortality, invisibility to bullets, peculiar to the young.

As Carlos turned to other papers, McLemore thought of his father. When had he received his orders, what were the circumstances, was he in an office at Langley or at some field station, or were they standing outside a safe house enjoying the bright Florida sun? "Jack," his boss would have said, "we need you to go down there. We absolutely must have someone on the ground. We've screened every possible candidate, and it all comes down to you. You have the best chance. You could make the whole difference. This is the greatest danger in our nation's history." Blah, blah, blah, McLemore thought. A conversation like this, together with phrases from the speeches during the ceremony at Langley a year afterward, had played itself over repeatedly in his mind since he was seven. What he couldn't imagine is what his father said in response. Did he quarrel with the decision, suggest someone better qualified, discuss the odds of getting away with it, talk about his obligations to his wife and son? Or did he do what McLemore hoped he did, what McLemore always remembered him doing? Did he just laugh?

■ ■ ■

A group of Soviet senior officers sat around a table in a farmhouse that they had commandeered and converted into their local officers' club in the middle of the Pinar del Río province. Wearing their guayabera shirts at the end of the day, they had finished a Cuban meal cooked by a campesina in portions that reminded them of home. The rum flowed freely. They were completing most of the basic construction required to establish the R-12 missile installations and were now laying the groundwork for a Luna missile base in close proximity to the Seventy-fourth mechanized rifle regiment near Artemisa a few miles to the north.

It was a few days before Soviet tractor-trailers containing the Lunas themselves, absent their warheads, rolled out of their warehousing areas. Under the command of Colonel Leonid Isakov, the smaller nuclear transport lorries had departed the Bejucal military base with warheads for three separate Luna batteries strategically placed to defeat an invading U.S. force. In each case the Luna launch sites were located, where possible, to the west of the projected landing site with the thought of reducing Soviet casualties from nuclear fallout drifting eastward on the prevailing winds. The following morning Isakov and his deputy Dankevich were to set out for the southern end of the Pinar peninsula to complete the Luna site on the island's western perimeter.

One of the officers, Gribkov, who was stationed at the central command headquarters for the Soviet Group of Forces in Cuba (code-named "Trostnik"), said, "Did you hear who's taken command?" The table quieted for the first time in the evening. "Pliyev. Issa Pliyev. We got a cable from Malinovsky today." One or two of the officers slapped the table. One of them said, "Good man. He takes care of the troops. Maybe he'll give us a few days off when this thing is over."

Another one said, "Yes, and if we have to use this hardware we've got over here, we'll all have a lot of days off . . . in heaven."

Gribkov said, "The funniest thing is that they're calling him 'Pavlov' in Havana. They don't want anyone to know we've got a senior Soviet Army general over here. If you don't have a big general, then you must not have a big army."

"It's like the fable, 'if you can't see the bear's nose, then there must not be any bear,' " one of the men said. They all laughed and poured more rum.

"Who's the deputy?" one of them asked.

Gribkov said, "That's the worst part. It's Grechko."

"Oh, God, not Grechko!" one of the officers said. "I served under him at the Strategic Rocket Forces base at Kamchatka. He's a demon. No vodka. No girls. He's the worst."

"*Never make it over here,*" *Isakov said with a wink. They pounded the table in agreement.*

"*The good news is that Garbuz is chief of staff. He's in charge of overall preparedness, so we will report to him directly.*" *There was agreement with Gribkov. They knew Lieutenant General L. L. Garbuz as a good man . . . easy to work with. So that was the senior operational command structure for the defense of Cuba. And maybe for starting World War III.*

Isakov held up his glass for a last toast, "*Here's to Pliyev . . . or should I say 'Pavlov' . . . we follow him into the jungle and hope he gets us out.*" *He put his glass down and said,* "*Let's go, Dankevich. We start early tomorrow. Down the coast to set up our fireworks.*"

At dawn a sleepy Dankevich joined his boss in the noisy cab of the second lorry in a four-vehicle caravan. They had special KGB security forces ahead and behind. In the lorry ahead and in theirs were the warheads for the Luna battery to be located near the Soviet military base at Artemisa. From their missile site they could cover potential landing sites from Mariel and Bahía Honda in the north of their position to a variety of beaches south of Havana. Several bays were bordered by mangrove swamps, not likely to attract an invasion force. On the other hand, if a division got ashore, they had a superhighway all the way to Havana. The location of this westernmost Luna site enabled the Soviets to drop a tactical nuclear warhead on any landing force in the area and obliterate a whole division, or more, at one push of the button.

Of course, as both Isakov and his nervous deputy Dankevich knew, if this were to happen it would be only a matter of minutes, if they were lucky maybe an hour or two, before an American bomber or short-range missile put an equally devastating warhead on them. They would be incinerated, reduced to atoms in a fraction of a heartbeat. So they represented the trigger to World War III.

For Isakov it simply meant live for the day. His idea of relief from nuclear stress was a full-scale Cuban dinner, a couple of bottles of three-year-old rum, and the same number of señoritas maybe a decade and a half older than the rum. Their warheads temporarily stored at the missile site and under strong, round-the-clock KGB guard, Isakov set about to create his own officers' club in the area. He commandeered, for a respectable fee, a farmhouse with campesina cook and ordered dinner, drinks, and companionship.

"*Loosen up, Dmitri Dmitrivich,*" *he said.* "*You worry too much for your own good . . . and for mine. Your nervousness is catching.*"

"Colonel," Dankevich said, "it's not so much the idea of marine landing craft on the horizon. If it happens, it happens."

"What is it, exactly?"

"Colonel, it's the extra Luna warheads. We've still got those two stored back at Bejucal. If someone finds them and reports that we haven't notified anyone, we'll be canned. I'll be court-martialed and shot. But you will be lucky. You'll have a post somewhere near the Arctic Circle where it will be as cold most of the year as here it is hot."

Isakov ordered the two very young women who had been serving dinner to bring more rum—he had quickly learned the word ron, ron—and to sit next to him, one on each side. He pulled them close and said, "Dmitri, you quaking birch, listen to me. Nichevo. Not to worry. When we get back to Bejucal, I will write a memorandum in my own personal hand. It will say: 'Lieutenant Colonel D. D. Dankevich has no responsibility for the two surplus Luna warheads, two kilotons each, which were sent to Cuba by some dumb-ass general in the USSR. These warheads are the sole responsibility of Colonel L. S. Isakov who will see that they are properly protected and disposed of.' How's that, Dankevich? Feel better? Have some ron. And, by the way, have a señorita. It is my gift to you. If you don't know how to handle a señorita any better than you do a little surplus warhead, I pity you. In fact, out of pity I will shoot you myself. Now, Carmelita, pour some ron for Dmitri Dmitrivich and give him some thrills before he dies . . . of fright."

■ ■ ■

 "Bejucal! I know Bejucal!" Manuel Lechuga was like a child. He hunched forward over a crude map, roughly one foot square. "I'll be damned. I used to go there as a little kid. At least that's what mia madre used to tell me. Her family lived near there. They had a country house in those hills." He laughed at the memory, and then at the irony. "That's where it is . . . in Bejucal?"

"As I know," said Viktor Isakov. He was busy with a spoon carving a large portion of ice cream cake into bites.

Except for Viktor's dessert and three coffee cups, the table was cleared. Manny sat with his back to the corner wall of the restaurant and had the hand-drawn map spread out before him. Tony sat close so that he could also look.

"Manny, that's not too far from Havana," he said.

"It's close," Manny said. "I'd say about an hour."

"What's there now, Vic?" Manny asked.

Viktor nodded his head sideways, mouth full of ice cream. "Don't know," he sputtered. Then he said, "This all I have." He reached into his ostentatiously expensive new briefcase and produced a plain brown envelope. It was tattered and had badly frayed corners. He handed it to Manny, who withdrew a single piece of blueprint paper. It crinkled and cracked with age as he carefully unfolded it. It was slightly larger than the map and was covered with intricate wiring diagrams. It could have been a map of the Moscow sewage system for all Manny could tell.

"Is this it, Vic? Is this the blueprint of your 'product'?"

Viktor nodded. "Very difficult to get, this. My partners have to pay a lot of bribes and do some funny things to get this. See marks at top? Is classification symbols, in Russian. It is saying—'top secret,' 'highly classified,' 'do not distribute outside this agency,' 'atomic secrets,' and so on. To be found with this in Russia, even today is . . . how you say? . . . 'bad news.'" He pointed a finger at his forehead. "Is quick bullet in brain. No questions asked."

"We have to take your word for it, Vic. But if it turns out to be a plan for a vacuum sweeper motor, instead of what you say, no second payment. Okay?"

Viktor ate some more ice cream quickly, afraid it might be taken away. He nodded vigorously. "Is promise, Manny. Vic don't know more about these things than you. But my partners risked a lot . . . even their lives . . . for this. I am trusting them. Is real goods."

"Okay, Vic. Now the last thing is the electrician. We need a guy who understands this spaghetti here and can replace the wires if the mice have chewed on them, or whatever. Who do you have?"

Viktor scraped the last drops of melted ice cream into his mouth, reluctantly pushed the plate back, and rubbed his hands together, satisfied for the moment. "You will not biliv what my partners have to do.

They spent many hours in records of former Soviet military . . . the files of those who handled nucl—these products—in Cub—in place where it is." He looked over his shoulder and leaned forward. "There are very few of them left, you know. They are very old men. In Russia today, people, men, are falling down on streets. Fifty, fifty-five years old. They die. Like that. So not many now around who were down there . . . on island . . . in those days . . . "

Manny pushed the sticky ice cream dish to the edge of the table, away from the precious antique documents, and signaled for more coffee.

"You are not biliving this," Viktor said. "My partners find . . . found . . . deputy to my father. He is called Dankevich. He is very old . . . maybe seventy-five or more years. He was down there with him in '62. They had the command of missiles which carried these war—these 'products.' He is engineer, highly trained in . . . how do you say . . . ?"

"Maintenance?" Tony offered.

"Maintenance of these instruments. Electrical. You know?"

They nodded. Manny looked at Viktor. "Vic, are you telling me that you got us a shaky old man to test the wiring on this thing? He's going to wire a modern timer, a clock, a trigger, on this thing? I can just see this." He held his hands over the table, imitating the gentle quaking of an elderly person.

Tony said, "By God, Manny, I don't want to be around while he's putting these wires together. He'll splatter us all over the Caribbean."

Viktor took his arm reassuringly. "Is okay, Tony. My partners tell me he's . . . how do you say? . . . solid. Like rock." He imitated Manny, holding his hands over the table, but still. "Better than you or me. No vodka. No smoking. Clean-living old man."

"How about sex, Vic? Is he still chasing girls?" They all laughed.

"Can you get this . . . Dinkevich, Dankewich, whatever . . . down there? Can he travel?"

"Very well, Manny," Viktor said. "We have talked to him about taking vacation. Like reunion trip. To see old places. He is very excited. He is already packing little bag. He hardly waits to go."

Tony said, "Does he know he has a job to do down there? It's not going to be just rum, and sun, and *señoritas*. Does he know what we want?"

Viktor nodded. "My partners are talking to him carefully. He understands completely. They said was very strange. Was like he went back almost forty years in his mind. He became like young man . . . like us. We told him about money. He was surprised. He was ready to go for free. We said, no. Is big job. Is important job. This is now capitalism. So you must be paid." Viktor smiled and shook his head. "Was kind of sad, they say. Dankevich say to them, 'With so much money, I will buy dacha outside Moscow for children and grandchildren.' Then he cried. Such is modern life."

Viktor looked under the restaurant table. Manny followed his eyes to the large black leather bag between his feet. "Speaking of getting paid, Vic. We have something for you." Viktor smiled happily. "But first, we need to understand this map. Exactly."

Viktor scooted around the banquette until the three men were scrunched together over the badly creased paper. "Now," he said, "here is . . . as you say . . . area around Bejucal. Road coming down from Havana, up into these mountains. . . ."

"Small mountains . . . large hills," Tony said.

"Large hills. Then, area in square in center is, I biliv, still Cuban military base. It was used by Soviets to store war . . . 'products.' Soviet Army got there before missiles. They built . . . how do you say? . . . bunkers. Heavy, buried compartments, under ground, for war . . . for 'products.' Now you see here an X mark. This is place where it . . . they . . . are stored."

"Who gave you this, Vic? How do we know where it came from?" Manny asked.

"Is directly from my father. He was commander of this base. Or at least he had responsibility for these . . . things . . . devices. He gave to me himself. Before he died. Was his gift to me."

"Like an estate, an inheritance," Tony offered.

"Exactly," Viktor said. "He had nothing else. Just military pension. After Gorbachev was practically worthless. Then came Yeltsin and everything is worthless. Then he died." Viktor touched the edge of the map proudly. "But before that, he personally gave me this and he tells me what is under the X." Viktor made a fist and stuck up the thumb. "This my estate."

"What do they call this thing 'under the X'?" Tony asked. "What was the Russian name for it?"

"Luna," Viktor said. He exaggerated the pronunciation. "Loo-nah." "Is moon. I guess could go over moon, maybe."

Manny said, "No, Vic. When this thing goes off, it sends you over the moon."

As Manny and Tony chuckled at the joke, Viktor nodded soberly. He was fixated by the black bag between Tony's feet. It looked to him like one of the large rectangular file containers used by airline pilots and lawyers. Without looking, Manny shoved it under the table until it was between Viktor's feet. Viktor smiled broadly.

Manny said, "One more question, Vic. What happens when we get to the X? What do we find?"

Viktor had them lean together and described in detail what his father had told him. How the storage was constructed, the materials, the dimensions, the precautions against the elements, the care taken to preserve the contents. Using his hands, he repeated his father's description to him of the size of the crated warheads.

All the while, Manny was beginning to estimate the tools that would be needed to rescue the product, the amount of time required, the need for another storage site in or around Havana, the transportation required, the number of men, the precautions to be taken, the chances of detection, the punishment if caught. This swirl of action excited him. He felt like a teenager again.

They then addressed arrangements for linking up with the ancient Dankevich in Havana, the codes to be used, and, for Viktor most important, the process for payment of the second installment once the goods were delivered satisfactorily.

Manny said, "Here's the deal. Our group meets in . . . ten days." He checked a pocket calendar and specified a week from Thursday. "Go out to the beach to the Doral . . . the old hotel. Behind the hotel, on the beach, is a giant palm tree. Don't let anyone see you. Tony and I'll be there after we make sure no one else is around. We'll have a plan for Dinkwitch . . . dates, times, places."

He moved closer to Viktor, fixed him with a black laser stare. "When we've found the nukes," he said, tapping the map, "and they're where you say, then you will get"—he thumped the black bag under the table with his polished loafer—"your second payment."

Remembering Manny's vivid lesson in business finance—his blackmail lever—Viktor knew they would produce the case—and that every dollar would be there.

"Well, Vic, it's been a pleasure doing business with you," Manny said as they concluded.

They stood to go. Viktor gingerly lifted the black bag, surprised by its weight. They were out on the sidewalk. Manny said teasingly, "Vic, aren't you interested to know who we are planning to send over the moon?"

"I don't want to know, Manny," he said. "I can only imagine. But better for me if I don't even think it. I am businessman, you know. For me, is just the business."

They parted, and Viktor hefted the bag, holding it securely in both hands. It felt like all the ice cream in the world.

11 By Friday afternoon, McLemore had spent three full days in the Foreign Ministry file annex and had made his visits to Bejucal and the missile site in Pinar del Río province. His week was up, and he felt, in spite of all his efforts, that he understood little more about the missile crisis than before he came. Based on the visits to the missile sites, he had concluded that little would be achieved by a trip eastward from Havana merely to see the same kind of missile sites in the Santa Clara region. Missile sites, especially old overgrown ones, exhibited few clues and even less charm. Sifting through the abandoned forum of yesterday's rocketry for insights into the minds of dead leaders was not a method calculated to yield great wisdom. Thus, he would catch the morning plane from Havana to Cancún, then on to Dallas, Chicago, and eventually Madison, as originally planned. On the other hand, he did not even begin to have enough fresh material to write anything insightful. In fact, he had only scratched the surface in his search. He had the remainder of September, then all of October and November and most of December, all the weeks until the holidays, to find some nugget to produce a monograph and justify his project.

What was the central thesis of his grant proposal, the pretentious title that had won the committee's support? "The 1962 Cuban missile crisis: lessons for U.S. foreign policy in the post-Communist world." It was the kind of inflated intellectual blossom that flourished in the knee-high manure carpeting the groves of academe. From extensive reading about the fall of 1962, reading he had begun as a grade school boy, he thought the only lessons to be learned were ones concerning hubris, confused communications, and the kind of pyramiding miscalculation that would have been comic had it not been so dangerous. Much of McLemore's skeptical attitude toward politics and government, indeed political history itself, was conditioned by his lifelong obsession with the events compressed into this fleeting, but startling, scene in the human drama. Did not accident play an overwhelmingly greater role than calculation? Did not leaders blunder into and out of danger, like children with hammers, much more than they consciously managed events? In spite of all the information and "intelligence" that vast secret expenditures produced, were not policy makers really just blind men in dark rooms? On what theories, aside from the usual ones about "national security" or "survival" or some other expediency, did one person, a "leader," send another to his almost certain death? McLemore had undertaken history as a discipline and teaching as a profession as much as anything to provide time and space to find an answer to this question.

The more he studied history, the more Tolstoyan he became. Chance would trump calculation every time.

His reverie was interrupted by the thought that he would see Trinidad that night. To his surprise she had suggested a kind of going-away dinner on his last night—at least for a time—in Havana. Curious woman, he thought. No question he was attracted to her. Difficult not to be, he thought. But the complicated layers of her life made the idea of intimacy remote at best. Her commitment to the ideal of a continuing revolution was, without doubt, sincere. On the other hand, she was clearly too intelligent to overlook the queues for food, for clothing, for transport, for everything. When one lived in a country where systemic disrepair—in buildings, cars, clothing—threatened to give way at any moment to physical collapse, did familiarity breed acceptance? Whatever the *revolución* had offered in the past, in the form of health, education, shelter, was quickly being forgotten as her country drifted sideways into the backwaters of history. The perfidious Yankees could only be blamed for so long, then the failures of the system would demand to be acknowledged.

Beyond her orthodox politics, what did she believe in? What were her hopes for the future? His project of humanizing Trinidad Santiago had succeeded in part. She had clearly accepted him as different from the loathed image of his countrymen. But she possessed a lot of moving parts whose purposes could only be guessed at. Maybe tonight would offer some clues.

As before, she met him in the lobby of the Deauville shortly after nine in the evening. "*Profesor*, tonight you complete your introduction to touristic Cuba." By now he was entranced by the way she said "Coo-bah."

"You are very kind to spend so much of your personal time with me. Your hospitality is much greater than I had bargained for."

"We are friendly people, *Profesor* McLemore. Despite what you are told, we like U.S. people. It is your government we have difficulty with." Then she said, "It is a perfect evening. Do you mind to walk?"

They strolled eastward from the Malecón five blocks to the Prado, now called the Paseo de Martí, the broad boulevard linking the Castillo de San Salvador de la Punta—which together with the Morro castle guarded the entrance to the port of Havana—to the Parque Central. At the north end of the *parque* they went two more blocks east then two blocks south until they came to a charming little square, a *plazuella* called Albear, where Calle Obispo meets Avenue Bélgica, also known as Monserrate. Here they arrived, with a smile from Trinidad, at El Floridita restaurant.

"You see," she laughed, "it is the touristic spot *mas importante*. Here your famous Hemingway ate and drank—a lot. Here is invented the daiquiri drink. The great Ernesto himself improved upon it with his own invention, the '*Papa Especial*.' "

"What's so special?" McLemore asked.

Trinidad's eyebrows raised and her eyes rolled comically. "Two times rum—mostly old rum—lemon, and smashed ice."

McLemore thought he could love a woman who said "smashed ice."

Once again a place had been arranged for them at one of the best corner tables. Influence she has, thought McLemore. The bust of Hemingway had greeted them from the left end of the bar upon entering. The place had filled up, with a queue of tourists already forming outside for a late sitting.

Trinidad said, "As you must have the *mojito* at La Bodeguita, so here you must have the *Papa Especial*." McLemore shrugged amiably, up for anything with only a plane ride facing him tomorrow. Presently the drinks arrived. He said, "Here's to you, and, if you do not mind, here's to Ernesto." Suddenly remembering the watchword of sophisticated world travelers in the 1930s, he added, "Have one in Havana."

"I don't mind at all," she said. "To be linked to the great writer is not so bad." She looked around. "It has changed a lot since those days. Here it used to be a very simple place. Now it is modernized for the tourists and made very expensive, so that very few Cuban people can come here. Maybe the great Ernesto would not like it so much now this way."

McLemore said, "Before I came down here, I heard someone use the phrase 'tourist apartheid.' You have beaches . . . Varadero, places like that . . . where tourists come from all over. They spend a lot of money, but they don't see very many Cuban people or very much of Cuba itself. The Cuban people can't afford to visit these places. Is it true . . . *es verdad?*"

"*Es muy verdad,*" she said. "It is our cruel fate. The *revolución* was to make everyone equal owners of everything. So all could enjoy this natural paradise. But now, because of our isolation . . . your embargo . . . we must convert our paradise once again into an economic attraction. We must have *una subasta* . . . how do you say, auction . . . of our natural beauty. It is a crime, I think, because it is almost a prostitution . . . *una prostitución* . . . of nature herself. It is I think what you call a 'necessary evil.' "

McLemore reflected to himself how much her tone had shifted from bitter rhetoric to an ineffable sadness in the short space of a week. "Is there no other choice?" he asked.

"Very little choices," she said. "Our refineries are not working. Our sugar cannot be sold in the United States. Much of our transportation and our machinery are broken down, as you can see. In the north, you cannot even buy our famous *los puros*—cigars. Cohibas, you know." She smiled. "Except I hear that many Yanquis do anyway . . . somehow."

"Somehow," McLemore said.

"May I give you some to take back with you?" she said, with the inflection of a tease. "Then you will have something to remember about us."

McLemore smiled. "You mean from jail. I can remember you as I sit in *el cárcel*. It might be worth it if they let me keep the cigars. But, I hear, they also take them away. Besides, I don't smoke. I remember, though, as a young boy, my father used to smoke a cigar . . . usually when he was very happy. Celebrating some occasion."

Their dinner had meanwhile arrived, and they ate. They divided what looked like a small leg of pork. "On it is *mojo criollo*," Trinidad said. "It has some juice of the *naranjo*—orange—some olive oil, some cloves, and cumin, and many other things." Her description made it taste even better, McLemore thought as he savored the dish. "Then we have here," she said, pointing, "*fufu*. It is *plátano*—you say plantain—which is crushed down and fried with some olive oil." McLemore thought Cuban food the most seductive he had ever tasted. Was it the spices—or the company?

Trinidad said, "Does he still smoke them?"

His mind on the combination of Trinidad and *mojo criollo*, McLemore was momentarily lost. He? Smoke?

"*Los puros.* Your father. Maybe you could take a few as a present. I'm sure they wouldn't throw a distinguished professor like you in jail for just a few Cohibas."

McLemore took time to chew. Then he said, "He is no longer alive. He died many years ago."

"I'm very sorry, *profesor*," she said. "I did not know. I did not mean to be familiar."

"It's okay. I was a young boy. He went away . . . on an assignment, I guess . . . and never came back. I don't know exactly what happened. He just seemed to disappear. Then he was never found."

Trinidad signaled the waiter to bring more daiquiris, then said, "Was it connected with his work, if you don't mind? You mentioned before that he was engaged in some kind of . . . what did you say? . . . intelligence work." She hesitated. "It is very mysterious. But I guess it isn't appropriate for me to ask, is it."

McLemore touched her hand. "It's all right. I don't mind. It was a long time ago." He gazed absently across the dining room as he ate. "It was mysterious, especially to a little boy. I thought my father was like all fathers. He put on a necktie and a suit every day and he went to an office. At that age, I thought all daddies did the same thing. Whatever it was. Sometimes he was gone on trips. He would show me on the map where he was going and tell me how many days before he came back. I looked forward to these trips because he always brought some interesting present. It was like Christmas. I would get toy soldiers, or exotic little cars, or a puzzle, or a book different from any at school." He took a large swallow of daiquiri. "It was a very long time ago."

"When he did not come back that last time," Trinidad said, "did your mother explain it to you? Did she tell you about his work?"

"Not really. She was in pretty bad shape herself . . . for a long time." He drained the second daiquiri. He was feeling relaxed and pleasantly drunk. McLemore suddenly reflected that, on none of his occasional "dates" since his childless marriage had disintegrated a few years before, had he been this relaxed. Maybe it was being outside his own borders— could it be the exotic climate?—but most likely, it was the company. Though the initially icy Señora Santiago had thawed somewhat, she maintained her barriers against him and his Yanqui countrymen. Oddly, he found her reserve appealing. Her manner had become less severe; but the real change had come in those dark eyes—less challenging, more warmth.

Right now she was looking at him questioningly, and he realized he had been talking about his mother. "She went away for quite a while," he continued. "I later found out to a psychiatric institute . . . she never really got over it. I guess the whole time they were married she was under a great strain. She didn't let it show. Then, he's gone . . . and she fell apart. I spent a lot of time with my grandparents, my father's parents, until she got on her feet. But it was never the same for her . . . or for me."

Trinidad sensed that McLemore wanted to talk more. "Did he travel all over the world?"

"Europe some," he said. Then he laughed ironically. "Actually, he spent a lot of time down here. In Latin America, I mean. He spoke Spanish fluently. It was a second language." He gave her a loopy smile. "His mother, my grandmother, was from Cuba. Isn't that something?" He wondered vaguely if he had pronounced it "shumthink."

"You are Cubano?" she asked, her face alight. Then she laughed out loud. "You are Cubano?"

"One quarterish," he said. "I guess." He looked at the table and saw, with delight, a pitcher of daiquiris. He filled both glasses. "Good old Ernesto," he chuckled. "Sure knew his drinks."

Trinidad, animated, asked, "What was her name?"

"Sarah," he said. "My mother, you mean."

"No, your grandmother. The Cubana."

"We called her 'Espie.' But her real name was Esperanza." He smiled broadly. "She looked like you. A lot." He tapped her glass. "Here is a toast to Esperanza. The 'hope' of the past . . . and the future."

Trinidad shook her head, and the dark hair swayed. "*Profesor*. I had no idea. . . . Did your father not teach you Spanish then?"

"No," McLemore said, dazzled by her sudden wide smile, "he seemed to want to put that part of his life . . . his partly Cuban background . . . behind him. Especially after Castro . . . the *revolución*." He gazed across the room. "I guess he thought it would not help him professionally. Maybe he would be suspect to his superiors." He thought again. "Or perhaps he thought that his bosses might use his background to focus him too much on Cuban matters. And maybe there was some reason he didn't want to be used against Cuba."

"Your grandmother, Esperanza, how did she come to the United States then?"

"My grandfather McLemore was a marine stationed at Guantánamo at the end of the First World War. He met this beautiful *señorita* . . . it's an old story, I guess . . . married her and took her back to the United States."

Trinidad excused herself, and McLemore marveled at the dancer's grace of the slender figure. Ballet, he guessed. He had to remember to ask her. McLemore thought he glimpsed the blondish white shock of Ramsay's hair pass the front of the restaurant and the red face look in. He refilled the daiquiri glasses. Why was he feeling so lightheaded when Trinidad seemed so sober?

Trinidad returned, white teeth and dark eyes flashing, and ordered coffee for both of them. "Will you come back?" she asked with what he believed to be a tone of hope.

"If your government lets me. I haven't learned enough from this trip to write anything worthwhile. I need to study more documents and I need to talk with some people who were involved in the missile crisis. I have to do some work in some Washington files to try to figure out what was happening on our side during this period. I have a feeling that no one was really in control of the situation . . . on either side."

"Your return trip has already been arranged on this side. Your project is of interest to us as well. Even though we are so close . . . maybe too close . . . to the United States, we really do not understand the strong feeling against us. We know our 'cousins' *del norte* are behind much of it. Even so, it's surprising to us how this small island with so little strength can make Uncle Sam so angry always." She sipped the steaming espresso. "Maybe you can help us understand."

McLemore said, "How do you mean?"

"I am not sure, *profesor*. You seem interested in the truth. Perhaps, when you come back, we could organize some meetings—a dinner, perhaps— with some officials of the Foreign Ministry who have responsibility for our U.S. relations. They would like to meet you and hear your views." She put her very warm hand on his. "You might have friends in Washington, in your government, that you could ask about their feelings toward us. We would like to know if there is any hope of creating a normal relationship . . . how that might be achieved."

McLemore laughed. "I'm anything but a diplomat. I wouldn't even begin to know how to get myself into the middle of anything as complicated as Cuban politics." He surprised himself by drawing his fingers across the hand she had placed, and kept, on his. Even as his mind swam in a rum-induced haze, he knew instinctively that he didn't want to undermine a fragile bridge she seemed to be trying to construct.

Trinidad now seemed in a rush. Her face came close enough that he could practically taste the fragrance of her breath. "We are trying to find out if our old 'friends' in Miami are carrying out terrorism against us. We have had bombings and shootings. They are increasing. We are trying to find out who is behind it." Her hand tightened. "Maybe you have some friends who can help us find this out. Yes?" It sounded always like "jess."

McLemore put his other hand on hers, and without thinking, he blundered into her carefully constructed bridge. "Trinidad, *mi amiga grande,* are you asking me to become a spy? Are you trying to get me to find out information for you?" His laugh was laden with irony. "It must be a joke. What is going on here? What am I getting myself into?" He drained the third daiquiri and emptied the pitcher into his glass. "Do you want me to become an *espía Cubano?* Is that it?"

She withdrew her hand. Her eyes, then her voice became cold. "If that is what you think, *Profesor* McLemore, then we have not understood each other. You have misinterpreted my meaning entirely. I did not suggest anything such as you have said. You have shamed me by this suggestion." She quickly collected a small purse on the table, pushed back her chair, and stood up. "We will have a car for the airport tomorrow at your hotel two hours before your plane. I will ask Carlos to accompany you to help you with the formalities. You have my card. Please let me know if you expect to return." She headed quickly for the door, the long dark hair tossing like the mane of a Thoroughbred.

By the time McLemore sorted through the rapid-fire events, called for and paid the bill, she was gone. He weaved uncertainly across the restaurant and out onto the street. He found himself surrounded by *jineteros,* hustlers and con men offering everything from postcards to erotic enter-tainment. He was confused and disoriented, unclear how to get back to the Deauville. He started down the narrow sidewalk toward the Parque Central, the way they had come earlier in the evening. As he waved away the *jineteros*, he arrived across the street from the *parque*, targeted an empty bench in the moonlight-dappled park, and started toward it. He hoped to sit long enough to clear his mind and sort through the rubble of the eve-ning's close. Through his stupor and clumsiness, he had created a disaster.

As he started across the street, he stumbled badly, almost crashing head-long into a passing taxi. He was suddenly aware of a thin but firm hand under his arm, guiding him to the bench and sitting him down. The *parque*'s murky darkness was interspersed with bright patches of moonlight, and the figures sitting and strolling around its perimeters seemed to McLemore like actors on a silent stage. He rubbed his forehead. He had entered a surreal world that bore no landmarks. He felt very drunk.

Suddenly he realized that whoever had saved him was sitting silently next to him. *"Muchas gracias,"* he mumbled. *"Muchas gracias."* He hoped he had not slurred the words beyond intelligibility.

The figure said, *"De nada. De nada.* It's okay."

McLemore tried to make out the dim figure next to him, but his eyes would not focus in the blurry darkness. The man's voice resonated hol-lowly, as if echoing from a forgotten cavern. McLemore made out a profile dominated by a sharply beaked nose and pointed chin covered with pale whiskers. The man wore a large straw hat and white clothing. He looked straight ahead, not at McLemore.

"Are you *del norte*, an American, a Yankee?" McLemore finally mum-bled.

"Not exactly," the man said. "Some time ago, *sí*. But now, *soy uno Cubano.*"

"You were from the U.S., but now you're Cuban?" McLemore struggled with this notion. The man nodded up and down solemnly.

"Let me show you to your hotel," the hollow voice said.

"My hotel?" McLemore said as he struggled to stand up. "How do you know my hotel?"

"The Deauville, I believe. *Es verdad?"*

"Es verdad," McLemore slurred. It sounded like "isferthought."

The man took his arm as they crossed the Parque Central. Figures

melted in and out of shadows in a dreamy ballet. Nearby a couple inter-
twined against a tree like a living, struggling vine. The moon intermit-
tently revealed the walkway.

Startled, McLemore said, "My God, you're the wraith."

"The what?" asked the man. "What do you call me?"

"You know, the guy who's always around . . . outside the hotel . . . in
the square . . . everywhere I go. You're him." He almost shouted, "I know
you're him."

The man continued on silently, propping McLemore up as they went.

"Do you know me?" McLemore demanded. "What do you want? Why
are you a shadow? Do I know you?" he insisted.

Half a head taller than McLemore, the man continued on, holding the
weaving McLemore on course. After a time he said, "We do not know
each other, not directly. But, in a way, our paths crossed a long time ago."

"I've never been down here before," McLemore confusedly insisted. "If
you're Cuban, how could I know you?"

The man said, "*Es complicado*. It's complicated." They were nearing the
Deauville, and McLemore was gradually regaining a small degree of com-
prehension and confidence. "But you said you used to be a Yankee. Did I
know you then?"

"No," the man said. They walked, and then he continued, "I came
down here a long time ago. You would have been very young then." They
were nearing the edge of the last darkness before entering the lights of the
hotel front. The man stopped and held McLemore's arm. "I was an idealist.
I came with others a long time ago. We came down to help with the *zafra*
. . . the sugarcane harvest. We wanted to help the *revolución*."

"But you're still here," McLemore slurred. He tried to do the time calculation and couldn't. "You've been here . . . it's been . . . how many years?
. . . you've spent a lifetime here."

"You could say that," the old man responded. "Yes, a lifetime . . . or
maybe several."

"Hey," McLemore said accusingly, suddenly remembering something.
"Why are you following me? You are following me . . . aren't you? I mean,
you've been everywhere I've been since I got here." McLemore remembered something else. He put his face near the old man's and produced a
crooked grin. "Hah! I bet you know a guy who calls himself 'Ramsay,'
don't you!" It was an indictment.

The old man smiled grimly. "I am afraid half of Havana knows 'Ramsay.'

He is not exactly easy to miss, shall we say. But no, I have no dealings with him . . . at all."

"Then what is it?" McLemore said. "What is it you're after with me?"

The old man looked about him, as if for ways of escape. "Will you be coming back?" he asked anxiously. Then he said, as if to himself, "Of course, you'll be coming back. You haven't finished here, have you? You couldn't have found what you are after so quickly. This is, after all, Cuba."

McLemore said, "As a matter of fact, I am coming back . . . probably sometime next month. Second half of October. You going to be around? Maybe we can talk. Love to hear your story." He still weaved a bit, standing still, as he tried to focus on the old man's face. "You didn't answer my question. Why have you been trailing me . . . all this week . . . everywhere . . . not everywhere . . . almost everywhere I go?"

The gaunt wraith surrendered McLemore's arm and stepped away, as if to leave. Then from the hollow cavern came the voice: "It is about your father," he said. "I knew him."

And then he was gone, in a blink. He simply disappeared into the dark.

■ ■ ■

In a jungle not so far away lived every animal in the world. But the most powerful animals were the eagle and the bear. And then there was also the little fox.

Because he could fly far and fast, and because he was the most powerful of all the winged creatures, the eagle ruled almost half the jungle. His kingdom spread throughout many different parts of the jungle.

And because he was also large and powerful, and among the most feared of all the clawed, walking creatures, the bear ruled almost all of the other half of the jungle. His kingdom was mostly the territory surrounding his great cave.

These two great creatures often struggled for greater power and for control over the parts of the jungle that were not in either kingdom. The eagle let the other creatures in its part of the jungle do as they please and did not try to force them to behave. The bear was a fierce master and kept all the creatures in his part of the jungle under his tight control. Sometimes creatures in the bear's kingdom, especially those on the edges, tried to escape and live in the happier kingdom of the eagle.

Then one day a very surprising thing happened. The little fox, who always had lived in the eagle's kingdom, grew angry at the eagle and cried out that he was tired of living under the shadow of the great bird's wings. "I want my freedom," he shouted, "and I don't want the eagle telling me how to live."

So the little fox called out to the bear, "Great bear, I want your protection against the eagle—I want to join your kingdom." The bear smiled. He knew he could use the fox to trouble his enemy, the eagle.

"You are welcome, Comrade fox," said the bear. The bear called everyone in his kingdom "comrade." "You are now part of my kingdom and I will protect you from the greedy eagle."

Then the bear taught the little fox how to bring other creatures from the eagle's kingdom into the bear's kingdom. "We small creatures are tired of living under the eagle's wings," said the fox wherever he went. "The eagle is a terrible tyrant. Let's go live in the bear's kingdom."

But because he was good, the eagle would not let the fox be misled or mislead others. "I will rescue the fox from the evil influence of the bear," said the eagle. So the eagle asked his most trustworthy subjects to enter the fox's den to persuade him to return to the eagle kingdom.

Meanwhile the bear, fearing the loss of his new subject, the fox, sent his strongest warriors to protect the fox from the eagle's subjects. The two sides began to fight inside the fox's den, and soon the whole jungle was in an uproar. All the creatures feared that the fight between the eagle's subjects and the bear's subjects would end up destroying the jungle.

—Bedtime fable told by a father to his son
Bethesda, Maryland (September 1962)

∎ ∎ ∎

PART TWO

October 1998

12 As the plane lifted off from Cancún airport on the fifty-minute flight to Havana, the noise of the engines' thrust muffled the question from the passenger across the aisle.

"Sorry," McLemore said, putting a hand to his ear on that side.

"Have you been down here . . . to Cuba . . . before?" the man asked.

McLemore said, "One time. I enjoyed it. It's an interesting place." Then he said, "And yourself? Is this your first trip?"

The man looked slightly confused. Then he smiled at a companion in the next seat and turned to reply. "I guess you could say this is the first trip." Then he volunteered, jerking a thumb at his companion, "We're from Mexico . . . businessmen . . . just looking around. Possible opportunities."

McLemore was perplexed. The man's English was perfect colloquial American. "What kind of business?"

"We are"—then he looked at his companion, as if deciding the nature of their business on the spot—"we are in the . . . hardware business. We buy and sell hardware." He smiled. "And you? You can't be a businessman. You are from the U.S., aren't you? You can't be doing business down here." It was an assertion rather than a question.

McLemore said with an ironic smile, "I'm afraid I'm not clever enough to be a businessman. I'm a teacher, a professor of history."

The two men across the aisle looked at each other and raised their eyebrows in mock respect. "A professor. Of history." The man on the aisle leaned across and whispered, "You looking into Fidel's history? There might be some interesting stuff there," he ventured suggestively.

"Not exactly," McLemore said. "I'm more interested in the Cold War period . . . missile crisis . . .'62 . . . that period."

The flight attendant came down the aisle with Cokes. The man across the aisle drank his down, then stuck out his hand. "My name's Jimenez. Juan. My partner is Jorge. Easy to remember. John and George." They both laughed, conspiratorially McLemore thought.

"My name's McLemore." They shook hands.

"Where do you stay when you're studying your history, Professor?" the man asked.

McLemore said, "The Deauville. Nothing fancy."

"We're at the Victor—" the other man started to say but was cut short by his partner's elbow.

McLemore thought the two men seemed nervous, perhaps afraid of an unknown environment. Then there was a kind of confused Yankee-Latin aspect to them. As they engaged in a furiously whispered exchange in Spanish that seemed to have something to do with their hotel, McLemore studied the flight magazine, then put his head back and closed his eyes. He dozed, then suddenly felt the plane's wheels jolt onto the José Martí International Airport tarmac.

Once inside the terminal, McLemore found himself in the passport queue directly behind the two Mexican businessmen, John and George. They seemed stiff as they approached the control desk. Occasionally they muttered a terse exchange. One, then the other, submitted his passport for inspection. McLemore noted that the passports had shiny new covers; unusual, he thought, for exporters experienced enough to be willing to market in a difficult climate like Cuba. The passport official studied each of them carefully, referring repeatedly to the passport picture then to their faces. He asked several questions in Spanish. Each man in turn shifted from foot to foot uneasily and responded tersely. The guard showed the passports to a superior standing behind him who studied the men carefully and himself asked several questions. Each of the men answered the questions with a "*sí*," or "*es verdad*," and one of them said "*ferretero*" several times, which McLemore took to mean something to do with hardware. After a considerable time the men were permitted to enter. But McLemore noticed that the superior made a handwritten note, presumably of their names.

The men were distinctive enough that McLemore was sure he would remember them. The tall one, Juan, stood out in a crowd. Black wavy hair and penetrating black eyes. He wasn't movie-star handsome, but he had a clear presence. Looked like a well-preserved college athlete. He would naturally be in command of anything he was involved in. He moved gracefully and had that kind of wealth-induced ease. He seemed to have eyes in the back of his head. And then there was also that intangible sense of danger. McLemore thought he had the smell of gunpowder about him. Juan's nails were perfectly manicured. And Jorge, his softer, friendlier companion, was a perfect counterpart. Totally unobtrusive, a genial traveling salesman. He was the guy who made the reservations, took care of the luggage, tipped the doorman, picked up afterward. Jorge chewed a hangnail as he shifted from foot to foot in the queue. McLemore marveled at the sudden insight, one he recognized even in the academic world. The hard-charger always needed a sidekick. One broke the crockery, and the other picked up the pieces. The shark, and the pilotfish.

Manny and Tony, McLemore's fellow passengers, did in fact spend that and several following nights at the Victoria Hotel, a small, relatively obscure hotel in the Vedado section of Havana, which was known to be frequented by visiting businesspeople. They tried to change hotels on their second day in Havana but, curiously, found that all the other hotels were fully booked. Needless to say, they were there more to buy than to sell, and the particular hardware of interest to them possessed its own peculiar values. Indeed, they were in Havana to establish a base for Bravo 99 and to recover a unique piece of hardware left by the Soviets many years before.

Their principal task on this advance trip into the belly of the beast was to establish a headquarters, an operations center for their excursion into mass terrorism. Over a map of Havana the next morning in the restaurant of the Victoria they explored their options.

"Here's what we do," Manny said. "First we visit the Plaza, like tourists, you know. Get an idea of the layout and this tower. Then—look down here, Tony. In south Havana, only a dozen blocks or so from the Plaza, is the Cerro section. I checked with my uncle. He says it's quiet and seedy. The kind of area where you can rent a place for a few bucks. We'll stroll around and pick out a few places and see if we can do a deal."

"Manny, I can't believe how that Commie son of a bitch has run this place down," Tony said. "It's tragic. The buildings falling apart. They got no gasoline, no cars. People packed into buildings like animals. If these people had any self-respect, they'd throw the bastard out."

Manny said, "Soon, Tony, soon. We gotta help them. We're gonna help them."

They took a cab to the Plaza. Standing near the Martí tower and looking northeast toward the gigantic image of Che, as Lazaro Suarez and his group had done only a month before, the two men imagined the Plaza packed with people, belly-to-back and shoulder-to-shoulder, shouting revolutionary slogans, waving great red banners, perspiring in the midday heat, thunderously cheering the provocative proclamations of *el Jefe, el Commandante.*

Seeking cool shade, they entered the large glass doors opening into the museum of José Martí, which occupied the entire ground floor of the tall monument to authoritarian architecture. They were directed by an elderly lady guide to the beginning of the panorama of the revolutionary leader's life. There were portraits of his birthplace, family, and early life. Schoolboy essays and later poems. Pictures, large and small, of Martí with fellow revolutionaries planning the overthrow of their colonial oppressors. Martí surrounded by *campesinos*. Finally, Martí saddled on a white horse riding bravely at the front of his men into his first and only battle. The pistol that he wore on that fateful charge was in a glass case under the larger-than-life picture of Martí a moment before the bullet struck, which would end his life and transport him forever into the pantheon of patriots, the Valhalla of revolutionaries.

Tony whispered, "Poor Martí."

"How do you mean, Tony?"

"He got rid of one set of dictators only to be given this sainthood by another set," Tony said.

Manny said, "You're right. He must be shaking his head. But that's what history is all about. Once you're dead, you can be used by anybody to prove anything."

The elderly guide approached and asked them to be more quiet. Manny asked her if there were any further exhibits. She said that much more material on Martí was stored in the basement of the tower. But they had no room for everything.

Manny gestured toward the elevator across the lobby area. "Is it possible to go to the top?"

The lady said, "Usually, visitors may go for a small fee. But today it is closed down for repairs." She shook her head topped with a knot of her gray hair. "This is as usual. The lift is always breaking. It will not stay fixed." She gestured toward a glass case nearby. "You are invited to contribute to the preservation of the memory of our great national hero."

The men quickly reached into their pockets and deposited several pesos each, for which she nodded her gratitude and said, "Please come back. The lift will be repaired and you will have an excellent view of Havana."

They reluctantly emerged into the powerful sunlight. Tony said, "Can't we stay in there longer, Manny?"

"Can't take the risk of that lady remembering our faces. Before we leave, we're going to come back one more time to try out the elevator," he said. "Then, come D day, we'll be back again, who knows how many times. We don't want Grandma picking us out of some book of mug shots."

They walked down the sloping Plaza to the bustling boulevard below. They turned and looked back up more than four hundred feet to the top. They were both thinking about that fateful second two months hence when an overpowering light would flash, everything within two-thirds of a mile in all directions would be vaporized, and a booming shock wave would issue forth across the city. Neither one wanted to risk a mundane word.

"What do you think, Manny?" Tony finally said, as if seeking reassurance.

"What do I think? I think we better go find a command post and get on with it."

Manny referred to the Havana map, pointed southeasterly, and they set off walking. They crossed the wide Avenida Rancho Boyeros, then walked down Calle Pedro Perez until they passed the Estadio Latinamericano. They turned south four blocks and then turned right on Calzado del Cerro, which wound around the giant complex of the Hospital General Salvador Allende, named for the late leftist president of Chile assassinated, many believed, with U.S. complicity while in office in the 1970s. A few blocks beyond, now perspiring freely, the two men found themselves in the heart of the humble structures of the Cerro section.

Here were low one- and two-story houses and small workplaces. Every second or third open doorway revealed a woman preparing a simple meal or one or two men repairing furniture, tinkering with an elderly car, or merely sitting on a stoop smoking a cigar. The buildings were in sad shape. Occasionally, patches of recent plaster could be made out. But there was no fresh paint or serious restoration.

Most of the structures were seriously overcrowded. The two men were silently calculating how much it would cost to dispossess several families. Near the middle of a block on Macedonia Street, they came upon a young man of perhaps twenty years, more sharply dressed than others in the neighborhood, leaning against a garagelike structure unfamiliar with any notion of repair for many years.

"You 'tourists' lost?" he asked, seeing their classier clothing and the map sticking up from Tony's back pocket.

"Not at all, amigo," Manny said, trying to remember inflections from Cubans recently off the boat in south Florida. "Just visiting the barrio."

"You gringos?" the cheap-hip young man asked bluntly.

Manny said, "No, amigo, we're visiting from Mexico. Thinking about doing some business here."

The young man smiled knowingly. "You're from Mexico?" He winked conspiratorially. "And I'm from Chicago." He pronounced it "chee-kah-go." "What do you want from us poor Communists?" he asked.

Tony cleared his throat. "We are thinking about selling some hardware here. You know, small tools, hammers, nails, stuff like that."

"Selling to who, for what?" the young man said with a harsh laugh. "*No tengo dinero*, comrade." He said it with the mechanical diction of a first-grade student. "We got no money. Besides"—the idea amused him greatly—"what do we want with hammers and nails." He gestured sweepingly. "Do you see any dumb Cuban anywhere around here who looks like he needs hammers and nails?"

He pushed himself off the building two steps into their faces. "Tell you what, 'Mexican' brothers, you got some VCRs, some tapes, some portable radios, stuff like that, we make a partnership and we make a lot of money on this *mercado negro*. You hear what I'm saying? No hammers and nails. Bring some stuff people want. You and me are both rich."

Tony started to shake his head and walk away. Manny took his arm and said, "Amigo, maybe you have an interesting idea. Now electronics is not exactly our line of business. But maybe we can learn. Let's say, for example, we brought some electronic stuff in here. We'd need a place to put it, and for sure we'd need a local partner. Somebody who knows the territory, who knows how to distribute, how to deal. Am I right?"

Skeptical but intrigued, the young man nodded.

"Now let's say we brought some stuff like that in here. And we had a really smart partner who would sell it and collect the money." He rubbed his fingers together, and the young man was briefly hypnotized by the motion. Manny put his face a few inches from the young man's. "How do we know we can trust this partner? How do we know when it comes time to collect, we can find him? What if we have to search real hard to find him and collect from him?"

The young man shifted uncomfortably backward, briefly thrown off by Manny's sinister tone implying that there would be punishment if there were any trouble in the collection process. He struggled to reconstruct his macho bravado. "You get the right partner, someone you trust, there's no problem."

Tony said, "You know anyone like that . . . anyone we can trust? It's difficult for us, you see. We're just stupid gringos." Now it was his turn to get in the young man's face. "We're not exactly as smart as, say, some young Cuban gentlemen. So, how do we know if we find a partner to help us out we can trust him on payday?"

Now the young man was thinking fast. "You got three problems. Bringing it in . . . the tapes and stuff. Storing it and distributing it. And collecting your profits." He smiled his *jinetero* smile. "I got friends who know how to bring it in. Trucks at the port. Cousins at Customs. It can all be arranged." He jerked a thumb behind him. "Here is for storage. It's mine. I live here. I can do with it whatever I want to do."

Manny and Tony stepped forward and peered into the open window. It was a hovel. "You *live* here?" Tony asked.

"Yeah," the kid said defensively. "Needs a little sweeping up . . . or whatever. But it's okay. Lot of room. You can put lots of things in here. Next trip from 'Mexico' you bring me some locks, everything will be safe."

Manny said, "Tell you what. Let's say we give you . . . fifty bucks U.S. now . . . fifty more in December. You clean this place up . . . good! You understand? Put a couple of cots in here. We'll stay here while we're planning our business. Only a few days next month. When we get all our plans made, you check your friends about getting our stuff in, then we start business the first of the year. How does that sound to you?"

The young man had already spent the first fifty in his mind. He grinned, looking more like a fox than he realized, and said, "One hundred U.S. up front. I got to find a place to live. And I got to bring some people in to clean up." The thought of doing it himself never crossed his mind.

Manny handed him a twenty. "Start now. We'll come back in a couple of days. We want this place straightened up. If it is, we give you the rest. You stay here until we come back next month. Then we put locks on, we use this as our base, and you guarantee the security. If you have set up your contacts for getting stuff in here and distributing it, then we will discuss a partnership. We work out the percentages, then we start our business after the first of the year. How's that?"

The young man nodded, tasting the possibility of endless wealth, girls, nightclubs, maybe even his own car.

A touch of menace in his voice, Manny said, "What's your name?"

The young man said, suddenly respectful, "Osvaldo."

"Okay, Osvaldo. I'm Juan and this is Jorge. Let's say we meet you here in two days about this time"—he looked at his watch—"three in the afternoon. You get your work done, you get the rest of the money and we discuss a partnership. Okay?"

Swept up in a moment of possibilities, the young man nodded again, still lacking access to the vocabulary of commerce. His life was about to change in ways he had only dreamed it might. These two "Mexicans," appearing on his doorstep like entrepreneurial angels, represented his golden future.

As they started to go, Manny turned and said, "By the way, we'll need a truck . . . you know, for distribution. You find us a truck, a solid one, we'll rent it by the month. And there's another hundred U.S. in it for you." It wasn't a request. It was an order.

"That's easy," Osvaldo said. "It'll be here when you come back." The young man now seemed surrounded by a golden aura. In the space of an hour, the future had become his.

Manny and Tony walked back to the Calzado del Cerro, where they flagged down a car that took them back to the Victoria. They hired a car for later in the evening and managed to convince the hotel concierge they could do without a driver. After a siesta and a couple of early evening drinks they set out for Bejucal.

Working from directions provided by the concierge, and after several unnecessary detours, they found themselves near the former Soviet armory just after sunset. They had changed into black khaki pants and pullover sweaters but carried no equipment for penetrating the compound. They parked their car off the narrow road and behind a clump of trees a quarter of a mile away from the compound's main gate, and with the aid of a pocket flashlight, they studied Colonel Isakov's primitive map of the compound.

As they pondered methods for carrying out their reconnaissance, a jeep carrying two Cuban soldiers emerged from the compound gate, made a right turn, and proceeded at moderate speed along a road that seemed to skirt the perimeter of the military base. Prudently, they waited to see how long the jeep required to make its rounds. In forty-five minutes, it was back. As the jeep stopped at the gate, the passenger tapped his watch, then entered the gate. The driver waited until his compatriot emerged with what looked like two cans of soda or beer, then they set off on another round.

"Let's go," Manny directed.

The two men dashed two hundred yards down the road to the compound's perimeter fence, then crouched at the edge of the adjoining cane field. Tony puffed audibly and marveled that Manny hadn't broken a sweat. The compound gate, thirty or forty yards away, was only dimly lit. They proceeded southward down the fence line, noting that its six strands still retained, after forty years, considerable tension. Manny had paced off, even as he stumbled around the cane stalks, about a hundred yards. He pointed to the nearby fence. Tony gingerly tapped it with the metal flashlight to test whether the Cuban Army could afford electricity. Receiving no response, they clambered to the top, where they met a double strand of barbed wire. Manny held the strands down for Tony, who climbed across, then did the same for Manny. Manny slipped, straddled the wire, and cursed in sharp pain. The barbs caught him in the groin. Through clenched teeth he hissed, "GodDAMNit!"

They dropped to the ground, Manny doubled in pain. Tony grabbed his arm, and they hobbled to the deep shadows of the nearest low shed. Manny caught his breath. They glanced at the amateur map by their dim penlight. Tony pointed behind them and then made a sharp left with his hand. He led the way for the still-grimacing Manny. They crouched low, pausing every ten or twenty hurried paces to listen for noise. All they could hear was the contrapuntal barking of two dogs communicating their loneliness at a nearby farmhouse. After fifty yards Tony glanced briefly at the map, then paced a dozen steps to the right. They were near the bunker door that McLemore had entered with Trinidad some six weeks before.

"This is it, Manny. I'm sure it is," Tony whispered. "It's right here."

Now they had to decide whether to use the small flashlight. Manny said, "We've got to look at the map. If we get it wrong, we're going to waste a lot of time . . . and probably get caught."

They crept to the end of the long, low bunker and stretched out on the dry soil, using the slightly raised bunker wall as shelter. Otherwise they were out in the open. Manny said, "Okay. I'll spread out the map. You get the light ready. Wait a minute . . . let me get the top pointed north, so we know where we are." He pointed toward the distant lights of Havana barely glowing over the low hills and oriented the top of the map toward them. "Okay. Now, when I say go, shine the light for no more than five seconds. Get down here beside me. Let's see if we can find out where we are and then where the X is." They listened for noises. The dogs continued their dialogue. Manny looked at his watch.

"We still got twenty to thirty minutes before the jeep's back. Ready? Go."

Covering the beam with his hand, Tony flicked on the light. They drank in the scrawling map like lost miners. "Shut it off!" Manny hissed.

They both thought in silence. Then Tony said, "We're close. It's right here . . . close . . . somewhere."

"Got to be sure, Tony," Manny groaned, rubbing his stinging crotch. "When we come back, we gotta go right to it. We gotta bring a bunch of shovels . . . picks and stuff. It could take most of the night."

Blessed with better-than-average night vision, Tony stared at the barely perceptible map. He uttered a low whistle. "Manny, I can't believe it. I think we're right on top of it. Look . . ."

"Look, nothing, Tony. I can't see a goddamn thing."

"No, Manny. Right here it shows the X mark at the north end of the major bunker. This has gotta be the major bunker. We followed the Russian's directions exactly to get here. Now the X is just at the end of the bunker. That's where we are. We're at the north end of the major bunker." He paused, reverentially. "I think we're lying right on top of the thing." The idea gave him a sudden chill. What if it chose this moment to fulfill its destiny?

As they let the seriousness of the moment settle in, they listened for noises from farther up the compound near the entry gate. Aside from the dim movements in the main guardhouse, they saw and heard nothing.

Manny said, "How do we get in? From the top . . . like straight down? Or do we go in through the wall of the bunker . . . inside?"

Tony was the leader now. Manny assumed that, as the successful owner of a small construction company in south Florida, his partner would know the mechanics of breaking into a secret bunker constructed, God knows how, thirty-six years ago.

Tony thought a minute. "Victor's old man had to do this quick . . . without a lot of notice. Digging a separate bunker would have got a lot of attention. What's he up to? What's that about? You know . . ." He thought some more. Manny checked his watch, then he made a circular "hurry up" motion with his hand. Tony held up a hand for patience.

"The easiest way would have been to use something, some storage already available. Cause the least notice. Then after he puts in the treasure, he seals it up so nothing can get in . . . you know, water and stuff . . . and so you can't even tell it's there."

They heard an engine approaching, then a slight mechanical cough. During their discussion about Colonel Isakov's motives and movement four decades before, they had lost track of the guards. Here they came, and they were halfway down the central roadway of the compound with only small running lights on the jeep.

In a second they were both on their feet running back the way they had come to the east fence. They could barely make it out ninety feet away. As they came to the low shed where they had first sought their bearings, the jeep pulled up. The front-seat passenger swung out and approached the bunker. Manny whispered "Jesus" to himself. The lean figure of the guard, rifle in hand, stood silhouetted against the dim distant gate lights. He motioned for the jeep driver to join him as he approached the bunker. Tony saw lights come on in nearby barracks. My God, Tony thought, they still use this as a base. Together, the two guards cautiously approached the bunker, one with his rifle at present-arms position and the other with drawn handgun. If either Manny or Tony made a noise, they had no doubt it would draw fire immediately and intensely. The guards got to the bunker steps and looked down into the blackness beyond the slightly opened doorway below. Manny and Tony held their breath. Then, reluctant to take the chance, the two guards backed away, as if from a freshly opened grave. The jeep paused inside the gate until it was relocked, then, with its passenger on board, headed for the compound command post at the end of a short road that directly passed the long bunker where Manny and Tony had just been conducting their calculations. The taillights of the jeep winked in the blackness and grew closer together. Covered in sweat, the two spies waited.

Finally they breathed, and Manny said, "Let's get out of here." Crouched as low to the ground as they could and still move, they headed for the fence slowly at first, then faster. They reversed the process, and there being justice in every detail, this time Tony got the barbed wire in his privates. His dark wash pants tore, then split as he hurled himself off the top of the fence. He left the tiny patch of trousers dangling from the upper barb and followed Manny across the small field toward the car. The dogs set up a howl. They could hear sharp voices shouting and the sound of the jeep starting in the distance.

"Come on, Tony. Run like a son of a bitch," Manny urged. They got to the old rented car just as the jeep got to the gate. Manny tried to start the car as the soldiers opened the gate and gunned the jeep out onto the road. The soldiers were certain that someone had tried to penetrate their perimeter but did not know which way to go. As they hesitated briefly, the battered car's engine turned over and spluttered into life. Manny eased the car around the cluster of trees that sheltered them from the jeep now pausing before the compound gate. He kept the lights off. As the two men watched the jeep some 250 yards away, its driver and passenger quarreled over which direction they should go. Suddenly, the driver lurched the jeep to his left, and they started around the perimeter road counterclockwise. As they made another left turn, Manny eased his car around the trees and started back down the main road to Bejucal and on to Havana. The nearby dogs set up a mournful howl and a *campesino* in undershorts and nightshirt piled out onto his porch, convinced now that something was amiss at the military compound. Manny continued to drive at an even pace to avoid attention. However, the *campesino* pointed a finger in their direction.

Lights were coming on in the compound as their car settled gradually over the top of a rise in the road and began to descend the sharp grade leading to the main road. In the rearview mirror, Manny thought he could see the lights of another jeep appear at the compound gate. He speeded up and in a minute or two they joined an irregular trickle of traffic. They both took a deep breath, the first in an hour.

Tony looked out the car window for a few minutes, then said, "He used the last room in the bunker and sealed it up."

"What?"

"Isakov. The old man. He put the nukes in the far end of the bunker and then sealed it up so that it looked like the original wall. We were right on top of the warheads."

"So, what does that mean?"

"It means when we come back we go into the door of the bunker that we went past and we break through that wall at the end . . . just below where we were looking at the map."

Manny said, "That means we can do our work underground and nobody can see us. Right?"

"That's not the best part," Tony said. "Did you notice anything when we ran past that bunker door?"

Manny hesitated, thinking. "Not that I remember. Why?"

Tony smiled triumphantly. "The door was open."

 It had been a mistake, earlier in the evening when he met with Trinidad, to drink the coffee. Now McLemore was wide awake at eleven o'clock and walking through streets of the old city he could now recognize. He suddenly realized that, consciously or not, he was looking for the wraith, the old shadow who had haunted him six weeks before. What was he talking about, that he knew my father? McLemore wondered.

Upon their reunion, Trinidad had been the soul of professionalism, never mentioning the clash at their departure when she seemed to Mc-Lemore, rather crudely, to be recruiting him for the Cuban intelligence service. Uncomfortable with her reserve, McLemore had brought up the subject himself.

"Look, I want you to know that I'm sorry for reacting badly the last time I saw you. Too much daiquiri, I'm afraid. I'm sure I didn't interpret our discussion properly and I overreacted."

"It is quite acceptable, *profesor*," she said. "I am sure that I presumed a friendship that did not exist and was not careful with my words."

McLemore said, "I want you to presume a friendship." She looked at him from the corners of her eyes. Highly provocative, he thought. He wanted to re-create, and hopefully expand, the deepening friendship they had begun to develop before he rebuffed her political advance. In the six weeks since he had left Cuba, he had thought of her constantly. It surprised him how often she appeared in his mind, wide smile, glistening sideways glances, flowing hair. But she had reverted to her original professional demeanor, and he was finding it difficult.

Deciding to get the politics out of the way, he answered an unasked question. "I spent some time in the libraries and archives of Washington and read everything I could find on the 'Caribbean crisis' since I saw you last. I have a pretty clear picture of my own government's official position."

"And what is that, *Profesor* McLemore," she asked with a playful smile, "that mighty Cuba was going to blow up the helpless United States?"

"More like the mighty Soviet Union was playing nuclear blackmail using Cuba as a convenient launching pad," he answered, matching her smile. "The whole argument, I'm sure you know, gets down to the definition of 'offensive weapons.' There is a repeated pattern of insistence on the part of Soviet officials—Mikoyan, Zagladin, even Khrushchev himself—that they would not introduce 'offensive weapons' into Cuba . . . and that the military buildup was a means of preventing a U.S. invasion."

"This is true, I think," Trinidad said more seriously. "There was every indication that you were preparing a major invasion. Military exercises, troops moving, planes collecting, ships sailing about. It looked serious to our country."

"Maybe so," McLemore said. "But medium- and intermediate-range missiles are not used to repel an invasion. They're used to launch an attack . . . a nuclear attack . . . World War III."

"Our fate was to become caught up in the nuclear confrontation. We simply wanted to be left alone by the Yanquis. The Soviets wanted you to know—at least this is what Khrushchev said—how your own medicine tasted. What it was like to have nuclear missiles near your border. Did you not have similar missiles on the Soviet border . . . in Turkey?"

McLemore said, "We did. But they would only have been used if the Soviets had invaded Western Europe."

"And the Soviet missiles in Cuba would only have been launched if the U.S. had invaded Cuba."

McLemore sensed that he was sliding into a debate that could never be won and, further, one that would once again alienate a woman he was becoming more and more fond of. "There are several differences. The most important is that we had a policy, more or less supported—but certainly understood—by other nations that no power outside the Western Hemisphere would be permitted to establish a permanent military presence in the hemisphere. Monroe, you know. A long time ago. Before nuclear weapons."

They had been having coffee the morning after his arrival in the restaurant at the Santa Isabel, a new hotel arranged by Trinidad. She looked out the hotel window, picked up a small purse, and looked at him as if to say let's go. She stood, and he put pesos on the table. They walked outside and started to stroll down the Malecón. The air was fresh and the sea was up. Periodically a large wave smashed against the nearby seawall, sending a shower high into the air. Gulls wheeled and dove through the spray. Despite the crumbling buildings, the queues and shortages, the creaking, antiquated transportation system, the neurotic politics, McLemore was glad to be back and was now convinced there was much here, not the least being Trinidad Santiago, that he could embrace.

These people have to get on with life, he thought as they walked; they have to pull themselves out of a stagnant struggle nobody cares about anymore. What a waste. A paradise stuck in an ice age. A political *Jurassic Park*. Leaders trying to perpetuate a fight that the rest of the world considers irrelevant. The atmosphere felt at once politically claustrophobic and socially liberating. He was visiting an island from a different age. He suddenly understood the pop notion of the time warp.

"What's the latest on the bombings since I was here before?" he asked the pensive Trinidad.

"They continue. The government has arrested a few people." He noticed she didn't say "We have arrested. . . ." "Our security forces have evidence of the connection between this terrorism and interests in your country . . . the exiles, you know."

McLemore steered her away from the spray of a breaking wave. "Can they be stopped?"

"We can try . . . at Customs and the ports. But the materials, the explosives and timing devices, and so forth, can still be smuggled in . . . from Miami and elsewhere." She walked on, thinking. "There are so many beaches, landing points to patrol. And we are so close to your country." Even though her tone was not accusatory, he somehow felt responsible.

McLemore said, "Do you think we should do more . . . the U.S.? If we don't have proof, how do we clamp down on the exile groups?"

"We have provided proof to your government. We give it to your government and we get no response. And you have your own sources. You must know what's going on. Your security forces . . . FBI and CIA . . . they have knowledge. It is impossible this could go on without them knowing."

"So we know but won't stop it. Is that it?"

She shrugged, unwilling to escalate the conflict. He had a sudden urge to embrace her, to seek in the embrace an escape from the hopelessness of politics. He wondered how she might react. Probably not well. Walls had to come down. She could not see him apart from his country. And his country was once again, as it had been for ages before her birth, the Yanqui villain. Perhaps later.

After walking in silence, Trinidad stopped, sat on the seawall, and looked at McLemore. "Is there a way, *profesor,* in which your study of the Caribbean crisis in the 1960s might help break the curtain between our two countries today?"

McLemore sat down beside her. "I'm a teacher. I teach history. I'm not a politician. I wouldn't know how to practice diplomacy or negotiate a peace treaty. Politicians don't study or try to understand history. That's where the trouble begins. How could my project . . . which, by the way, was originally undertaken to get *me* out of the academic rut . . . possibly be used to get *Cuba* out of its political rut?"

"I don't exactly know," she said. "But I somehow have a feeling there is a connection. There is some destiny," she ruminated.

McLemore said, "It would be nice to believe it, Trinidad. Never having had a destiny, it might be interesting to meet one . . . even briefly."

His ironic tone made her smile. "Perhaps I will consult a Santeria priest . . . *el babalao* . . . to penetrate this mystery." They started back toward the Santa Isabel. Trinidad said, "I have arranged for you to meet some people from the crisis time. Quite a few have died. But most of those still alive were very happy to talk with you and cooperate in your project. You are here for two weeks now, are you not?" He nodded. "Then we have some time to organize these interviews. Also if you wish to continue with the documents, Carlos from before is happy to help you in the Ministry of Foreign Affairs archives."

After making arrangements for the following day, they had parted. Trinidad politely deferred his dinner invitation, pleading work at the office. So as evening settled in, McLemore restlessly roamed the narrow streets of *Habana vieja,* brushing aside flocks of tiny *jineteros* pleading for ballpoint pens, gum, or any giveaway. Now back in the city of the woman who occupied his thoughts, he felt suddenly extremely lonely to be apart from her. He had to sort out his priorities. Had she become part of his project, or had his project become an excuse for being with her? His mind said project. His heart said woman. He smiled at the identity she bore with her country. The one unassailable connection was that she was Cuba and Cuba was Trinidad. He ruffled a hand through the light salt spray collected in his hair. Did he have to convince her that he was not the United States and the United States was not him?

Thinking about his last departure, the other preoccupation—the thin old man . . . the man who claimed to know his father—returned. For some reason he had half expected the old man, *el viejo*, to be waiting for him, prepared to reveal the intricate mystery of his vanished father. Now that he was nowhere about, McLemore was increasingly inclined to believe the old man was nothing but a disturbed dream, a restless specter from his repressed subconscious. During their only direct encounter, the night of his departure in September, McLemore had, after all, been sailing without a rudder on a sea of rum and triple sec.

Remarking to himself on the vivid contrast between the occasional restored building containing a shop and flats or perhaps a museum and the crumbling facades it was propping up on either side, McLemore rounded a corner only to see the bleached mop of surfer curls atop the florid face of Sam "Ramsay" who, together with a man and a woman, was very nearly upon him. The animation of their conversation prevented them from noticing him as he pressed himself into a doorway around the corner from which he had just emerged. As they passed, Ramsay gesticulated largely, and McLemore heard him say in a stage whisper, ". . . damn dummy wouldn't tell us anything, wouldn't help." And they were gone. McLemore was instantly reminded that, at least for Yankees, Havana was a very small town.

▪ ▪ ▪

The Soviet Union had never placed nuclear-capable missiles outside its own borders. Chairman Nikita S. Khrushchev would later say: "The installation of missiles in Cuba would, I thought, restrain the United States from precip-

itous military action against Castro's government." Cuban officials had a more strategic perspective: "We were doing this not so much to defend Cuba as to change the correlation of forces between capitalism and socialism."

Khrushchev states his policy more bluntly: "It was high time America learned what it feels like to have her own land and her own people threatened." We will "give the Americans a little of their own medicine."

Aware that something is, or might be, afoot in September 1962, President John Kennedy publicly sends a warning to the Soviet Union by saying that if the United States ever found "offensive ground-to-ground missiles in Cuba, the gravest issues would arise."

On an overflight of western Cuba in late September 1962, a U-2 spy plane photographs a trapezoidal pattern characteristic of Soviet offensive missile launch facilities with the town of San Cristóbal at its central point. About the same time Nikita Khrushchev uses a Soviet military intelligence officer assigned to the Soviet Embassy in Washington, Georgi Bolshakov, to assure John Kennedy that only "defensive weapons" were being sent to Cuba.

A U-2 flight on the morning of October 14 obtains film evidence of an R-12 (or SS-4 missile, as the U.S. military designated it) medium-range ballistic missile installation in western Cuba. Confirmed by highly sophisticated photo analysts on the fifteenth, it is promptly reported to national security adviser McGeorge Bundy that night. Bundy notifies the president early on the morning of the sixteenth. The Cuban missile crisis has officially begun.

The president calls together his senior advisers, a group soon to be called Ex Comm (the Executive Committee). Dean Rusk, secretary of state, says: "We have to set in motion a chain of events that will eliminate this base. I don't think we can sit still. The questioning becomes whether we do it by sudden, unannounced strike of some sort—or we build up the crisis to the point where the other side has to consider very seriously about giving in." He continues to say that this situation "could well lead to general war."

The secretary of defense, Robert McNamara, says that an air strike against the missile installation and other military facilities "could be done almost literally within a matter of hours," but that it might have to continue "for a number of days" to get the job completed.

General Maxwell Taylor, the new chairman of the Joint Chiefs of Staff, says, "Once we have destroyed as many of these offensive weapons as possible, we should . . . prevent any more coming in, which means a naval blockade. . . . At the same time, reinforce Guantánamo [the permanent U.S. military base at the eastern tip of Cuba] and evacuate the dependents."

He says that once the air strike is evaluated, it will provide the basis for a decision "whether we invade or not." But that's the toughest decision, he says, "one which we should look at very closely before we get our feet in that deep mud in Cuba."

The president's brother Robert Kennedy says that with a surprise air attack, "you're going to kill an awful lot of people"—he doesn't specify whether Cubans or Soviets, civilians or military—"and we're going to take an awful lot of heat on it."

After much discussion, the president says, "I don't think we've got much time on these missiles. . . . We're certainly going to do number one—we're going to take out these missiles. The question will be . . . what I describe as number two, which would be a general air strike. . . . The third is the—is the general invasion. At least we're going to do number one, so . . . we ought to be making those preparations."

Robert Kennedy, as he did customarily, remained behind after this initial meeting of Ex Comm and followed the president into the Oval Office. "Bob," the president says, "these pictures [from the U-2] are spectacular. They're all the proof we need to confront Khrushchev. The son of a bitch has been lying to us on this since last spring. Through his teeth. 'No offensive weapons!' Shit! He either thinks we're stupid . . . or he thinks we're weak. Either way, we have to show him he's wrong."

Robert says, "I agree, Jack. But it would help a lot to have an on-the-ground assessment of what they've got down there and the kind of preparations they're making."

The president says, "Sure. The pictures aren't good enough . . . to make any big decision . . . like air strike or invasion. As soon as McCone is back [the CIA director is in Seattle for the funeral of his stepson, who has been killed in a car crash], I want you to talk to him and have him send some of his best people . . . three or four, maybe five, six . . . down there. People with the language and background. No exiles. They'll pick a fight or try to blow something up. Our own people. Arrange to have them report directly to me when they get back."

Robert says, "When they get back. That's a problem. Getting them in is going to be hell. Getting them out even worse. We did it a few times in '61 [before the Bay of Pigs, which he will not refer to by name]. Now it's ten times tougher. I figure if we send four, we're lucky to get back one. It's a trade-off. The more you send, the better the chance of getting one back. But the more you send, the more chance there is of Castro finding out."

Distractedly, the president says, "Send four or six. You and McCone work it out. But don't tell any of the others. And find out if John can figure out a way for them to send information back . . . you know, even if they can't get back themselves." He turns away.

▪ ▪ ▪

14

McLemore's glazed stare rested vaguely on the documents spread out on the table before him. Having peered around the open doorway three times in the past half hour, the antique Foreign Ministry archivist had let McLemore know he was more than ready to leave. Normally, McLemore would have been gone by six in the evening. But an hour or so ago he had shuffled through an otherwise inconsequential file of documents that were largely routine carbon copies of Ministry of Defense memoranda having to do with the 1962 missile confrontation. In that file he found inventories of weapons, missiles, and warheads removed in the aftermath of the crisis. The Soviet military guests had permitted the Cuban political hosts to participate in the packing up and shipping out of the nuclear, and much of the conventional, arsenals. For McLemore, however, there seemed to be a problem. Either some military bean counter had made a simple error in numbers—or the Soviets had brought in a couple of warheads that they had not taken out. The small, stifling room, coupled with the bizarre notion of missing nuclear warheads, caused a reverie to descend on McLemore:

How in God's name had this island outpost managed to become the great fulcrum in the political taffy pull between democracy and communism? What had made a Santeria-worshiping, rum-drinking, cigar-smoking, samba-shaking sand-and-sun hideaway the O.K Corral of the twentieth century? There was something wrong with this picture. Either history was a potpourri of coincidences, mistakes, miscalculations, and accidents-waiting-to-happen, or Cuba meant something. If you believed in any kind of reason in human affairs, then this growing instinct that Cuba was the platform for one of the great dramas of all times—that it didn't just happen to be the remote crossroads where the great train wreck almost occurred—had to have some foundation. The missile crisis wasn't just about a catastrophe that didn't happen. It really was thirteen days that shook the world. History turned here. Khrushchev backed down and his slide into obscurity began. His vacillation on the missiles provided the glue that bound his critics in the Politburo together and led to his forcible removal in favor of Brezhnev, the apostle of detente. For his part, Kennedy abandoned his commitment to depose Castro—one way or the other—in exchange for removal of the missiles. The CIA might swallow this. But it's a long stretch to believe its coalition allies—the Mafia and hard-line Cuban exiles—ever would. Did this decision set off the complex chemistry that brought Kennedy down thirteen months later? You didn't have to be either Gibbon or Shakespeare to sense the number of historical dominoes the missile crisis—played out on this blissful island stage—may have knocked down.

McLemore had a headache. This was a kind of macrohistory he felt ill-equipped to deal with. The notion that large parts of twentieth-century history may have been triggered by a chaotic thirteen-day period in this small way station of the globe—a period where the behavior of titanic political forces was characterized more by confusion and miscalculation than by wisdom and deliberation—was the kind of Big Idea he wasn't used to managing. But perhaps that was the lesson he was looking for. Maybe history was simply a series of catastrophes divided between those, like World War I, that escaped their cages like wild beasts because the keepers were stupid, or those, like the Cuban missile crisis, that were kept in their cages by some fumbling human instinct for survival. But, as always happened when he reflected on those thirteen days, the picture of his father, his eyes reflecting both reassurance and apprehension, appeared—a picture formed by a small boy listening to his father's bedtime stories. Even when the predatory beasts of history are kept in their cage, someone has to sacrifice. Someone has to stay there keeping the lock on. Had that been Jack McLemore's role thirty-six years ago, almost to the day?

McLemore looked at the dusty memoranda, the inventory of missiles, warheads, artillery, tanks, and light armament. Did the confusion of the moment cause anxious officers and confused subordinates to miscount? There had to be chaos on the docks at Mariel and the other major ports.

Just get the stuff out of here! Load it up and get it out! The Yanquis have the U-2s overhead. Let them worry about counting. The bosses in the Kremlin just want this goddamn stuff out of here. Load it up! Jittery sergeants sweating over their clipboards could easily have missed a couple of medium-size crates. McLemore conjured up the scene in his mind.

Seeing the librarian, twice as old as this paper, peering through the doorway yet again, McLemore pushed back from the table, stretched his arms, and stood up. When the old man turned away, relieved that he could now go home for his supper, McLemore did something he could later not account for. He folded the weapons inventory memorandum and put it in his inside jacket pocket. It seemed at the time a necessary thing to do, if for no other reason than to study it again in his hotel room. He promised himself, as if in exculpation, that he would return it to the file where, in any case, it would never be seen again.

After profuse thanks to his elderly keeper, McLemore left the confines of the Foreign Ministry annex and started for his hotel. He had by now become familiar with Havana's streets and could make his way without concern about wandering into strange culs-de-sac. Still caught up in his reverie and not distracted by the now familiar buzz and hum of the Havana street life flowing around him like a busy stream, he considered the enigma Cuba had come to represent for him. There was the rich and complex cultural stew—Indian, Spanish, African, British, French, Yanqui, Mafia, in all their complex varieties—Sicilian and otherwise, and even, improbably and comparatively briefly, Russian. What made this otherwise typical Caribbean island such a magnet for pirates, dabblers, intriguers, renegades, and fortune seekers? How did it happen that these lizard-shaped outcroppings became such a political crossroads? He could understand the attraction of the great natural harbor, which Havana city was constructed to guard, to sixteenth-century fortune seekers whose great sails billowed forth from Spanish ports driven by hyperbolic Columbian winds promising unbounded treasure. He could understand also the magnet that same harbor held for every pirate in the New World drawn ineluctably toward the same Spanish galleons laying over in Havana before raising sail for the long and treacherous dash back to the Old World bearing but a token-size portion of those same treasures. Perhaps, he reflected, Cuba's troubled destiny resulted from the mystical crossing of some fabled east-west, north-south lay lines that generated an electric resistance to serenity.

As if by transubstantiation, he had a companion. "How do you do," the old man said in that voice from beyond the ages. "It is good that you came back."

No longer shocked when the specter materialized from nowhere, McLemore greeted him with a wry smile. "Somehow I knew if I didn't look very hard, I would let you find me." They walked half a block in silence. "What are the chances that you are going to give me your name?" McLemore finally asked.

"Prescott," the old voice rattled. "My first name's John. But everyone has always called me Prescott."

"Where do you come from . . . in the States?" McLemore pressed his temporary opening.

"California. Salinas. I went back there after seminary. Had a small parish. Never left . . . until I came down here. I don't remember whether I told you before . . . I was . . . am, I guess . . . a priest."

They were at the top of O'Reilly Street headed east through the old city toward the Santa Isabel hotel. It was a small place, twenty-seven rooms, on the Plaza de Armas, only a block from the harbor. It cost more than the Deauville, but there was enough in the study grant to handle it. McLemore liked the old city better in any case, and whatever ghosts the Santa Isabel might have, they were not those of the 1950s Mafia shuffling along the musty corridors of the Deauville.

McLemore stopped and grasped the old man's thin elbow. "How about a *cerveza*? Or even better, let me give you something to eat." He looked at his watch. "It's dinnertime. Let's go." He started tugging his companion back down a side street.

Prescott looked confused. "I don't know," he said. "It . . . it doesn't seem right. I don't mean to beg," he stammered. "Maybe next time."

"No. Come on," McLemore said gently but insistently. "This time. We have some business to take care of. From last time. Come on, it won't wait."

Prescott let himself be pulled along as they made their way down a broken street littered with unused boards and construction materials, old cars, pitiful, cowering dogs, people chattering in stifling doorways, and small stagnant pools of water from a late-afternoon shower. They went two blocks down the street from the small square where the Floridita was located, the restaurant where, on the last trip, he had managed to offend Trinidad.

By now, McLemore knew where he was going. He found the tiny sign saying JULIA, and he stuck his head in the narrow doorway. One of the three tables was empty, so he pulled Prescott in behind him. *"Por favor,"* he said, gesturing toward the table. He did not see the ebullient Julia, but a young woman, possibly a cousin of Carlos, pointed him to the table, happy in any case to see someone who obviously had Yanqui dollars. *"Dos cervezas, por favor. Cristal,"* McLemore said.

Nothing had changed, McLemore noted as he inspected the small, crowded room. Two small oscillating fans blew the flies about while providing a slight breeze. The tile floors were worn by the ages. The place was a monument to Cuban kitsch. Behind their table was a short bar decorated with blinking Christmas lights. At one end was a figure of the Buddha, with a cigar. At the other end was a taller ceramic American Indian which, unlike the Buddha and its counterparts in the United States, had no cigar. Against the opposite wall was an aged green couch on which several family members and friends rested from the day's labor. Above the couch was a creche of old Venice, complete with gondola, gondolier, and tiny honeymoon couple doomed to transit the Grand Canal till the end of time. In one corner was a pot of flowers, decaying despite the fact they were plastic. There were several tiny deer heads on both sides of the creche. Above Prescott's head on the near wall was a formidable tapestry dominated by an Amazon of Xena-like proportions, mostly naked, but framed between a thoughtfully serious lion and a tiger with a very bad toothache.

Through the beaded curtain doorway opening to the kitchen in the back burst the effervescent Julia looking for someone to feed. She glanced at McLemore, then stopped, confused. Suddenly she remembered. The friend of Carlos! She charged the table, preceded by a volley of *"holas."* The men stood, and she embraced them warmly. She pressed every dish she had on them: *congri* with "Christians and Muslims," fried plantain, yucca, *mas cervezas*. She retreated to the kitchen to prepare the heaping plates.

McLemore explained his connection with Carlos, his translator, and thus his aunt Julia. Then he said, "But of course you must know this. The second time I saw you was down the street in the square." He paused to think, then said, "Where you found me tonight. You've put yourself in my path pretty effectively, both last trip and this one. If I didn't know better, I'd say you had quite an intelligence network. But since I do know better, I'll have to just say that you're lucky."

The ancient white head was down, eyes on the table. "I knew someday you'd show up here. I knew it. And I hadn't given up. It became almost a vigil for me. Like something I was put here to do." He seemed ready to go on. Then the beer arrived and he stopped.

As they sipped the welcome, mostly cold liquid, McLemore resolved to go at this indirectly, sensing that Prescott was still reluctant to pick up the thread of his father's fate. "I've been thinking about Cuba a lot since I left here last month and since I've come back. This place is an original. I'm trying to find out why and how. And I'm trying to figure out how this place gets itself out of its historic cul-de-sac . . . without violence and without returning to the 1950s and with some shred of honor on all sides." He drank the beer and waited.

Finally Prescott said, "How we resolve this matter . . . Cuba . . . will tell us a lot about ourselves and whether we . . . Americans, human beings . . . have made any progress toward civilization." He gazed out the front of the restaurant. "When I first came down here, many years ago, I was so naive. I thought maybe something good might happen here . . . that these people had a chance to escape colonialism, and the dark side of capitalism, and all the isms. That they might actually build a just republic here." He shook his head. "It was too much to ask, too much to expect. After all, they're only humans. They've got too much history on their backs, too much distrust . . . of us, of Yanquis, of big corporations, of mafias, of gangsters and plunderers. These people have seen too much to be innocent. But they had a chance, for the first time in their long history of slavery, to create a republic of the people here, to put up a monument to justice and to worship it."

Babbling as she came, Julia brought dishes and dishes of food, more beer, and then rubbed her ample hands in satisfaction as they waded in. Through mouthfuls of *congri*, McLemore said, "What kind of justice are you talking about . . . the kind they provided to the Batista agents they swept up here and put in the castle"—gesturing with his fork—"across the harbor?"

Prescott shook his long head sadly. "No. I had something else in mind. Along with some other people, I was willing to overlook that kind of revolutionary justice at the time in the hope that, when the *barbudos* got rid of all that hatred, they'd discover real justice . . . the kind they claimed they believed in."

"What kind of justice do you believe in . . . ah . . . , Father?" McLemore asked.

"Don't call me that," Prescott said heatedly. "I'm not a Father . . . a priest. . . . Haven't been for a long time. Won't be anymore. Couldn't be even if I wanted to, and I wouldn't even know how, anyway."

Prescott pushed the rice and beans back and forth across the plate, Christians and Muslims. Then he looked up at McLemore, staring at him hard. McLemore couldn't hold the heat of his gaze and briefly wondered if the old man had gone mad. "I'll tell you what I'm talking about. I'm talking about human justice . . . what I guess they now call social justice. I believe in enough for everyone. A place to live, enough to eat, medicine for children, whether they can pay for it or not. Decent work, honest work. This is what Jesus taught. It's why I joined the Church. Because that's what he preached. Jesus wasn't a capitalist or a Communist. He was a human being who believed we're all divine. We're all children of God. What's more divine than a child? Children are the kingdom of heaven. What kind of a country . . . a society . . . can't find a way to feed its children? First! Before anything else. Before guns and bullets. Before highways and tax cuts and handouts to corporations. When schools look like dumps and banks look like Greek temples, that's not civilization. For rich people, justice means putting criminals in jail. Punishing kids who steal a bicycle. That's all they can think about. Punishment and prisons. That's their definition of justice. But that's not much more than vengeance. What about the kind of justice that's about fairness and forgiveness and kindness? Whatever happened to that kind of justice?" The old man's lips trembled slightly, but his gaze was fiery and fearless. "Someday I'm going to find a country where children are the gods and the kings. I'll sweep the streets there every day and I'll be happy to do it. That'll be my country."

Prescott ducked his head and turned away at the same time, embarrassed, apparently afraid that McLemore might walk out on him, the madman, or worse yet, start laughing.

McLemore put out a hand to touch the bony shoulder, but suddenly found that he had his own emotions to deal with instead.

15 Standing in front of Colonel Nuñez's desk, painfully aware he had not been asked to sit down, Lazaro Suarez shifted tensely from foot to foot. Nuñez studied the papers before him as if they were meant to be memorized. He had not said a word since Suarez entered almost five minutes before. Although it was against his nature, on occasions like this Suarez found himself noting Nuñez's great ugliness. Behind his back, he was called "pineapple face" after the American-supported, drug-running former president of Panama, Manuel Noriega, and in recognition of the devastation of his corrugated skin. It was widely known that Nuñez kept his position as senior deputy in the secret service because of respect for his ruthlessness not out of any promise of congeniality.

Nuñez hummed under his breath, a cracked monotone that sounded like a generator with a faulty fuse. He looked up with mock surprise, as if he had forgotten the presence of the man who, minutes ago, had received his urgent summons. "Sit down, Lazaro. Don't always be a fool." He waved dismissively with his hand even as he turned back to the papers. Suarez retreated to the only chair available, one against the wall. "Goddammit, Suarez, bring that chair up here where it belongs," Nuñez bellowed with exasperation. Suarez knew he was being humiliated, an increasing pattern, but he did not know why.

"Goddam hell!" Nuñez said, punishing his innocent desk with a beefy left fist. Finally, he pushed the papers across the desk at Suarez. "Read this!" He did not say "you imbecile," but it was implicit in his tone.

Suarez sighed and read the intelligence report, apparently from an agent in Miami code-named Nightlight according to the source block. Suarez was not cleared to know who Nightlight was, but he knew, through his own sources, anyway. After the usual preliminaries establishing dates, places, circumstances, and so forth, Nightlight states:

> Several members of the group calling itself Bravo 99 left the dinner meeting at La Casa Blanca early. No more than six stayed behind, apparently including the top leadership. Approximately an hour later, I observed (from a secure spot across the street) this

second group leave. They whispered together, in what appeared to be an excited fashion, before they split up. Then I went back to the hotel and picked up the tape. With the help of some sources, I had picked up "Ulanov" when he came back to town, took the room next to him, and put a wire on his phone. The important parts of the tape said: ". . . pick up the first installment soon. . . . Will deliver maps and diagrams required by buyers. . . . They are in a hurry . . . something about the end of the year. . . . Complicated deal about 'Pay for one, but get rights to two' . . . or something like that. . . . Don't get it. . . . (Laughter) Yeah, Americans for sure . . . even though from down South. . . . Very eager. Very." Then some more I could not understand. Watched him days later. Back to La Casa Blanca. Met with two guys, both from the meeting the night before. A big bag changed hands. From them to him. From him to them, two big envelopes. More later.

Suarez looked up. Nuñez had been studying the top of his head as he read the report. "Well, Lazaro, what do you make of it?"

"The same as you, I'm sure, Colonel. This Bravo group is buying some weapons from the Russian. The only three important questions are: One, who is this Bravo group? Two, why are they buying from a Russian? And three, what are the weapons?"

"What do you think, Lazaro? What are your answers?"

Suarez hesitated, knowing he would be roasted for missing something obvious or for telling Nuñez what he already knew. "Well, the Bravo group is either a spin-off of an old hard-line outfit or maybe the next-generation hard-liners. They are buying from the Russian either because he is selling the usual stuff—small arms, C4, grenades, and so forth—cheaper. Or, he is selling something new. Last-generation Soviet stuff, optics, nightscopes, triggers, detonators. Who knows. Could almost be anything."

Nuñez waited, dreadfully, to see if he had anything more creative than this. "Lazaro. I can't tell you how sad this makes me. You're the best we've got. And yet . . . you just don't get it. We're at war. War!" he suddenly shouted, standing up and resuming the thrashing of the helpless desk. "They want to kill us. All of us. Don't you see? Don't you understand? They are conspiring with the Russians, our old 'friends,' to kill us. I tell you, Lazaro, they are going to start a real war down here. That's what they're up to."

Suarez studied his shoes briefly and said, "We have almost doubled the number of Customs officers at the airports and harbors, Colonel. We have put many more people on the streets, watching any 'tourists' that fit our terrorist profile, as you suggested. Not just in Havana, but all the cities. We have all the leading dissidents under complete surveillance, and we have infiltrated all their groups." He shrugged and raised his hands, palms up. "I have done everything, and more, that you have ordered. Please tell me what I can do."

Nuñez steepled his fingers and studied the stubby cathedral. "I'll tell you what you can do. You can turn over these responsibilities to Hernandez. Felix. He's good at managing things that other people organize. He'll report directly to me. And I'll kick his ass if he doesn't perform," Nuñez added gratuitously. "What I want you to do, Lazaro, is to take over the investigation of this goddamn Bravo group."

Suarez straightened up in his chair. This was either a serious demotion, or he was being told to focus on the greatest threat. "As you wish, Colonel. But I'll need to see all the intelligence traffic and get to know the agents involved . . . presuming there's more than one." He thought a moment. "How much do we know about this 'Ulanov'?"

"Aside from the fact he's a Russian, and an arms dealer, not much," Nuñez said. He massaged the pocked landscape of his face and began to pace the office space behind his desk. "You know some of the people we have in Miami. But not Nightlight. In fact, you don't need to know who Nightlight is. Just get the traffic, identify yourself, and become Nightlight's keeper. Find out everything you can about 'Ulanov,' and this Bravo outfit. That is now your job . . . full-time. Nothing else. I'll help you fashion the shopping list for Nightlight. Questions to ask. But focus everything on the product he's selling and what Bravo intends to do with it."

Suarez, entering the stream of thought, said, "Whatever it is has to be brought in here. If we watch those six Bravo guys, and the Russian, we can tell when they intend to bring in the weapons . . . whatever they are . . . and be waiting for them. We can track them at sea and be on the beach when they land."

"It's not so easy," Nuñez growled. "We don't have enough people in Miami to put round-the-clock surveillance on all of them. We could easily lose them if they cast off from some remote dock in the Keys. And we don't have enough coastal patrol to watch every landing spot. Besides, we don't have a clue what they're buying from the Russian. Could be a tank.

Could be a transistor radio. Could be some new high-powered explosive in a video camera in a tourist suitcase. Or several of them. Could be some tiny new pistol or poison pen or something . . . someone gets close to *el Presidente* and kills him." Nuñez's eyes bulged, as if a tiny but wicked hurricane was building behind them. "Goddamn Russians used to kill people with poison umbrella tips."

Nuñez was now pacing around the room and behind Suarez's back. Suarez got up and moved to a far wall. He feared his boss, in a fit of fury, might attack him from behind. An idea was forming in his mind, and he briefly wondered if Nuñez were clever enough to have maneuvered it there. "Colonel, what's coming to me is that we have to double the Russian or . . . get inside the Bravo group."

Nuñez smiled wickedly. "Now, Lazaro, now you are thinking."

Suarez feared, briefly, that Nuñez might embrace him. "Can Nightlight do that? Can he get inside?"

"I don't think so," Nuñez said. "It's not impossible. But I don't think so. We may have to try it. But I don't think so."

Suarez had a sudden chill. "Nobody from here can do it, Colonel. We can't get visas, and besides the Americans know all of us . . . or at least think they do."

"I've been thinking about sending Trinidad up there," Nuñez said, "to seduce one or two of those bastards. We could probably get her in illegally . . . put her ashore at night, or something. She has good English." He put his hand up as Suarez started to protest. "It's risky. I agree. But we don't have too many choices."

"Colonel, you can't do that. They'd find out and they'd kill her. She—"

"Don't tell me what I can and cannot do, Suarez," Nuñez growled, doubling his fists. Would it be the desk or him? Suarez wondered. "I told you this is a war. Those bastards want to kill us. If we don't find out what they're up to before the anniversary celebration, they are for sure going to try to kill *el Jefe* . . . and probably as many others of us as they can."

"But, Colonel, this—"

"This is nothing, Suarez. It would be a great honor for her. Besides, she's a real revolutionary. If she saves the boss's life, she goes down in history . . . no matter what else happens. Think about it. If she could help us bring these guys down . . . at least warn us what they're up to, we'll build her a monument about as big as Martí's."

"It's too dangerous," Suarez said firmly. "If someone new shows up in

Miami and starts knocking on the door in the middle of a big operation
. . . if that's what it is . . . they'll smell it right away. Too dangerous."

"You have a better idea, Lazaro?" Nuñez asked. "You're telling me what
to do now, maybe you want my job." Miserably, Suarez shook his head.
"Then let me offer you another way," Nuñez said softly. "You and Trinidad
get that Yanqui professor of hers to do it for us. Get him to find out what
those bastards are up to."

"Colonel, he's a professor," Suarez said with exasperation. "He doesn't
know anything . . . about anything. He's a confused academic. He's a Yanqui. He doesn't work for us. For all I know, he hates us. Why should he
risk his life for Cuba?"

"Find a reason why he should. Make him fall in love with Trinidad.
Turn him. Pay him. I don't care. Let me give you the choices: We send
Trinidad; we turn the professor; or, Lazaro, you come up with a better
idea."

Nuñez dismissed Suarez with a flick of the wrist. In Nuñez's outer office,
Suarez filled out a form requesting access to two files, one code-named
"Bravo 99" and the other "Ulanov."

He went down the hall on the top floor of the Ministry of the Interior
and asked his assistant to send for Trinidad Santiago. When she came, he
simply took her by the arm and led her out of the building. It was widely
assumed that Nuñez tapped all of the phones and bugged all of the rooms
in the Ministry. Trinidad knew that Suarez only behaved this way when
he had a run-in with Nuñez or was otherwise very upset. They walked in
silence two-thirds of the way around the Plaza de la Revolución and then
sat down on the grass of the Plaza.

"He wants to send you to Miami . . . to penetrate this wacky Bravo
group," Suarez said.

"That's crazy, Lazaro," Trinidad said after a while. "I can't get a visa
. . . surely not soon enough to do any good. They'll spot me as a plant
from a mile away. Why would they bring a woman into a wild plot . . . if
that's what it is . . . almost at the crucial moment?"

"He's talking about infiltrating you . . . putting you ashore."

"That's about a one-in-fifty chance right there," she said through
clenched teeth. She shook her head. "He is crazy, Lazaro. This business
has pushed him over the edge. The difficulty of getting inside that group
is ten times greater even than getting in under the U.S. Coast Guard."

Suarez sighed. "He has an alternative plan." He paused, and she held her breath, expecting the worst. "He wants you to get the professor to work for us."

"Dammit, Lazaro, that was your idea! I said I wouldn't do it. Then I tried to do it. And he brushed me off. He wouldn't have any of it. Using McLemore to spy on these madmen isn't any more logical than using me. The only advantage he has is his ability to get into and out of the U.S. And"—she hesitated, pondering for the moment—"there is that business about his father. I told you. He had some kind of intelligence background. He also had a family connection to Cuba." They considered that, then she asked Suarez, "Do you think Nuñez has maneuvered us around to focus on McLemore? Is he clever enough to use me as a lever on you to recruit McLemore?"

"I don't know, Trinidad. But he has put me full-time on this Bravo group and the Russian they're dealing with. He knows I'm soft where you're concerned. And he's not above using any trick he can to get what he wants. All I know is that I have to come up with some idea pretty fast or I'm going to be working in the *zafra* for the rest of my life."

They stood up and started back to the Ministry. Suarez said, "Think about this. Maybe you introduce me to McLemore. Maybe I give him some kind of vague idea of our problem. And maybe we try to find out if he has any ideas how we can solve it. That doesn't go as far as Nuñez insists. But it does show we're making an effort." Then as they entered the shadow of Che Guevara, the outline of whose giant face guarded the Ministry entrance, Suarez added, "Besides, maybe he *can* help us."

▪ ▪ ▪

About the same time as the Ex Comm meeting in the White House on the sixteenth, Chairman Nikita Khrushchev calls a meeting of the Presidium, the senior leadership of the Communist Party of the Soviet Union and thus the ruling body of the USSR. The agenda includes a lot of official business, only one item of which is a plan from the KGB for managing the announcement of the secret Soviet missiles in Cuba.

Vladimir Semichastney, head of the KGB, has previously submitted a six-point proposal that is basically a propaganda initiative. "The KGB suggests the following measures which could create a broad social movement in defense of Cuba and by which to criticize the colonialist and aggressive character of American imperialism." Communist rhetoric uses colonialist and imperialist interchangeably. The plan mostly involves recruitment of respected cultural and intellectual figures to condemn the U.S. embargo as an effort to starve the Cuban people. The only part of the plan explicitly adopted by the Presidium is an effort to organize a privately led European boycott of American products as a protest against U.S. policy.

There is a greater concern for a meeting between Soviet Foreign Minister Andrei Gromyko and President Kennedy two days later. The Soviets are mystified that no word of complaint is heard from Washington about the Cuban missile emplacements. There are twenty-four R-12 missiles in Cuba; eight of them are operational and therefore detectable. Yet not a word of protest from the United States. Perhaps, Khrushchev is thinking, I am right about the immaturity of this young president. We'll find out from Gromyko what he says about this matter. Meanwhile, we'll have Gromyko continue to say that we're only giving defensive equipment.

Gromyko and Anatoli Dobrynin, Soviet ambassador to the United States, meet with Kennedy and Secretary of State Rusk. Rusk, Gromyko later reports, is "red like a crab." Kennedy reads a portion of a statement he made in early September which says that the United States will not accept offensive weapons in Cuba. But he has not yet reached a consensus with Ex Comm on a plan of action. So he says nothing more about the Soviet missiles.

Instead, Gromyko launches an attack on U.S. Cuban policy. Cuba, he says, is "a baby facing a giant," and attacks by Cuban exiles against Cuban shipping is "piracy on the high seas." He refers to notes that contain explicit instructions from Khrushchev. Soviet military assistance to Cuba is "by no means offensive." All military assistance (he does not refer at all to any nuclear missiles) is defensive in nature, he assures the U.S. president. (Years later, Gromyko says that he did not mention nuclear missiles because Kennedy did not ask about them. "The words 'nuclear missiles' did not figure in the conversation. If he had asked me about it, I would have answered." Answered what?)

Gromyko returns to the Soviet Embassy in Washington and sends Khrushchev this report: "Everything we know about the U.S. position on Cuba permits the conclusion that this situation is in general wholly satisfactory."

Based largely on this assessment and U.S. silence on Soviet missile *deployments in Cuba, the Presidium orders full speed ahead on completion of Operation Anadyr, especially efforts to make all R-12 missile batteries operational as soon as possible and deployment of longer-range R-14 missiles as well.*

■ ■ ■

16 After dinner, McLemore and Prescott set out from Julia's *paladar* toward Prescott's tiny two-room apartment in the Cerro district of south Havana. It was still midevening, and McLemore insisted on accompanying the older man despite his protests. As they walked, McLemore could not help but speculate as to whether they were being followed.

"Do the authorities here still take an interest in you?" McLemore asked.

Prescott laughed softly. "Of course not. What could I do to them . . . even if I wanted to do something . . . and there is nothing I would want to do to them anyway. I came here to help them. And I still care about the ordinary people here. I don't have much goodwill toward the government anymore. But I'd still like to find some way to help these people. They're good people . . . decent people. Despite all the political rhetoric over the years, these people still like the U.S. They don't understand our policy toward them, for sure. But they still like us."

"Do they treat you all right?" McLemore asked with concern.

"For sure. Mostly they leave me alone." The old man shuffled on a few steps. "The few of us who stayed . . . after the *zafra*, in '60 . . . were heroes here. They had us at all the political rallies. Took us all around the country, like circus animals. Then things gradually got more and more anti-Yanqui, and I got more and more uncomfortable being used as a puppet against my own country. So, I quit showing up. And that made them unhappy. Then after '62 . . . the 'Caribbean crisis' as they call it . . . things got very bad for the few Yanquis here. Most of the others left . . . went back home. Only three or four of us stayed on. I thought it was just a passing thing. They'd get disenchanted with the Russians, and we'd gradually work things out. But it just got worse and worse."

"Did they harass you?" McLemore now wanted the whole story. This interview, framed in his mind every day over the past month since he had first encountered Prescott, had a relentless direction.

Prescott now seemed eager to have his story out. "Well, about that time . . . '62 . . . the paranoia really set in. They decided, after all, that I was sent by the CIA. So, I was interrogated . . . endlessly." Prescott studied McLemore from the corner of his eye. "About that time there was an 'incident.' I spent two or three years in jail." McLemore waited to see if there would be more on the "incident," but Prescott continued on. "They had some of their people in the States do a little covert search of my background. My family. My schools. Even my little church in Salinas. Some of my parishioners were visited by people who said they were Mexicans, asking about my politics . . . was I truly a priest? . . . did I work for the U.S. government? . . . stuff like that. Of course, this confused everybody in town, because they had all decided that I was a Communist. So here are some Cubans, posing as Mexicans, asking if I was with the CIA. I guess it's sort of the story of the Cold War, isn't it?" Prescott shook his head and laughed with a soft barking sound.

"How did you find all this out?" McLemore asked. "Have you been able to stay in contact with anyone in the States?"

Prescott nodded. "I couldn't get or send any messages for a long time. Then, gradually, they began to let letters come through . . . after they read them, for sure. And, then, in the last few years, when Americans—Yanquis—started drifting back, I occasionally get a letter out through them."

McLemore said, "Do you still have family in California?"

"My sister. She's a few years younger. Still in Salinas, where we grew up." Prescott stopped, preoccupied and sad. "I haven't seen her and her family for . . . I guess almost forty years."

"I'll take some letters," McLemore offered. "In fact, I'll call her, if it's okay . . . when I go back this time."

Prescott put a long bony hand on the younger man's arm. "Would you do that? Oh, that'd be mighty fine. I haven't had a letter in . . . maybe a year or two now." They walked a block, then he said, "You know, I could die down here . . . *will* die down here . . . and nobody will ever know."

McLemore stopped. "Prescott, why not go home? They'll let you go.

I'm sure. I'll talk to them. I've gotten to know some people in the Foreign Ministry. Let me talk to them. It's time."

"Oh, that's awful nice of you," Prescott sighed. "But I can't."

"Why not? Of course, you can. Just pack up and go."

Prescott shook his long white-capped head. "No. It's not the Cubans. It's the U.S. You see, in about '65 or so, they canceled my passport. Wrote me off for good. They won't let me go back." He shuffled on, head down. "You see, about twenty years ago, I gave in. Got homesick and wanted to go back. Carter and Castro had opened these 'interest offices' in both countries. So, there was somebody, finally, to go talk to. So, I got my courage up one day. And I went around to that 'Interest office' and told them who I was and said I wanted to go back home. This nice young woman looked at me like I was some kind of a ghost. She asked for my passport. And I gave her the old one . . . from '60. She looked it over and said, 'Come back at the end of the week.' So, I went back in. Cubans taking my picture coming and going every time, of course."

"What happened when you went back?"

Prescott looked skyward, studying the early stars just beginning to gleam through the evening dusk. Finally he said, "I had to sit in the waiting room for a long time. Seemed like an hour or two. I knew something was up. Then an official-looking young man came and got me and took me into his office. The first young woman was there, looking like she was about to cry. And there were one or two other people, I think." He hesitated, trying to recall the scene. "This young man said, 'Mr. Prescott . . . ' " Prescott chuckled. "I think he even called me 'Father John.' He seemed very official, but very nervous . . . like he was delivering a prison sentence. 'I'm afraid we have some bad news for you.' I thought maybe something had happened to my sister at first. Then I realized it was about the passport. He said, 'Our government has considered your case, and particularly the circumstances surrounding your original travel to Cuba, and a decision has been made in your case.' I remember now, very clearly. He said, 'The Immigration and Naturalization Service has made a decision that your passport is now invalid. And'—then he swallowed real hard—'therefore, I'm afraid it will be impossible for you to return to the U.S. . . . . at this time.'

"So, I said, 'At this time? You mean I should reapply, down the road. Or what?' Then the young man shook his head and said something like, 'You can appeal this decision through the courts, in the United States.

But, frankly, it could be long, and complicated, and very expensive.' I said, 'I don't have any money. And for sure I don't have any lawyers. And I'm down here. How can I do this?' The official-acting man just shook his head and said he was sorry. Meantime, the young lady was crying now and she had to leave. I felt very bad for her."

Heatedly, McLemore said, "Prescott, it's not too late. I can get some pro bono lawyer in the U.S. to take this case. It's outrageous! They can't take your passport away. It's the kind of thing the Communists would do. You're still a United States citizen, and you've got a right to that passport."

The two men, one of ordinary size, the other tall and somewhat stooped, walked on in the late twilight through south Havana. Again, the older man put his long fingers, drawn by arthritis, on the younger man's shoulder. "No, I think our government was right in a way. I had come down here. I had stayed. We had become enemies. And," he said, hesitating, "it is what I was meant to do. Of all the Yanquis who came down here in those days, excited by the revolution, starry-eyed idealists caught up not so much in socialism but in the possibility of justice . . . what we were talking about at dinner . . . with the ideal of enough for everyone. Of all those people, you see, I was *the only one* who bought a one-way ticket."

Puzzled, even slightly stunned, McLemore said, "What do you mean, what you were meant to do? I don't understand that. What does it mean?" He had spent a good part of his adult life trying, more in spirit than in mind, to fathom what it would be like to have a purpose. What does it mean to have a purpose? What if that purpose changes your life, alters your plans, casts you into exile . . . like Prescott, or even costs you your life . . . like his father?

"I don't quite know," Prescott said. "Maybe it's something I picked up in the seminary. Or maybe I went to the seminary because I already believed it. It's just that sometimes you do something because you feel you should or because you have to. You just *know* something is right. You have a choice in your mind . . . but you really don't have a choice in your soul. I came down here partly because I was caught up in the excitement. Keep in mind, I was much younger then. But it also seemed like the right thing to do . . . for me, it *was* the right thing to do. I've been able to help quite a few people here . . . help young people learn English . . . I still do that . . . help old Catholic people who want to keep the faith. I'll tell you something," Prescott said, looking around, "but you shouldn't mention it to your friends at the Ministry. I still say mass sometimes. There are a few of the old people in the neighborhood, still Catholic, still religious. We've been friends for years . . . more than years . . . decades." He chuckled, then lowered his voice. "I'm still their priest." The thought made him smile. "In Salinas, I would have been just another Catholic priest . . . going through the motions . . . by now burned out and ritualistic. Down here, I'm an illegal priest, a renegade priest." He gave a soft laughing bark at the excitement of the idea.

They were now in the Cerro district, and Prescott pointed the turns in the streets toward his small flat. McLemore said, "You said . . . last time . . . that you met my father."

Prescott was silent.

"I want to know how that happened . . . whether you really got to know him . . . how it came about."

The old man straightened, studying the stars again. They walked a block or more in silence, McLemore waiting for a response.

"It was in '62 . . . during the crisis time," Prescott finally said, reluctantly. He thought some more, as if calculating. "You know, it was almost exactly . . . thirty . . . thirty-six years ago . . . this very month." It was as if, through his aging pale blue eyes, his mind could be seen to be drifting backward. "There was this young man, maybe my age, dressed like a Cuban, could have been a Cuban. But there was something different about him. I can't describe it exactly. But it was like the way his eyes looked. He was watching everything. Very keen, those eyes. Watcher's eyes. He was by himself, at the edge of a crowd at an anti–*Tio Sam* rally down at the Plaza de la Revolución. Big crowd. I kept at the back, even though I was told I had to be there . . . to show solidarity. There were a few Russians toward the back. They stuck out. They all wore these gray pants . . . and the same loud plaid shirts. I don't know where they got them . . . but they all wore those shirts. It was a joke with the Cubans. They all laughed about it. Here were forty or fifty thousand Russians. All wearing these plaid shirts. Somebody sold them a shipload of these crazy-looking shirts . . . apparently on the basis that this was the kind of shirt the Cubans wore." Prescott barked a laugh. "Crazy Russians. You could spot them a mile away."

The older man was beginning to enjoy the reminiscence, one that he had been able to share with no one else for almost four decades. "Anyway. This different-looking man was hanging a few yards back of the Russians. At first, I thought he was Cuban intelligence . . . you know, a secret service type. Then, suddenly, I decided he was a Yanqui. I don't quite know how. It's one of those things you just feel . . . if you see one of your own in a strange situation. He kept moving around, pretending to listen to the speeches. But it seemed to me that he was really watching the Russians. Strangely enough, it wasn't too common to see Russians out on the streets in the cities. When you did see them . . . like these men at the rally . . . they were usually senior officers. But never in uniform."

"So," McLemore asked, wanting to get to the main point, "how did you finally meet this man you thought was a Yanqui?"

"Well, he kept shifting sideways toward the Russians, like he was trying to hear what they were saying. Then, all of a sudden, I saw two or three guys, Cubans, moving back through the crowd, as if they were looking for someone . . . someone in particular. They each had a piece of paper . . . I later saw, when they came past me, that it had a picture on it. These guys were cops, intelligence, for sure. Just before they got to me, though, this guy, the Yanqui, came around behind the Russians, brushed past me and pulled my sleeve, and jerked his head . . . like he was saying let's go. He took off. I waited a minute, then I started toward the back of the crowd slowly, so as not to draw attention. I knew something bad was up."

They were nearing Prescott's street, and he slowed his pace, both from fatigue and the desire to finish his long-secret tale. "Pretty soon, after I got out of the crowd, I saw this guy, the Yanqui, half-leaning, half-hidden behind this tree. Very nonchalant. As I started toward him, he took off. So I followed him for a few blocks. I didn't have any idea what I was doing. I just knew he was in some kind of trouble and needed some help . . . from someone. And, probably out of desperation, he picked me. Of course, I looked more Yanqui than he did, and I had even been down here a couple of years by that time. At one point, I remember, I stopped to tie my shoe . . . just to check things out. For sure, here came the Cuban cops, looking up and down every street, in every doorway. So, I picked up the pace." He chuckled. "I was a little spryer then. So, finally, we get into the old city. Narrower streets. More hideaways. I passed by a doorway, and this guy reaches out and pulls me in. Very scary. He started talking very calmly, but very fast. 'I'm U.S. I need your help,' he said. 'Give me your address.' I knew I shouldn't, but I felt like I didn't have any choice. So I took an old pen . . . neither one of us had any paper . . . and I wrote a street and number on the palm of his hand. That's all. Then he took off."

They had by now stopped near a low rock wall, part of an abandoned ruin of a house. Prescott sat down and McLemore joined him. "Then what happened?" McLemore asked urgently. Prescott was stunned. It was the same low, quick, insistent voice he had heard thirty-six years ago, almost to the day. "Nothing," he said, "until two nights later. I remember because it was the Saturday night when everybody down here . . . maybe in the U.S. and Russia, too . . . thought we were going to fire all those missiles headed in three different directions. I was scared. Everybody was scared. The radio here kept announcing the call-up of the remaining militia . . . to go to all the preassigned defense points on the beaches . . . for the Yan-qui invasion. The rest of us were told to stay in our houses. I didn't have a radio, but I listened to the people outside the window. I kept inside, because it was very anti–*Tio Sam* at that time, but I could tell what was going on by all the racket outside. So I went to bed, but I didn't sleep because I thought, 'This is it.' "

McLemore said, "Then . . . ?"

"Well, sometime before dawn, very early in the morning, I heard this knock. Maybe I had dozed off because at first I thought I was dreaming. The neighborhood people left me very much alone at that time. And the other Yanquis I knew had almost all gone home. No one came to my door at that hour. Then I heard some cars and feet running in the distance. So I went to the door and he said—the same voice as the guy at the rally— 'Let me in, let me in.' I'll never forget it. So, I let him in. And right away, he scooted under my bed. He told me to get back on the bed . . . it was just a little cot. I still have it." Prescott studied Orion, remembering.

McLemore said, "Then . . . ?"

"Then the Cuban police went up and down the street, looking for your fa—for this guy. Apparently they knew they had him trapped on my street. So, after a while, they started going door-to-door. You could hear them breaking doors down when people were too scared to open them. Then, from under the cot, this man—your father—said, 'When they come to the door, open it. Try to look like you're asleep. Let them come in . . . they'll come in anyway. If they look under here and find me, I'll tell them I had a gun on you . . . that you resisted and I threatened to kill you.' "

Eyes burning, McLemore hissed, "Then what . . . ?" as if afraid the old man might lose his memory or die before the end of the story.

"They came in and got him."

"Did they shoot him right away, or did he say anything else before they came in?"

Sorry for the younger man, Prescott patted him on the back. "Part of the reason I'm still here is to tell you this. It's what I was saying about destiny. He said to me, very calmly, 'My name's McLemore, Jack Mc-Lemore.' He was still breathing hard, but he had to get it out. He knew they were going to get him. 'I will not tell you who I work for. It's safer for you not to know. You can make your own guess anyway. I have a wife and son in the States, in Bethesda, Maryland. You can track them down. Someday find my son. He's a little kid now. He doesn't understand.' I could hear the doors coming down close by. The last thing he said before they pounded on the door was 'Tell him that I wasn't here to hurt these people. We had to find out, firsthand, what was going on here . . . what the Soviets are doing . . . whether they're going to fire their missiles. If they do . . . if we can't talk our way out of this . . . the first missile will kill my wife and son. . . .' "

Prescott was silent. Then he said, "About then the door almost came in. And it was all over. They took him away. They roughed him up. He didn't say a word to them. They took me away, too. I spent a couple of years in jail. It wasn't too bad."

McLemore exhaled deeply. It was a profound sigh, almost like giving up the spirit, Prescott thought. "Was there anything else? Any other message?"

Prescott stood up, painfully, from the low wall and summoning Mc-Lemore to follow, slowly walked down the street to the door—the door upon which the fatal summons had landed—to his tiny two-room, ground-floor apartment, the same apartment he had occupied for almost forty years. He slowly opened the unlocked door and lit a very dim light as McLemore entered the doorway through which his father had been dragged to his summary death almost the same number of years before. Prescott went into the second room, which doubled as kitchen and bath. He reached to the back of a single small wall cabinet containing only pitifully meager plastic-wrapped bags of coffee, rice, and black beans. He drew out a battered box that had, many years before, contained rice. He shook it slightly, satisfied its single content remained, then turned it up until a tiny ball of cotton fell out. He held it a moment, then handed it to McLemore.

"When I came back from prison and even after others had used this place, I found this tucked in the underside corner of the cot," Prescott said. "I don't know why, but I thought someday you'd show up for this.

He did, too." Then, as if remembering for the first time in an age, Prescott said, "As I started for the door that night, your father did say one more thing. He knew, for sure, somehow, who I was—that I was not just a priest, but that I was an American priest called Prescott. He said, 'Pray for me, Father. . . .' And, you know, I have . . . every day since then."

In the dimness of the cell-like room, filled with the presence of a father he barely remembered but who had haunted every day of his life, McLemore slowly pulled at the ball of cotton, congealed and hardened by age. Inside he found merely a thin, tarnished chain containing a single ornament, an equally tarnished silver Saint Christopher medal.

17 Even though the old priest's story came very close to the one he had conjured in his mind since childhood, McLemore was too startled by the vivid details to contemplate his small hotel room and the thought of sleep. Instead of seeking a taxi, he headed due east of Prescott's neighborhood, thinking as he walked how this tiny room, a prison cell, had suddenly become a personal shrine for him with Father John Prescott as its own personal keeper. He walked through the darkened streets, hearing voices from doorways, radios and television sets, murmurs of love, shouts of anger, children crying . . . all the sounds of life . . . and all against the constant vibrant backdrop of the endless Cuban music, like the beating of the heart of Havana.

Occasionally, in spite of himself, his eyes misted. It was one thing to imagine his father's final hours, yet another to know firsthand. The picture of the young man, torn between fear and courage, under the cot, then dragged out the door, as blows and kicks rained down, and then thrown into some Cuban paddy wagon, replayed itself over and over in his mind. Knowing you would never see home again, never see your family and your friends again, never live the rest of your life. Was it enough for him, McLemore wondered, to know he had done his duty, that he had sent back scraps of information, invaluable or not, important or not, to his country, to try to protect his son and others like him, to inform the decision makers in the White House, and the Pentagon, and at Langley? Did those same decision makers, those politicians, and generals, and spymasters appreciate it? Did they think about him, the lonely American, Jack McLemore; or had they merely, in the drama of the moment, the tension, the fear, the apprehension, the concern for the nation, the world, had they merely taken it for granted? Another good soldier lost. Too bad. Tough job. But it had to be done. The epitaph for all the scouts on all the frontiers of all of human history. Nice guy. But there's the greater good.

McLemore followed the Avenida del Puerto until it became the Desamparado at the outcropping of a fragment of the southern end of the seventeenth-century wall of the old city. He walked slowly along the harbor with its long, largely abandoned wharves reaching out into its petroleum-polluted waters. He turned northward for the last few blocks before the Plaza de Armas and the Santa Isabel hotel. He decided he would try to find one of his father's old colleagues, by now pretty old, at the Agency, someone who had worked with him on the Cuban missile crisis. There must have been others who came down. Did they all perish? Were they all rolled up by the Cubans? Did anyone get out? Was one of them even now sitting on some porch somewhere, maybe at a retirement home, willing to tell the son of a casualty of those wars what it was really like . . . what it was like not in the trenches but in the back alleys and political souks and dark sewers of the third world where those wars were fought?

In that strange, claustrophobic, paranoid community of espionage, there were heroes. But only the cognoscenti knew *who* they were, and only the priesthood knew *why* they were. Medals were given. McLemore had his in the bottom of his underwear drawer in Madison. But then they sank without a trace. No public ceremonies or services. No walls or monuments on the Washington Mall. No stories to pass down in children's textbooks. These were heroes we could not talk about because they were heroes for reasons we could not talk about. It had been a strange little war. No official heroes. No official victories, or defeats. No parades for the victors. But, McLemore mused, now that it is over, why can't we bring them all out?

Why can't we tell the story, have the official histories, present the parades? Why can't everyone celebrate the end of the war? Now, we're all on the same side. We all won. You show me your heroes and I'll show you mine.

But even that wouldn't work, he thought, glancing across the calm harbor at the outstretched arms of the giant Jesus atop the lookout hill above the community of Casablanca. For here he was, in one of the two or three last holdouts in that war. Couldn't celebrate here, now, yet. Wouldn't you know that the place that had cost him his father would be this little Caribbean-Spanish-African holdout. This gorgeous butterfly frozen in the amber of history. The place time left behind. The place where the war was still on, even though most people on both sides couldn't remember why. The place where the politics drove you mad and the music made you ecstatic.

Where had they buried him? As he entered the Plaza and approached his hotel, the question struck McLemore like a thunderclap. They had to bury him somewhere. Where was he buried? Or maybe they had just thrown him out, onto some waste heap somewhere. Maybe they took him out to sea and tossed him to the sharks. How many ways are there to dispose of an unwanted organism? Would anyone today know? Would anyone today care? Did a hostile country even keep records of such things? There's a doctoral dissertation in history for you, McLemore thought wryly, deciding he would recommend it to his graduate students—if for no other reason than to test their sense of humor: The Patterns of Selected Nations in Disposing of Executed Spies. Before he could entertain even the notion of sleep, this was going to be a two-, maybe three- mojito night.

He entered the glass doors of the Santa Isabel, picked up his room key from the concierge desk on the right, and passed into the open-air courtyard, which served as a bar and lounge, on the way to the elevators. Two-thirds of the twenty-seven rooms were occupied, mostly by European tourists. He'd recognized the languages spoken in the small dining room at breakfast time. Two of the courtyard tables had guests enjoying nightcaps, and one of the far tables had a figure whom McLemore, with a sidelong glance, thought familiar. As he continued toward the elevator, he chose not to stare. Then he heard his name called.

"Mac, Mac, come join me." The voice had the familiar cheerleader's reach and zest. The other tables took brief note, then dismissed the scene as two Aussies finding each other, according to their tribal custom, in a strange corner of the world.

Determined to hush the noise and the attention it drew, McLemore turned toward the bar and looked to the back of the compact courtyard. Ramsay was standing, beckoning with both muscular arms. His red face beamed, his tousled surfer locks a pale white in the moonlight penetrating the open courtyard. McLemore decided to join him, if for no other reason than to keep him quiet. "You make a lot of racket for someone in your line of work," he said as he approached the table.

Of all his theatrical repertoire—brash con man, hurt small boy, threatening thug, sinister spy—Ramsay chose the new role of hearty frat brother for the evening. "Mac, old pal, whadyasay? Long time no . . . however it goes. Good to have you back in town. All your friends have been missing you, pal. Now listen, I know you've been working hard"—how would he know that? McLemore wondered—"so whatsay I stand you a tall one?" Up went a beefy arm to summon the sleepy-eyed bartender-waiter, who moonlighted, McLemore assumed, for Cuban intelligence . . . or vice versa. "My money's as good as yours here," Ramsay blustered. "Actually, it may even be better."

"Mr. Ramsay . . . ," McLemore said.

"Mac, we're old pals. You've got to call me 'Red' like all my other pals."

McLemore said, "I think when I met you before you wanted me to call you 'Sam.' Which is it . . . 'Sam' or 'Red'?"

"Sam's the name; good government's the game. But my *real* pals call me 'Red.' "

McLemore continued, "Please explain to me how you do what you do in such a . . . ah . . . visible manner. I thought you people were supposed to be quiet and unobtrusive."

"Wrong, wrong, wrong, Mac. Hide in plain sight, don't you know. An old trick of the trade. It's the sneaky, creepy ones that get rolled up . . . as they say in the business. Besides, I keep trying to tell you, I'm not a spook. I just try to gather information—as part of my job."

"What is your job exactly, 'Red'?"

"Gathering information, Mac. Boy, you really are an academic, aren't you?"

"I suppose it's no accident your outfit sent a guy named Red to this country, now is it?"

Ramsay spluttered with laughter. "Hahaha! Goddamn, Mac, you are a card . . . for a professor. That's rich. Red . . . in Cuba. Goddamn, I wish I'd thought of that. Hahaha!"

"You will," McLemore promised with confidence. This set Ramsay into another peal of braying as the waiter arrived with the *mojitos*. Ramsay and the waiter eyed each other. Different weight classes, but both in the boxing game, shadow and otherwise. The waiter was no slouch, McLemore decided. He could spot Ramsay thirty or forty pounds and still maybe turn him into a rather thick pretzel. Maybe. On consideration, McLemore decided not to back Ramsay into too small a corner.

"So, your keepers have not recalled you from the island paradise," McLemore ventured.

"So much to find out; so little time," Ramsay countered. "And, likewise, I am happy to see that the sabbatical still stands and that your grant committee has not caught onto your elaborate academic scam."

"What scam exactly might that be?"

Ramsay assumed his hurt-little-boy face. "Mac, you know, pretending to look for historical treasures in the already finely sifted sands of the Cuban missile crisis. Christ, Mac, if I had been on the grant committee of the foundation you brought that proposal to, I would have absolutely toppled out of my overstuffed, leather-covered chair with laughter. You've got to have the *cojones* of a bank robber to pull that old chestnut out of the fire."

"I'm surprised at your scruples, 'Red.' It's not your money." McLemore took a long drink of the *mojito* and quickly began to enjoy himself with this heavily upholstered fraud. "What do you care if I take a little time off from the toils of academe to roll around in the sunny rum . . . or the rummy sun. Besides . . . although I'm sure you wouldn't have noticed . . . the girls are pretty here."

"And they all get prettier at closing time," Ramsay added. He put on his dorm counselor face. "Mac, you watch yourself with these girls. Do you hear me? They're pretty, all right . . . especially those really dusky ones. And they dance . . . among other things . . . like dervishes. All night, I hear, although I wouldn't know firsthand." He leaned forward conspiratorially. "In my 'line of work,' as you call it, we know these things. These pretty ladies can steal your *cojones*, and all the plumbing with them, and everything north of there up to and including your mind and its most private secrets. Do you hear where I'm coming from?"

McLemore finished the *mojito* and waved for two more. "Got no secrets, 'Red.' That's where I've got it over you. You have to worry about those things. Me . . . I can just enjoy the pretty ladies . . . and let 'em steal whatever they want. He who steals my purse . . . or my plumbing . . . steals trash."

Ramsay wagged his shaggy head sadly, as if watching an alcoholic enter a wicked bar. "No joke, Mac. I'm giving you the straight poop. You *watch these girls*," he whispered as his nemesis approached with the second round.

McLemore leaned in and whispered, "I intend to, 'Red.' That's the whole point, if you want to know the truth. I'm not here to rebake some overbaked history. I'm really here to watch the girls. But, please, please, whatever else you report, don't report that to my grant committee."

Sighing with defeat, Ramsay rolled his glass around the table. McLemore waited for the real business to begin. Ramsay was not here as drill sergeant ordering the recruit to button up around the town girls.

"Okay, Mac. Here's the deal. I came on a little strong last time. I'm really sorry. That approach works with some of the rubes we get down here. But you're a man of sophistication. I should have seen that when you walked in the joint. So, let's go back to square one. We know about your research project. Obviously, we know about your father. He's a genuine hero in our shop. Honest to God! One of the first stories they told me when they got me ready to come down here. He was a truly great patriot. You should really be proud of him. I would suppose . . . just as one human being to another . . . that you didn't cook up this missile crisis project out of some detached academic interest alone. This has to be some kind of pilgrimage for you." The big man sat back in his chair and drank half the *mojito*. "I like to believe I would be doing the same thing if I were in your shoes."

McLemore was silent, aware of the softening up, waiting for the pitch.

"I told you last time," Ramsay went on, "that we know the locals are concerned about their big party on New Year's Day. This is the last hurrah for some of the good old boys in Miami. If they're going to make one last effort to topple *el Jefe*, this will be the time. We know it, and they know it. Besides, our brothers at the Bureau have picked up some new activity in Little Havana. So, we have a pretty good idea of *when*. What we don't know is *how*."

McLemore said, "I don't get this. We're opposed to Castro. We've had this idiotic embargo on for more than thirty years. We'd be happy if this whole house of cards toppled. And you're concerned about some fracas on anniversary day?"

"I guess you'd say it's a PR thing, Mac." Ramsay ran thick fingers through thick hair. "If somebody comes over here from Guatemala, say, and starts a tussle, there's very little we can do about it. Not our business, don't you know. But if some folks up in the States . . . let's just say Miami, for example . . . decide to cook up something really nasty, it's a big black eye for *Tio Sam*. We've taken a courageous stand against terrorism. Big issue for our president. We made war on Saddam Hussein. We bombed Gaddafi. We wag our finger at Assad, and the ayatollahs, and the Hezbollah, and the Hamas, and the North Koreans. So how does it look if we let some folks up north carry out their own little bomb-and-strafe down here . . . from our soil? We can't let any of our folks be in the terrorism business, Mac. Makes us look like hypocrites. Simple as that."

"Just so I understand, 'Red' . . . U.S. policy, according to you, is that it's okay for innocent Cubans to get killed, so long as Yankees don't do it. That's the kind of policy we innocent taxpayers always find interesting." As if resigned to a world of folly, McLemore sighed. "You do seem to have a big job on your hands, at least for the next couple of months, and I wish you very good luck. It's all very interesting. I just don't know what it's got to do with me."

Ramsay scooted his chair around toward McLemore. "We could do our job better if we knew what the locals know. I know it sounds strange, but they've got better sources inside the exile community in the States than we do."

"Get your own sources. Put your own people inside those organizations."

"Can't, Mac. It's too late. It takes years to penetrate those small closed 'social clubs.' Your man has to develop a level of trust. That takes a lot of time. Doubling somebody already in the group is even riskier. One or two of these hard-line outfits just got started recently. We're not even sure who they are. And, besides, politically it's like dealing with nitroglycerin. These people are Americans now. We get caught trying to penetrate them . . . particularly without some concrete evidence to go on . . . and all hell breaks loose. Congressional hearings, investigations, newspaper editorials, Civil Liberties Union, lawsuits. Hell to pay. We went through that in the 1970s. Nobody alive then wants to go through that again."

McLemore waited, still uncertain where this baring of the intelligence soul was headed. Finally, he said, "Sometimes the most obvious answer is the right answer. Sit down with the locals and offer to help."

Ramsay released a great sigh, whether out of frustration or exasperation,

McLemore was unsure. "Can't do that, Mac. We have no diplomatic relations. My outfit is not supposed to be here anyway. We surface, and we're
out of here for good. Besides, I kind of like the place. Not ready to leave
. . . yet." He winked. "Pretty girls and all, don't you know." The demor-
alized face of the hard-working bureaucrat returned. "Basically, it's just
too awkward. *Tio Sam* asking Fidel for help spying on Cuban Yankees in
our own country so we can keep them from doing bad things to him."
Ramsay's eyes rolled skyward. "Think of the headlines . . . 'CIA and Castro
Bag Cuban-American Terrorists.' We'd never live it down."

"Sounds to me like you're going to earn your salary in the coming
weeks," McLemore observed with detachment. He was forcing Ramsay to
show his hole card.

Finally, Ramsay said, "Cards on the table. We need a favor, Mac. Even
more, we need your help. We've tried every way we can think of to crack
this nut, and all the arrows keep pointing your way."

Tired suddenly of the game, McLemore said, "Spit it out, Ramsay. What
do you want?"

"Use your sources in the Foreign Ministry. They're all Cuban intelligence anyway. Find out whether they've identified a threat . . . who it is
. . . what they're up to . . . what is their plan . . . how are they going to do
it? All those things. Anything you can find out. We'll take it from there."

McLemore shook his head as he would at a terminally naughty child.
"They are not 'my sources,' Ramsay. Señora Santiago merely helps organize my research and my trips outside the city. That's all. I don't have
'sources.' That's your world. The rest of us don't operate that way . . . in
case you have forgotten. Don't you see? The minute I try to get inside
their intelligence operations, they're going to conclude I really do work
for the Agency . . . that the history project is my cover . . . and that I've
been sent down here to identify their agents in Miami so you and your
outfit can roll them up." McLemore felt deep fatigue from all this maneuvering and the tension of reliving his father's last moments. "I say this
respectfully, Ramsay. You're on a fool's errand."

As McLemore started to stand up, Ramsay put a hand on his arm,
almost forcing him back into his chair. Across the courtyard, a large wicker
cage containing a dozen or more songbirds, brilliantly colored and as mu-
sically vibrant as their island, suddenly came alive, and the birds chirped
and chattered at the departing customers. The two men, attended only by
the observant waiter, were now alone.

"I can help you with your father," Ramsay said, now the serious professional. McLemore marveled at his dexterity, thinking he must have interrupted a stunning theatrical career to serve his country. "We can help you find people who worked with him . . . his boss . . . his compatriots. There are things you must want to know. What happened. How it happened. Otherwise, you wouldn't be hanging out with that rummy old priest."

McLemore marveled now at Ramsay's ability to foul his own nest and understood why the theatrical career would finally have failed. "Yes," he said slowly, "there are a lot of things I'd like to know. I can probably find out quite a bit without your very kind bribery offer. And, yes, it is part of the reason I wanted to get in touch with Prescott. He knew my father. But dismissing him as 'rummy' is contemptible in my book. So, with all due respect, go to hell." He started to leave, then said, "You're really good at what you do, Ramsay, but only up to a point. Then, somehow, your real character ruins it all. You'd be a lot more effective if you'd lose the bullyboy. Maybe a little psychotherapy might help."

Ramsay's face reddened, and he put his hands flat on the table. "One more thing before you go," he said fiercely, as if to a fool. "We've intercepted some traffic between a known Russian arms dealer in the States and his suppliers in Moscow. It's all in code word and euphemism. But we *know* it has something to do with Cuba and . . . we *think* they're talking about something nuclear."

McLemore sat down at the table again.

18 The more he looked into the events of 1962, the more Mc-Lemore felt compelled to try to re-create the era in his mind. Trinidad had introduced him to a number of veterans of the era, and she and some of her friends had spent evenings with him telling stories, mostly passed on by parents and families, about those emotional days.

It all began, of course, in the Sierra Maestra mountain range of eastern Cuba in the late 1950s, where the rebel Fidel Castro Ruz held off President Fulgencio Batista's army for four years. These were not easy years. Supplies were sparse. His ragged forces lived off the land. Volunteers, many teenagers, drifted in, and defectors, usually under cover of night, slipped out in almost equal numbers. Little help came from sympathizers in Havana. Government forces, first disdainful of their ragtag opponents, under pressure from the Havana oligarchy, bombed and strafed the pesky rebels, managing in the process to kill local *campesinos*, burn their crops, and drive them into the arms of the rebels. Later, when lashed into the hostile mountain terrain by furious officers, government troops encountered deadly rebel ambushes supported by the alienated *campesinos*.

Early on, Fidel Castro saw himself as the fly that buzzes in the ear of the giant, the pesky mote in *Tio Sam's* eye, the rabble youth chucking stones at the carriage of the gross and greedy merchant. He meant to be, from the start, a reproach to the American autocracy. But, true to his chameleon nature and a love-hate ambivalence toward *el norte*, Castro cultivated U.S. support even as he attacked U.S. policy. His strategy was to drive a wedge between American public opinion and the conservative American government and American corporations that dominated the Cuban economy. In anticipation of a situation that was to reverse itself within months, Cuban exiles from the repressive Batista government staged rallies in New York and quietly collected financing in Miami for the bearded rebels in the Sierra Maestra even as *el Commandante* thrashed the perfidious Yanqui government in interviews carried in the U.S. press that were reported by U.S. journalists smuggled into the harsh mountains.

But all that was forty years ago . . . ancient history. Now, Trinidad says—presumably on behalf of officials senior to her—things have changed. Now *el Commandante* is seventy-three years old, a lion in the warm Cuban winter. A historic anniversary is weeks away, and everyone in the top levels of the Palace of the Revolution knows their ancient enemies, continuing to try to foment rebellion against the rebels who dispossessed them, will make one last supreme effort. *El Presidente* has been briefed on the threat. He has told the minister of the interior that he expects him to deal with it, to prevent it from marring the historic anniversary, to protect the Cuban people and the *revolución*. The minister has deputized Colonel Ernesto Nuñez to supervise all security arrangements and has also given him absolute authority to requisition all the forces and resources required to guarantee success. Success in this instance means prevention of treachery.

Trinidad has yet to tell McLemore that Cuban intelligence in south Florida, supplemented by international telephone intercepts, has confirmed a vague plot to disrupt the anniversary ceremony in the Revolutionary Plaza. The source of the plot is believed to be a hitherto unknown radical group calling itself Bravo 99, supposedly composed of a small group of second-generation heirs of Brigade 2506. This group, it is known, has had contact with a Russian arms dealer. The key to Bravo's proposed operation, and perhaps to defeating the threat itself, is the nature of the purchase. U.S. intelligence agencies know less than Cuban intelligence, and highly sensitive political considerations are hamstringing their efforts to penetrate Bravo 99 and confirm suspicions, based upon telephone intercepts of discussions in Russian concerning *yadernoye*, Russian for *nuclear*. Colonel Nuñez has made it clear that one of his chief deputies in the Cuban secret service, the disillusioned Lazaro Suarez, is responsible for discovering and, if necessary, defeating Bravo's plan. How he is to do this seems largely up to him.

Meanwhile, a pattern of terrorist attacks, largely focused on tourist facilities, continues to escalate, a pattern totally preoccupying the State Security Department. In the last week of October 1998, bombs have gone off in two separate hotels on the beaches of Varadero and in the disco of the Sol Melia Hotel in Havana. Eighteen casualties were reported at Varadero and one fatality at the Sol Melia. Security forces are at a loss to find the perpetrators. To his relief, this is one can of worms for which Lazaro Suarez is no longer responsible. Nuñez, under pressure from the minister and, indirectly, from *el Presidente*, begins to lock up dissidents. Any Cuban suspected of dissent, and the list is not long, is jailed. Airport Customs searches are taking longer, delaying arrivals and frustrating tourists. Hotel rooms are routinely searched, further angering visitors whose currency is needed to keep the fragile economy afloat. Indeed, revenues from tourism are down measurably in the fall of 1998. Security forces, primarily in plainclothes, now stop anyone on the streets with a bag or backpack. Confrontations between security police and tourists have become routine and noisy. Tension is palpable. Even the loose-jointed street music now sounds jittery.

Since most of his colleagues in the security service are Nuñez's lackeys, Suarez has chosen to rely primarily on a small group of loyal friends in the service, including Trinidad Santiago, his long-standing close friend. "We have no choice but to continue to try to get *Profesor* McLemore to help us some way," Suarez said to Trinidad over dinner in the small flat a few blocks off O'Reilly Street she shares with her mother. It is just past 10:30 P.M. on October 28, approximately the same time on the same night that McLemore is listening to Ramsay talk about the remote possibility of a nuclear detonation in the center of Havana in just over sixty days.

Trinidad sighed. "We've tried that, Lazaro. It doesn't work. Each time he says he is not a spy . . . for anyone . . . including his own country. And, by the way, I believe him. So, he says, why should he become a spy for Cuba?" They sipped coffee in silence. "It's a waste of time, Lazaro. We have to think of something else."

"I don't know anything else," he said, resigned. "I can't go up there. You can't go up there. No one can go up there. And even if we could, we don't have enough time to get inside this Bravo cabal. We keep going over and over the same thing."

"What about the Russian?" she asked.

"We can't get our hands on the Russian. He's not about to come down here. And our people in Miami say they haven't seen him around there for a while. My guess is, he's lying low . . . particularly if he's done a big deal with Bravo." Trinidad poured more viscous coffee, which they drank in silence. Then Suarez said, "What if we ask McLemore to talk to the Russian? Would he do that?"

She shook her head. "First, how is he going to find the Russian? Then, what does he say . . . I want to be your friend . . . tell me what you've sold these crazy Cubans here . . . how are they going to get their purchases into Cuba . . . tell me all your secrets?" She continued to shake her head. "It won't work. He has the same problem we do . . . time. You can't get some-body's trust in sixty days, especially if they're involved in some dangerous deal or operation."

Suarez, desperation now overtaking him, pushed on. "There is still the old trio . . . alcohol, money, and sex."

Trinidad snorted derisively. "Drink, maybe, particularly with the Russian. But again you have to find him. Money, no. The Russian's getting his money . . . for the deal . . . whatever he's selling. The Yanqui-Cubans are in this for revenge and politics, not for money. And, as for sex, Lazaro"—her face flushed—"I don't want you to talk about that with me—ever again. You understand? If you are willing to use me to seduce McLemore, then I get the idea you're willing to use me the same way with those thugs in Little Havana. Don't do that, Lazaro. It makes me very angry. It makes me lose respect for you and not like you very much."

Suarez put up his hands and quickly said, "Trinidad, I'm not talking about you. I'm just trying to think about what's left that we can do. We're not just trying to save an aging revolution . . . one I know you believe in more than I do. We're trying possibly to save a lot of lives. I don't have enough idealism left to care about the *barbudos* and all that ancient history. I'm trying to do my job. And, frankly, I'm scared to death."

His protest worked. Trinidad put a hand on his arm. "All right. I'll talk to McLemore. But just once more. We get together at the end of the day tomorrow to talk about his project. I'll try to get him interested in helping us. But I don't expect much success."

Suarez said, "There are two new things you should know. When he was here before, he was followed by a peculiar old Yanqui who's lived down here practically since the revolution. An old priest called Prescott."

Trinidad gasped. "I know that old man! I've seen him on the streets from time to time. He's lived down in Cerro for years. I think I even saw his file one time, years ago, during some briefing on characters to keep an eye on. I guess there was a time . . . a long time ago . . . when Nuñez claimed he worked for the CIA."

"That's the one," Suarez said.

"Why in hell was he following McLemore?"

"That's the second thing. The old man was in jail for a few years in the 1960s."

"Is he trying to get McLemore to help him get out of the country?"

"No. He can't get out. He can't go home. The U.S. took his passport a long time ago. We would be happy to get rid of him. But the U.S. won't take him."

"Then why would he follow McLemore around?"

"The old man knew McLemore's father."

"What!" Trinidad practically shouted. "He did what? You mean before he came down here?"

"No," Lazaro said, "after. After he came down. During the Caribbean crisis."

"*Madre de Dios!*" Trinidad gasped. "Then he did work for the CIA."

"Not the priest," Suarez said. "McLemore's father. He came down here as a spy . . . during the crisis. It was about this time in '62 . . . during the time of the crisis. They put him ashore someplace down the coast. We were never quite sure where. He made his way up here and managed to operate for over ten days. His Spanish was almost like a native's. He was probably in his late thirties at the time. Apparently, he was very good."

"How did you find all this out?" Trinidad asked, still shocked. "What happened to him?"

"Nuñez was a young officer in counterintelligence. They were sure the U.S. put some agents ashore. So they tracked them down. He was the last one. They got on his trail. He had no place to go. He was desperate to find out anything he could about the Russians and the nuclear missiles. He could have gone into the mountains and probably have disappeared forever, or until they could come get him. But he stayed around here, apparently trailing Soviet officers. So, when Nuñez and his team got onto him, the only place he could think of to hide was with Prescott down in Cerro. He had been briefed on Prescott's presence here, and when we got on his trail, he found him. He made for Cerro and barely got into Prescott's place, then Nuñez got him."

Knowing the answer, Trinidad asked anyway, "What happened to him?"

Suarez studied the coffee grounds, looking for a forecast of his destiny. "What do you think? They beat up on him for a day or two. And after they couldn't get anything out of him . . . they shot him. Nuñez himself did it."

"My God!" Trinidad breathed. Suddenly things came together. McLemore's admission, with the help of some rum, that his father had been in intelligence. His statement that his father had a Cuban mother. That he spoke Spanish very well. That he had died young and that McLemore had barely known him. It all suddenly made sense now.

Still stunned, she looked distractedly out of the window opening onto the street below. The coincidence of it all was a shock. So that's why he came down here, she thought. It's not to study the missile crisis at all. That's his excuse. He is here to find his father . . . finally. "When did you find this out?" she eventually asked.

"One of our street agents, routinely checking out McLemore, spotted the old man outside the hotel a couple of times last month. He reported it to Pedrito in our office, and he told me. I didn't think much about it until you told me McLemore was back in town. So, I had Prescott's file pulled. I went through it and found out about his arrest in '62. Then I found all of Nuñez's reports on his arrest and his connection with Mc-Lemore's father. Then the whole thing finally fell into place sometime yesterday. That's why I wanted to talk to you tonight. I thought you should know all this."

"Have you told Nuñez?"

"Not yet."

"Please don't, Lazaro. God knows what he would do."

"The first thing he would do is throw McLemore out. That mind of his would automatically assume that McLemore is with the CIA. Like father, like son. It wouldn't do any great damage to McLemore. But, frankly, it would eliminate any chance we have to get McLemore on our side." Lazaro watched the woman's eyes as she struggled to put the pieces together. "Now, Trinidad, now do you understand why I insisted on talking to you about this tonight? All of this makes McLemore a much more complicated presence on our doorstep at this highly dangerous time."

■ ■ ■

Ex Comm meetings on the sixteenth, seventeenth, and eighteenth of October, and beyond—often two a day—wax and wane on the issues of air strikes, invasions, and naval blockades. Participants change sides. Some originally for air strikes decide against. Some for cautious diplomacy decide for stronger military action. The debate is intense. Metamorphosis between dove and hawk, hawk and dove, transpires on an hourly basis as new information comes in from U-2 films, lower-level flights, from exiles still arriving from Cuba, and from President Kennedy's own human intelligence sources. Meanwhile, Soviet missile crews are working literally around the clock to bring their batteries to launch capability. In a word, Soviet policy is a "fait accompli."

On Thursday, the eighteenth of October, the Joint Chiefs of Staff are in their cloistered Pentagon command post. The chief of the air force, General Curtis LeMay, says, "Are we really going to do anything except talk?"

Saturday, the twentieth of October, is decision day for the president. Ex Comm meets and receives this report from CIA analysts: "We believe the evidence indicates the probability that eight MRBM missiles can be fired [at the United States] from Cuba today." The president calls for a vote. A majority of Ex Comm recommends a naval blockade as the first response, to be followed if necessary by air strikes, to be followed if necessary by a United States military invasion.

President Kennedy announces his decision on nationwide television on the twenty-second of October. For all practical purposes, the entire nation is watching:

"This government, as promised, has maintained the closest surveillance of the Soviet military buildup on the island of Cuba. Within the past week, unmistakable evidence has established the fact that a series of offensive missile sites is now in preparation on that imprisoned island. The purpose of these bases can be none other than to provide a nuclear strike capability against the Western Hemisphere. . . .

"We will not prematurely or unnecessarily risk the costs of worldwide nuclear war in which even the fruits of victory will be ashes in our mouth—but neither will we shrink from that risk at any time it must be faced."

The president announces a "strict quarantine" around the island of Cuba. Shipments of "offensive military equipment" will be turned back by U.S. warships. "I have directed the armed forces to prepare for any eventualities," the president announces. "We will," he says, "regard any nuclear missiles launched from Cuba against any nation in the Western Hemisphere as an attack by the Soviet Union on the United States, requiring a full retaliatory response upon the Soviet Union." Everyone knows the missiles are all pointed at the United States.

After the televised speech, the president and his brother walk back to the Oval Office.

"Did McCone send those people down there?" the president asks.

Robert says, "Yes, he told me tonight that he had successfully landed three and that he was trying to land three more." Then he says, "But he doesn't really expect any of them will get out again."

▪ ▪ ▪

19 "Trinidad, what will you do if . . . say, tomorrow . . . the *revolución* ends? If you were to discover suddenly that Castro is dead or deposed or replaced?" McLemore asked.

"The question isn't what I would do," she responded. "The question is what the *campesinos* would do, what the children would do, what the old people would do. What I would do doesn't matter. But your question cannot be answered without knowing what comes next. If the alternative is to return to a U.S.-dominated oligarchy, U.S. corporations giving us a few jobs in exchange for exporting profits from our resources to New York, some sophisticated modern version of colonialism, then it would be a catastrophe for us."

They were in Doña Eutimia, a popular *paladar* at the end of Callejon del Chorro, a short street just off the Plaza de la Catedral. Much like Julia, but without its kitschy charm, Doña Eutimia was situated in a prerevolutionary house and served spectacular roast pork.

"Profesor," Trinidad continued, "I know the revolution will not last forever. We understand that. Though it may not seem so, our history has made the Cuban people realistic. It's because young people have no history . . . no memory. I know about the Batista days from my parents. And perhaps I can tell some young people . . . even possibly my own children

sometime. But soon people forget. Instead of politics, they want jeans and watches and a Walkman and the latest rock music. And they are willing to pay some price . . . possibly even some independence . . . for those things."

"Is it wrong to want these things?" McLemore asked. Despite the political nature of the conversation, McLemore sensed a genuine warmth on her part toward him. She touched his hand often and her eyes smiled.

"Of course not. It's a question of price, isn't it? We let the big U.S. companies come back. They bring money . . . rebuild our sugar mills and oil refineries. They don't like our politics—Fidel, or who comes after Fidel—then they must put their own puppets in power, people who will not tax them and who will make sure their workers don't make wage demands. They can't help it. It's their . . . how do you say? . . . economic self-interest."

McLemore said, "So is political stability. And democracy has proved to be the best way to get that. Political freedoms."

"Political freedom becomes less important the more hungry you are. Democracy does not tell you how to distribute wealth fairly—especially where there is so little. It's like your 'free press.' One of your people once said, 'There is a free press in America for everyone who owns one.' Well, maybe there is political freedom for everyone who has plenty of food."

"Democracy doesn't have anything to do with wealth," McLemore responded.

"Why are we not intelligent enough yet to find a way to create economic democracy," she responded, "where people are free but also have enough to live decently?"

McLemore said, "What do you mean . . . workers owning the means of production? So far no one has been able to figure out how to make Marx work—let alone how to make Marxists work."

Trinidad said, "If workers' pensions can be invested in the shares of capitalist corporations, why can't the workers help decide whether the companies they invest in should produce chemicals that poison their children? There have to be better solutions . . . more human politics in the world. Don't you agree?"

"Of course," McLemore said with a grin, deciding to lighten the atmosphere. "If it were left up to me, I'd lift the embargo—swamp Cuba with tourists and businesspeople, dollars and cellular phones and fax machines, CNN and MTV. That'd cause a real revolution."

Trinidad smiled in return, her voice wry. "It's already happening. Tourist dollars are everywhere now. We now have two economies. What you call 'tourist apartheid.' It is a much more effective invasion than Playa Girón." She seemed more resigned than angry.

They were almost nose-to-nose over the table, their frequent intellectual debates more and more difficult to separate from sophisticated flirtation. McLemore felt that, in fact, the usually combative Señora Santiago was unusually preoccupied. He suspected it had something to do with the impending threat Ramsay had hammered him with the previous evening. If Trinidad were in fact more than a middle-level bureaucrat in the Foreign Ministry, if she were somehow involved in the Cuban state security network, then most likely she would know of any threat, including an extremely violent one, to disrupt the impending anniversary celebration. That would be more than enough to preoccupy anyone, McLemore thought. As the dinner arrived, he noticed that she seemed totally uninterested in eating. McLemore wondered, in passing, what it might be like to have the lives of a lot of people . . . thousands, possibly many more . . . in your hands and on your conscience. Suddenly, Trinidad did not seem to him an abrasive Communist functionary, the aloof, impatient bureaucrat. McLemore instead saw for the first time a frightened, vulnerable woman, one who apparently had little life outside her job and the perpetuation of the revolutionary cause, one now harboring the knowledge of a threat whose dreadfulness mankind had actually experienced but once.

For reasons he was not especially compelled to analyze, McLemore felt a sense of protectiveness toward Trinidad. He was surprised by its intensity and frustrated that this feeling had so little outlet. He reflected that she had made her way well enough in her world so far without his help. But that human landslide Ramsay had unsettled him. Normally possessed of an equanimity tinged only by bouts of melancholy, now McLemore felt a foreboding with an aspect of doom about it. Edginess was in the tangy Cuban air. Nervousness among leaders in small countries is quickly registered among the people, especially a people accustomed by the caffeine of their existence to rely on their senses more than on their intellect for survival. Tension rippled through the ether. And Trinidad's sensors were especially refined. She projected the tension right back.

Suddenly swept up in concern for her, McLemore said, "When I was here before, we talked about whether I might be able to help get information from the U.S. government about some of your former countrymen and whether they may have anything to do with the problems . . . the attacks . . . you're having down here. After I left, I knew right away I hadn't been quite as understanding as I should have been. It's just that I have some personal reasons for avoiding that whole world . . . espionage, intelligence, spying . . . all those things. It's a world some people find intriguing. But it's not a world I want to have anything to do with. Besides, Cuba's a . . . what should I say, diplomatically? . . . Cuba's a problem."

The warmth of her smile dulled the edge of her response. "It's a matter of point of view. For you, Cuba's a problem. For us, the U.S. is the problem."

"I guess what I'm trying to say is that if there is some way I can be helpful to you . . . without getting in the spy business . . . I want to help you. I don't have bad feelings toward this country. Certainly not like your former compatriots. I don't have any stake here, one way or the other. As far as Cuba's concerned, it's live and let live. I've been reading Cuban history. Given your history, U.S. policy here is neither very bright nor very productive. But, the U.S. doesn't care about my opinion anyway. All I'm saying is that I'd like to help you in any way that doesn't require that I pretend to be James Bond."

McLemore saw Trinidad's face soften and her eyes reflect something like relief. "*Profesor*, I knew you would help us. I knew it." She neatly converted his personal offer to a collective one but clearly understood the difference.

McLemore said, "I'll try to do what I can. But, it's an impossible situation. As I understand it, somebody is trying to damage your economy— maybe destroy tourism and agriculture. You obviously believe it is Cuban Americans, probably from south Florida. You can't figure out what they are up to. So you want an ordinary Yanqui . . . not in the U.S. government . . . to collect information about them? How do I do that? I told you, I'm not a spy and I don't intend to become one."

"We don't want you to spy, *profesor*," Trinidad said. "We want you to ask your government, anyone you know in your government, whether they know anything about these attacks and, if so, what they are doing about it. We cannot do this, you understand, through diplomatic channels. The people involved . . . the people we *know* are involved . . . are now U.S. citizens. We have lodged protests with your government through your Interest office here. We get no response."

"Can't you provide the information you have . . . how you know Cuban Americans are involved . . . directly to the U.S. government?" McLemore asked.

"It is impossible. If we do that, then we reveal the methods we use— and perhaps even some of the people involved—in collecting this information. Information concerning those who help us could well fall into the hands of those who oppose us. Our enemies will then take steps to prevent our collection in the future . . . even endanger the lives of those who take great risks to keep us informed." Trinidad raised her hands, palms up, and shrugged, suggesting the impossibility of his proposal.

McLemore was frustrated by her representation of the collective. He wanted to help her. "What exactly do you want me to do?" he asked.

"We do not want you to 'spy' in any case, *profesor*," Trinidad said. "If you have friends, or can make friends, in your government. . . ."

"When you say 'your government,' you really mean the CIA, don't you, Trinidad?"

She flushed even as the wide-set brown eyes held him steadily. "I suppose," she said. "Whomever. It is for you to decide who best to talk to. Please tell them, once again, of the terrorism continuing to come from the U.S. Although, for some reason we do not understand, the U.S. press does not report these stories, people are being injured and even killed here. It goes without notice in the U.S. It is as if, to us, that we do not matter to the American people, as before in our history. But, most important, say that we know, that we have *firm* evidence, that the direction and the money and support for these operations come from a hundred miles away . . . to the north."

"And that's it? That's all you want me to do?" McLemore asked.

As she had several times during the evening, Trinidad glanced uneasily at the close-packed tables on either side. They had by now finished the traditional Creole dinner, McLemore with relish, Trinidad with little interest. "May we walk before having coffee?" she asked.

McLemore paid and she led the way out of the *paladar*, through the Plaza de la Catedral filled with street musicians, *jineteros*, tourists, and natives hanging out, and down the three blocks to the harbor entrance. The Morro Castle and La Cabaña Fortress were brightly lit, creating a panoramic scenario more vivid than an epic movie. McLemore never tired of the dramatic sight, indeed saw it in his mind even when back in the States. They turned left at the seawall to walk up the Malecón. Presuming them to be fellow sufferers from the maladies of love, the young lovers, some sitting, some lying on the wide seawall, followed their progress, little guessing at the consequences of their intense conversation.

"There is something else," Trinidad said softly.

McLemore's mind flashed briefly on Ramsay the night before. He waited.

Presently she continued. "We have very reliable reason to believe that our tormentors are planning something very destructive on the anniversary of the *revolución*. As you know, it is New Year's Day. It is not so far off."

"I suppose it would do no good to ask how you know this."

"Not really," she sighed. "I could not tell you, in any case. But we know it for sure. We even think we know who it is . . . a specific group. We think it is the same one organizing all these terrorist incidents for the past year or more."

"Do you know what they plan to do?" McLemore asked. "Can you tell me?"

Trinidad headed for an unoccupied stretch of seawall. Over the walls of the Morro, a three-quarter moon peered brightly and inquisitively. McLemore sat beside her, again waiting as she sought to frame her case without endangering others.

After a moment she said, "No, we do not know enough. We know one thing, possibly an important thing. But you must not tell it to anyone . . . except appropriate U.S. officials. This group has met with . . . has had several meetings with . . . a Russian living in the United States. We think he is selling them some kind of weapons."

"For example . . . ," McLemore said.

"We do not know. Possibly something new . . . from the Russian military. Something we do not know what it is, something we cannot prepare for."

"But, to do much damage, wouldn't it have to be something big . . . something you could find if they tried to bring it in?"

"Perhaps," she said. "But maybe the Soviets had developed some new miniature weapon or explosive that we don't know about. Perhaps they could also bring in something in smaller pieces . . . pieces that look innocent by themselves. Then they get them here, put them together . . . maybe like a missile . . . and blow us all up." She paused, remembering the harsh crackdown initiated by Nuñez and the jails filled with innocent countrymen. "Believe me, we are alert. We are watching our own people.

Everything coming in is searched. Ship cargoes. Airplane cargoes. Tourist bags. Everything you can imagine. But, as everyone knows, we have hundreds of miles of shoreline, beaches, places to land with small boats. We are doing everything we can think of. But we cannot be everywhere . . . look everywhere. Until we know what to look for, what they are going to try to do, it is almost impossible."

McLemore said, "I understand. But what makes you think our people know any more than you do? Believe it or not, it's against the law to spy on U.S. citizens, at least without pretty good evidence that they're up to something illegal."

"It's a chance," she said. "It is a chance we want you to take for us. We can't think of anything else. I have confessed to you . . . it is no great secret . . . we do have friends in the U.S. who send us information. They are continuing to do their best. But this group we are dealing with, we have not known before. So, besides following them, we have very little chance to find out what they are planning."

"So, I should tell someone in authority . . . CIA or someone . . . about your suspicions, about the evidence you have, identify the group . . . and then what?"

Trinidad said, "I do not know. Whatever you can think of that would help keep these people in hiding for the next two months . . . until we can have our celebration, at least. If they know they are under suspicion, perhaps it will keep them from . . . how do you say? . . . mischief making."

"It would be helpful, I suppose, to have the name of the group," McLemore said.

Trinidad hesitated, then said, "They call themselves Bravo 99, sometimes just Bravo."

"How many are in the group?"

"We are not sure. But it is a very secret organization. We think no more than twenty or thirty."

A raucous band of teenagers camped nearby with a small but vibrant boom box playing Afro-calypso, and McLemore, placing his hands around her waist, helped Trinidad down from the wall. They started back toward the Morro at the harbor entrance, and the rising moon lit their way like a spotlight.

"Buying weapons, particularly sophisticated weapons, is expensive," McLemore observed as they walked. "Does this group have money? Or do they get it from somewhere?"

"We believe they are mostly successful businessmen. So they contribute to their cause. But we believe they also have other support."

"From where?" McLemore asked.

"From the Mafia."

20 Juan "Johnny" Aragones, Jr., had made a small but substantial fortune in the travel business. Over four decades, he, his father, and his brother had expanded their first travel agency into a chain of thirty offices throughout Florida and the Southeast. They specialized in tours to Central and South America and throughout the Caribbean. With the travel boom of recent years, business had been phenomenal. Retirees had money to travel, and the Latin American expats were always taking their kids down to see the relatives in the homeland. The Aragones family had recently acquired a network of bus lines serving several major Latin capitals and were negotiating investment partnerships in a series of hotels to be built in six of those capitals. As the last of his five guests arrived and his security man closed the entry gate at his luxury home in South Miami, it was clear that life had been extremely good to the Aragones family.

The only demon plaguing Juan senior, and thus the whole family, was the Commie son of a bitch in Havana. The old man had treated the ravages of cancer and old age with the elixir of hatred. He refused to die before Fidel Castro did. He went to sleep hating Castro. He woke up hating Castro. And he spent the hours in between devising new ways to ensure his nemesis's slow and painful death. Once a week, he and several of his aging compatriots from the Brigade, a rapidly declining number, got together to toast the impaling of el Barbudo on a long, sharp stake.

Under the relentless barrage of his father's hatred, Johnny sought desperately to find a way to transport the old warrior to his Cuban Valhalla on a raft constructed of Castro's bones. His last best hope was Bravo 99, which he helped found with his friends Manny, Tony, and several others. Like them, he now had financial resources. He had inherited the supremely intense antipathy to the present rulers of Cuba. He was still in good physical condition. And he wanted to please his old father. All these factors together provided both motive and opportunity. Like virtually his entire generation, he had no desire whatsoever to move back to Cuba. Why would he? He had more than he had ever dreamed of already. Why leave all this in the richest country on earth to live on an impoverished Caribbean island?

As he watched his boyhood pal José "Joe" Hernandez approach his pillared porch, he looked at his Rolex. The twenty-eighth. They had just over sixty days, and it would all be over. Then his father could die in peace. The ultimate gift from son to father.

Johnny took his old buddy into the den to join the four others already there. Now complete, they formed a band whose respective attributes fortuitously fit the mission they were now committed to undertake. There was, of course, Manny's overall organizational and leadership skills, his remarkable network of connections, which had turned up Isakov the Russian, and finally his fearless response to a challenge. He had the guts of a burglar. Tony, Manny's pal as Joe was his, was more cautious but had an uncanny ability to spot a phony or a danger. He was great with details and logistics, remembered everything; he could always cut to the chase. Joe was as successful in the electronics business as Johnny was in travel. He had won a lot of science awards in school and a full scholarship to MIT to study electrical engineering. Now he had more computer shops than Johnny did travel agencies. Joe had brought Orlando Menendez into Bravo 99. Orlando was just Orlando. Plain vanilla. No Anglo nickname. He had always liked the idea of being named after a major Florida city. Like the others, he was a successful businessman. His family's elevator company had made a lot of money with the building boom in South Florida during the last two decades. Then there was Pete. What a card. Class clown, a million laughs. Pedro Medina was not only a joker, he was also an incredible athlete. He had nearly qualified in two Olympic weight-lifting competitions. And his dream of a great Saturday afternoon was routinely fulfilled on the shooting range—long guns or handguns, it didn't matter.

Since their decision to undertake Project Luna, Pete had punished the group at his health club, requiring them to endure serious workouts three times a week. They had all attended the regular October meeting of the original Bravo group, but Manny had made a point of telling the larger group that the dramatic scheme discussed in September had been abandoned. Project Luna was something for just the six of them—Bravo ultra. After their colleagues had walked out of the September meeting, refusing to sign on to some unidentified major attack on the anniversary celebration in Havana, for all practical purposes Bravo 99 did not exist. It was becoming simply one of many Cuban-American organizations lobbying for tightening the embargo. Now it was the six of them. They had a secret no one else would ever know. They had a common goal. The six of them. They would liberate Cuba. This would be their gift to their fathers.

"Okay, let me tell you about our trip down south," Manny said as Johnny served the last of the drinks and passed the elegant humidor filled with Cohibas. "Tony and I looked over the Plaza and took a little tour of the Martí tower. We also located a 'clubhouse' and hired a young kid, who rented us the place, to help us out. He found us a truck. It's old but in pretty good shape."

Johnny said, "Did you get out to Bejucal? Did you find out where the 'product' is?"

Manny and Tony nodded like schoolboys with a secret. "Bastards almost caught us." Tony chuckled. "But the map worked like a charm and we're positive we know where the treasure is. We were right on top of it." He described their penetration step-by-step. "It's going to take a little work to get it out . . . one of the things we gotta talk about tonight . . . but it's do-able."

The two advance scouts told their story in detail from the flight over until the flight back. Passport control had been suspicious but had let them in. Thanks to Johnny's travel contacts in Mexico, their fake passports had worked. The six men sat around the large coffee table, a map of Havana spread out before them. The two men pointed out their hotel, the layout of the Plaza, the street in the Cerro district where they had located the hideout. They talked about the second visit to the Martí tower and the elevator trip to the top. The Cuban government had opened the observation deck on the top, the twenty-second floor, as a new attraction to offset growing tourist discontent. They all agreed that this policy would surely be suspended during the duration of the celebration. Tony had, typically, made a mental note of the manufacturer's name on the elevator plate. Orlando rubbed his hands with silent satisfaction. It was the standard brand of a well-known, traditional European manufacturer.

Tony then opened out yet another map, this one of Havana province. He pointed to the town of Bejucal thirty-five or so kilometers south of Havana and traced the roads they had taken to get there. He then drew a small square box some four or five kilometers north of the town on a small, little-used road that represented the Bejucal military compound and the storage area for the Soviet nuclear warheads in '62. Tony then took a clean sheet of paper, drew an outline of the compound, and fixed the bunker, which they had identified using Isakov's father's drawing, as the exact storage site.

The group became suddenly silent. They knew, they had seen and touched, the very hiding place of their contribution to the celebration of the fortieth anniversary of the Cuban revolution.

Pete broke the silence. "How do we get the fireworks out of there?"

"We figured you'd go in and just carry it out yourself . . . in broad daylight," Manny said. They all chuckled.

"Hey," Pete said, assuming a flex position, "you think I can't?"

"All right, big man," Manny said with a solid pop on a massive shoulder, "you may need some help. Tony and I talked about it coming back. We thought this over. The map shows Isakov's old man sealed up these fireworks in the end of the bunker. Considering the circumstances . . . the pressure, soldiers—Cubans, Soviets—walking around, big-shot generals giving orders, the Cubans mad at the Russians, all that stuff . . . we think he had to act fast. He didn't have all the time in the world. And he could rely on only a few people. So, probably late at night, he got a couple of guys down there, told them it was top secret, and got them to seal up a couple of medium-size crates at the far end of the bunker."

Pointing at the hand-drawn diagram, Tony said, "We go into the bunker late at night. We go down to the far end, and we break through the false wall. It's got to be something like cinder blocks. We break through the wall. We have to do it very quietly, which will take time, or we have to create a distraction. Get the night security patrols to chase a squirrel, while we do the damage and get out of there."

"How many guys?" Joe asked.

"Four guys to go in. Two guys to drive the truck and make some distraction. We found a spot about fifty yards down the road from the gate to ditch the truck. We'll make a couple of trial runs to get the timing and reduce the uncertainties. When we get inside, we've got to move quickly, quietly, and efficiently. No mistakes."

"Then what?" Joe asked.

Tony said, "Back to Havana. If we get out of Bejucal without being followed, we go right to Havana. Take the crate or crates directly to our place in Cerro. It's going to be late at night. So when we get to our place, the 'clubhouse,' we get the crate out fast, so no one sees, with no noise, so we don't wake anybody up, and we park the truck around in back. The hardest part is done."

Johnny said, "What day is this?"

Manny pulled out a pocket notebook and checked dates. "It's the twenty-fifth of December. Christmas Day. Maybe a day or two later. We'll see."

"How do we link up with the old Russki?" Pete asked. "He's got to check the wiring of this whizbang. When does he show up?"

Manny said, "Tony and I got a meeting later tonight with Isakov to work all that out. Basically, he's going to get the old guy—Dinkowitz, Dankowitch, whatever—down there the last week of December. About the time we get the package. We'll set up a contact point, get him to the clubhouse, and he'll work his magic. If this thing has been sealed up as tight as Isakov promises, he won't have much to do."

Johnny said, "The Commies are going to be checking passports very carefully from now on."

Manny said, "He's an old man. Seventy-three or -four. Like our pops. An old Russki back for a sentimental journey. Showing his respects for the revolution and all like that. Harmless old guy." He puffed on his cigar. "Besides, we got 'em really whipped up now with the hotel bombings. They're locking everybody up, shutting everything down, got all the tourists angry with the searches. We let this go on for a couple more weeks, then we let up. Like we're done. No more bombs. We let 'em think they stopped us. They hold their breath for a while . . . then they exhale." He took a puff on the cigar, held it, then blew it out. "Like that. Storm's over. They slap one another on the back. They relax just in time for the anniversary."

Tony grinned. This was his plan.

Johnny said, "What's the plan with the whizbang?"

Manny waited while Johnny, to Pete's disapproval, recharged their glasses. This was breaking training. "Once the old man has checked the wiring and set the timer, we load it into the truck. Orlando," he said to the silent member of the group, "you and Pete go over to the tower ahead of time, maybe the afternoon before the celebration. We'll get you some outfits that look like maintenance. You are there to check the elevator. Make sure it's okay in case the big shots decide to view the city, take up some VIPs on the anniversary. You find something wrong with the elevator motor. You tell the museum guards that it's got to be fixed . . . maybe even replaced . . . for safety. You come back. You get the truck and the gizmo. You take it back to the tower. Two more of us go . . . Johnny and Joe . . . along to lift and carry. You put this thing on top of the elevator carriage and set the timer. That's it. Then you get back in the truck and come back to the clubhouse."

Johnny said, "How are we getting in and out . . . of the country?"

Tony said, "Manny and I will go in first, with our Mexican passports. The other four come by boat by way of Cancún. Your boat. It's the fastest one of all of ours. We got friends going to give us some landing sites—probably in Pinar." He checked his pocket calendar. "You come down on the twenty-fourth. We'll meet you and take you to the clubhouse. You bring all the supplies, help get the whizbang, guard it, and get it in position on the afternoon of the thirty-first. After that's done, we all get back to the boat. When the balloon goes up on New Year's Day, we get the hell out of there." He sat back. "That's it."

"Why not get out on the thirty-first?" Orlando asked quietly.

"And miss the fun?" Pete responded with a harsh laugh. "I wouldn't miss that for the world. We'll be well out to sea as the fireball drifts eastward carrying all that Commie dust."

Tony got out several sheets of paper and distributed them around the group. "Here are the supplies we need. Joe, we'll need some sophisticated timers, electrical wiring, connectors, whatever. Use your imagination for a forty-year-old nuclear warhead. Orlando, get whatever you need to look like an elevator repairman. But remember, these guys would have tools from the fifties. So nothing too new-looking. Pete, you're the arms guy. A couple of assault rifles, a couple of shotguns . . . fast-action pumps . . . and at least one nine-millimeter for each of us, with plenty of ammo. You decide what we might need to get out of a tight spot. Johnny, you're transport. Get your boat up to trim, plenty of fuel for a round-trip. Have the engines tuned up. Whatever. Also, you might have a mechanic show you the basics of a '59 Chevy ton-and-a-half. I'll coordinate with all of you over the next few weeks." He turned to Manny sitting next to him. "And I nominate Manny for commander in chief. It's his idea. He found Isakov. He got the whizbang. He's been the brains all along."

Manny put his hands up, as if in surrender. They all applauded. He was elected by acclamation. "Tony and I will go down about the twentieth or twenty-first of December to make sure everything is ready to go. We'll be waiting for you at the landing spot in Pinar. It's just down the coast . . . right here," he said, pointing at a red X on the map of the province. "But we've got six or seven more weeks to get ready in the meantime. So let's plan to get together, either at Pete's health club, or here at Johnny's place, at least once a week to compare notes and go over the plan. Next week, Tony and I will have the details on linking up with old Dinkowitch." He checked his watch. "We gotta go. We meet Isakov in forty-five minutes."

The group broke up. They left one at a time over a half-hour period, Manny and Tony first, Joe last. The collective mood was upbeat and excited. They were finally getting down to business, entering the homestretch. As they shook hands on the vast porch, Johnny said to his old friend Joe, "I can hardly wait for the old man's reaction. He'll probably have a heart attack from happiness. Those old guys are going to be so happy. Finally . . . finally . . . no more Castro. No more Commies."

Among the many factors bonding the six conspiratorial brothers was the lack of any sense of what would come after. They were not motivated by power lust. None wanted to return to Cuba to live. None contemplated a position in a successor government. Indeed, they had given no thought to what kind of government there would be in twenty-first-century Cuba. There was an unspoken, unquestioned assumption that a solid, corporate-democratic government would probably emerge, as if by the laws of nature. There would be a return to the status quo ante; a benign oligarchy would guide Cuba's destiny, and perhaps the old veterans of the Brigade would form a governing council to direct Cuban affairs . . . who could run for office, who could own the media, who could invest in the land and factories. Everything would be copacetic.

Manny and Tony parked their car near the venerable Doral Hotel in Miami Beach and, according to prearrangement, set out down the beach toward the tall palm closest to the water just north of the old hotel. It was just minutes after 11 P.M., and the three-quarter moon lit their path. As they approached the tree, a large figure emerged from behind its equally large trunk. It was Isakov.

"Manny. Tony. Here is Victor. How's things?" came the thickly accented voice.

"Okay, Vic. And you?"

"Okay, for myself," Viktor said. "How is everything with your big project?"

"Our planning is fine, Vic. Not to worry. How's your old buddy Dankovitz? He got his bag packed?"

"He's cold," Isakov said.

Tony said, "Cool, don't you mean, Vic?"

"However," Viktor said. He hated to have his American slang corrected; it made him feel foolish. "He is being ready. He has plane reservation. He has visa. We will make for him hotel reservation . . . near you, but not same."

Manny said, "What about the electronics lessons, Vic? How's he doing with the refresher course . . . you know, getting back up to speed with his old business?"

Viktor said, "My friends are providing original manuals and he is studying them every day. Is amazing, they say. His mind is sharp, very keen. He remembers everything from original expertise. He can draw all diagrams . . . link up all connections. He can go back into strategic rocket forces even today, probably."

Manny said, "We don't exactly need him to go that far. Just check out the systems on the 'product' your old man left behind." He paused. "Then just that other job."

"Which other job, Manny?" Viktor looked puzzled.

Manny moved in closer. Nose-to-nose in the moon shadow under the giant palm. "You remember, Vic. Hooking up the timer. He has to show us how to make the whizbang . . . what should we say? . . . operable."

"Whizbang?"

"The product, Vic. The device. It's a word for a tricky toy. You understand?"

Viktor Isakov nodded, noting the word. He would remember to use it.

Tony said, "Speaking of understanding, Vic. How do we communicate with the old fellow? Will he have a translator? Or how's his English?"

"English is good, Tony," Viktor said. "Not so good as me. But he understands everything, and he can speak pretty good."

"Okay, Vic," Manny said. "One last thing. Where we meet. We want him in Havana on the twenty-fifth of December. No sooner, no later. Understood? Here are the instructions. He goes to the hotel, checks in, and he waits. Tell him to get some rest. Have food sent up. Get over the jet lag. At noon on the twenty-sixth, we send somebody around to knock on his door. This person will call himself 'Señor Cruz.' He will say he is the guide from Cubatur. Dinkovitz should bring his luggage. Nothing but a small bag. We'll have somebody take care of the hotel bill. He will not be going back there. We have a place for him to stay. When he finishes his work, there will be plenty of time for him to visit the old places, have a good time, relive the good old days."

Viktor held up his hand. "He wants to know can he meet some of his old Cuban officers he work with." He handed over a crumpled piece of paper. "Here are some names he remembers. Is amazing, don't you think?"

Tony coughed. Manny said, "Vic, it may be a problem. We don't want him too visible, you understand. It's not like he's down there on a real tour. In spite of how careful he is, he might have a little rum and let something slip." Noting Viktor's dismay, he added, "But tell him we'll do what we can. We want him to have a good time, enjoy himself. A memorable time even."

Viktor kicked sand with his new canvas shoe. "What should I tell him about his pay? You know, money we promise him. He is not demanding, you know. But he want to make help for his children with it, and he is asking me this very shyly. He doesn't know how it work . . . business . . . capitalism, you know."

Manny patted him on the back. "You tell him he's dealing with honorable men. All expenses paid in Cuba. Airfare. And he goes back home with ten thousand . . . in cash . . . in his little bag."

Viktor nodded happily.

"But, Vic, tell him not to spend it all on those Cuban girls." They all laughed as they departed.

■ ■ ■

The Presidium waited in its Kremlin conference room for a copy of the president's speech. It came from the U.S. Embassy after 1 A.M. the morning of the twenty-first. Thirty Soviet ships are making for Cuba at that hour. One of them, the Aleksandrovsk, contains twenty-four nuclear warheads for the intermediate-range R-14s and the forty-four remaining warheads for the FKRs, the land-based cruise missiles. Additionally, four ships—the Dubna, the Nicolaeev, the Divnogorsk, and the Almeteevsk—containing the missiles for the two IRBM regiments were racing for Cuba at flank speed.

Relieved that Kennedy seems to have precluded invasion in favor of "quarantine," at least for the moment, the Soviet leadership debates the orders to be given its ships at sea and the Soviet Group of Forces in Cuba. "Continue with rapid construction of the missile batteries," Khrushchev orders. With regard to the thirty supply ships, a compromise is reached. With several exceptions, all ships that have not arrived should turn back to Soviet ports.

Concerned that top secret nuclear equipment might fall into U.S. hands and committed to the full completion of Operation Anadyr, the Presidium orders the Aleksandrovsk and the four missile ships to make for any Cuban port they can reach. The KGB resident in Washington destroys all secret documents and checks his emergency generators so that communications with Moscow can be maintained in case the U.S. cuts off the power supply to the embassy. Chairman Khrushchev stays in his Kremlin office all night, with his street clothes on, ready for any emergency.

The simultaneous decisions of Ex Comm, as announced by the president, and the Presidium, as carried out by Khrushchev, set the stage for the most dangerous six days in history.

■ ■ ■

21 Havana's energy level seemed to rise even as its life became more precarious. McLemore could not decide whether he imagined this or whether some law of Caribbean nature was at play. As he walked past the stalls of the booksellers surrounding the Plaza de Armas, on his way to the Foreign Ministry, carrying with him not only the notes from his research but also, in his mind, the sinister prospect of a terrorist threat against the city, the collective human temperature and energy output seemed to mount. It was as if, collectively, the people, out of centuries of conditioning in sensing danger, thought they could ward off evil by dancing. Calypso-Afro-Caribbean rhythms blared from doorways of bars and shops. Along the tiny streets leading into the Plaza de la Catedral and in tourist bazaars, hawkers promoted Afrocentric carvings and paintings, the faces of the sellers mirrored in their wares. Through the doorway of La Bodeguita, still being repaired weeks after a small bomb had blown the original entrance away, musicians, surrounded by locals and tourists, sang and swayed to Cuban favorites. On the streets, the tourists swarmed. Light tourist gentlemen could be seen appraising dark local ladies. And light tourist ladies could be seen appraising dark local gentlemen. Here belonged the solution to the mystery of racial division. Along the streets, doors opened directly from the crumbling sidewalks onto tiny rooms and apartments already sweltering in the late-morning heat. Pathetic scruffy dogs slithered away from the dangerous feet of *jineteros* hustling "Cohibas" made in back rooms from sweepings from the floors of second-rate tobacco factories. And everywhere, the omnipresent Che guarded the revolution, a stern conscience against *any* compromise.

Havana, McLemore thought, is inimitably feminine, a fading beauty preserving the mystery of her allure even as the facade wrinkles, cracks, fades, and crumbles. Except for the mansions of the Batista millionaires, now restored as embassies and consulates, corporate offices and executive residences of foreign companies, the houses were subdivided and subdivided yet again, overrun with excess people, eroding under the assault of sun and salty air.

A few blocks on his right toward the ocean, McLemore could see the top of the seven-story glass tower, perpendicular to the water, the U.S. Interest office. Together with its low, one-story annex, it was encased in a seven-foot wire fence symbolizing, whether on purpose or not, its separation from the host country. It was set apart, a kind of modern, high-tech reproach to its shabby neighbors.

McLemore continued on past a vacant lot next to a kindergarten, where two dozen elderly women practiced tai chi among the blooming butterfly jasmine and dusty royal palms, hummingbirds, and yellow-shafted flickers, and laughing children clung to the neighboring fence, bemused by the strange andante antics of their elders. Along the streets of the more modern Vedado section of the city, everyone was hitching. Masses in slow motion sought a foothold or even a handhold on a fuming truck or bus. No vehicle escaped carrying ten times its designed capacity. The antique cars, rustic survivors of the General Motors factories of the 1950s, spluttered past, tributes to the mechanical genius of Cubans having neither spare parts nor tools. Everywhere the faces, history's maps, Indian-Spanish-African-Caribbean, mulatto and mulatta, the offspring of generations of plunderers, natives, pirates, soldiers, fortune hunters, bounty hunters, visionaries and missionaries, and restless refugees from dozens of foreign shores swept westward in the never-ending search for one kind of El Dorado or another.

Over it all, like a brooding presence for forty years, restlessly pushing and prodding, haranguing and harassing, urging, promoting, preaching the evangelistic message of *revolución*, loomed the relentless figure of *el Jefe*. Still imposing, taller than most of his generation but now graying with age, wearing layer upon layer of history like sackcloth and ashes, he dominated the history of his own country and bedeviled an entire hemisphere for half a century. He had buried Che thirty years after he was killed, and he had lived to see Batista buried. He had seen U.S. presidents come and go. He had survived an embargo carried out by the dominant economic power of his hemisphere, indeed of the world, for almost four decades. He had been in power longer than almost any leader in the world. He had seen the Cold War begin and he had seen it end. He had used it, been used by it, been a central player in it, been betrayed and abandoned by it. But, defying political wind and weather, there he stood. Implacable.

One who knew him well said, "You do not understand Fidel. He is not a Communist. He is a Jesuit." They raised him and educated him, after all. They made him a true believer. They taught him a single-minded discipline, so crucial to the revolution and yet so uncharacteristic of this culture of sun, sand, and salsa. On top of this, he absorbed with his mother's milk a love-hate ambivalence toward the giant political cloud constantly hovering over his country's northern horizon. It is not true he hates the United States of America. It is true the United States makes him very angry. The degree to which that anger continues to manifest itself in both large and petty ways is a measure of its endurance. One would not look to twentieth-century Cuba to find a Fidel Castro. One would look to early sixteenth-century Florentine Italy.

McLemore had seen the three black cars late one night. *El Jefe* on the prowl. Maybe headed in the small hours to a nearby beach to see if the long-awaited—perhaps even secretly desired?—invasion was finally under way. Disappointed—possibly?—not to be able to face his ancient foe one more time. *Tio Sam.* He couldn't live with him . . . and he couldn't live without him.

Approaching the now familiar Foreign Ministry archives, McLemore wondered whether Castro could survive normal relations with the States. Would it deprive him of his purpose? Would it leave him feeling empty and unfulfilled? What was there to live for if not to thumb your nose at the greatest power in history, day after day, year after year? Outliving them all. Surviving everything . . . invasions, embargoes, crises, hostility, endless demented assassination attempts. What a reason to get up in the morning, to run up the flag yet again, to survive *one more day*. McLemore thought with amusement—end the embargo, normalize relations, and the *revolución* would end in a fortnight . . . and *el Commandante* would probably die from boredom. This is what the Cold War had come down to—*mano a mano* between *el Jefe* and *Tio Sam*.

McLemore started up the steps of the Foreign Ministry thinking, There truly is something going on here. How else can you explain Cuba's attraction to Richard Henry Dana, Jr., Ernest Hemingway, Graham Greene, and Gabriel García Márquez, among many others? He laughed out loud at something he had read just before his return. "Cuba seems to have the same effect on American administrations," an American diplomat had said, "that the full moon used to have on werewolves."

The ever-patient Carlos waited for him, as usual, with the files of memos from the Foreign Ministry spread out on the bare table in the dusty archive. There were inventories of weapons coming in and inventories of the same weapons going out. All within the space of weeks, even days. McLemore imagined, as he gave Carlos a pat on the shoulder and sat down, the frustration and anger of the Soviet forces, not to say their Cuban hosts, who had been lashed to get weapons out by the same Kremlin officials who, mere hours before, had been lashing them to set up the launch sites, lay the electrical cables, get the missiles set up, the warheads targeted and secured, communications established, preparations made to go to war. The Yanquis are coming and they're just over the horizon. The Kremlin's overnight reversal had angered the fifty thousand Soviet military personnel in Cuba; angered them either because they believed in what they were doing—confronting the capitalist menace in its own backyard—or because they were enjoying the sun for the first time in their lives. It had infuriated the Cubans to the point of apoplexy.

Carlos proceeded to read the headings of the files, McLemore as usual waving off the routine ones. He had, by now, focused his research on an issue almost untouched in Cuban missile crisis historical literature—what happened between the Soviets, the Cubans, and the Americans during the period between the culmination of the crisis at the end of October and the removal of the last of the weapons at the end of December 1962. During the period between his trips to Cuba, while he was back in the States between the second week in September and the third week in October, McLemore had performed a thorough search of the literature of this sixty-day period in late 1962, and he had found almost nothing. All the historians had focused on the infamous "thirteen days" and few had bothered to find out what happened afterward. Thus McLemore had his topic and his grant project had a focus: How had the three parties carried out the agreement made between the most powerful two of them, and what had happened in the sixty days following the agreement? Now he kept returning to the very narrow question of how the United States knew that all the weapons that came in also went out.

The documents Carlos was now translating for him had to do with the agreement between the United States and the USSR, Kennedy and Khrushchev, to place the outgoing missiles, on their return from Mariel and other ports back to Soviet ports, on the decks of the Soviet freighters, usually covered with canvas so they could readily be uncovered for the U.S. counting planes flying low overhead. There seemed little doubt that these missiles were all present and accounted for. What good would it have done for the Soviets to try to cheat by one or two? Not enough to start a war, and only enough to sour relations with the United States and its allies even more. No, the missiles had all gone home. And, of course, the warheads would have gone with them. What good is a nuclear warhead without a delivery vehicle, a missile to carry it to its target? Besides, with the Soviet military pulling out, abandoning its revolutionary allies, relations between the Soviets and the Cubans were hardly the best. Castro was so angry that, given some leftover nuclear warheads, God knows what he might have tried. It was hard to tell whether his fury was directed more at the sinister Yanquis, who had avoided the confrontation he so urgently desired, or at the perfidious Russians, who had gone eyeball-to-eyeball with the United States and had blinked.

"Carlos, see if you can find anything referring to 'Luna' warheads," McLemore asked. He wanted to find some confirmation of the document in his pocket.

Carlos's bright black eyes rapidly scanned line after line, page after page. Presently he said, "Señor, here it says that the Soviet foreign minister Mikoyan has ordered General Issa Pliyev, the senior commander of all Soviet military forces in Cuba, to remove all tactical nuclear warheads from Cuba."

"What is the source, Carlos?" McLemore asked, making a note in his pocket notebook.

Carlos flushed. "*Profesor*, from the routing of the memorandum it is a Defense Ministry copy of a message between Minister Mikoyan, who was here in Havana at the time, and General Pliyev. It was . . . ah . . . it was intercepted by Cuban intelligence."

"What is the date?" McLemore asked.

"The date is 22 November 1962."

From previous documents Carlos had translated for him, McLemore knew that the original Soviet position, encouraged by the Cubans and endorsed on October 30 by Soviet Defense Minister Rodion Malinovsky, was to remove the strategic missiles and warheads, the R-12s and the R-14s, but to leave the Luna tactical missiles and warheads and the FKR cruise missiles and warheads and train the Cubans in their use for their own defensive purposes. Indeed, on November 5, under orders from Marshal Malinovsky, the Soviet ship *Aleksandrovsk*, already loaded with nuclear warheads for the R-14 intermediate-range missiles that never arrived in Cuba, completed loading of the remaining warheads for the R-12 medium-range missiles and left port for the Soviet Union. All tactical nuclear warheads and delivery systems remained in Cuba.

What continued to puzzle McLemore was the original inventory of a hundred tactical warheads, counted at the dock as they were unloaded, and the memorandum in his pocket that confirmed ninety-eight nuclear warheads shipped out, also counted at the dock as they were loaded. The returned tactical warheads were loaded over the period of time between November 22, when the Kremlin overruled Malinovsky and ordered the tactical nukes removed, and the end of December 1962, when the last warhead was shipped home to the USSR. Why the discrepancy? And did it matter?

"Carlos," McLemore mused, "are there any names of Soviet officers who had responsibility for the warheads . . . bringing them in, storing them, shipping them out, counting them?"

Carlos surveyed a number of documents. "Pliyev is mentioned often. 'Pavlov,' as he was called. Garbuz, Gribkov, both senior and mentioned quite often. Ah, here, on these two documents regarding the tactical warheads . . . 'Luna' you call them . . . here is a Colonel L. S. Isakov. He is also mentioned again as responsible for warhead storage at Bejucal. His deputy, a lieutenant colonel, is called Dankevich. They are referred to together in both documents." Several minutes passed as Carlos quickly scanned three or four other files. "It seems that Dankevich reports to Isakov. Isakov to Garbuz, a general, deputy chief of Soviet forces in Cuba. Garbuz to Pliyev, senior commander of all Soviet forces. Pliyev to Gribkov, a member of the Soviet general staff. Gribkov to Malinovsky. The marshal who is Soviet minister of defense."

McLemore said, "Look for Isakov's name to see if he was anywhere else besides Bejucal."

More minutes passed as Carlos scanned page after page, occasionally turning down the upper left corner. McLemore made notes of the names Isakov and Dankevich as he waited. Presently Carlos said, "Isakov and his deputy went to the motorized rifle regiments at Artemisa and Managua where the Luna batteries were. They played some role in setting up the batteries and supervising the warheads. They seemed to go back and forth often to Bejucal."

McLemore said, "*Por favor*, one more question. See if you can find any reference to Isakov, or the other one, in connection with the Luna warheads being shipped out."

Carlos scanned two more files, then came to the last. Being chronological, this file dealt with the last few weeks of Soviet missile forces in Cuba. Ten minutes passed. "I do not find it, *profesor*. There is reference to the loading and shipping of the remaining missiles. But there does not seem to be any final report of the numbers or who was responsible. Everything else is carefully reported. It seems strange there is no final report or record."

Suddenly remembering the purloined document in his pocket, McLemore coughed and reddened. "Carlos," he quickly said, "we need some coffee, *mi amigo*. You've been working hard." Carlos smiled shyly and pushed a hand through his bushy brown hair. "I think so, *señor*." As Carlos began to organize the files, putting documents back in their proper folders and sorting the files according to dates, McLemore said, "I'll meet you at the front entrance in a minute."

Trying to conceal his awkward secret, McLemore headed out of the archives for the fresh late-morning air. Once outside, he walked to a tall palm in the corner of the front yard of the Ministry building. He stood in the shadow of the palm, back to the trunk so that he was not visible from the Ministry. He pulled the document from his pocket and scanned its contents once again. He confirmed, as before, that ninety-eight nuclear warheads had been loaded on the Soviet naval transport. It looked like an official inventory, certifying the contents of the ship about to depart the port of Mariel.

Then he looked at the bottom of the page. On the line marked *Certi-ficado* was the typed name "Col. L. S. Isakov" and the handwritten signature "Isakov."

McLemore looked at the top of the page. The date was 25 December 1962.

22 Because of the nature of his last message to headquarters, Sam "Red" Ramsay was recalled to Langley for "consultations." The Cuban government, meaning of course the Cuban intelligence services, took note. When foreign intelligence officers, especially ones from the U.S. Interest office, went home for "consultations," it was worth noting. Something was up. Ramsay would report to his masters at the CIA either that the Cubans were concerned about disruption of their anniversary celebration, or that they had additional evidence involving Cuban-American groups in the support of terrorism against Cuba, or that he had uncovered evidence of some plot in Cuba, or that he was off on some wild goose chase involving a very unobtrusive U.S. history teacher. His masters at Langley knew of McLemore's presence in Cuba because his name had appeared in at least two of Ramsay's reports on current activities in Cuba. And because Jack McLemore was one of the Agency's great Cold War heroes.

Hot coffee in hand and safe in the arms of his colleagues in the Cuban section at Langley, Ramsay said, "McLemore refuses to help us. He knows something . . . I . . . I'm not sure how. But he has been putting some pieces together . . . maybe from his new 'friends' at the Foreign Ministry. Maybe he's running some kind of game of his own. Who knows? All I know is that he knows more than he's saying."

"Is he sympathetic to the Cubans?" a younger officer asked.

Ramsay said, "That's probably not the right word."

"Even though they killed his father?" she persisted.

"He seems . . . it's hard to explain . . . he seems . . . neutral," Ramsay said with a snort. "He doesn't seem to have a side. It's like he's standing outside the whole goddamn thing . . . sitting there and laughing at all of us. I've never seen anything like it . . . from an American."

"What is he doing down there, anyway?" someone asked. "Surely, he must hate Castro."

"He says he's working on some research project . . . oddly enough, about the missile crisis. Got some money from something called the Huntingdon Foundation. At least that's what you guys told me when you checked him out. Anyway, I've pitched him twice," Ramsay said. "I asked him to find out what he could from the Foreign Ministry. First, just about things in general . . . anything he could collect that would help us . . . in general. Then, last week, I brought him inside . . . just a little. I told him we had a problem. The Cubans had a problem. Something was up around the celebration. Maybe something very bad."

"Did you tell him about the Russian?" the section chief, Mr. Worthy, asked.

"Not exactly."

"Did you tell him we . . . did you tell him about the . . . that we think a device may be involved?"

"Let's say I hinted at it . . . to try to bring him over."

"Do you think it was a good idea . . . to tell him as much as you did?" Mr. Worthy persisted.

Ramsay swore and threw the empty paper coffee cup across the room. "We need him, goddammit! He's all we've got right now."

"You've got some other people down there, Red," the woman officer said. "What do they have to say?"

"Nobody knows anything, except that every screw in the system is being tightened down. They've tossed everybody who spits on the sidewalk in the slammer. Right now, it's tighter than a drum. Our regulars can't find out anything, except the *jefes* are nervous as they can be. The Cubans have some info . . . we just don't know what it is. That's what I asked this half-assed professor to find out. What are they so worried about? What do they know?"

"And he's not buying?" the section chief asked.

"He's not buying," Ramsay said, "at least right now. But I've got him thinking. And he still might come around."

"What did you offer him?" a washed-up field agent in the corner asked.

"I offered him help in finding out exactly what happened to his father."

"How did he respond?" Mr. Worthy asked.

"Frankly?" Ramsay said, kicking the cheap federal coffee table. "He told me to stick it up my ass." Then he kicked the table again.

"When is he coming back up here?" a researcher named Sandy asked.

"I'm not sure. I think in three or four more days."

"Will he go back down again?" the chief asked quietly.

Ramsay said, "You want my guess? I'll give you my guess. Yes. Yes, he's going back down there, at least once more."

"Why?"

"Why?" Ramsay said mockingly as he stood up. "Why? Because he hasn't found his old man yet."

Eyeing Ramsay as if he were a highly volatile explosive device himself, the chief said quietly, "See if you can get him to come in and see us when he comes back up."

∎ ∎ ∎

On Wednesday, the twenty-fourth of October, the Joint Chiefs of Staff order American military forces to Defense Condition (DefCon) 2. DefCon 5 is a condition of peace. DefCon 1 is all-out war.

The order is issued en clair (uncoded, in the clear). Unless you are pre-

paring for a surprise attack, there is no reason not to let the world, including all real and presumed enemies, know what you are up to. That message is part of the purpose of the higher alert status.

On the same day Khrushchev invites William Knox, a very surprised American in Moscow on business, to the Kremlin for a three-hour meeting. He admits to Knox that the Soviet Union has placed nuclear-capable missiles in Cuba but argues that this was done purely for the defense of Cuba against U.S. attack. The issue can be resolved only by a summit between himself and Kennedy, he says. "But if the U.S. insists on war," he concludes, "we'll all meet in hell."

Later that night, President Kennedy was read a letter from Chairman Khrushchev. It says, in part:

Imagine, Mr. President, that we had posed to you those ultimate conditions which you have posed to us by your action [the naval quarantine]. How would you have reacted to this? . . . Who asked you to do this? [Khrushchev firmly believes the Pentagon governs the United States.] . . . You, Mr. President, are not declaring quarantines but advancing an ultimatum and threatening that unless we subordinate ourselves to your demands, you will use force.

Consider what you are saying! . . . You are no longer appealing to reason, but wish to intimidate us. . . . And all of this not only out of hatred for the Cuban people and their government, but also as a result of considerations of the election campaign in the U.S.A. [He also believes this is an election ploy by Kennedy.] . . . The actions of the U.S.A. toward Cuba are outright banditry or, if you like, the folly of degenerate imperialism.

Unfortunately, such folly can bring grave suffering to peoples of all countries, not least the American people, since the U.S.A. has fully lost its inaccessibility with the advent of contemporary types of armament. If someone had tried to dictate these kinds of conditions to you, you would have rejected it. And we also say—no. . . . We shall not be simply observers of the pirate-like actions of American ships on the high seas. We will be forced to take measures which we deem necessary and adequate to protect our rights.

The Soviet Union is serving notice that it intends to challenge the United States' naval blockade and thus create a military confrontation.

*Shortly after midnight that same night, Kennedy sends an equally uncom-
promising response through the Soviet Embassy in Washington. We have, he
says, "learned beyond doubt what you have not denied [in your letter]—
namely, that all these public assurances," which he describes as "most explicit
assurances from your government and its representatives, both publicly and
privately" that there were no offensive nuclear missiles in Cuba, "were false
and that your military people had set out recently to establish a set of missile
bases in Cuba." He urges Khrushchev to take all steps necessary to correct the
"deterioration in our relations." He writes, "I ask you to recognize clearly
that it was not I who issued the first challenge in this case, and that in the light
of this record these activities in Cuba required the responses I have announced."*

*Khrushchev thinks the United States is preparing to invade Cuba. Given
a major call-up of reservists, large-scale redeployment of U.S. air, sea, and
land forces, and intelligence reports of invasion rumors all over Washington
and south Florida, there is ample evidence to support this conclusion. Khrushchev is also told that, after the failure of the Bay of Pigs invasion and the
disastrous summit in Vienna, Kennedy must do something tough, to show
strength and resolve, before the congressional elections in November.*

*On his part, Kennedy thinks Khrushchev is secretly placing missiles in
Cuba to blackmail the United States into signing a peace agreement over
Berlin that will permanently isolate the city from the Western world.*

■ ■ ■

23 Trinidad listened to the deputy director of the immigration
security services explain to Lazaro Suarez the procedures being
used to screen visitors at airports and harbors who might fit the
profile of potential terrorists. The most suspicious were placed under surveillance. Additional personnel were being seconded from other security
services to carry out this manpower-intensive task. For those who could

possibly be something other than mere tourists, spot checks at hotels and surveillance by members of local committees to protect the *revolución* would be used. Tourist groups were being followed to ensure that individual members were not breaking away for clandestine meetings. The entire network of local vigilante committees had been activated to watch for packages being passed from tourists to locals or foreigners behaving suspiciously or unusual activities in local neighborhoods. As for Cuban dissidents and troublemakers, the jails were filling up. Nobody would criticize *el Commandante* or question the *revolución* or suggest that the time for free speech had arrived. Individual cases would be dealt with later. For the meantime, at least until the anniversary of the *revolución*, critics were guests of the state.

Lazaro listened patiently as the apparatchik paced the small office, strutting and preening, thumping the paper-laden desk, pointing a bony finger like a rapier at an invisible terrorist, and issuing grand promises. After years of close friendship, Trinidad well knew that Lazaro was heavily skeptical. The crease of doubt between his tangled eyebrows, his inability to applaud the bureaucrat's performance, his preoccupation with the papers on his desk, all signaled to Trinidad that he knew that none of these measures, however rigorously undertaken, would finally frustrate the threat they faced. What little they knew about those they were up against suggested that their unknown adversaries possessed enough canniness, resources, and demented determination to bypass the puny, unimaginative measures the immigration forces were taking.

When the self-important security peacock had finally moved on, Lazaro wearily stood up from behind the desk and followed Trinidad out of the Ministry of the Interior. She had been thinking how much he had aged in the fifteen years they had known each other. Always a compact man of ordinary height, now he had begun to slump slightly, as if carrying a great burden of unrealized ideals. His once rich brown hair was now almost totally white. His wide, spontaneous smile was now less frequent and more constrained. His natural shyness now seemed to mask a deep disappointment. Lazaro's early revolutionary idealism had been squeezed out by life. Trinidad's youthful passion for Lazaro had long since been converted to sisterly concern for his sadness and disillusionment.

They made their way on foot several blocks north into the Vedado section of Havana where Trinidad shared a flat with her aging mother.

Through skillful trading of some clothing she no longer needed, she had acquired enough food coupons for a chicken, some fresh vegetables, and an extra bottle of rum. Her mother would have most of the food ready for cooking and then would spend the evening with her sister who lived nearby. Trinidad had arranged the evening as a forum for introducing McLemore to her boss, Lazaro Suarez.

On the way they discussed the script for the evening. Lazaro was to be charming, open, and solicitous. Trinidad would carry the burden of the early conversation, introducing Lazaro gradually, then moving to the real business after dinner. Lazaro would close the deal by laying as much of the threat as he could on the table and asking, perhaps pleading with, Mc-Lemore to do what he could to help, possibly even to intervene with U.S. intelligence.

Trinidad's third-floor apartment had a view of the ocean a dozen blocks away. Cramped and hot, but with two bedrooms, it was slightly larger than those of most Habanistas. She made Lazaro comfortable. He was already familiar with the surroundings, having spent many pleasant hours there some years earlier during the brief but passionate romantic collision with Trinidad. By the time he had managed to overcome his scruples against abandoning his wife and young children, his wife's illness surfaced and Trinidad's ardor transformed itself into affection. They had rescued a friendship from the ashes of passion. The occasion was still surprisingly frequent when he regretted his earlier sense of duty. He felt he had missed part of life itself.

She finished preliminary preparation of the dinner, poured Lazaro some rum, and finished her debriefing on her last conversation with McLemore.

"He said he would help . . . actually, that he would *try* to help," she said. "He may not be effective. He dislikes the spy world. He dislikes politics. It's about his father."

Lazaro said, "Then why will he talk with us . . . help us?"

Trinidad shrugged. "Maybe he finds it interesting. Maybe it is an intrigue. Maybe he thinks he will learn something more about his father's experience . . . a kind of reliving. Maybe he has now got a conscience."

"Maybe he has some personal purpose . . . something to do with his feeling for you," Lazaro tendered.

Trinidad flashed a glare at him. "Don't, Lazaro. We have discussed this before. Don't try to create a romantic drama out of this. You let your own emotions get involved, this is going to get very complicated." She poured more rum in his glass. "I must go downstairs to collect him. He knows the street and number. But he will get confused. I'll be right back." She shook her dark hair as she swirled out of the flat.

On the street outside her apartment building, Trinidad glanced at her watch, nervously lit a cigarette, and peered up and down the street. She was furious about Lazaro's miserable jealousies and more furious at herself for her emotional response. Why did the idea of a romance with McLemore make her so angry? Was it because it was so unlikely? Or was it because he was such a Yanqui? Was it because Lazaro seemed so preoccupied by it? Was it because the idea really interested her?

Rounding the corner a block away came the now familiar figure of the bemused, slightly unfocused professor looking rumpled and ill at ease in the loose-fitting *guayabera* shirt that he had now taken to wearing. It was as if he had assumed a disguise that he knew fooled no one. He waved awkwardly and smiled as he approached, happy that he had found the right location.

"*Buenas noches, profesor,*" Trinidad said with mock formality. They had not quite worked out the transition from professionalism to friendship. And the vague possibility that even more might be at stake made it that much more problematic.

"I am so happy to see you . . . right where you said you would be." They shook hands awkwardly, and he leaned forward slightly as if to kiss her, then veered away as though tilted by a strong breeze.

She gestured for him to follow her up the stairs. McLemore observed the peeling walls, the flaking paint on the stairway bannister, the strong odor of food cooking in the flats they passed, the darkness of the hallways. He suddenly realized he had inadvertently become nervous at the prospect of an evening with a senior Cuban intelligence official. His mental picture was not a good one. He steeled himself for a rough evening with a rigid ideologue, an inquisitorial defender of the revolutionary faith, some jumped-up latter-day, Yanqui-hating acolyte of Che himself.

She led him through her doorway, and a genial-looking, stocky, middle-aged man with almost white hair and a wide smile rose to meet him. As they shook hands, McLemore liked him immediately.

"*Buenas noches, señor.* It is a great pleasure to meet you," Lazaro said.

"Likewise," McLemore said. "Trinidad promised that you would not arrest me . . . at least this evening."

They all laughed, and the ice was broken. Trinidad poured rum for all three and, after some abstract explanation that she and Sr. Suarez worked together at the Foreign Ministry, excused herself to finish dinner preparations.

After an awkward silence, Lazaro said, "If I am not too bold, I am interested to know about the work that brings you here and whether you are enjoying your time here in Cuba?"

McLemore appreciated his directness. "What am I doing here? It's a good question. Looking for something. Escaping from something. Maybe boredom. Who knows? Let's just say I am an archaeologist of the Cold War—and here I have discovered . . . with great respect . . . the last living dinosaur."

His composure shaken, Lazaro said, "I am not sure it is a compliment. But I am sure that you 'nortes' cannot seem to leave us alone . . . with great respect."

"We can't," McLemore said. "It's not in our nature to leave things alone. We're like children who find pretty wrapped boxes and always assume they're presents for us. And if they are hidden in a closet at holiday time, we can't wait. We can't stand anything closed up. We are frustrated by puzzles and mysteries. We have to open the packages up. The world is our Christmas tree, Señor Suarez."

"Por favor, Lazaro."

"Nevertheless, it is an interesting mystery and I am enjoying very much the effort to solve a small piece of it, Lazaro. Trinidad and the young assistant, Carlos, whom you have provided, have been extremely helpful." Lazaro smiled and nodded. McLemore hesitated, uncertain how much explanation of his work was required and how much would be repetitive of what Trinidad had already told him. "I'm studying the Caribbean crisis of 1962 generally and focusing especially on the way in which the Soviet nuclear warheads were managed during that period."

Lazaro nodded pleasantly.

"The way in which the agreement between the United States and the Soviet Union was carried out . . . after the crisis . . . seems not to have been studied very much. It has come to interest me. How the U.S. knew that the Soviets carried out their part of the bargain in every detail. The warheads particularly. The missiles were easier to count. But I can't find out how we could have been sure about the warheads."

Lazaro said, "All nuclear materials are dangerous, of course. But what could we, or the Russians, possibly do with warheads? Carry them to Miami or Washington and explode them like fireworks?" His tone was light and his smile wide.

"Who knows," McLemore responded. "People do strange things. Much of the information that has come out from all sides in recent years shows that the Cuban government was at least as angry at the Soviets for letting them down as they were at the U.S."

"Even so, the Soviet forces were rigid in denying the Cuban military access to their weapons. They counted everything coming in and everything going out." Lazaro shrugged. "They let us touch nothing. They had no interest in leaving nuclear warheads behind."

Trinidad brought in full plates from the kitchen, which was partly open to the single sitting room that served also as dining room. She gestured for them to join her at the table. Again she filled their glasses. She had been listening to this discussion intently.

"Do you suspect something, *profesor*?" she asked as they began to eat.

"Not at all," McLemore said. "I agree with Señor Sua—with Lazaro—that warheads by themselves presented no real threat. But, historically, it is interesting . . . the period after the crisis . . . between late October and the final weapons pullout in late December. Not much has been written about it. The popular literature sort of ends with the understanding between Kennedy and Khrushchev on the twenty-eighth of October."

"I suppose, as a historian, this could be interesting for you," Lazaro mused, leaving open the strong possibility that it had little relevance to the problems of the day.

They ate in silence. Then both men simultaneously congratulated Trinidad on the quality of her cooking. They ate with relish. McLemore had come to understand that shortages made this kind of dinner exceptional and vaguely wondered how she had managed it. He decided to open the discussion that had brought them together.

"Trinidad explained that you have heavy responsibilities for planning the celebration of the revolution at the New Year," he ventured to Suarez.

Lazaro ducked his head modestly, acknowledging his role. He drank some rum. He was storing courage for a tricky passage.

"You will have a lot of people?" McLemore patiently tested.

"We will have many people," Trinidad responded. "Maybe too many," she added ominously. Her meaning was clear.

"You expect trouble?" McLemore offered, trying to ease Suarez's burden.

Lazaro nodded. "It is a concern for us." He sighed deeply, then plunged ahead. "I must . . . we must . . . trust you, *señor*. We have deep concern about this." McLemore's thoughtful nod showed that he understood, that Trinidad had prepared him well. "We have information . . . actually, very reliable information . . . that some 'interests' are prepared to take drastic and probably very dangerous steps to disrupt this event. Many people . . . many, many people . . . could be hurt by this."

McLemore pushed back his empty plate, stretched out his legs, and lit the Cohiba offered by Suarez. Trinidad took the plates and returned with Cuban coffee. He waited.

Suarez ignored the coffee, sipped more rum, and looked squarely at McLemore. "We must find out exactly who these people are and what they plan to do. We are almost certain *when* they intend to act . . . when one million of our people are in the Plaza de la Revolución. It could be a catastrophe."

McLemore nodded again, accepting these assertions, and waited for the pitch. Suarez had to come to him. He could not help with this.

"We are certain that our 'adversaries' are from the United States. We must believe, because we have no other choice, that they are not motivated by the United States government."

"Why do you believe this, that the U.S. government is not involved? It certainly was 'active,' shall we say, in the past," McLemore said evenly.

"*Señor profesor*," Suarez said, "it would make no sense. There has not been sabotage against us for many years . . . only the embargo. Despite everything, I simply cannot believe even the CIA would think about killing many innocent people. The facts would come out and the whole world would be outraged by some act like this."

McLemore puffed on the cigar and stared out the open window into the dark sky above the ocean. Trinidad and Lazaro studied him intently. "The U.S. government is concerned by this matter . . . this threat . . . as well," he said.

Lazaro's eyes widened. "How do you know this?"

McLemore smiled. "There is a man here called Ramsay. I think you know him. He has been talking to me."

Lazaro said, "He has been talking to you? May I know for what purpose . . . and how it might affect our 'problem'?"

McLemore looked directly at Trinidad. He was making a decision, a decision about his life. He turned to Suarez and said, "He wants me to spy on you."

In that moment, McLemore realized how much he had changed since coming to Cuba. By nature ironic, he was politically detached and lacking in the professional ambition required for success in the academy. He was, as Solzhenitsyn said of himself, a state within a state. If he continued down the path now opening before him, would he therefore, as Solzhenitsyn also said, become a threat to the state? He was, without exactly knowing it, unfinished and capable of great deeds—if only he might know what they were. Like his country at the close of the twentieth century, he was adrift and undefined, flotsam on a sea of materialism that neither sufficed nor satisfied. He studied history as a detective might a crime—searching for clues that might produce definition. He resisted—truth be known, resented—authority. Authority had destroyed his family and cast him adrift, a stranger in his own land. Although he could not admit it to himself, he searched for a belief and a cause. He seemed, even to himself, vaguely preoccupied, as if listening to a melody for one. The experiences of the past few weeks now brought him to reflect on the true meaning of patriotism and had delivered him to the threshold of a kind of definition.

"*Señor?*" Lazaro's soft voice fetched him from a reverie.

"I said no," McLemore said. Then his eyes twinkled mischievously. "But I didn't say hell no."

Realizing they were being teased, Lazaro and Trinidad smiled wanly. "But how does this . . . shall we say, proposal . . . cause you to believe that your government knows about the threat to us?" Lazaro asked.

McLemore said, "When I brushed Ramsay off, he sobered me up by saying that they know about a major threat to your celebration."

"Did he say more?" Trinidad urged, her elbows on the table and her face a foot from McLemore's.

"Not much. Said he couldn't. But he knows . . . something." McLemore shook his head wryly. "Actually, he wants me to try to find out from you what you know." McLemore drank more rum, washing down the strong nicotine. "I think they . . . his group, his . . . ah . . . Agency . . . have run out of clues. They're stuck."

"Did he identify any sources and names or groups? Did he tell you whether he knows what is planned?" Lazaro asked with intensity.

His head back to blow smoke toward the ceiling, McLemore chuckled with amusement. "See. Now you want me to cross the line. When exactly does a spy become a spy? When he tells the first secret? When a lot of little secrets make one big secret? When he loses track of which side he's on?" He laughed again. "Maybe when he's working for both sides."

Lazaro looked taken aback by his cynicism. "I'm sure Trinidad explained to you, *profesor*, we do not want you to 'spy.' "

"What shall we call it, then?" McLemore asked.

Trinidad traded looks with Lazaro. Were they about to lose him?

McLemore filled the gap. "Look. I have a great idea. Why don't I just introduce you to Mr. Ramsay or Mr. Ramsay to you. Eliminate the middleman, as we say. You tell Ramsay what you know and he tells you what he knows and . . . *voilà* . . . you are working together on the same problem."

Lazaro went to the kitchen, brought the remains of the bottle of rum, and divided it equally three ways. "This cannot be done for many reasons. I would need authorization from my superiors, and that will not be granted. Officially, Mr. Ramsay does not exist. He is on the Interest office list as an immigration specialist. We do not enjoy normal diplomatic relations with the United States and therefore we cannot have direct discussions, especially on a matter as sensitive as this. Most important, it would be difficult for us to tell your side *what* we know without also facing the question *how* we know it. This is impossible for us to discuss, as you might imagine. I would also suppose that Mr. Ramsay is in the same box. If we are correct that the bad guys here are U.S. citizens, he and his superiors must be concerned that it might be revealed that U.S. intelligence cooperated with Cuban agencies to surveil and possibly apprehend U.S. citizens. It would be a scandal involving a country that has already been too scandalous for the CIA."

"What do these guys intend to do?" McLemore asked.

"We don't know. But we know it is something big. Something at our celebration." Lazaro hesitated. "There is a Russian involved."

"Trinidad told me," McLemore said, then wondered if he had put her in jeopardy.

Suarez didn't blink. "We believe these people, really a radical exile group, have met with a Russian who sells weapons. We think they bought something from him. But we cannot find out what it is."

I wonder what they would do if I told them what Ramsay told me last night? McLemore mused. He considered how labyrinthine must be the minds of those who spy for a living. "Not that it matters, but I understand these people call themselves 'Bravo' something. . . ."

"So far as we know, that is the name they were using among themselves. They are a new group of the sons of Brigade veterans, some of the most anti-Castro of the exiles. It was a small group and difficult to know about."

"Was?" McLemore asked.

"They have disappeared," Lazaro answered. "They no longer go to their monthly dinners . . . at least at the places they usually use. We are sure they continue to meet. But perhaps because their project is drawing near, they seem to have gone underground . . . disappeared."

McLemore stood up. Trinidad glanced at Lazaro, afraid McLemore might bolt. He paced the room. He had a feeling Trinidad's family lived better than most. But this place had not seen a paintbrush in decades. "And you want me to see if I can find out if the U.S. knows anything about this Bravo bunch. Who they are . . . what their plans are . . . so that you can stop them. Is that it?"

Lazaro shrugged. "If it is possible. This is a puzzle . . . how do you call it? . . . jigsaw puzzle. Perhaps the U.S. has some pieces, some important pieces. Anything would help us know what to look for, how to prepare. We have only"—he thought briefly—"some sixty days to solve the puzzle. We must find out what they look like. We must find out what they plan to do. We must find out what they have bought from the Russian."

McLemore said, "Just search everything at the border . . . the airport, the seaports. You've got the manpower. Open up all the boxes. Weapons . . . especially big weapons . . . shouldn't be hard to find."

"We will do that. But keep in mind we have hundreds of miles of uninhabited beaches. The coastal patrol can catch most things coming in. But not all. It is always possible some clever people could come to one of these faraway beaches with a fast boat, dump something or some people off, and hide waiting for them or simply run away."

McLemore sat down and held up one finger of rum. "I'll see what I can find out. Here's to your celebration."

Lazaro and Trinidad were dumbstruck. One minute McLemore was out the door. The next minute he was signing up. They numbly clicked un-matching glasses and downed the rum.

Catching her breath, Trinidad said, "What convinced you to help us, *profesor*? You seemed at first so opposed."

"Trinidad, it was your cooking. Great dinner. You should open a *paladar*."

Lazaro managed a tense smile. He still had not absorbed the success of his recruitment. "Perhaps when all this is over. Then I might join her as waiter."

"I guess I shouldn't ask whether you two really are with the Foreign Ministry, should I?"

Trinidad hastily collected the remaining dishes and headed for the kitchen. Suarez looked at the floor and shook his head.

"No," McLemore said. "I didn't think so."

"Is there anything else you need from us, *profesor?*" Trinidad asked softly, returning from the kitchen. "We have told you almost everything we know. We cannot tell you how we know it."

McLemore smiled. "I'm learning the rules. I know that much." He paused, then said, "Two things."

"Anything you need," Lazaro said.

"I have a friend here. He's an old man. An American. Kind of a priest."

Lazaro nodded his head. "We know. He is called Prescott. We know of him."

"I'm leaving in two or three days. I'll be back one more time. Probably the last few days of the year. I'd like to spend Christmas here . . . see what it's like."

"You are most welcome," Trinidad said with transparent pleasure. "You may even be surprised to see some Christmas trees and even Saint Nicholas."

"Somehow I think down here Saint Nicholas will look something like Che Guevara."

Trinidad smiled, and for the first time, Lazaro laughed out loud.

"About Prescott. Look after him for me. He's getting very old and he lives on very little. Your government treats him poorly. I will leave you some money and I want you to see he gets some food and, if he needs it, some medicine. Just send it around to his little flat." McLemore handed them a small piece of paper. "But, I expect you know where to find him . . . even after all these years. Don't make a big deal about it. Just make sure it's done."

Trinidad took the paper and reflexively put it to her breast. A promise.

"Is there something else?" Lazaro asked.

"Yes," McLemore said quickly. "I want to see the Defense Ministry files for the period of November to December 1962, regarding the removal of Soviet missiles and warheads. Can it be done?"

Lazaro looked slightly confused. "For your project? Of course." He was now deeply in McLemore's debt. "There might be some very secret materials—"

McLemore waved his hand. "I don't want to know which Russian general was sleeping with which *commandante*'s wife. I simply want to know how the missiles and warheads left here and who was in charge."

Lazaro turned to Trinidad. "Remind me to call the minister tomorrow. I will explain the circumstances"—meaning, McLemore thought, that I'm on your side—"and ask him to cooperate. I believe he will do so."

McLemore shook hands with them both, then started for the door. "If things don't go well in Washington, I may need a place to live down here." He turned again and said, "Next time, dinner is on me."

24 By the following afternoon, McLemore found himself ushered into the Cuban Ministry of Defense with the faithful translator Carlos tagging along. He noticed straightaway that the treatment was distinctly more professional and more serious than he had initially received at the Foreign Ministry. Someone had made some phone calls, and someone else had received a message. He wondered whether he might soon be invited into a secret brotherhood of *barbudos*, issued fatigues, and asked to grow a beard.

He was shown into an upper-floor conference room where a large table held six stacks of files. A young uniformed officer, whom McLemore guessed to be a lieutenant junior grade, greeted them and gestured toward the seats in front of the files. He explained in very good English that the files contained all the information the Ministry had on the removal of Soviet strategic and tactical nuclear weapons and that only a very few documents, containing especially sensitive materials, had been removed. These, he assured McLemore, were highly classified communications between senior Cuban and Soviet officials, some of whom were still alive . . . read *el Jefe*, McLemore thought . . . and therefore could not be made available. Otherwise, he was free to review and request copies of any of the remaining documents. He understood that Carlos had been cleared by the Foreign Ministry to translate documents for McLemore's convenience. An even younger private served them coffee, and then both soldiers disappeared through a side door.

Now experienced at working together, McLemore and Carlos waded into the files, Carlos audibly skimming the headings of memoranda for telltale words, phrases, and topics, and McLemore asking for elaboration on the ones that sounded interesting. Once the routine was established, the work moved quickly. By now Carlos understood that McLemore wanted especially to know about the warheads and, of those, the Lunas were the most important. Given that focus, they moved through two stacks of files by late afternoon and obtained approval from the officer in charge to return in the morning to continue. Mostly what they found were the originals of memoranda sent between senior Cuban military officers and between Cuban and Soviet commanders. Copies of many of these had been sent to the Foreign Ministry. So they had already seen much of this information from their previous research. By and large these were chronological files. So they had progressed through the first two or three weeks of November 1962. McLemore was confident they would complete their search by the end of the following day.

Having committed himself to operating as a go-between, if not actually an agent, for the Cuban government upon his return to the States, McLemore found himself curiously eager to penetrate the world of the U.S. intelligence establishment. Besides, he was now beginning to share the sense of urgency that clearly possessed Trinidad and Lazaro, and in his own bizarre way Ramsay, as well as their respective keepers higher up. To his surprise, McLemore found himself disappointed when, at the end of that evening, he had not heard from Trinidad. She had made no promise to contact him. But he had hoped that she would. He wanted to hear her opinion on the dinner and how Suarez had reacted to it. More important, he wanted to see her and feel the warmth of her touch.

At nine-thirty the following morning, McLemore and his helper were at the Ministry of Defense table and hard at work. The work was tedious but occasionally interesting. Throughout the Cuban-to-Cuban communications, and even occasionally in Cuban-to-Soviet correspondence, there was a powerful underlying tone of bitterness and betrayal. It was not uncommon to find Spanish references to impotent bears, neutered Cossacks, drunken Slavs, incestuous blockheads. The Cuban military had not been amused by the Soviet retreat under the Yanqui guns. Even more interesting were the Soviet responses, which clearly showed a breach between the forces that had come to defend Cuba and the perfidious politicians in the Kremlin. Many senior Soviet officers shared the Cubans' sense of betrayal and hated the humiliating retreat ordered by the commissars. McLemore imagined that he could smell the odor of mutiny emanating from the lines of type. Comparisons were drawn to Napoleon's disastrous retreat from Moscow during the vicious winter of 1812.

As Carlos read on, a kind of suspicion formed in McLemore's mind. Could a Soviet commander, this man Isakov, say, have become so embittered by the reversal of orders that he undertook to subvert them, to prepare for his own private war? As preposterous as it seemed, a man whose anger had tilted him to madness might be up for anything. What might he do? Press the button on a missile before it could be dismantled? Obviously that had not happened. Leave blueprints for rocketry construction behind for the Cubans to follow on their own? Not a chance. The Cubans would have used it for wipe. Stow some nuclear materials for the day when the Cubans could design a warhead? Too unstable. Too many people radiated into the bargain.

He shook his head as a confused Carlos watched. There was little if anything a renegade officer could do. At least there was nothing he could think of. There was always the option of going native—shedding the Soviet epaulets for a *guayabera,* taking up with a local girl, sipping *mojitos* as the sun goes down. That sort of thing. Making a separate peace. Faced with the prospect of retreating back into the teeth of yet another bitter Slavic winter, just chucking it all for early retirement in the sun. That Soviet officer would be interesting to interview—and he made a note to ask Trinidad if such a man existed—but it could hardly shed light on some undefined terrorist threat thirty-six years later.

By now the indefatigable Carlos, voice hoarse from reading and eyes wide from an abundance of caffeine, had moved well into the December chronological files. The Soviet expeditionary force was winding down its presence in Cuba. Heavy equipment was being crated, troops were bivouacked at Mariel and other ports, command headquarters were being cleared out and abandoned. The communications still carried the under-tone of bitterness all around. There were oblique references to Comman-dante Castro's persistent efforts to retain the medium-range Soviet aircraft and defensive missiles and at least a token force of Soviet troops. He was convinced the United States would attack in force the day after the last Soviet soldier embarked. The United States, of course, insisted on total withdrawal—although this had not been explicitly agreed to in the dra-matic negotiations of late October 1962 between Kennedy and Khrushchev. Soviet officers were resigned, drowning their frustration in bottles of rum. Cuban officials stoked their fury in the same manner.

The documents occasionally contained a copy of a Soviet inventory of weapons and troops as they were loaded aboard Soviet military freighters. There were also Cuban documents containing similar figures. It was not so much that anyone was concerned that a stray Kalashnikov or grenade or service revolver might be left behind. It seemed more a function of fantastic boredom and timeless military practice—when there is nothing else to do, count things.

Virtually all the documents from December 1962 reflected the logistics of a retreating army. Timetables for troop embarkations. Schedules for ship arrivals and departures. Lists of military units departing on which ships and on what dates. Some documents dealt with serious policy issues such as the Soviet willingness to meet Cuban demands for conventional weap-ons. Requests went from General Issa Pliyev, commander of the Soviet expeditionary forces in Cuba, to the Soviet Ministry of Defense transmit-ting Cuban requests for armaments needed to repel an impending inva-sion. The Cubans really did believe that Uncle Sam was just over the horizon waiting for the last Soviet ship to clear the harbor to make way for a Normandy-scale fleet of landing craft. There was little in the files to reflect a Politburo greatly concerned with Castro's fate.

Late in the afternoon, Carlos opened a file dated "Week of December 24, 1962." It was the last full file. These dates covered the last week of the Soviet nuclear force withdrawal. After a few minutes of leafing through documents, Carlos sat up. "Señor. Here it says 'Luna.' "

McLemore said, "Read what it says."

"It is another . . . what do you say, inventory? . . . inventory of these warheads. Here you see"—holding the memorandum up for McLemore— "here is a list of numbers of trucks with the number of warheads on each truck. They are brought to Mariel during this week . . . the last week of the year. The freighter is waiting, and they are loaded aboard as they arrive. It all seems very businesslike. The Soviets did not seem to want these weapons sitting unprotected on the docks."

McLemore asked, "Is it a Soviet or Cuban document?"

"It is a Cuban translation of a Soviet document, which is attached to it," Carlos answered. He turned a page. "Here it shows the final totals of weapons. Lunas. At the bottom, see, it is the Spanish word *total* and the number. It says 'ninety-eight.' "

McLemore followed his finger. After *total* the figure was clearly ninety-eight. As with the document he had purloined from the Foreign Ministry files, there was a signature in the lower right-hand corner of both the Russian and Spanish versions. It was typed in both cases "L. S. Isakov."

So, McLemore thought, this man Isakov, who had responsibility for the care and feeding of the Luna warheads, received one hundred and sent ninety-eight home. He had confirmation in both the Foreign Ministry and Defense Ministry records. Why would he do that? Either he was sloppy—and there was every evidence that the Soviet senior command was scrupulous in its management of its nuclear weapons inventory—or there was a separate game going on. Maybe he went into business for himself. Sold the warheads to the Cubans. For what purpose? How do you use a warhead without a delivery system? Conceivably, the Cubans might have seen two small-scale nuclear warheads as insurance against a U.S. invasion. But he had seen virtually every historical record in the Cuban archives for the period, and there had been no discussion of such an idea. Maybe Isakov simply went over the side of the sanity lifeboat. Cracked from fatigue, frustration, and pressure. Hid some warheads as part of some mad scheme to get even with the United States or his own bosses in the Kremlin. But there was still the delivery problem. McLemore shook his head. None of it made any sense.

McLemore noted the date of the inventory, the date the freighter sailed from Mariel, and the signature on the document. At his gestured urging, Carlos plunged ahead and finished the file. Nothing else about Lunas. All of the other weapons inventories matched up with the numbers of weapons brought in during the September–October buildup. Over the past two days, McLemore had made sufficient notes to finish his study project— withdrawal of Soviet forces from Cuba following the Kennedy-Khrushchev agreement in the fall of 1962. A little obscure, but focused and quirky enough to pass muster with the foundation grant committee and possibly even appeal to one of a number of little-known historical journals.

McLemore and Carlos thanked the young officer who had been deputized to look after them. With a shy smile and embarrassed apologies he had insisted on inspecting their papers to assure that nothing had been removed from the files. McLemore then led Carlos out onto the street and gave him an envelope. Carlos was genuinely mortified to find out that McLemore had given him money. But McLemore insisted on the grounds it was standard practice and that it would help Carlos and his family as he finished his schooling. He assured Carlos that professional translators around the world routinely were compensated for their services. The young man was reduced to a confused mixture of reluctance and gratitude. McLemore promised to get in touch when he returned in late December to complete his work.

As he walked back to the Santa Isabel hotel to pack his bags, McLemore considered his options. If he became a spy-courier for the CIA, perhaps they would introduce him to someone who could explain the uses of missileless warheads. He could even dump this curious anomaly in the Agency's lap. Look, fellows, a couple of small warheads went missing in Cuba thirty or forty years ago. Probably doesn't mean anything. But I thought you'd like to know. Might be interesting additions to the CIA's secret museum. Ancient weapons we might have known.

25 There are few instances in modern history of the birth, life, and death of an ideology—in this case communism—in one forty-year lifetime. Cuba is an exception to this rule. It was a colony for three and a half centuries. It was independent, but under United States suzerainty, for sixty years. Then it became a Communist satellite of the Soviet Union and, in one of those quirks of history so characteristic of its

fate, outlived its sponsor. How Cuba would manage the next act of its life
was one of the most interesting political questions of the impending
twenty-first century.

The now underground Bravo 99 had its answer: restoration of the ruling
oligarchy, possibly with a new generation of entrepreneurial Mafia in its
wake, even at the massive cost of lives. The United States had its idea,
however vague: a democratic republic, albeit one that cooperated fully
with its benevolent northern neighbor. Whatever plan the aging Cuban
leadership had in mind for their nation's future seemed not to take account
of the factor of mortality. In the end it would be up to the Cuban people
themselves to manage a perilous transition to an uncertain new future that
provided freedom with autonomy and justice with independence.

In the meantime, the Cuban government had more immediate problems on its hands. In the current hand it was holding, there were few cards
to play. Now, at the end of October 1998, it played one. At ten o'clock
in the morning on Friday, October 30, three officials of the Cuban Ministry
of Foreign Affairs appeared at the United States Interest office in the
Vedado section of Havana and announced they were there for an appointment with Mr. Samuel Ramsay, head of the political section. One of the
members of the delegation was the deputy director of the U.S. desk at the
Ministry, Sr. Lazaro Suarez.

Ramsay showed them into a small conference room, served coffee,
and said, "I am at your service." The visit was unusual. Contact between the Interest office and the Ministry mostly involved immigration
issues—boat people, illegal immigrants, undocumented aliens—and occasional negotiations over aircraft incursions into Cuban airspace or
ships penetrating Cuban coastal waters. Ramsay knew the officials across
the table were senior political officials and therefore represented an extraordinary agenda.

"*Muchas gracias*, Señor Ramsay, thank you for seeing us on short notice," said Eloy Oliverez, the second secretary of the Ministry. "You know,
I believe, my colleagues Señor Gutierrez and Señor Suarez. We are grateful
for the opportunity to meet with you. Unfortunately, our purpose is not a
pleasant one. We are here to register an official complaint with your government. It regards serious threats to Cuban national security, threats we
have strong reason to believe originate in the United States."

Ramsay waited silently and impassively.

"Señor Ramsay. We have information, very reliable information, that individuals and perhaps organizations in the United States are planning—possibly even beginning to implement those plans—to carry out a major terrorist act or acts against our country." Oliverez referred to typed notes, as if delivering an official protest. Protocol insisted that he get it right. If it turned out to be an official protest, he would leave a démarche behind. Ramsay was unsure, so he withdrew a pocket notepad and began to jot.

Still Ramsay waited, passively absorbing the whole story.

"We believe the pattern of terrorist attacks in recent months on our hotels and tourist facilities is most probably attributable to these same individuals and organizations."

Ramsay remained silent.

Oliverez looked him in the eye and continued. "Our information tells us that these people have had contact with at least one known arms dealer—in this case, Russian—and we believe, based on evidence, that we may expect some serious incident in connection with the celebration of the anniversary of our revolution on the first day of the year."

Ramsay waited for the punch line. Therefore . . .

"Therefore, Señor Ramsay, in the interest of the safety and security of the Cuban people it is our duty to insist that the government of the United States take all steps necessary to halt these activities and take measures to apprehend those in the United States responsible for these terrorist acts."

Ramsay knew Oliverez and liked him. He was a straight shooter. He was more polished and urbane than the average run of Cuban diplomats. He read the scripts prepared by the hard-line commissars. But he didn't pound the table and spout the usual rhetorical abuse. He got to the point, made his case, and then moved on. Ramsay poured more coffee, gestured with his hands, palms up—as if to say, Is there more?—then sat back in his chair.

"Do you plan to issue a press release?" he asked Oliverez, his tone businesslike.

The question threw the Cubans off. It was not what they had expected, and they looked at one another.

"If you do," Ramsay continued, "it changes things. Then we get into this 'he said,' 'we said,' accuse-deny business."

Taken aback momentarily, Oliverez said, "What do you advise?"

Ramsay chuckled. "You're asking *me* to advise *you* on how to handle the press? That's your business. All I can tell you is, if you make a big political circus out of this, my people are writing this off as a stunt, another political charade, and we don't take it seriously. So, number one, decide whether you are serious or not, then we'll react accordingly. If you are serious, then button it up and we'll respond accordingly."

Oliverez nodded. "And your response will be . . . ?"

"Hell, Eloy, I don't know what our response will be. Your guess is as good as mine. I suppose it all depends on whether you have any real evidence, and if so, how much of it you'll show us. We can't do very much if we don't know what the hell you're talking about." Ramsay swigged a half cup of coffee. "Who're the guys? What's the group? How do you know what you think you know? Dates, names, and places. Cards on the table. If you seriously want us to do something, you've got to work with us."

Oliverez was now operating on the edge of his authority. He looked at Suarez. The Interest office had Suarez on its intelligence list for some time. Ramsay's eyes narrowed and his ears opened.

Suarez had an ability to deliver a shy, wide smile while his eyes remained deadly serious. "You know, Señor Ramsay, that we can tell you only so much as will not jeopardize our sources. Which means you will have to trust some of the assertions we make."

Ramsay shrugged, as if to say, go to it. Everyone in U.S. intelligence knew the Cuban government had penetrated the exile Cuban community, not only in Miami but worldwide, since the early Mongoose days in the 1960s. How else could *el Commandante* still be alive? On the other hand, it would be a real coup to find out who some of their agents were. Maybe we could double them, Ramsay thought. The chess game was on. Ramsay was about to earn his salary.

"The group is based in Miami," Suarez said, as if to state the obvious first. "It organized itself as an offshoot of Alpha 66. Its members are younger—second-generation successful businessmen—who believed Alpha had become too old and ineffective. It is small . . . maybe twenty to thirty members, tops. Its organizing principle seems to be that time is running out, that something must be done soon to destroy our leadership. It splits from the other groups on this central point. Most of the others are content to wait for our president to . . . for our leadership to change . . . and then to exploit any weakness in the transition. The traditional position is that the embargo, together with a change of leadership, will finish the revolution. This group believes it must act now to eliminate any chance of succession."

From the beginning, Ramsay had decided to play ignorant. "What do these guys call themselves?"

"Bravo 99 or just Bravo," Suarez said. He hesitated, calculating, then said, "Our information is that leaders of this group met with a Russian some months ago. We believe the Russian is an arms dealer who is selling off weapons from the Russian army."

Ramsay picked his way carefully through the minefield of political intelligence. He had to temper his bulldozer temperament to do so. It was a struggle. Already knowing the answer, he said, "Are you going to tell me this guy's name?"

Suarez looked at his companions. Then he said, "We are not authorized to do so, at this moment. We believe it might put certain lives in jeopardy." Translated this meant: If we work out an arrangement, and we decide you are serious about this problem and willing to cooperate, we might. Otherwise, there is the problem of reverse intelligence . . . like reverse engineering. Give us the product and we can figure out how you put it together.

Ramsay probed in a different spot. "Do you know individual names of this Bravo crowd?"

Suarez, knowing the conversation to be recorded, nodded.

Ramsay, theatrically, thrust a hand forward and made a beckoning sign with his fingers. Give me what you've got.

Suarez continued the charade by then shaking his head. "Again, not for now . . . for the same reasons."

Ramsay snorted. "You want my help. You give me nothing. You want me to arrest these guys . . . lock 'em up for a couple of months . . . in violation of U.S. laws . . . and you won't even tell me who they are."

Oliverez said, "We are noting your request, Señor Ramsay. We must receive further approval regarding these details." The note taker Gutierrez was busy at his task.

Ramsay released a deep sigh and said, "I suppose you're not even going to tell me what these guys bought from the mysterious, unnamed Russki."

Suarez looked at Oliverez who said, "This we do not know. Indeed, if we knew what they were buying, we would know more clearly the threat. This is the main area where we need your help."

Ramsay was tempted to say, *We* know who this son of a bitch is and we know in general what he sells. But this particular deal went down before we could get a wire on or near those involved. "Okay," he said, "so we've got an unnamed Russian selling an unidentified product to a bunch of anonymous Cuban-American cowboys, and you want me to solve the crime before it happens." He laughed derisively. "Who do you think I am, Sherlock Holmes? Or maybe Inspector Clouseau?"

"Señor Ramsay," Suarez said, "it would be a black mark for the United States if people from your country killed a lot of Cubans." This is as much your problem as ours, he was saying in very clear terms.

Ramsay perceived threats even where they did not exist, and he did not react well to them. He lunged forward, led by a pointing finger as thick as a gun barrel. "Listen, amigos, don't start this with me. It's been a long day." In this context a long day meant a long forty years and a very unhappy relationship. "You walk in here, deliver some kind of protest, accuse the United States of harboring terrorists, demand that we solve your problem, give us no information, leave it to us to figure out, and threaten us with a trash can full of propaganda if we don't do so. This is no goddamn way to carry on a love affair."

The good cop Oliverez said calmly but with force, "*Por favor,* Señor Ramsay. We are 'threatening' nothing. If people living in the United States are discovered to be involved in an awful terrorist action, and many are killed, it will require no propaganda on our part to cause world opinion to condemn your country."

At that moment Oliverez and Ramsay shared a common thought, one familiar to political leaders, warriors, and intelligence agents throughout the world. Whatever happened on New Year's Day in Havana, two months hence, would be shown on international television instantaneously.

Except, as they could not know, if Bravo's plan succeeded there would be no cameras left to transmit picture or voice.

As if to calm the large, red-faced man, Oliverez said, "We have information that, sometime after the first meetings with the Russian, the Bravo group split. We guess that, whatever was being bought from him and however it is to be used, it caused a division in this group. We believe that an even smaller group . . . perhaps no more than a dozen . . . split from the main group to pursue whatever plan they have. From this we conclude that their plan must be desperate. Knowing this Bravo group to be *radical* in its purpose, if a plan caused this group to divide, then it must have been too drastic even for some of the group's own members."

"Or maybe not radical enough," Ramsay said.

"We think the former," Suarez said. "They have certainly been willing—according to our sources—to sponsor terrorist actions against our hotels. Therefore, if this were more of the same, we see no reason for the split. It can only be because one *facción* wanted to try something even more destructive and dramatic, and the other found it too *horrible*."

"Okay, Eloy." Ramsay spread his hands and put them firmly on the table. "Let me understand. You are filing a protest against terrorist actions you say are coming from the States. You are alleging—based upon information you will not share—that a group called Bravo something—or some piece of it—has bought something you do not know what it is from a Russian you will not name to do something really bad at your New Year's Day party. And you want us to do . . . what?"

"Find out for us what these Bravos bought from the Russian and help us stop it from coming into Cuba." Oliverez raised his hands, palms out, as if in surrender. "We can take care of pretty much all the rest." Looking slightly uncomfortable, Oliverez pulled an envelope from his jacket pocket and handed it to Ramsay. "Señor Ramsay, on behalf of our Foreign Ministry, here is our official protest to the incidents against our hotels during the past several months. It says almost exactly what I have said to you this morning. My minister respectfully requests that you present it to your government. *Muchas gracias para su hospitalidad.*"

Ramsay accepted the envelope and extended his hand as they all stood. Oliverez really was a class act, Ramsay thought, for a Cuban. "It will be off to the State Department today, Eloy. But tell your government," he said, glancing at the intelligence man Suarez, "that we can't be helpful to you on the Russian matter . . . Bravo matter . . . whatever, without knowing what you know. It's as simple as that." Ramsay knew, however, and Oliverez knew he knew, that their conversation now constituted notice to the United States of a threat, that enough information had been given regarding the threat to make it real, and that, if the United States refused to take action and something terrible happened, this fact would become known. The Cubans had achieved much of their purpose, though Ramsay would not acknowledge it.

* * *

Perhaps an hour later, just as Ramsay prepared to go to the Interest office mess for lunch, the main receptionist rang. "There is a Professor McLemore here asking if you are available. He says he does not have an appointment." She whispered down the line, "If you wish, I can say you are not here."

Ramsay paused, genuinely surprised. "Put him in the downstairs conference room. Say I'll be there in a couple of minutes." Now what? Was this a mere coincidence, or was this his lucky day? Much as he disliked surprises, he did like action. This seemed as if it might be one of those rare action days.

"Mac, old pal! What a treat! And even more so for being unexpected." Ramsay always reverted to cheerleader until he could gauge the mood and decide what else to be. "Just passing through the neighborhood, I'll bet, and you decided to drop in on old Red and see what's up."

They sat in two worn easy chairs in the corner of the room. McLemore asked for coffee to buy time to polish his lines. Ramsay's beaming face was as uncharacteristically silent for McLemore as it had been earlier for the Cubans. His eyes twinkled with suspicion. He was calculating the odds that McLemore back-to-back with the Cubans was a coincidence, then decided to suspend judgment. "Will the coffee do, or did you have something more along the lines of business in mind?"

"I'm headed back to the States tomorrow," McLemore said, "and I thought I'd drop by to say good-bye."

"What a swell thing to do, Mac! You're a real thoughtful guy." Ramsay's voice was so heavy with irony that it almost fell through the floor. "Will this luxuriant isle know your presence ever again?"

McLemore shook his head at Ramsay's never-ending charade. "Of course. I have to come once more . . . to finish my research. It's coming along well," he offered. "I've finally focused on a question that my brother and sister historians haven't sifted to dust."

Feigning interest, Ramsay said, "And what might that be, Mac?"

McLemore said, "The issue of what the Russians did with their missiles and warheads between the time of the Kennedy-Khrushchev deal in late October and the time the last nuclear weapons left at the end of the year. There's all that new stuff from the Kennedy tapes and the Politburo files that came out a year or so ago. But it all builds up to the climax on October twenty-eighth and then, with the exception of the resolution of our missiles in Turkey, it sort of meanders off."

"Interesting," Ramsay said. McLemore thought he was stifling a yawn.

"So, I'll come back in December, finish up with the files they're showing me, and probably spend the holidays on the beach."

Ramsay said, "Give you a chance to join the party."

"Which one is that?"

"You know, Mac. The New Year's Day party. Big blowout. Lots of speeches. Music. Dancing." His tree-branch arms swayed above his head and his bulky body did a rumba sitting down.

"That's an idea," McLemore said. "Except I thought you said something bad was going to happen. Wasn't that the occasion? Doesn't sound like the kind of thing an innocent professor like me ought to get involved in."

"But, Mac, you've become pals with these people. Sauce for the goose, sauce for the gander. Whither thou goest, I will go, don't you know." His voice was mock-pleading.

"Tell you what, Red, you go, I'll go. How's that?" McLemore mocked back.

"I'm not much into Commie celebrations, Mac. The only revolution I like is the one celebrated on the Fourth of July. Ramsay bleeds red . . . and white and blue." Ramsay paused, waiting. McLemore smiled and sipped the awful coffee.

"Anything else I can do for you, Mac, before you go?"

McLemore said, "If I'm going to be your employee, shouldn't I have a letter of introduction?"

Ramsay sat up. "How's that? Employee? Did we discuss employment?"

"Close to that, Red. I recall the last time we met you wanted me to work for you. 'Help me out,' you said. Something like that."

On this rare occasion, Ramsay was baffled. "You want to be paid? Is that what you're talking about? Ah . . . that was not exactly what we had in mind."

McLemore now leaned forward. "Come off it, Ramsay. You know what I'm talking about. I want to see your bosses in Washington. If I'm going to become a spy, I want some understandings higher up. No offense. Can you do it or not?"

"Of course I can do it. Say when."

McLemore said, "Next Monday. I'm going directly to Washington tomorrow."

Ramsay reached for a yellow legal pad on the conference room table and scratched a number from memory. "Monday morning, call this number. Identify yourself. You'll be told where to go and when." He was already calculating how long it would take to draft a cable and whether, if it were received after hours on this day, Friday, anyone would get it before Monday. Of course they would. He'd mark it to set off some sirens.

"Then what?" McLemore asked.

"Then they'll brief you on the case. Tell you what we know . . . or at least what we know that's not ultra classified. And they'll tell you what we need."

McLemore smiled like a small boy. "Does this mean I'll be a real spy, Red?"

Ramsay was not amused. "Believe it or not, this is not cops and robbers, Mac. This is the real deal."

McLemore was tempted to say, Couldn't tell by the way you behave. But he was afraid he would get his lights knocked out. McLemore folded the paper as he stood to go.

Ramsay said, "Know what this reminds me of, Mac? That movie . . . the one with Bogart . . . what is it? . . . *Casablanca*. At the airport the guy says to Bogart, 'Welcome back to the fight. This time I know our side will win.' " He seemed genuinely moved. "What did the job, Mac?" Ramsay asked. "Just curious to know what works . . . for the next case, don't you know."

Over his shoulder on the way out, McLemore said, "Your charm, Red. It's just magnetic."

The following Monday, McLemore sat on the bed in the small hotel off Dupont Circle and dialed the number Ramsay had given him. A man's voice answered, "Yes." McLemore said, "My name's McLemore. Sam Ramsay said to call." McLemore could here a muffled discussion, then, "Take a taxi to Langley. Tell them to take you to the McLean entrance. Be here in half an hour. Someone will meet you and bring you in." That was all.

He was met at the Agency guardhouse by a woman in her thirties. She checked him past the sentry who gave him a visitor's pass. They got in a car that delivered them to the front door of the main CIA building. As they passed the security checkpoint at the far side of the large lobby, she said, "How do you like Cuba?"

"I have come to like it," McLemore said, deciding on the spot at least to be an honest spy. He wondered briefly if they would polygraph him. He hoped not. His sex life had not been that interesting recently.

He was taken through an outer office where the name on the corridor wall outside the door seemed to be "Worth" or "Worthy," chief of the Cuban section. Then into the large corner office. Except for a small shield bearing the CIA emblem and what McLemore supposed to be some small snapshots of the great man with former directors, there was little to distinguish it from any other government office. He had no way of knowing that Ramsay's cable, received late Friday evening, had indeed set off alarms. These days almost anything political from Cuba was given higher alert status. Then there was the name "McLemore." Jack McLemore, the legendary hero from the Cuban missile crisis. The man who had walked into the jaws of death and hadn't come back. In fact, was virtually certain not to come back. All the old files were pulled, if for no other reason than to give the younger people in the section an idea of what it had been like. The real Cold War. Ninety miles away. Nuclear weapons. Missiles configured to fire. The brink of catastrophe. Jack McLemore was at the heart of the heart of the Cold War. Many still believed that the signals he managed to get out . . . the movements of senior Soviet commanders, troop deployments, eyeball sightings of missiles erected on launchpads at two separate sites in Pinar del Río . . . had gone right to the Oval Office and had provided information based upon which Kennedy had faced Khrushchev down and had thus begun the long slow process of untracking the Soviet behemoth. Jack McLemore.

And there, thirty-six years later almost to the day, stood his son. Word had gone out, and unbeknownst to McLemore, the strangely congested hallways through which he had just passed and the number of people passing back and forth beyond the outer door did not betoken sudden action in the Caribbean. They were there to see him, to see what he looked like, to see if he was his father's son. What was he doing there? they whispered. Was this some kind of sentimental journey?

For his part, McLemore felt eerie. The only time he had been inside any CIA building had been thirty-five years ago, at the memorial service in the auditorium outside, where they had given his mother the medal now buried under a tangle of shorts and mismatched socks in a drawer in Madison. Like Cuba, which it symbolized, the medal now seemed a relic.

"How do you do, Professor McLemore," said the tall, gray-haired man now coming through the door. "It is an honor for me. I knew your father many years ago." He did not introduce himself, not that it mattered. McLemore wondered if this man had hesitated when volunteers were requested to go to Cuba back then. If this man had gone, would his father still be alive?

He gestured for McLemore to sit on the couch. He sat on a chair nearby. "Sam has sent me a long cable, which follows some earlier reports he has made, about your visits to Cuba and your research project there." McLemore nodded, wondering how this recruitment process worked. "Well, I'll get to the point. He told us he has tried to get you to help us, on several occasions, but that you have resisted. From your point of view, that's very understandable. But, apparently, you have had a change of heart and might be willing to help. Is that a fair summary?"

McLemore said, "In general, yes. But I've explained to him that I have not formed the kind of friendships with the kind of people that might interest you during my two brief visits that would put me in much of a position to be helpful."

The man said, "Professor, in this business, our motto is, Every little bit helps. Basically what we do here is solve puzzles—jigsaw puzzles. You can't create the picture without all the pieces. We try to rely on our own people to collect most of the pieces. Sometimes, someone like yourself comes along and they help us find pieces that we can't. That's basically it. And unless you know the kind of picture you are trying to create, you don't even know what kind of pieces belong to your puzzle. So we pull in as many pieces as we can and then sort them out here. This, you might say, is the puzzle factory."

In more ways than one, McLemore thought. "What kind of picture are you working on at the present time?"

"It's a picture of Cuba on the brink of collapse on the occasion of the fortieth year of its failed experiment with socialism. It's a picture involving those who might wish to hasten that collapse out of frustration and impatience."

I wonder if this man has ever met a Cuban like Trinidad, McLemore thought. I wonder if he has ever met any Cubans. "Why shouldn't we let them?"

"Because it's not in our interest to do so. If people inside Cuba take action, that is one thing. We might even applaud that—"

"As we have in the past," McLemore said.

"As we have in the past," the man responded.

His temper suddenly up, McLemore asked, "Do you agree or disagree with the way we've handled Cuba over the years?"

"Oh, Professor, I cannot begin to answer that question. Contrary to popular impression, we do not make policy here, we carry it out."

"I hope you will not take this personally," McLemore said, "but could you tell me how many people out here actually resign if they are given a policy to carry out . . . say, like assassination . . . that they think is wrong?"

The tall man shifted in his chair, now faced with an unexpected inquisition from a man he was seeking to recruit. He was beginning to appreciate Ramsay's oblique references to McLemore's prickly nature. "It happens," was the best he could offer.

McLemore merely uttered a hmmmm. He didn't sound convinced.

"Professor McLemore, I am happy to try to defend our mission as long as you would like. But it would really be, if I may say so, a kind of academic exercise, and it would not get me any closer to solving my puzzle. May I be blunt? We would like for you to help us. Mr. Ramsay has explained a bit about the rumored threat that we . . . that is, the Cubans . . . face. If there is such a threat, and if it should emanate from our shores, it will not be good for the United States."

"What exactly do you need to know?" McLemore asked. "And how do you propose that I find it out?"

The man said, "We need to know what the Cubans know. If they can identify specific individuals here in the States, if they can give us information on a mysterious Russian arms dealer whom, I believe, Mr. Ramsay has mentioned to you, if they will tell us what we need to know, then perhaps we can help protect them."

"Why don't you just ask them?" McLemore said.

The man said, "We can't, Professor. You must understand that. It doesn't work that way."

McLemore said, "I tell you what. You tell me what *you* know. Then I will have a much better understanding of the exact pieces of the puzzle still missing. That's simple enough, isn't it? If you trust me to spy for you, then you have to trust me all the way."

The man looked out the window, pondering. Then he decided. "We are becoming concerned enough with this threat that we must take some chances. Although we usually do not do business based on trust, in this case we must trust you." He paused, then pressed an intercom button on a nearby phone and said, "Send Sandy in." Presently the woman who had met McLemore at the gate came in with a thick file. She nodded and sat down as the man said, "Tell Professor McLemore what we know about the Bravo matter."

She nodded again, somewhat surprised, then began. "There is a group of radical second-generation-exile Cuban Americans that was formed under the name Bravo 99 some months ago. They intend to do some harm at the anniversary celebration of the Cuban revolution on New Year's Day. They have had at least one and probably more meetings with a known Russian arms dealer. We do not know what they have bought or have on order. We believe, whatever it is, that it is related to these disruptive plans. We do know that Cuban intelligence knows much of this already. We need someone . . . you . . . to find out, if you can, whether they have identified the Bravo group, the whereabouts of the Russian, what Bravo has purchased or is about to purchase, when and how the scheme is to evolve."

"Now tell me what you know," McLemore said.

"We know the following names of the Bravo group." McLemore jotted on a small pad. "Manuel Lechuga. Antonio Varona. Juan Aragones. José Hernandez. Orlando Menendez. Pedro Medina. We know that the Russian uses the Anglicized name Isaacs but that his real name is Isakov." McLemore's pen halted. He kept his head down until he was sure he showed no shock. He nodded as though he had heard nothing extraordinary. "We know that the Bravo group fractured, quite possibly over this project. We believe that the most radical faction of this radical group expects to deploy some weapon or weapons associated with their deal with Isaacs at the anniversary event." She closed the file. "Except for identifying our sources and methods, which of course we are not going to do, that's the story so far as we know it."

"Why don't you arrest these Bravo characters?" McLemore asked.

The chief said, "Without more specifics on the Russian deal, no probable cause. We could have them detained and try to question them. But they wouldn't talk and their lawyers would have them out in ten minutes. Then they disappear and we are in trouble. They're becoming difficult enough to track even as it is."

"Where's the Russian . . . this 'Isaacs'?" McLemore asked.

Sandy said, "Don't know. He's gone to ground. Made himself scarce."

McLemore asked, "Has the weapon or have the weapons changed hands yet?" He was beginning to think he might have the answer to that himself.

The man said, "We don't know that. To do much damage, say, like a rocket or major explosive, it would have to be large. We know the Cubans are searching everything. So, if it has changed hands, we think it may still be here in the States or offshore somewhere."

McLemore pushed his hair back. "So basically you want me to get inside the Cuban tent on this, pretend to go over, or whatever you call it, and find out what I can. Seems both straightforward—and improbable."

The man said, "Remember, all we need are one or two pieces."

McLemore stood up, and from the corner of his eye saw two or three figures scurry from the outside door. "There is something I need. For my project."

"How can we help?" the man asked.

"Let me see your files on the period from late October until the end of the year, 1962, on the removal of Soviet missiles and warheads from Cuba. That's the topic I'm working on. And I don't have time to go through the bureaucracy of the Freedom of Information Act."

The man said, "Sandy, see what we can do. Get whomever you need to help you. Remove any remaining sources and methods stuff and turn over as much as you can to Professor McLemore."

26 In a small park on the beach in South Miami, Viktor Isakov waited nervously for his clients. The moon played hide-and-seek behind the low, fast-moving clouds. Traffic half a block away provided some ambient light and enough human proximity to slightly reduce Isakov's anxiety. He experienced conscious fear that he might be mugged by some roaming gang. He experienced less conscious fear that his Cuban-American clients might, once they had acquired their precious "whizbang," not need to complete payment or might even decide they did not need its putative owner anymore.

Though half a million dollars heavier, Viktor was not feeling any better for it. He didn't much enjoy the game in which he found himself. Small arms, conventional rockets, even high-performance combat aircraft were one thing. Nuclear weapons, even old, low-yield, tactical ones, were yet another thing. His epiphany came the week before when he attended a parade down Fifth Avenue in New York for the heroic crew of astronauts who had safely brought their crippled space shuttle home. The police estimated the crowd to be near one million. When he heard that, it rang a bell. The number of people down in the middle of Havana on New Year's Day. The number of people who would be in the neighborhood when Manny and Tony set off the device, the "product." He remembered the huge number of people that was. He had seen their faces. There were children there.

This wasn't the same thing as his regular deals, he thought. He sold weapons to military people to be used in wars, against soldiers in combat. This deal . . . this was a different deal. His growing discomfort wasn't helped much by the fact that he was on the run. He was pretty sure he was being followed. At least it seemed to him that people were watching him all the time now—getting on and off elevators, parking his car, going in and out of restaurants. He thought people were probably listening to his phone calls. He just wasn't sure who they were. They could be Cubans. They could be Americans. They could even be Russians. What a great mess he had gotten himself into. The thing to do now was to just get out of here. He would meet with Manny and Tony, he would manage the successful handover of old Dankevich, he would collect his last payment, and he would take a long holiday.

He was thinking about Cyprus, or Santorini, or Dubrovnik, when a raspy voice behind him said, "Put your wallet over your shoulder or I'll blow your head off." He felt a hard object against the back of his head. Then there was laughter.

"Hey, Vic. Did we scare you?"

He turned and saw Manny and Tony slapping each other on the back. Isakov suddenly realized how close he had come to soiling himself.

"Funny for you, maybe, Manny," Viktor said. "But for me, not so funny. Next time, watch out." He had the apoplectic demeanor of an angry, helpless man.

"Sorry, Vic," Tony said. "You looked off in another world."

"Where I hope to be soon," Isakov said. "Away from customers like you. World is scary enough place without someone playing these kind of jokes . . . which are not so much funny."

"Take it easy, Vic. We're just enjoying the evening." Tony was unusually talkative, and Viktor concluded that, at this late hour of the night, they had consumed a lot of wine at dinner.

Isakov pulled an envelope from his jacket pocket. He unfolded its contents and placed them on the picnic table where the two men now joined him. Looking around first, he pulled out a small pen flashlight, and motioning the others to huddle up, he shined its thin beam on a wallet-size photograph of the quality taken in amusement park photo booths. He turned the picture toward them and said, "Here is Dankevich, Dmitri Dmitrivich. Colonel. The glorious Red Army. Strategic Rocket Forces." The two men studied the photograph for two or three seconds and the small light went out. Isakov handed it to Tony. He was still angry at Manny for his cruel "joke."

"My friends in Moscow have made all the arrangements. Dankevich will arrive in Havana on twenty-fifth December. He will wait for you until next day. And he is perfectly prepared to carry out his job." Isakov folded his hands in his ample lap and looked out into Biscayne Bay.

Manny said, "Vic, you don't sound quite as enthusiastic as you used to. You haven't spent all that money we gave you, I hope. You didn't go out to Las Vegas and lose all that money gambling, did you?"

Isakov shook his head. "No. Is safely put away. You should not be concerned about such matter."

Manny's black eyes focused on Viktor like a laser. He put his face directly in front of Viktor's. "Hey, Vic, what's up? You're not sounding like the friendly Russki we know and love. Do you have some problems in your life? Is there anything we can help with?"

They could barely make out Isakov shake his large head in the dark.

Manny looked at Tony and made a gesture. Tony pulled a silver flask from his back pocket. He handed it to Manny, who put it on the table in front of Viktor. "Help yourself, Vic. We're here to help. We're your friends."

Viktor stared at the flask and shook his head. "Come on, Vic. Let's have a little sip, and then we'll talk about it." He led the way. Tony drank, then passed it back to Viktor. Finally, like a man preparing for his execution, he tipped the flask up and drained half of it. Manny and Tony looked at each other in the dark.

Presently, Viktor said, "I want to know, for sure, what you are doing with 'whizbang-gizmo.' "

"Well, Vic, that's kind of our business, isn't it? You know, in capitalism you sell things and you buy things, and you don't much ask the people who buy things what they intend to do with the things they buy." Manny sounded offended. "Now, do they?"

Viktor said, "This is not just 'thing,' this thing. This is very"—he struggled for the words that would suitably express his deep concern—"big monster thing." He stared at the flask, picked it up, and finished it off. Manny looked at Tony again.

"You're right, Vic. It is a big monster thing. That's why it's better we have it than the Cubans." Tony had finished a year and a half of law school and, on appropriate occasions, liked to pretend to counselorship. "Think what might happen if that nutcase Castro was digging around someday and found this thing. Just think what he might do. He might put that big monster thing on a boat, ship it up here to Miami . . . say, right up the bay there close to the center of town . . . or how about the port of New York, right there on the West Side . . . and he just blows the goddamn big monster thing right up? Think about that for a minute."

Viktor picked up the flask, turned it upside down, and shook it, disappointed. He started to stand up, then sank back, defeated. "I know what you are doing. You are blowing that thing up in middle of Havana. There will be many people there, like at astronaut parade. Little kids. Think about that for just a minute."

Manny said, "You want to give us the money back? Okay. Give us the money back. Give us the money back," he was almost shouting, "and we'll call this whole thing off." Tony looked at him, eyes gleaming from a brief peek of the moon, and Manny waved him off. "You got twenty-four hours, Vic. You give us the money—with interest—and the deal is off. You keep the goddamn whizbang and we keep our money. But, listen to me, the interest is high . . . like maybe twenty to thirty percent." Viktor looked up startled. "Twenty–thirty percent! Our 'financiers' charge high interest rates. Understand? You give the money back, this time tomorrow, and come prepared to add, say, a hundred, maybe a hundred and fifty thousand. You keep the goddamn 'product' and try to find some other dummies like us who want to buy it." He snorted with derision. "I got a big picture of *you*"—he gestured at Isakov's ample middle—"carrying that goddamn bomb out of Cuba."

Now Viktor was both angry and afraid. He was in well over his head. He was in a conspiracy that would incinerate thousands of children on the one hand; he was being blackmailed by a bunch of madmen on the other. Thirty percent interest rates! To hell with that. He stood up unsteadily. "I want rest of money. You keep bomb. Kill as many people as you want. Is your business—so I think."

Isakov wandered toward the water's edge. For a moment, the two other men watched, secretly hoping he might simply keep going until the bay closed over his shaggy head. Then Tony thought, What if he washed up in Cuba? Wouldn't that be something? They huddled briefly. Then Tony started after him, shuffling through the wet sand, until he corralled the reluctant businessman and brought him back. They had agreed that Tony should conclude the precarious negotiations.

"Vic, listen, we need to straighten this thing out." Tony was the good cop. "We're friends. We're more than friends, we're business partners. We don't want the money back. We want you to have the rest of what we owe you, so you can go off and get some rest and not worry about this business. It's getting you down. We understand. It's a complicated matter. You've gotten into a lot of old politics here that don't really concern you. It's a little fight we Cubans are having among ourselves. Doesn't really concern you. You shouldn't worry about it. We're going to get it settled, once and for all. Get our country back on track. It's all going to be okay."

Tony had an arm around Viktor's great round shoulder as they circumnavigated the area around the picnic table. "People will die, Tony," Viktor said.

"We know, Vic. It's a war. People die in a war." Tony sounded less like a lawyer now and more like a priest. "Look at it this way. Let's say the U.S. had to go down there and wipe out Castro. Think about it. Tens of thousands of marines. Hundreds of thousands of soldiers. A lot of sailors and air force pilots. A lot of them get killed. A lot of them. They've all got families. They've all got kids. Then you've got these poor Cuban people—*our* people, Vic. These U.S. troops are going to have to kill a lot of those poor Cuban people. Women and children, Vic. Just think about it."

The two men continued to walk around the table, Tony still guiding Viktor with his brotherly arm. Viktor nodded his head slowly, contemplating the awful possibility.

"What we're trying to do, Vic, we're trying to avoid all that. We're trying to just get that awful goddamn Commie-son-of-a-bitch leadership. We're trying to *save* lives. We're trying to avoid war and bloodshed. It's clean, Vic. It's kind of a one-shot deal. Don't you see?"

Viktor nodded his head. Whatever had been in the flask had not served to clarify his already confused thinking. He continued to nod his head like a great contemplative horse. Manny and Tony studied him intensely. Finally, he emitted a huge, troubled sigh. "I am now businessman. I must keep my word. I will go through with deal." His head now shook sideways. "But it is great trouble to me."

Manny was thinking to himself, You better keep your word, you dumb Russki. We know where the gizmo is, and you've only got half of our money. He stood up and resumed control. "All right, Vic. Attaboy. Now listen. Here's the way this works." He reached in a side pocket of his coat and retrieved a piece of paper. "Here's an address and a name. This is our principal financier . . . the guy who has contributed to our cause. He personally wants to meet you and thank you. He thinks you're a very great patriot, and he wants to shake your hand. It would be an honor for him. And besides, he's put up a lot of dough for this operation. It's a big deal for him. So we promised he could meet you and thank you personally. How's that?"

Isakov stared at the paper dumbly, unable to make out the writing in the dark. Then he said, "It is probably not so good that I meet new people. Too many people should not know me, I think. Maybe for my own safe-keeping."

Manny patted him on the back, pals again. "This is an important man, Vic. He is tied in with some important people, in this area and in many other areas. You get to know him, you may find yourself developing some big new business. These are very serious people. They do business around the world. They can use your products. You meet them, you're doing us a favor and you're doing yourself a very big favor."

"Why are they financing your 'operation,' Manny?"

"Because they believe in our cause. Because they used to do a lot of business down in Cuba . . . entertainment business. They want to go back. It was a very good business for them until this Commie son of a bitch took over. They believe in democracy—and capitalism." Manny looked at his watch, its numbers glowing eerily in the dark. "Vic, we got to say good-bye. Tony and me have to go see these guys to tell them we are carrying out our plan—thanks to you. Now listen. You go around to that address at ten next Tuesday night. You get a payment and you get a big hug of gratitude from our friends. They can set you up for a long time."

Then they were gone, up the sloping grass to the parking lot and into Tony's dark Cadillac. They drove in silence for a few minutes. Then Tony said, "It's too bad, you know. I like the guy. He's really trying to make a go of it."

Manny snorted, dismissing sentimentalism. "He's a wacko. He'll never learn how the world works. No wonder those Russkis are so screwed up. Czars. Commissars. They're all peasants. Got to have a strong boss. Look at him down there. He's turned to Jell-O. Shaking and quaking. I tell you, we could have taken those guys. We'd had somebody with guts in the White House, we could've taken those guys." Manny's education in Russian history had not extended to Hitler, let alone Napoleon.

They arrived at a wrought iron gate, gave a name to the voice from the gate box, and presented themselves at a dimly lit mansion door. They went inside, were served brandy, and sat for five minutes in an even more darkened study until a portly man in his early seventies emerged slowly through the door, greeted them familiarly, and ordered them into heavy leather chairs. "How did it go?" he asked.

Manny said, "He's coming apart. Nerves are shot. He's totally paranoid."

"Even paranoids can have enemies," the man said. They laughed, respectfully. "A Kissinger line," he added, dropping the name as if it belonged to a near acquaintance.

"We did what you suggested," Manny said. In fact, the man had ordered it. Manny's manner was very much that of a supplicant. "He wants the money. So, he'll come around."

"You didn't send him here, of course," the man said.

Manny's hands came up, and his eyes widened. "Oh, no. No. We sent him around to the clubhouse. That's what your people told us. We set it up for Tuesday night. My guess is, he's planning to grab the dough . . . the payment . . . and head for the Riviera. Someplace like that where he thinks he can hide, but where in fact he can be picked up by Interpol in a heartbeat."

The man sipped an espresso. "If you're sure he's unstable, then we have no choice."

"Unstable is the best thing you can call him," Tony offered. Though resigned to this outcome, Tony was made unhappy by it. He sighed. "He'd finger us in a minute if they nail him."

The man nodded, understanding.

Manny said, "Eventually, the Bureau and maybe even the Agency will catch up with him. If Castro's weasels don't get him first. We think they may already have his number. Could be who's following him . . . if he is being followed. We thought at first he was a pro. We thought he had a serious spine." Manny feigned sadness. "But he doesn't. He's a Russian jellyfish."

The man peered into the tiny cup, possibly searching for the pathway to the Big Casino when his rampant cancer finished off his spleen. "We'll take care of it. You get your job done, then clean up the mess. Our people will work with you in reestablishing order down there." His voice was as certain as destiny. "And, of course, you will honor our arrangement." It was not a question. Whether he himself saw the day, the family would live on, and it would reclaim what it had lost forty long years ago.

Whatever reassurance Viktor had gained from his midnight séance with the Bravo ultra leaders retreated like a phantom at dawn. Between that Friday night and the following Tuesday, he was reduced to emotional rubble. He had flown to New York, rented a lady for the weekend, and then, after three hours, had grabbed his belongings and raced, half-naked, from the Brighton Beach hotel. The phone had rung and the caller had hung up when he answered. He rented a car and drove through New Jersey into eastern Pennsylvania. He started to check into a roadside motel and suddenly remembered he had used his real name in renting the car. He abandoned the car at the Philadelphia airport and flew to Tampa Bay. He spent the rest of Saturday, Sunday, and Monday driving across Florida. He stopped at Orlando to hide out in Disney World until he decided that Mickey Mouse was a special agent from the Bureau, or maybe a friend of Manny's. By Tuesday evening he was back in Miami, dressing for his ten o'clock appointment.

Suddenly, he had an inspiration. He put his belongings in the back of his rental car at the small beachfront motel and drove an hour early to the agreed meeting place on Miami Beach. After several wrong turns and repeated inquiries at neighborhood shops and gas stations, he finally found the place. It had once been a residence, apparently a very handsome one. It was now a bit run-down. A high rock wall opened onto a courtyard with the art deco main structure set well back. As he peered through the front gate, he heard the low guttural noise of at least two dogs back near the house. He quickly stepped away and returned to his car parked across the street almost a block away. It troubled him that his legs were shaking and that he was perspiring on an otherwise cool evening. He was quickly losing his nerve.

Viktor Isakov had to make the most important decision of his life. Did he wait another half hour until ten o'clock and then go collect his money? Or did he leave the half million dollars and for sure keep his life? He had really been stupid. If he had been smart, he would have required the customers to deposit the money in his bank. How could he have fallen for an obviously phony line about the "financier" wanting to meet him? He had spent the weekend imagining the "financier," first with a gun pointed at his head, then with a sharp knife across his throat. Now operating on a full infusion of adrenaline, Isakov decided on a bold move. He started the rental car and drove around the block. On the street behind the house wherein his fate awaited was a vacant lot. He parked, crossed the lot, and came to the back stretch of the rock wall. He found an abandoned milk crate, placed it against the wall, and stood on it. Barely able to see over the wall, he made out a large black van backed up to the rear doorway of the house and, in a kitchen window, four or five very fit young men wearing shoulder-holstered pistols. Not one of them looked like a "financier." One of them looked at his watch as the others, at least in Viktor's mind, prepared to dissect him before carrying what was left of him away in the van and to the nearest auto compactor somewhere in industrial Miami.

With a crash, the milk crate shattered under his bulk. The dogs, unquestionably Dobermans, set up a vicious roar. Momentarily stunned as he sprawled in the alleyway, Isakov saw large floodlights illuminate the back parking area and heard angry voices spilling out from the kitchen door. He was up and headed across the pocked surface of the vacant lot faster than he ever believed possible. He got to his car as the dogs rocketed out of the back gate followed by serious men waving flashlights. By the time he got the car started and headed away, he was convinced the sprinting men were close enough to get his license plate. As he hurtled down the street, he jammed his bulk as far down into the car seat as he could, convinced that bullets were even now beginning to overtake him. In fact, by the time he turned the first of many corners the men were back at the house and into the two large cars parked in the front drive. The electronically controlled gate was open by the time the first of the two cars burst through and squealed onto the street in hot pursuit.

By the next morning, a contact the men had inside the Dade County sheriff's office confirmed that an Avis car bearing the license plate they were seeking had been found, apparently abandoned, in rural south Dade. Well-paid contacts inside the airlines, bus companies, and rental car agencies reported no sightings of the missing driver. Nor would they anytime during the coming days and weeks. One Viktor Isakov, bearing a valid Russian passport, had just installed himself in a luxury cabin aboard the outbound *Caribbean Calypso*.

27 The only person at the time who knew that the man on board the *Calypso* was really a burly Russian merchant seaman whose name was Pyotr Kudriavtsev and not Viktor Isakov was a Cuban intelligence agent named Juanita Jimenez. Or at least that's the name she was using these days. She had been following Isakov/Isaacs for the past three months, roughly since his first meeting with representatives of Bravo 99. She had lived in Little Havana for almost twenty years. The fact that she was one of the few aboard her raft to survive the trip that started from Mariel in a driving rain at two in the morning and ended in the Keys was not accidental. She had trained for the mission for months and had conditioned herself to survive with little water. To say she had been accepted with open arms into the exile Cuban community was a great understatement. She had been the heroine *du jour*—until the next raft arrived. Thereafter, she had slipped quietly into the verdant life of Little Havana, had attended all the anti-Castro rallies, and had reported routinely to her bosses ninety miles away. She had risen to become the local station chief of the Cuban State Security Department. Her code name was Nightlight.

Juanita's specialty was the more virulent of the anti-Castro organizations. She had watched the venerable Alpha 66 age by two decades. She had watched original members die and new ones join. As age eroded the potency of the hard-liners, new ones grew up to take their place. Or new organizations were created to carry on the cause of hanging Fidel heels first from the tallest lamppost in Ciudad Viejo. Juanita had seen it all. That is, until Bravo 99 came along.

She identified a number of its members. So it wasn't too difficult to tap the grapevine for meeting times and places, to count the heads, and to identify the activists. She had been particularly interested to observe the lunch at the Casa Blanca in September where two Bravo 99 leaders met with an overstuffed Slav they subsequently hustled down the street to the park where they scattered the slumbering domino players. And then there was the night ten days later at the same restaurant where she delayed dinner with an agent companion long enough to watch ten or twelve Bravos walk out buzzing like bees around eleven o'clock, and a half dozen more, including one Manny and one Tony, leave about midnight in ones and twos.

Using the small Leica with the 135mm lens, she got Manny, Tony, and the Russian from a phone booth across from the park and then, after the dinner and using the fancy nightscope, got all six of the lingerers, including the same Manny and Tony, from a dark observation post across the street. When the pictures got to Havana in a shoe box full of old family papers and weathered pictures, her boss Lazaro Suarez increased her rank to major in the State Security Department. Juanita was the best of a widespread network in Miami.

In the preceding three months, Cuban security had developed considerable files around the six pictures Juanita had sent. The pictures also had been distributed widely within the Cuban security network. Cuban security, relying on remaining contacts with former KGB officers in Moscow, had also developed some background on Viktor Isakov, aka Victor Isaacs. They knew him to be an arms dealer with a network inside Russian military circles. Most interestingly, they had only in the past week learned that the father of "Victor Isaacs" was one Colonel L. S. Isakov, late of the Strategic Rocket Forces and a veteran of the Soviet Expeditionary Force in Cuba in the fall of 1962. Researchers from Cuban security were at this minute reviewing the very files that McLemore had examined, during his September and October trips, for references to Colonel L. S. Isakov.

Based upon the more than coincidental meeting in September between "Isaacs" and the Bravo leaders, Juanita had been instructed to lock on "Isaacs" and report on every move he made, particularly anything involving Bravo, in the Miami area. Using the Cuban intelligence network that extended throughout the travel, accommodations, and tourist industries in Miami, Juanita had picked "Isaacs" up on several subsequent trips. His efforts to cover his tracks had proved absolutely amateurish. She observed the second meeting at the Casa Blanca with the Bravo characters Manny and Tony in which a large briefcase had been passed from them to "Isaacs." From the veranda behind the Doral, she had observed the late-night meeting among the three men two weeks ago. Last Friday, she sat in a car at midnight near the beach park in south Miami while the three men talked again. Then the following Tuesday she had tailed "Isaacs" to the Mafia clubhouse and continued to track him on his Odyssean escape. In the early morning hours, she had watched and even photographed "Isaacs" meeting in an all-night coffee shop near the Miami International Airport with a man whose age and description were remarkably similar to those of "Isaacs." After dawn, "Isaacs" had driven his twin to the tour ship docks and dropped him, luggage and all, at the pier for the *Caribbean Calypso*. When she later checked back with the shipping line for the manifest of the *Calypso*—because she needed to reach her boss, Mr. Isaacs, due to a family medical emergency—she discovered that, indeed, one Victor Isaacs bearing a valid U.S. passport was on board.

Only he wasn't, Juanita reported to Havana. He had returned to the Washington, D.C., area, on board a regularly scheduled Delta flight at 10 A.M. that same day using the name D. D. Dankewitz. Everyone in the Cuban intelligence network noted that name for future reference. You never knew when such incidental things might prove to be important.

Operating under instructions from Havana, Juanita then focused her attention on the Bravo group. By now, with the help of her network, she knew the business locations, residences, clubs, and hangouts of the six renegade Bravos. Other agents were assigned level-two surveillance of the other five, but she assumed responsibility for Manny Lechuga on the grounds that very little important would happen without him. About a week after "Isaacs" faked his own vacation, she followed Manny and Tony from their dinner at the Cracked Crab with its famous key lime pie to a fitness club in the tony South Beach central area. Since it was almost eleven o'clock, she deduced that something more was involved than working off extra calories. Although the discreet sign saying PETE'S PECS still glowed, the club had been closed for two hours. There were, however, three cars parked in the adjacent lot in which Manny parked his Mercedes.

Juanita parked her car as she saw Manny and Tony enter the lot and quickly moved up on foot to a cluster of bushes near the club's back door. The time the men took to stamp out their cigar butts gave her an opportunity to move within ten feet of the door undetected. They knocked on the door, and momentarily a very muscular man, whom she recognized from the internal light to be Pedro Medina, the proprietor, admitted them. As the door's hydraulic slowly closed the door, she slipped a credit card into the catch, preventing it from locking. She waited for an eternity of five minutes by her watch. Then she slowly opened the door wide enough first to look into and then to enter. She found herself in a back corridor off which were the management offices of the fitness club. As she moved quietly up the hall toward the sound of voices she passed offices for accounting, then membership, then staff, and the next, from which the voices came, would be for the manager.

Juanita was now operating well beyond her experience and her capability, but not beyond her mandate. Instructions from Havana, always conveyed in elliptical telephone calls to her boss at the photo shop, had recently become more and more urgent. "We must know how poor Manuel is doing . . ." or "Your uncle says he must know how you are doing before the anniversary . . ." and so forth. She got the message. Something big was up. It would make sense that it would be connected with the anniversary of the revolution. And it would make even more sense that, if somebody was planning something, that somebody would be in Miami. Juanita understood that the focus was upon her flock, and that her boss, Suarez— and undoubtedly everyone up to and including el Jefe—needed to find out what they were planning. She didn't need to be told that it had something to do with "Isaacs." She could figure that out for herself. But someone farther north had to watch him now.

Juanita went into the office designated STAFF. In the near dark she could make out three desks and a single file cabinet. In one corner were a medicine ball, a pile of towels, and a set of small five- and ten-pound barbells. At the top of the wall between the staff office and the manager's office, a small vent transmitted a little light and a range of voices. Moving carefully, Juanita slid papers back on the desk positioned against that same wall, took off her sneakers for fear they might squeak, and one knee at a time climbed up on the desk. Now in her early forties, even this exertion made her breathe more heavily. She took time to calm her breathing and her heart, then stood on tiptoe to look through the vent. Of ordinary height, she could only make out the tops of three male heads on the far side of the adjoining room, but could hear at least two more distinctive voices.

". . . so where is he?"

"How the hell should I know, Manny? I'm not his baby-sitter."

"Why the fuck didn't you guys take him over there?"

"You don't think he would have smelled through that? Besides, those guys scare me."

"They must've scared him, too. Out of there like a bat."

"He sure as hell has disappeared. I've had all my guys looking all over town."

"Well, Tony, they didn't look hard enough. 'Cause I found him."

"You what . . . ?"

"Found him! Where?"

Chair legs fell forward. Juanita saw the three heads lean in reflexively. The room was silent. She held her breath.

"The *Caribbean Calypso*."

"The what?"

"*Caribbean Calypso*, Pete. It's a ship. A tourist ship. Left here the morning after good old Vic slipped the leash. It's cruising down south. The manifest shows one Victor Isaacs, Westchester, New York, on board from Miami. Returns in five days."

"I think we should meet him, Manny."

"I got a better idea," the voice Juanita now identified as Manny's said. "Let's let those bad boys meet him . . . the ones he got away from."

"What if he gets off someplace before he gets back?"

"Joe, I thought about that. I alerted Mr. Big . . . who by the way is not amused by this little hide-and-seek . . . and he is putting someone on board at Cancún . . . the next stop . . . to look after our Vic. See that he gets home safe and all like that."

"Why can't they just dump the son of a bitch overboard? Feed him to the fish."

"He's too fat. He'd float."

The laughter cackled and ricocheted.

The Manny voice said, "Somebody on board might miss him. They'd stop and search. There'd be a big investigation. Newspapers. All that stuff. There's a chance . . . him being Russian and all . . . that it would even get into the Russian papers, say. What if old Dinkowitz heard about it? He'd get scared. We'd never see him. He's our main man now."

A couple of voices said, "Yeah."

"So we got to get him back here. Then we lock him up until our 'project' is over . . . then have the wise guys off him. So that's the plan with Victor . . . the slimy son of a bitch. Now listen. D day is two weeks off. I don't know about you guys, but I think I'm being tailed. Can't pick it up exactly. But I just have a feeling that it's there."

Joe said, "You too? I *know* someone is on me. It's the creepiest goddamn feeling."

Juanita saw two more heads nodding vigorously. She suddenly got an ice-cold chill.

"We can't meet again . . . until we take off. So this is the last time. We're going underground," the Manny voice said sternly. "Tell your families and your partners you got to go away on business. Call them before we leave and make some excuse for being gone on the holidays. It's tough. But we got to do it. Don't be too mysterious. But do it. Now, let's report. Me first. Tony and I are not going back by air. If they've made us, they'll be looking for us at the airport. We're changing plans. We're all going down in your boat, Johnny. Take the boat to Cancún, as we agreed. The rest of us will fly down and meet you, then you drop us off at separate beaches in Pinar del Río two at a time. I'll show you a cove to hide the boat in. There'll be ordinary work clothes for everybody on board. We'll have to leave a day early to give enough time for everyone to get across country to our meeting place in Havana. Directions will be available on board the boat. Now, everybody tell me what you got."

A quiet voice said, "I got the tools, for the elevator. They're old ones. But you could change a motor with them. I'll get them down to Johnny's boat."

Another voice said, "My friends are going to provide Mexican passports for all of us. Just in case. They'll be here . . . FedEx . . . next week. Just in time."

"I got the firepower," another, hearty voice said. Juanita thought it probably came from Pete the jock. "Everything we need . . . and more. We can wage a little war down there if we need to."

"My mechanics have checked out the engines and have built a little fiberglass locker against the engine housing that looks like its part of the original. There's plenty of room for the armor."

Juanita had heard enough. She had rough dates and places, numbers of people, even something about an elevator. This meeting was breaking up soon, and she had to be out of there. She would get her report off tonight. And in ten days to two weeks, the Pinar del Río coastline would be patrolled by every coastal craft in the Cuban navy. Just as she got down to one knee, she heard . . .

". . . a couple of pickaxes, a couple of sharp chisels, and a couple of sledgehammers. We'll need them to get the 'package' out of that bunker at Bejucal."

It was the Manny voice. Now Juanita knew the what. Whatever they were up to was located at the military base at Bejucal.

She dropped to the other knee as she stepped off the desktop onto the floor. Her foot came down on a ten-pound barbell free weight under a towel and it rolled away from her, throwing her leg up into the air and bringing her crashing down onto a desk chair on rollers, which in turn fell over backward with a crash. Coming down on the back of her head, she lay stunned but conscious. Conscious enough to be aware of an ominous silence. Then the overhead light came on and the office door was full of bodies and faces. Reflexively she tried to pull her dress down to cover her bare legs, but her arm would not move.

The largest of the men in the doorway, the one who had let the others in earlier, came forward and knelt down beside her. He gently felt for a pulse in her throat. Someone else came in and handed him the credit card she had reinserted once inside to keep the door from locking. He studied it, as if it were in a foreign language, then handed it back to the others. The big one picked her up gently in his arms and carried her down the long corridor into an exercise room. She heard the one with Manny's voice say behind her, "Juanita. Juanita Jimenez."

As the big man laid her down carefully on a workout mat, she wondered why she could not feel her arms and legs. The big man knelt down, facing the top of her head and gently put his hands on both sides of her head. His fingers touched in the back.

"Juanita Jimenez. I remember her. She came over on a raft a long time ago. Now she's working for that Commie son of a bitch," the Manny voice said.

That was the last thing Nightlight heard. The big man, Pete, snapped her spinal cord.

28 In the small bar toward the rear of the Bentley Hotel discreetly located in a residential neighborhood three blocks from Dupont Circle in Washington, McLemore looked over a small glass of Irish whiskey at Mr. Worthy, the head of the Cuban section in the Latin American division of the Central Intelligence Agency. Mr. Worthy had been McLemore's host during his visit to the Agency some days earlier. Since that time, Mr. Worthy's assistant, Sandy, had made a lot of low-classified files covering the missile crisis available to McLemore. His search of the files had turned up little that was helpful in the nature of warhead inventories. The files did confirm a negative. The Agency had no agents in Cuba in November and December of 1962, at least none positioned well enough to count exported warheads and no agents among the Soviet forces capable of observing the packing, counting, and shipping. During their dinner conversation, Mr. Worthy confirmed as much.

"We had practically no assets down there then, and the ones we did have had gone to ground," he said.

McLemore said, "So, you would have no way of knowing if the Soviets left any nuclear material behind. Say, a warhead or two."

Mr. Worthy studied him. "Whatever would make them do a thing like that?"

McLemore shrugged. "No reason, I guess. I just have to explore all the options . . . for my research project, you know. My central argument is that, following the Kennedy-Khrushchev agreement on the twenty-eighth of October, the United States had the ability to count large objects, such as missiles, by airborne surveillance and therefore that smaller objects, including potentially lethal ones, might have remained behind."

"For what purpose?" Mr. Worthy asked.

McLemore shrugged again. "Don't know. Maybe some Soviet officer went over to the Cuban side. There is a lot of evidence, including from recently declassified files on our side, that the Soviet forces were angry as hell at their own politicians for making them pack up and leave. It was a kind of small Vietnam without the bloodshed for them. Maybe if the military feels emasculated, they leave a couple of balls behind as a consolation prize for their buddies."

Mr. Worthy said, "It's a novel theory." But it was clearly not a theory that he found interesting enough to pursue. "May I ask you a question, Professor McLemore?"

"Of course." McLemore was still unclear why Mr. Worthy had asked for this evening. But he thought he was about to find out.

"Your father. We thought you would probably want to know about your father. But, so far at least, you haven't asked."

"All right," McLemore said, "I'm asking." He was about to enter a memory tunnel he didn't think he wanted to enter.

Mr. Worthy was a bit of a stiff, McLemore thought, but he liked—and even more important, trusted—him. Mr. Worthy resembled nothing so much as a proper upmarket Presbyterian minister. He combed his neatly parted gray hair straight back and used some kind of old-fashioned stay-put on it. No blow-dry for this one. His conservative gray suit matched his hair and, for off-the-rack, fit his trim figure nicely. McLemore imagined he had gone to prep school and then on to the Little Ivy League. He probably rowed a scull on the Potomac for exercise. He wore precise, round wire-rimmed glasses, of course.

"That he was a hero goes without saying. You received the tangible evidence of that thirty-five years ago." McLemore wanted to say, Yes, and that and thirty-five cents gets me a cup of coffee. But he didn't. "He was one of six whom we . . . the Agency; I was just beginning . . . sent down there. One landed just as the agreement was reached, and we were able to get him out. The other five, including Jack McLemore, never came back." So far, nothing new. McLemore waited. "He sent back some remarkable information really. He confirmed the location of the headquarters of the Soviet Expeditionary Forces just outside Havana. We then targeted it, number one. He confirmed one of the IRBM—intermediate-range ballistic missile—sites in Pinar del Río and two of the Luna tactical missile batteries in the same region. Being smaller, the Lunas were harder to find from the U-2 footage. Their location was important. If we had to go in and we couldn't take those batteries out, they would have wiped out a couple of divisions . . . maybe our entire landing force. Up to that time, we were not even sure they had tactical nukes down there. So, your father carried off a huge intelligence coup. Finally, and equally importantly, he located the warhead storage depot at a town called Bejucal. That was targeted number two. Have you run across Bejucal in your research?"

McLemore's head came up from the Irish whiskey. "Yes," he said, "I've been there. Went there first thing in September. I heard about Bejucal from that book that came out a year or two ago . . . *One Hell of a Gamble* . . . from the Soviet archives."

"After he got the word out about Bejucal and the Lunas, we told him to come back," Mr. Worthy said. "He wanted to spend a couple of more days. He thought he might be able to recruit a Soviet officer." Mr. Worthy shook his head and smiled wryly. "From all I can tell, he had the guts of a burglar and the tenacity of a bulldog."

McLemore smiled to himself. So that's where it comes from.

"Do you want to hear the rest?" Mr. Worthy asked, his tone kindly.

McLemore shrugged and nodded, Why not?

"He apparently began to pop up so often that he attracted attention. In those tense situations, it can happen. Everyone is on the lookout. Everyone is suspicious. Plus, he didn't actually look Cuban. His language was perfect. But there was too much of the Irish there. The eyes were green . . . like yours. The gait was loping . . . like yours." Mr. Worthy pushed a picture across the cocktail table. Jack McLemore was grinning, arms crossed, leaning against an early '60s convertible. The shadow of the photographer stretched forward toward him. His mother. He was an athlete, a thoroughbred. Despite himself, McLemore smiled. The figure dared you to smile. He started to push the picture back, and Mr. Worthy shook his head no.

"Anyway, they almost caught him at Bejucal. He would go out there at night, on a bicycle or somehow, and watch the trucks come and go. He had studied Soviet equipment enough to know these were special lorries designed to haul nuclear warheads. He counted them and somehow figured out from the number of containers per truck and the size of the trucks that these were tactical . . . Lunas . . . not strategic. It was a huge discovery for us. It went right to the White House. All of his stuff went right to the White House. Kennedy didn't know who he was, but he thought he was a saint. We think he went out there once too often and they got on his trail until they evidently picked him up at a big war rally in the Plaza de la Revolución. He went to ground and tried to hide out with a—"

"Priest," McLemore said, "a priest named John Prescott. I know him. He found me. He had been waiting for me . . . all these years."

Both men were silent. New whiskeys had arrived and McLemore finished half of his. Mr. Worthy adjusted his glasses with care and said, "They apparently treated him pretty badly. I am truly sorry to say this to you. And we'll leave it there, if you like."

McLemore shook his head no.

"So far as we are able to tell, he didn't give up a thing. He didn't know it, but the others had already been captured and killed. If he had given their identities, he couldn't have hurt them, and he might possibly have saved himself. But we are virtually certain that he didn't give them the time of day." Mr. Worthy looked away, then chuckled.

McLemore looked at him quizzically.

"There is a legend in the Agency," Mr. Worthy offered, "that toward the end of his . . . mistreatment . . . Jack McLemore said, 'I wouldn't walk across the street to see Fidel Castro slit his wrists.' If so, it would have been characteristic, and it would have sealed his doom."

McLemore downed the whiskey, excused himself, and went to the men's room. He fumbled for a towel, his eyes moist. Goddamn it! His hands were shaking. He hated that. After a moment, he regained composure and returned. "Thank you very much, Mr. Worthy. I appreciate all you've told me. Strangely enough, it helps a lot."

Changing now to a drier, more businesslike tone, Mr. Worthy said, "Which brings us to the present day. History repeats itself . . . or something like that."

McLemore waited.

"We have mentioned to you a Russian. Someone we believe may be involved in present or future terrorist operations against Cuba. He is an arms supplier. And you will recall that we mentioned some Cuban Americans having meetings with him."

"I remember, of course," McLemore said.

"He is the key to whatever mischief is planned for Cuba—planned, we think, for New Year's Day."

McLemore waited, then said, "Why don't you bring him around to your office for a visit. I am amazed that the people in your business are not more direct."

"We cannot do that, Professor. We have had him under surveillance . . . the Bureau has . . . for more than thirty days, since we focused our efforts upon him as the key. He is becoming extremely erratic. We believe also that, for reasons we are unclear about, his customers in Miami have turned against him. It may be that they are concerned about his stability and are trying to eliminate him. In any case, if frightened or provoked, we believe he will bolt and remain in hiding, at least through the critical New Year's period. Then, if our other information is correct, it may be too late."

McLemore raised his hands, palms up in a shrug. "What in hell can I do. I'm a run-of-the-mill academic. Contrary to your wishes, I'm not even my father's son. I don't like your business. If you don't believe me, ask your man Ramsay."

"You are anything but a 'run-of-the-mill academic,' Professor," Mr. Worthy said. "You are ideal for this purpose. So ideal, you may have fallen from the sky. You obviously know the depth of the Cubans' concern. You must believe the depth of our concern. The White House is now focusing on this matter and demanding that we . . . the Agency, the Bureau, ATF, everybody . . . prevent a disaster. Our problem is, we don't know what kind of disaster we are supposed to prevent. Aside from a small handful of Cuban Americans who, if confronted, would deny everything, the only living person who has the answer is this Russian. He has provided them whatever they intend to use."

"So I should just walk up to him and ask him what he's selling?" McLemore asked ironically.

"No, here is our scenario. You should put yourself in his way, introduce yourself, and ask to talk with him about your project. We will help put you in his way. You have done research on the Cuban missile crisis. You are a legitimate academic. You have found reference to his father, who played a key role on the Soviet side in this matter and you have spent a great deal of effort tracking him down to see if his father told him any of his experiences that might help in your research of those crisis times. You are searching for the survivors of key Soviet military officials to round out your research efforts. You have credentials. You look and act the part. You speak the academic language. You are believable."

McLemore held up his hand to prevent Mr. Worthy from begging. "Where is he?"

Mr. Worthy polished his glasses and looked at his watch. "Right now, he is about twelve miles away. In Potomac, Maryland."

McLemore sat up. "He is here? How do you know that?"

"Please, Professor, it is our job. The Bureau's job, really. They have him under constant surveillance. He recently shook off the Cuban Americans who apparently were out to do him harm. He cleverly faked a departure on a cruise ship, then he came back here. He is staying at the rather fancy home of a wealthy Russian-American 'businessman' who lives in the suburbs but is back in Moscow on 'business.' "

"And exactly how do I 'put myself in his way'?" McLemore asked.

"We'll do that. Do not worry. And we will help you make it very natural."

"What if he bolts? What if he takes off?"

"He won't," Mr. Worthy said. "And if he does, we'll be nearby, listening on the other end of the little device you will be wearing. We'll catch him and cut off his fingers until he talks."

McLemore winced involuntarily.

"I'm very sorry, Professor, that was a thoughtless comment. Please forgive me."

McLemore had decided that Mr. Worthy was a decent sort. Perhaps in the wrong line of work. But there he was. And he had been sensitive in relating his father's last hours. And he did have a big problem on his hands. Before shaking hands with Mr. Worthy for the night, McLemore wondered whether the information he knew he could get from the son of Colonel L. S. Isakov, late of the Soviet Strategic Rocket Forces, should go to the government of the United States or to the government of Cuba.

29 Arguably the most affluent of a number of affluent suburbs of Washington, the small village of Potomac, on the Maryland side of the Potomac west of downtown, could boast of some of the most stately houses in the area. It was home to the capital's most successful lawyers and lobbyists. And each of its estates was generally large enough to accommodate at least a couple of riding horses. Lately, however, its aura of exclusivity had been eroding under the invasion of arriviste sports stars and nouveau riche foreign "businessmen."

Among these was Alexei Shumatoff who had "liberated" several tens of millions in CCCP liquid assets in the chaotic fall of 1991. Those dollars now rested comfortably in the account of the Democracy Export Corporation in the National Bank of Cyprus. Shumatoff had then traded tips on where many more hundreds of millions of Communist dollars had gone to the CIA in exchange for a U.S. green card. Shumatoff, in turn, had staked Viktor Isakov to his new arms trading business in exchange for 25 percent equity in the Isaacs Security Company, LLC. As part of the deal, Shumatoff provided Isakov a key to his guest house on his plush estate in Potomac in case Isakov ever had to "rest."

Over the past few days, Isakov's pattern, confirmed by external observation and internal microphones, was to rise late, eat a lot, watch television, and go into Potomac village in the late afternoon to replenish his stock of food and alcohol. The internal bugs had been placed during the first of these forays, and his daily shopping trips were the occasion for examination of the trash and garbage. These examinations put the daily vodka consumption at just over a quart.

Two days following his evening with Mr. Worthy, McLemore drove his rental car to the small parking lot of the single liquor store in Potomac village. In his tweed jacket, corduroy trousers, and Timberland loafers, McLemore looked quintessentially professorial. The only new alteration to his authentically worn costume was the tiny microphone buried in the thick knot of his loosened knit tie. At approximately five-forty-five in the evening a Bureau agent in a nearby car gave him the thumbs-up signal. Isakov was on his way. When McLemore saw the beige BMW coupe stop at the corner stoplight, he went into the liquor store and positioned himself in front of the ample vodka shelf. Within a minute and a half he was joined by a large, sweating man in a black warm-up suit. From the corner of his eye he saw a red face topped by tousled, badly cut dark hair and from the middle of which blazed two bloodshot, frantic eyes.

McLemore studied a bottle of Smirnoff and, as the man reached in front of him for the Stolichnaya Cristall, he muttered, "Goddammit."

The man's arm stopped in midreach.

McLemore shook his head hopelessly. "Say, pal, do you know anything about vodka?"

The man grunted, then pulled the Stoly toward him.

"I gotta buy some vodka for some friends of mine in Russia, and I want to get the best. What's that you have?" McLemore asked as he reached for the man's bottle.

Isakov reluctantly permitted McLemore to study the bottle cradled in his thick hands.

"Is this the best? I've heard about it . . . seen people order it in bars . . . but I just don't know. What do you recommend?"

Isakov looked around furtively; then, observing nothing threatening, he let his natural congeniality take over. This looked to him like a typical confused American niceguy. "Is very much the best," he said, his accent sharpened by a sudden thirst. "I recommend it most for any Russian person. Is not drink Russian people get to see very much. Mostly, is sold for exporting."

"Say," McLemore said, stepping back slightly. "You're not Russian yourself, are you? You sound like you might just be from the old country. Nothing personal, you understand."

Isakov waved magnanimously. Naturally gregarious, he was now suffering badly from cabin fever. He had even been thinking about renting another lady for the weekend. But the last experience had been disastrous. She had thrown a shoe at him as he escaped through the motel door. And, on occasion, he appeared to enjoy being recognized for his singular quality, his Russianness. The confused American before him didn't seem to him like such a bad guy. "You are going to Russia, yourself?" he ventured.

"Yea," McLemore said wryly, "first time. I don't have a clue what to expect."

"Is not so bad now," Isakov responded. "I have many friends there who will give you good time." He winked.

Gotcha, McLemore thought. He had just become a spy. "Say, you wouldn't let me buy you a drink . . . maybe try out this 'Sto-litch-nay-a.' Like to get your views on where to go and who to see." He winked back. "I don't mean to be pushy. But you'd sure be doing me a great favor. McLemore," he said, sticking out his hand.

"Isaacs. Victor." The big man responded.

After paying for two bottles of Stoly, the two new friends headed around the corner to one of the two or three small restaurants at the village crossroads. Isakov pointed the way, somehow assuming that McLemore was a stranger to the area. It was early, so they beat the dinner crowd and picked a table in the back near the glowing fireplace. When the waiter asked if they would like dinner, McLemore said yes, and Isakov didn't object.

The Stolichnaya Cristall arrived. McLemore clinked glasses and said, "To Russia."

"With love," Isakov responded, and they both laughed.

McLemore was wondering how long his tenuous luck would hold when Isakov said, "So. You go to Russia. Why are you doing that?"

"Well," McLemore said, plunging ahead, "I'm a history teacher and I'm doing research on the Cuban missile crisis . . . you know, in '62. I want to find some Soviets involved in that period. Maybe some military people. Or maybe the families of key military people, who can tell me what it was like from the Soviet viewpoint. I've talked with some of the U.S. officials and I've even talked to some of the Cuban leaders. They're all getting pretty old. So, I'd like to interview a few Soviet officials who were there or who made decisions. It's important for history that these people tell their story . . . you know . . . before they die."

McLemore wanted to say more, but he was afraid he might already have gone too far. Isakov's eyes had widened when he said "Cuban missile crisis," and he sat now alert with all radars up and warning sirens sounding. If a rat had been smelled, his prey would bolt in the next sixty seconds. McLemore sipped the vodka as he waited to see which way the pendulum would swing. Isakov was struggling between the safe choice of another lonely, drunken night before the TV set or the potentially dangerous choice of talking about Topic A with someone he met fifteen minutes ago. The one thing he decided was that this man, whoever he was, didn't work for Manny and Tony. Not the type. Besides, if they had caught up with him, he would be dead by now. He decided to play chess, a game his father had taught him.

"Is an interesting subject for history," he said, moving a pawn. "Why is interesting you so far afterward?"

"My father was involved," McLemore countered, shooting the queen straight up to take the pawn.

Isakov seemed momentarily stunned by the move. "Your father? How involved?" He advanced a bishop one square.

"He worked for our government. I was very young, so I'm not sure exactly what he did. It was kind of secret." McLemore's knight leapfrogged a pawn.

Isakov seemed out of breath. He tipped up his empty glass and waved for two more. Urgently. "You mean like CIA kind of thing?" His rook maneuvered sideways.

"Don't know exactly. Whatever he was doing, he didn't come back. I guess I'm doing this project to sort of find him in a way—at least to find out what he was doing." The drinks arrived, and they both tipped them up at once. "Say, do you know any Russians I could talk to . . . you know, about this crisis?"

Isakov blinked his eyes. It seemed as if McLemore's pieces had all advanced at once. Isakov seemed to be trying to figure out what was going on here. He drank some water to buy time and clear his clouded brain. It didn't work, so he went for more vodka. Hair of the dog. "Well," he said slowly, "I might have some idea." He touched a pawn, then lost his nerve.

McLemore made a tactical move. He withdrew the queen. "Let's get some dinner." He waved to the waiter who brought menus. The waiter recommended crab cakes, and they both nodded. Isakov weighed his next move. Then he said, "I have friends in Russia for sure who know these things. Old men. In military in those days. We can discuss when you are making your trip and maybe I arrange some things. Give me some days."

McLemore nodded, waiting. Diners were arriving, men in their suits home from the office. He started to tighten his tie, then withdrew his hand, as if from a viper. He wondered if he had given the guy in the van outside a burst eardrum. Isakov drank and reviewed a parade of ghosts. His father. Dankevich. Other veterans his father had introduced him to. Then a small parade of angry Cuban Americans passed by his mental reviewing stand. They were armed. He drank some more. McLemore waited, and presently their dinners arrived. They silently dug in. Isakov ate like a condemned man, McLemore thought. Even though it was December, the fireplace, combined with the psychological heat, made him perspire freely. He mopped his face periodically with his napkin.

"You can talk to me," he finally blurted out. It was a release. He swept all his pieces from the board and the words flowed. "My father was colonel in Soviet Army. He had special responsibility for some nuclear weapons. It was his specialty. He told me many stories of those times. If you like, I will tell you what I remember."

"I would like," McLemore said quietly. With his hand behind the chair, he waved to the waiter for more vodka.

Isakov inhaled a crab cake almost whole. "What I remember from my father was that Soviet Army believe very much in its mission. There was strong belief that U.S. was about to invade Cuba or maybe continue to try to assassin Castro. Kremlin had decided to stop this kind of action. So they sent these men and these equipments to help Cuban people protect their independence."

McLemore pushed his plate back unfinished and, interrupting Isakov with a palm up, pulled a notepad from his pocket. "This is really interesting, Mr. Isaacs. Do you mind if I make some notes . . . for my study?"

Eyeing McLemore's remaining crab cake, Isakov said expansively, "Not at all. Not at all." He was enjoying the attention and his own performance. "When Khrushchev ordered forces to leave at end of October in '62, it made many of them . . . especially officers . . . very, very angry. My father, he stress this very much. Very angry, he said always. In Russian, you know, 'Goddamn angry!' But, they do it. They do as they are told . . . by these cowardly politicians in Politburo. But, you know, it divide Politburo. Even some of members say, Khrushchev now go too far. He embarrass us. He make us look weak. We go to defend Cuba. Then we back down to U.S. Now nobody trust us. They think mighty Soviet Army, great Red Army, is . . . how do you say? . . . paper lion."

"Tiger," McLemore offered, his head down, writing like a serious academic.

"Tiger. Correct. Paper tiger." Isakov drank vodka and snorted. "Is very funny . . . paper tiger. Good picture . . . paper tiger." He drifted back to his boyhood, his father hurling ashtrays and glasses across the room. Beating the wife. Beating the kids. No paper tiger this one. A real tiger. A drunk tiger. A mean tiger, his father.

"So, your father," McLemore said, "he was involved with the nuclear missiles. That's an important job. Very important, I would think."

"Of course. He is in top command. Special rocket forces. Is his training. He goes to nuclear weapons school. Very smart. Very tough. An engineer, he is. Would have become general, he told me, except . . ."

"Except?"

"Except, he . . . criticize politicians. He raise his voice against decision to go back . . . to Soviet Union. He tells commanding general is wrong decision. Mighty Red Army should stay on . . . protect Cuban people."

McLemore pressed forward. "Isaacs is not a very Russian name, is it? I hope you don't mind my asking."

Isakov thought. "Is Western business name. I choose. People here understand it better, I think."

"So, your father's name, originally, would have been . . . ?" McLemore was mentally leaning forward. But he knew the answer.

"No. Is okay. His name . . . my name . . . in Russian . . . it is 'Eez-ah-koff.'" He pronounced it slowly, as if for a child, and then spelled it. "I-s-a-k-o-v."

McLemore wrote this down, letter by letter. His hands suddenly were cold. A piercing headache began on the lower left back of his head. "Isakov. You said he was a colonel. Colonel Isakov." He put his pencil down and drank. Isakov had finished off McLemore's remaining crab cake and the waiter cleared the table. "Is that a common Russian name? Would there have been very many Russian officers with that name in Cuba in those days?"

"Is not unusual, but is not also usual. There are some others, but not many more."

McLemore said carefully, "This is such a coincidence. Because I was doing research in Cuba some time ago . . . about the missiles, and the warheads . . . and I saw this name . . . Isakov." He shook his head.

"In what way do you see it?"

McLemore looked toward the ceiling, trying to remember. "I think it was in some documents in the Cuban files that they let me see."

"Why do they let you see files . . . secret files?"

McLemore said, "Because I am just a historian. And it was so long ago. It isn't important anymore."

"What does it say, these files?" Isakov's shaggy head was a bit wobbly and his eyes unfocused.

McLemore looked at his watch and boldly checkmated. "You know, Mr. Isaacs. I've kept you a long time. I'm really sorry." He waved for the bill and, when it arrived, paid it promptly. He started to stand up. "This must all be very uninteresting to you . . . this old history."

McLemore had an image of the guy out in the van having a heart attack.

Isakov grabbed his forearm, both to detain him and to get help standing up. He struggled to his feet. "You must come to my house. Is near. I give you cap for night. You come."

His heavy arm around McLemore's shoulder, they weaved out of the crowded restaurant.

He lurched into the BMW and motioned for McLemore to follow in his small car. The three-car caravan, the Bureau van far back, weaved through the single stoplight at the village crossroads and proceeded down several turns to the north that finally led to the Shumatoff gate. After several tries Isakov got the gate remote control to work, the wrought iron gate swung inward, and two of the cars went in. The van took up its listening post down the road.

The guest house, Isakov's hideout, was a mess. He pushed a pile of dirty laundry aside as he waved McLemore inside, took the Stoly into the kitchen where stacks of dirty dishes went untended, and poured two drinking glasses two-thirds full. No ice. Isakov threw *Penthouse* magazines off the two chairs, fell into the most comfortable one, and waved McLemore into the other.

"Cuba is long ago. Is not so interesting," he offered. "You must study some other thing."

McLemore calculated swiftly. I have only until the bottom of this glass to finish the job, he thought. "My father. I told you. He was there. I want to know his experience." He raised his glass and watched with dismay as Isakov swallowed a third of his.

"Ah, our fathers. They plague us even after dead." Isakov waved his glass and the liquid swirled. "To our fathers. May the dead stay resting . . . and not bother us no more."

McLemore drank to that with mixed feelings. The toast covered half his feelings. He wanted to lay his father to rest, but he could not do so until he uncovered his story. His father was a ghost, doomed to walk the night, seeking some respite and demanding that his son avenge him. Across from him, slipping into alcoholic oblivion, was a Russian of his age, likewise bearing some family curse, pursued throughout his dreams by a father who refused to stay entombed. What in God's name had thrown them together half a lifetime later? How could the Cold War linger on, years after the unseemly collapse of one side had left the other standing triumphant but bewildered? What had their fathers wrought that so demanded closure? Were they players in the last act of a drama whose author forgot to finish?

McLemore tried to roust himself. He had work to do. "Victor, wouldn't it be something if my father and your father knew each other . . . back in those days? Wouldn't that be something?"

"How could it be? Your father is in Cuba then, he must be spy. You said he may be spy. You don't know. They don't tell us . . . our fathers . . . what they do. You saw my father's name. What he is doing there?"

McLemore said, "As you said, warheads. Nuclear. There is an Isakov. Colonel. He signs papers. He is respon . . . responsible . . . for bringing in warheads and then for taking out warheads. Maybe it is your father. Eez-ah-koff." McLemore was going fast himself.

"Of course is my father!" shouted Isakov, as if to an idiot. "Who else it can be? He has control of these warheads. Luna. Luna. Luna. Hahaha! Luna. Is moon. Moon. Moon. Moon. Nice sound, moooooooon. He is big man. Important man. He is waiting for Uncle Sam coming over the waves . . . onto beach . . . whoosh Luna. No more Sam. Hahahah." He raised his glass. "For Luna!"

"For Luna." McLemore said through gritted, smiling teeth. "Of course, they're all gone now. All the Lunas. No moons in Cuba. No Cuban moons. No moons over Cuba. Of course that's true." He lowered his voice and loosened his tie. "That's true. Isn't it."

"Hahahaha! Hahahaha! Of course. Hahahaha! How can not be true? Colonel Isakov. Leonid Sestanovich Isakov. Colonel L. S. Isakov. He control Lunas. Bosses in Kremlin, big men in Politburo, say, 'Isakov. Take out Lunas. Send back.' He salute. He send back Lunas."

"Correct, Victor. He sends them all back. But I saw some documents in Cuba. Colonel Isakov signs papers showing warheads coming in, and Colonel Isakov signs documents showing warheads going out."

Isakov started laughing, and McLemore laughed with him. Together they chant, "In and out. In and out." Then they laughed some more.

McLemore's mind was now dead cold sober. He had to move fast. He took off his tie, plucked the tiny black object out, placed it on the coffee table, and smashed it with an ashtray. "A bug," he said.

"Bugs in Victor's place?" Isakov said, "No way." They both laughed again.

McLemore leaned very close to Isakov. He spoke conspiratorially. "I don't want to surprise you, Vic. But the number of Lunas that came into Cuba is more than the number that went out. It's a secret. Don't tell anyone."

Isakov put a beefy hand over his mouth and giggled uncontrollably. He shook his head up and down. He leaned toward McLemore, his mouth a few inches from his ear. "I know. I know. My father tell me. He keep one or two." He muffled the giggles once again. "For himself. He keep one or two. You know what he tell me . . . before he go to Communist heaven . . . he tell me, 'Viktor, I don't tell bosses. But I keep one or two. You know what I tell bosses,' he say to me, 'I tell bosses—fuck you!' " Viktor was now laughing uncontrollably. "I tell bosses, 'Fuck you!' Hahahahaha!"

McLemore laughed with him. "Fuck you! Hahahahaha!" McLemore leaned toward Isakov and said, "I know a secret, too, Vic. I know where he hid them."

Isakov shook his head back and forth. "No way. Only I know. My father tell me. Only I." He punched himself in the chest with the hot dog finger.

McLemore shook his head back and forth. "No, I know. But what I can't figure out is how he moved them without anyone finding out."

"See. I tell you, you don't know," Isakov whispered furiously. He was slumped badly in his chair. He would go at any moment. McLemore marveled at his capacity. He had consumed the equivalent of a quart of 90-proof vodka. "He is genius. My father." He waved a hand vaguely in the air, as if to summon up the mad colonel's ghost. "You don't have to move something if you hide it where it is." Isakov giggled again. Then his eyes rolled back and his head fell sideways against the wing of the chair back.

McLemore grabbed for the glass and rescued it as it began to slip from the relaxing meaty hand. Now, even in his own vodka stupor, he moved quickly. When the bug went dead, the guy in the van would have called Bureau headquarters or Langley for instructions. The cavalry would be on the way. There would be concern to rescue McLemore from the possible stranglehold of the mad Russian. There would be even greater concern to find out Isakov's last words about the Lunas. They now would have a clue about the weapons they were looking for. But they would not know where they were or how Bravo intended to get a Luna warhead into Cuba.

McLemore turned off the lights. He quickly made his way out the door. He listened momentarily to the loud snoring, then locked the door behind him. He went to the BMW, holding his breath in the hope Isakov had not locked it. His luck was running. He opened the car door and punched the remote control for the gate. He got in his rental car parked behind the BMW as the gate swung open and eased himself in reverse out into the darkened lane. The van would be within a couple of hundred yards. He left his lights off and drove slowly by the dim lights coming from neighboring estates. He made one turn, then shortly another. He turned on his lights and picked up speed. Presently, he came to River Road and turned left to Washington. He now had to get to National Airport, catch the next flight to Milwaukee, get to Madison and pack his bags, get back to Milwaukee or even Chicago, and get back to Cuba.

McLemore had chosen sides.

PART THREE

30 The crossing from Cancún had been timed so that Johnny's boat, *Liberator*, would arrive off the Pinar del Río coast in the predawn hours of December 24. Anti-Castro sources in Cuba provided information, such as the routine schedules of Cuban coastal patrol craft, to any elements of the anti-Castro network that might want it. Armed with this information, the Bravo team lay twenty miles offshore at 5 A.M., waiting for the patrol craft to cross, then made their dash for the coast. Their sources inside Cuba had also given three alternative landing sites that would accommodate the draft of the fast boat and provide cover for the next ten days.

At precisely 5:20 A.M., just before the eastern sky began to glow, the *Liberator* began its run at eighteen knots for the Cuban coast. The men did not break out the assault rifles because the range of the guns on the Cuban coastal patrol boats was far greater than anything they carried. If they were spotted, they would be hailed. If they refused to acknowledge and stop engines, they would be blown out of the water. No chance for close proximity combat. There was only a slight chop to the sea, and they maintained a heading almost due east. There were low clouds and a slight drizzle that, with a darkened boat, provided a measure of stealth. Two of the men scanned the darkness, one northward and one southward, with high-powered binoculars. Except for the retreating lights of one of the coastal patrol boats running south, they saw nothing. And nothing saw them.

At the last minute, Manny changed plans once again. Instead of risking three separate landings—at Bahía de Cabana, at Bahía Honda, and at Bahía de la Mulata—and the dangers each landing entailed, he decided they would make for the southernmost bay, the Bahía de la Mulata, hide the boat, and make their way the seventy or eighty kilometers to Havana in teams of two. Bahía de la Mulata was farther from Havana, but it was also more remote and offered greater security for the men and the boat.

They bore slightly south by southeast. Johnny's sources in Mexico had provided a chart of the central Pinar del Río coastline before they cast off from Cancún, and Orlando, acting as navigator, guided him toward the bay. The two large engines were throttled well back as the lookouts reported scattered coastal lights. Soon they began to make out land two thousand yards to the northeast, and Johnny eased the engines down to two knots and felt his way through the slight chop. Dawn was breaking, thus permitting selection of a cove by natural light. Their timing had been perfect. Johnny made for the southeast corner of the V-shaped bay and then ran northeast along the coastline. Within fifteen minutes they found a small notch in the otherwise smooth beach line where a small stream fed into the ocean. Johnny guided the boat into the notch, headed the sharp prow westward out to sea, reversed engines, and expertly backed the boat into the mouth of the stream. Tony sat on the stern and took soundings between the two large propellers. The small cove provided adequate draft for the boat as well as abundant natural foliage. The cove narrowed and became shallower as the foliage thickened. Johnny shut down the boat. Pete dropped the anchor, jumped into the stream, and tied the line off on the sturdy root of a water shrub. Another line was secured, and the men then covered the boat with palms and branches from thick foliage nearby. The other four men waded ashore, and Johnny handed clothes and equipment and then finally the armor down the human chain until everything was ashore and stockpiled.

Manny went up the beach fifty yards, turned, and looked back. The boat was completely hidden. Studying maps and charts by the dawn's light, he calculated they were two to three kilometers from the coastal village of Playa el Morrillo and the village road that led to the paved road to Havana. The men huddled and confirmed their plan. They carried all the equipment inland two hundred yards under a small clump of trees. Using a trenching tool to dig a pit, they wrapped everything except three handguns in tarpaulin, stripped and changed into ordinary Cuban work clothes, and buried everything in the pit. When the loose soil and sand covered the pit, they brushed the surface with foliage as they backed away from the site. It was impossible to detect any disturbance. Once safely located at their "clubhouse" in Havana, and once they had taken delivery of their truck, they would return for all their gear.

They set off along the foliage line along the high beach and within thirty minutes they intercepted the village road east of Playa el Morrillo. It was now approximately 7:30 A.M. Pete noticed with pride that his insistence on hours of workouts in the health club had paid off. Even Orlando did not seem winded. Manny and Tony formed one team, Joe and Johnny another, and Orlando and Pete the third. Each team took a nine-millimeter Heckler and Koch pistol with an eight-cartridge clip. They embraced solemnly, and then, led by Manny and Tony, they set out along the country road in thirty-minute intervals. They all looked, more or less, like rural Cuban workers, dressed in slightly better than ordinary clothes, headed off for a day in the capital city. Depending on their luck in hitching a ride or encountering one of the rare fuming buses, they agreed to rendezvous sometime after midday at what they now routinely called the "clubhouse" in the Cerro district of Havana.

Manny and Tony arrived first. As they had prearranged, Osvaldo, the occupant of the clubhouse, had removed his meager belongings, acquired competent help to bring order to the place, and made it more or less habitable. There were primitive kitchen and toilet facilities, but it would be crowded for six people and, when he joined them on the twenty-sixth, Dankevich, the seventh. There were only two small cots. But each man had a blanket in his meager straw bag, and that would have to do for the handful of largely sleepless nights ahead. Tony opened the place up while Manny looked around and took stock. While waiting for the others, he jotted notes about the food and supplies they would have to acquire—not having coupons—on the black market. It would be a long week of rice, beans, plantains, and, if lucky, one or two fish or chickens. They could spend odd hours planning the steak dinners when they celebrated back in Miami.

At three that afternoon, a healthy Pete and exhausted Orlando showed up. And two hours later, the weary team of Joe and Johnny joined them. They had an adventure to relate. The ancient farm truck that had picked them up was already overloaded. When it stopped to take on more people, the engine had overheated and the road patrol had pulled up to check things out. Afraid that papers might be checked or, if confronted, that their accents might not be authentic enough, they had slipped into some brush on the other side of the truck. It had then left without them, and they had been forced to walk more than five miles before they were picked up again. Upon arriving at the block where the clubhouse was located, each of the men had entered the place separately to minimize the sense that a new group of residents had arrived.

As the men were considering a plan for acquiring provisions, there was a knock on the door. Manny waved the others into the tiny kitchen and opened the door slightly. It was their landlord, just checking up to see if his angels had arrived.

"You okay, Juan?" he asked, peering over Manny's shoulder.

"My partner and me just got in from Mexico City a little while ago," Manny said. "You got the place in pretty good shape." Truthfully, he wanted to ask the kid how he could live in such a hellhole.

Osvaldo said, "When you want to talk some business? You know, like we planned."

"I tell you what, Osvaldo," Manny said. "Let my partner and me get some food and some rest and maybe we can get together tomorrow. How's that?"

Osvaldo was confused and disappointed. How could these guys be tired after a short flight over from Mexico? And he had wanted a night on the town with these high rollers. "Food? You need some food? I show you a nice place tonight. Over by the harbor. Good Cuban food. The best." He displayed a foxy smile. "And some Cuban señoritas *también*. The best."

"In a couple of days, Osvaldo, *muchas gracias*," Manny said. He had moved just outside the doorway and realized that the sun would be setting soon. "Tell you what, though. You can help us out." He pulled ten dollars from his pocket. "Bring back some beans and rice, coffee, and anything else you can get, for when we don't feel like going to a restaurant. Any fruit you can get." Osvaldo stared at the ten, then started away. Manny called him back and gave him another ten. "*Cervezas, por favor*. Also a couple of bottles of rum." Manny knew, and Osvaldo knew he knew, that this was twice as much money as he needed.

"Sure," Osvaldo said, somewhat happier in the knowledge that he could buy one of his girlfriends dinner with the change.

Within an hour he was back, his arms loaded with supplies from the black market. And good thing, too. Aside from very early coffee and energy bars on board Joe's boat, Bravo team had not eaten all day. The men shared beans, rice, a scrawny chicken, a dozen beers, and a couple of rum chasers. Even though it was still midevening, blankets came out and the men collapsed. Before sleep came, however, and with the last drop of rum, Manny said, "Welcome back to Havana, Bravo. This time it's ours."

*   *   *

When Osvaldo had earlier come back with the food, Manny arranged to take delivery of their rental truck. Osvaldo showed him the lot behind the shabby quarters where it would be parked. His efforts to see inside the house were unsuccessful. The following day, the twenty-fifth, Manny and Tony set out for the hotel where Lieutenant Colonel D. D. Dankevich was to arrive later in the day. The four other men, maps in hand, were to return to Pinar del Río province and retrieve the buried equipment, tools, and hardware. Before they separated, Manny said over his cracked coffee cup, "Merry Christmas, amigos."

An inquiry at the desk of the hotel revealed that Mr. Dankevich was expected on the Madrid flight late in the afternoon. They were friends, they said, and they would check back. The two men reconnoitered the Plaza de la Revolución yet again to refresh their two-month-old recollections on the layout, approaches, and exits. Strolling around the Plaza, making mental notes, they casually calculated escape routes, fallback plans, contingency options, strategies, and tactics. Anyone observing the two men would have thought them to be discussing the economic hardships of the "special period" or the remittance that didn't arrive this month from the daughter in the States.

Except for the extra hour or two it took to relocate the exact site of the buried equipment and load it on their rented truck, the other four Bravo members carried out their mission with few complications. At one roadside ride-waiting post, an *amarillo,* the yellow armband ride-coordinator, made them pull over and load half a dozen riders on board. They had little choice; it was the law. So, there the riders sat, feet resting on arms lockers and break-in equipment, riding back to Havana with two-thirds of the team intending to level the center of the city within the next week.

The riders safely deposited near the city center, Joe, Johnny, Pete, and Orlando parked the truck in the space behind their shabby quarters. Once the sun set and darkness concealed their actions, they brought into the clubhouse two assault rifles, two pump-action shotguns, six explosive grenades and six stun grenades, and the three remaining nine-millimeter side arms. These were placed under one of the cots and covered with a folded tarpaulin. Under the other cot went the sledgehammers, chisels, and picks.

Three tasks remained: retrieval of the treasure; arming of the treasure; positioning of the treasure. Task number one would be carried out on the night of the twenty-sixth. Dankevich would arrive at the clubhouse on that same day. He would carry out task number two. While he was working his magic on the treasure, bringing it to problematic life after almost four decades, Pete, Orlando, and perhaps one or two others would reconnoiter the Martí tower at the Revolutionary Plaza, preparing for the most important task, number three: positioning the treasure on the day before the New Year's celebration of the fortieth anniversary of the revolution.

31 On the flight from Chicago through Houston to Cancún, McLemore confronted a fact he had up to now resisted: What had started out for him as an escape from the tedium of teaching had become a search for the deeper meaning of the Cold War and was becoming an even more emotional hunt, with a life of its own, for the secret of his father's life—and death. Jack McLemore and much of his generation had plunged into the Cold War full of patriotism and idealism. But that ideological struggle, carried out by cynical means in the back alleys of the world, had betrayed their ideals—their profound beliefs in the therapeutic value of democracy—and turned them instead into fatalists. Had his father's life and death become a microcosm for the corruption of the ideal of democracy?

Isakov's father had come to Cuba with some kind of vague belief in self-determination for the Cuban people. The Cuban people had overthrown their corrupt Yanqui oppressors, according to the Soviet doctrine of the day, and freely chosen a socialist future. But how could Khrushchev have convinced himself that nuclear missiles with a 1,500-mile range were purely for the defense of Cuba? And then, by reversing himself in his compromise with Kennedy, Khrushchev had disillusioned his own military and left them bitter and cynical. Could Kennedy have believed that nuclear missiles on the Soviet border with Turkey would not invite an equiv-

alent response from the new Soviet nuclear power anxious to flex its
muscles? From the clear heights of hindsight, McLemore thought it painfully obvious that Cuba inevitably would become the Soviet balance-of-
power base in the Western Hemisphere.

Was there anything to be learned from these madnesses, miscalculations, and misinterpretations? Based upon the bizarre plot now unfolding,
apparently nothing, McLemore thought. Cuba was the relic of a forgotten
quarrel. Virtually everyone old enough to remember its purpose was either
dying or losing memory of what it was about. The United States' singular
quarrel with Cuba was one that had outlived any real meaning it may ever
have had. Yet, here were grown men and women, the heirs of the original
dispute, seeking to kill one another—for what? Ownership? Power? Title?
It certainly couldn't be belief. The U.S. had long since recognized many
too many Communist governments to make that stick.

Once in his room at the Santa Isabel, McLemore rang the number in
Trinidad's office. They quickly arranged a dinner and agreed also to a
meeting the next morning with Suarez. He thought it interesting that she
had not invited her boss to dinner. He remembered the way to her apartment in Vedado and dutifully appeared at her door at eight-thirty that
evening, complete with bottles of wine, flowers, and scented soaps and
toiletries, which were practically impossible for Cuban women to find.
Once inside, he found Trinidad's elderly mother, dressed in black. Trinidad greeted him with a warm kiss on both cheeks.

"Mi madre, Maria," she said.

"Buenas noches, señora," McLemore said as he crossed the small room
to shake her hand. He noticed she had very recently been weeping.

"Profesor, I thought if you do not mind, my mother should join us. We
have had sadness here recently," Trinidad explained.

McLemore said, "I am very sorry. Was it something unexpected?"

"My sister, in Miami," Trinidad offered. "I regret to tell you that she
encountered a very bad accident. We are trying to find out the details.
But she was somehow killed."

"I am truly sorry," he said. "Please express my sincere regrets to your
mother."

Sitting next to her grieving parent, Trinidad spoke softly in Spanish.

"Is there anything I can do to help?" he continued.

Trinidad said, "We may need your help in getting some information.
We have tried through our Interest offices in Washington and New York,

but it has not been successful. It seems she was attacked on the streets of Miami at night, and someone killed her. About ten days ago. They just found her lying in some bushes. That is all we can find out from the Miami police." She moved toward the kitchen and said quietly to McLemore as she passed, "I will explain more later."

McLemore expressed more words of sympathy to Señora Santiago with Trinidad interpreting from the nearby kitchen. Feeling himself at home in this place, McLemore opened the wine and gave glasses to the two women. *"Con mucha pena,"* he offered as a toast. With much sadness.

Trinidad moved the conversation away from the recent tragedy as she concluded dinner preparations. She explained to her mother McLemore's mission in Cuba, alluded to the fact that his grandmother had been Cuban—which elicited considerable interest from Señora Santiago—and suggested that he might be interested in her reflections on the crisis times of 1961 and 1962.

The elderly lady closed her eyes, as if struggling to recapture an elusive dream. McLemore thought how much like his own grandmother she looked. Her narrow face, distinguished by high cheekbones and piercing brown eyes, was framed by silver hair pulled back from her face into a twist and held there by a long ornamented silver pin. A lifetime of struggle and tragedy had produced a striking mask of dignity. She began to speak slowly and softly, with Trinidad interpreting as she brought dishes to the table. The story unfolded between occasional sips of wine.

"My husband, a teacher, was exempted from military service due to poor eyesight, but like virtually all men who could walk, he was incorporated into one of the local militias in late 1960 against the day when the inevitable Yanqui invasion would occur," she began. "They knew it would come," she said, "but they did not know if it would only be the exile Cubans or also the U.S. military. Information was constantly coming to us of mysterious training bases in Florida and throughout the Caribbean. As the crisis mounted in the spring of '61, my husband's militia was called out and sent to reinforce regular army units guarding one of many southern beaches."

As she sipped wine, McLemore asked through Trinidad, "Did you and your husband have much contact with the Soviet forces that came the following fall?"

"Very little," she responded. "We would see them occasionally in the streets, with their funny bright shirts"—she smiled to recall the picture—

"and sometimes outside the city their caravans of trucks and jeeps would pass heading for some secret installation. Mostly," she said, "they stayed to themselves and, except for occasional rowdy outbursts or drunken parties, pretty much behaved."

Her head lowered. "Then," she said, "came the invasion in April 1961. It came at the Playa Girón in Matanzas province. Fate had put my husband's militia unit near there. When the attack came, they had been summoned there quickly as reinforcements. The fighting went on for two or three days. Some of the invaders made their way inland into underbrush and swamps. They were scattered about, and it was hard to know who was who. The Cuban commanders, believing that successful control of the beachhead by the attackers would lead to an even greater assault, possibly with U.S. forces, threw all their men into the desperate effort to kill or capture every last invader to prevent them from coalescing and establishing a solid foothold on the island."

Weeping softly now as she told the story, weeping for the nearsighted, quiet-mannered schoolteacher husband gone these thirty-seven years, she continued. "His unit plunged into the thickets, not knowing where they were going or what kind of enemy they were looking for. There was random shooting everywhere. No one knew who was on which side. Then suddenly my husband fell. He lost his glasses and could not tell where he was. He wandered near the hiding place of some of the invaders. Firing broke out. To this day, they do not know whether he was killed by the invaders or by his own forces who were shooting at every moving thing. This was all told to me," she said, "by one of my husband's closest friends, a boyhood friend who had also been our neighbor and in the same militia. This friend brought Severro's body back to Havana. He was only thirty-eight years old. Our Trinidad had just been born at that time and her sister was three." With the mention of the sister, both Trinidad and her mother embraced and wept.

Respecting their fresh grief, McLemore busied himself in the kitchen, opening more wine. Presently, Trinidad brought him out to sit with her mother, and dinner was served. McLemore asked Señora Santiago, "If Cuba remains Communist, can there still be good relations with the United States?"

In her soft, low, rhythmic Spanish, she replied, "It must be. The gods of geography have made us neighbors. Therefore, we must be friends. We do not believe in socialism so much," she said, "as we believe in owning our own destiny. We will not be a colony anymore, of anyone. There will be a debate, after Castro, about the socialist system for us. But there is no debate about belonging to ourselves. As we would not be Russians, so we would also not be Yanquis. Perhaps our fate is always to be poor. But we can be poor with dignity. If we belong to someone else, we cannot have dignity even if we are rich."

"Can you ever make peace with your fellow Cubans in the States?" McLemore asked.

She said, "It is up to them, not us. We wish only to be left alone and treated with respect like other people. They will never get this land back by terrorism. They should talk to us, not try to kill us."

She asked to know about McLemore's research beyond what Trinidad had already told her. He described his effort to understand the period after the missile crisis when the Soviets had withdrawn their troops and missiles. Then, with coaxing from Trinidad, he repeated John Prescott's memory of his father's final adventure in Cuba during the crisis period.

"Even though we find ourselves on different sides," she mused, "I am sure he was doing his duty and serving his country and trying to prevent harm to you. Just as Severro was doing."

Trinidad could see her mother fading with the evening. She gave her a kiss good-bye and, to his own surprise, McLemore found himself doing likewise. She gripped his hand and said, "Do your duty also, *profesor*."

Trinidad and McLemore walked through the old city to the docks on the western side of the harbor. They took a ferry across to the community of Casablanca on the eastern side and climbed the steep hillside above. There the giant Christ figure, just east of the Fortaleza de San Carlos de Cabaña, looked west across the harbor. The night was clear but unseasonably cool. They sat on a stone bench in the small park beneath the towering Jesus, and Trinidad settled comfortably into McLemore's arms. It seemed natural, as if they had been doing this for a long time.

Gradually, under the pressure of imminent catastrophe, the intimate welding by an intense common purpose, and finally by shared loneliness, McLemore and Trinidad had come to sense barriers of politics, culture, and distance crumbling. Whereas at first McLemore had been intrigued but indifferent, Trinidad bore a lifetime of resentment—resentment toward *Tio Sam* who had dominated or sought to dominate her people one way or the other for a century and toward the vanguard of Yanquis once more filtering back to use Cuba as a giant nightclub and house of prostitution. She hated most the idea of Cuba as a prostitute—socially or politically. McLemore had become a revelation for her, a Yanqui who respected her and her country, a Yanqui searching for a painful personal and historic truth, a man—a human—who genuinely cared what happened to her and to her people. She looked up, met his lips, and they kissed with little sense of present place or time.

As they crossed the harbor on the ten-minute ferry ride moments before, Trinidad related the details of her sister's death.

"She worked for our government," she said, the universal euphemism for spying. "She helped follow the militant exile groups. She was very good at it. She did it for almost twenty years. They caught her, I am sure. We have gotten some reports that she was found a few blocks away from a health club belonging to a member of the organization that concerns us the most now—the group that calls itself Bravo. Several of Juanita's colleagues in Miami are trying to get more information. They are trying to locate members of this group, but they cannot be found anywhere. We believe she was following them and they caught her and killed her. They broke her neck."

"You had not mentioned her to me before," McLemore said.

She had smiled apologetically. "I could not. Her life was always in danger. It would be enough, if someone knew that I was . . . that I was engaged in security work, and that she was my sister. This alone could have destroyed her. She was never afraid. She was very brave." Trinidad turned her face away in the darkness. He heard her say, "She was doing her duty. It was important. There are things that must be found out. I say with great respect that your father would have understood her mission completely."

McLemore hesitated. "Where is this Bravo group now?"

"We don't know. They have disappeared." She turned to him as they approached the other side of the harbor. "We think they may be coming here. We are watching all the airports and marinas. We have descriptions. Juanita took their pictures. She knew no fear."

"What will happen if the Bravos come here?" McLemore asked.

She said, "I hope they try. Here or there, I intend to avenge Juanita. Here is easier."

McLemore had no doubt she meant it.

*   *   *

Then they were at the top of the hill, and she was in his arms. She embraced him as if he had suddenly and unexpectedly returned from exile. He held her as if tomorrow exile might be forced upon him. They kissed, naturally and repeatedly, and did not want reality—a prospective brutal and dangerous reality—to intrude.

She felt him shake with some emotion. She pulled back and looked at him. He was smiling. "I was thinking of the first time we met . . . how angry you were."

"It is true." She smiled. "I thought I had better things to do than take a boring Yanqui professor around to old military bases. I did not know he would turn out to be not so boring after all."

McLemore put his hands to the side of her face, surprised at the softness of her skin. "You did intend to recruit me, though. *Es verdad?*"

She looked shocked. "Recruit you? For what? What does a professor know . . . about anything?"

"You might be surprised what a professor knows . . . about a lot of things." He poked his fingers into her sides, and she giggled helplessly.

"No! No! Don't! I can't stand it!"

McLemore held her again and they stood up still in each other's arms. "Starting tomorrow, I'll show you what I know. And then we'll decide what to do about it."

The following morning he was met at the main entrance of the Interior Ministry and escorted to Lazaro Suarez's office, where Trinidad waited. She greeted him cordially but not warmly, he noted, and he was suddenly jealous of her professional relationship with Suarez. Suarez was equally cordial and genuinely seemed pleased to see him again after his six-week absence.

McLemore got down to business immediately. "Our side is watching the Russian. We have confirmed that his name is Viktor Leonidovich Isakov, almost certainly the son of the late Colonel Leonid Sestanovich Isakov, a senior commander in the Soviet Strategic Rocket Forces with a specialization in the management and targeting of nuclear warheads. The senior Isakov served in the Soviet Expeditionary Forces here in Cuba from early September until early January 1962. He remained in the Soviet Army until his retirement in 1975. He died in Ekaterinburg in 1987. He was a hard-liner, and our people think Gorbachev gave him a heart attack."

Suarez said, "Is it simply a coincidence that his father served here and that this Isakov is selling weapons?"

"Yes and no," McLemore said. "It is almost certain that he has been using a network of his father's old friends in the Russian Ministry of Defense to acquire his inventory . . . the stuff he sells. Those connections have little to do with his father's brief service here. The military establishment in Russia is a sieve. If there's a profit in it, it's out the door. Place your order and name your terms."

Trinidad said, "Then what is the 'no'?"

"It is not coincidental in this sense," McLemore said. "There is a very good chance, as you know, that Isakov has done a deal with some Cuban Americans. If so, then it could well directly relate to his father's activities in the fall of 1962." McLemore added, "When I left here six weeks ago, I agreed to try to find out what I could about the connection between Isakov and the Cuban Americans, the so-called Bravos. I also said I would try to find out what Isakov may have sold them. The only way I knew how to do that was to cooperate also with the people on our side who are in the same business you are. Just so you understand the deal, in exchange for giving me information on what they know, they expect me to find out what you know. For example, what you know about this Bravo group, who they are, and where they are."

"It may be too late," Suarez said. "They've dropped out of sight in Miami and they may be on their way down here."

"Do you have any more information on what they might have bought from Isakov?" McLemore asked.

"We had one of our best people trying to find that out," Suarez said, glancing at Trinidad. "Tragically, she was killed. We think she was discovering the secret, and they discovered her."

McLemore said, "If that's the case, then there is no question these guys are serious."

"No question," Suarez said. "What success has your side had at finding the Russian . . . Isakov?"

McLemore hesitated. This was the moment of truth. "They've found him. He was in the Washington area when I left the States yesterday. He's hiding. Our people think the Bravo group tried to kill him, too."

"If they are in partnership," Trinidad asked, "why would they do that?"

McLemore said, "A couple of reasons. They probably concluded that he is unstable—and there is some evidence of that, drinking, for example—

and they don't need him anymore. Apparently they have what they bought, or they know where to get it, and they don't want him talking. It makes some sense."

Suarez said, "We have some reports that the Bravo group has been getting financing from the Mafia. We think that they have a deal to give casino rights back to the Mafia, in exchange for a bankroll, if they are successful at overthrowing our government."

"That's pretty far-fetched," McLemore said.

Trinidad responded, "Not so extraordinary. If these Bravo people are descendants of the *batistianas*, then their ties with the Mafia go back to those days. We know for sure that the Mafia wants to come back here. They made a lot of money here . . . gambling, hotels, prostitution."

"So they might finance an outfit like Bravo—including laying out a fortune for exotic weapons—with the understanding that they get their Cuban operations back?" McLemore asked.

"Exactly," Suarez said. "The question is, what kind of weapons? We have to assume that these people intend to do something more than kill a large number of our citizens with assault weapons and grenades. We would surely catch them or kill them. Very little damage would have been done. Despite the bloodshed, our government and our society would survive. They might try to assassinate our leaders. But people have been trying to do that for more than forty years. Our best theory is some kind of standoff rocket attack, where they would position themselves at some distance and fire some rockets and kill a large number of people, maybe even one or two thousand, depending on the munitions."

McLemore said, "Señor Suarez, do you know who built the bunkers at Bejucal where the Soviets kept the warheads for their rockets?"

Lazaro and Trinidad looked nonplussed. "You mean where we went in September?" Trinidad asked. "That place was built a long time ago."

McLemore said, "Let me ask your help. Check with the military— Ministry of Defense—whatever. See if there are any records—particularly construction drawings or plans. And do it as fast as you can."

Suarez made a note on a desk pad. "What can that have to do with our problem? It was so long ago. There is nothing there. Isn't it so, Trinidad? You were there . . . you saw."

McLemore put his hands up. "It's just an idea. Something I want to look at. Let's do this. See if you can find the records for the bunker. Then

I'd like to go back down there in the next day or two . . . whenever it can be arranged."

McLemore stood to go, shook hands, and said to Trinidad that he would wait to hear from her. Sooner rather than later, he hoped.

When McLemore had left the office, Suarez said, "What is he thinking about? Do you have any idea?" He was beginning to speculate quietly about the Trinidad-McLemore relationship, but he intended to subdue the speculation at least for the next week.

"He has a theory. It's impossible to know what it is. Maybe he thinks the Bravo group intends to store something in the bunker. I was with him when we saw it two months ago. It was abandoned and empty. There was nothing there."

▪ ▪ ▪

Dankevich had never seen his boss in such a rage. And he had seen some pretty good rages. Isakov stormed and shouted, threw things and cursed. Dankevich considered sending for help from the nearby encampment. The proprietors of the small family restaurant outside Artemisa, where the Soviet officers gathered two or three nights a week—certainly on weekends—for Cuban food rather than Soviet military rations, were terrified. This was now late November, and the Soviet military, under direct orders from the Kremlin, was packing up and leaving Cuba. Since the announcement of the agreement between the Soviet Union and the United States ending the missile crisis, these Saturday night performances were becoming routine. As before, it would cost somebody a lot of pesos to put this place back into shape. And Dankevich thought he knew who that would be. But the first order of business was to contain the madman.

"Goddammit to hell, Dankevich, I want to kill those fuckers! I want to kill them! They cannot humiliate our army this way. We work too goddamn hard. We sacrifice too much. We give our families nothing. And the fucking Politburo . . . sitting on their fat asses in the fucking Kremlin . . . shit all over us!"

Thank God, the other officers had gone, Dankevich thought as he rescued a rum bottle before it was launched against the back wall. Surely the unit commissar would have heard and put Isakov on report. Bad report. This kind of talk led to an army hearing, possibly a Ministry review, and certain demotion if not court-martial. You can't talk that way about the government of the Union of Soviet Socialist Republics . . . certainly not the very Politburo itself.

"They cannot do it. They cannot send us over here to be eaten by flies and bugs . . . to roast in the goddamn sun . . . to slog around in this goddamn mud, trying to get these fucking missiles ready, maybe get killed by the U.S. missiles or even worse the marines . . . what for . . . to protect our comrade Cubans who could give a fuck . . . all they want is some rum and some good times . . . dancing and fucking . . . and what do they care anyway. I tell you, Dankevich . . . this is too much . . . it's the last straw on the back of a camel. Enough for me, I tell you. They can have their goddamn Cold War . . . hot war . . . any fucking war. I've had it!" A rum bottle, half full, exploded against the back kitchen wall, just over the heads of the cowering Cuban family. In the corner, Isakov's now-regular girlfriend slept through it all. She was out for the count. Wouldn't remember a thing. The war of the cantina . . . the war between Isakov and the Politburo. How could you conceivably sleep through a war like that?

Thank God we put the side arms away, Dankevich thought. Those were house rules, though not Soviet Army rules. The house hadn't actually set the rules. Dankevich had. He had because he had refereed similar bouts . . . Isakov against the Turks . . . Isakov against the Chinese . . . Isakov against the Poles . . . the list went on. Oddly enough, Dankevich thought, as he set a fallen chair right, never Isakov against the Americans. Isakov had respect for the Americans, especially the marines. In a moment of more sentimental drunkenness, Isakov had once confessed that he would like to be a colonel in the United States Marine Corps. Behaving this way, he might make it.

Isakov paused for breath and possibly to rest his throwing arm. Dankevich respectfully suggested they sit down for a moment. He himself was breathless from ducking and dodging. Isakov's chest heaved. Sweat drenched his head and shirt. His head hung like a great bull preparing for the final lunge.

"It's orders, Colonel. We must obey. Nothing we can do. It's politics, you know." With that last comment, Dankevich felt he might have gone too far. Isakov groaned. "You know what I think, Colonel? I think we'll be sent back down here . . . soon. The Americans will violate the agreement, and the Cubans will want us back."

"Fucking nonsense, Dankevich. You don't know politics . . . or the Cu-

bans . . . for shit," Isakov muttered sloppily. "These people will never have us back down here. We've disgraced ourselves. We're pussycats. Look at those people back there. They're laughing at us!" Suddenly the rage was back. "You sons of bitches laugh at the Red Army, I'm coming back here tonight and blow this shithole off the face of the fucking earth!" In the back, the father got his wife and son out the back door but stayed to try to salvage anything he could. Isakov sank back down.

Looking ostentatiously at his watch, Dankevich calculated the risk of trying to call it an evening. He glanced around. Aside from chairs, there was very little left to throw. And Isakov was, at least momentarily, drained. Dankevich started to restore order to the three tables and dozen chairs. He thought about getting a frayed cornstalk broom for the glass but then thought better of it. He could pay for that.

Isakov finally looked up at him, his eyes narrow and fiery red. Hell to pay tomorrow. "I'll tell you something, Dankevich. I'll tell you something. That cowardly shit-ass Khrushchev will lose his job . . . and hopefully his head . . . over this. And I'll tell you something else. You must never tell. If you do, I swear I will kill you." His voice was low and eerily calm. "I will get even. I will find a way to avenge our army. Whatever it costs, I will do it. Do not forget. It is my oath. May God strike me dead if I am lying." He stood up and staggered into Dankevich's face. "I will get even." It was a promise delivered with a hiss.

∎ ∎ ∎

32 The ancient truck hissed and steamed as it rolled toward Bejucal. Manny sat in the cab with Orlando, whose accent and demeanor were the most "Cuban" of the group. On the night of the twenty-sixth of December, Bravo was out to reconnoiter the abandoned bunker at the Bejucal barracks of the Cuban Army. In the back with Pete, Johnny, and Joe were the tools necessary to break into the bunker—if they got lucky. Otherwise, armed with logistical knowledge and a tactical plan, they would carry out the main mission the following evening.

At noon that day Manny and Tony had gone to the hotel where former Lieutenant Colonel Dankevich was staying, as originally agreed with Isaacs. Manny stood watch in the corner of the lobby below to note if anyone followed Tony and Dankevich out of the hotel. Tony presented himself at Dankevich's door and identified himself as "Señor Cruz," the guide from Cubatur. The elderly man seemed relieved to have been found by friendly faces and was surprisingly spry from his daylong rest after the long flight from Moscow. They exited the hotel—unaccompanied, Manny noted—and proceeded toward the old city, where Manny joined them. They gave Dankevich a short tour of the colorful Plaza de la Catedral and other touristic sites, then gave him lunch, and in the late afternoon took him to the clubhouse.

Over lunch they explained the plan. The missile crisis relic would be recovered within the next day or two. Dankevich would make the clubhouse his home for the following week. He would be expected to make the device operational as quickly as possible. He would be paid, and then they would arrange for him to meet some old friends down in Pinar del Río, Cuban acquaintances from the old days in '62. He seemed delighted by the idea and even showed them, from his small plastic carry-on bag, what appeared to be watchmaker's tools. These, he explained, together with several rolls of fine wire he also had with him, were all that he needed to carry out his job. He had been practicing, he assured them, with mock-up models and blueprints from the old days, and was looking forward to the challenge. His eyes twinkled, and Tony noted with great satisfaction, his hands, as they held his coffee, were as solid as Gibraltar.

Manny assured him that modern, sophisticated timers were also being provided for him and that, after he had checked and restored the original wiring on the device, he would be expected to install the timer as well. Dankevich assured them he understood this to be part of the job. He thanked them profusely for the opportunity to be useful. It had been so long since he'd had a real purpose. Manny then, after administering a solemn oath of secrecy, undertook to bring him inside the operation.

It was a top secret, highly classified operation being undertaken by Cuban national security services with some friends from outside whose identity could not be disclosed. There had been serious rumors that the United States might undertake to carry out a lightning raid on Cuba on the occasion of the celebration of the fortieth anniversary of the revolution. Friends of Cuba, including some loyal former Soviet military and security officers, were pledged to prevent this from happening. They were going to arm this device and place it in a helicopter, since they had no launcher. If an invasion force appeared on military radar, there would be sufficient warning time to fly the device to the beach designated for the initial assault. It would be used to wipe out the assault and thus deter the invasion. The United States would not know how many more of these devices there were or where they were located. This operation was being carried out, Manny explained in an intimate voice, by a very small, secret, loyal group of Cuban patriots and friends of Cuba. Even many senior government officials were unaware, he continued, because there were surely CIA agents inside the Cuban government who would immediately warn the United States, which in turn would dispatch clandestine agents to destroy the device and defeat the plan.

Throughout the narration of this byzantine fiction, old Dankevich nodded solemnly, nodded with understanding, appreciation, and sympathy. He counted himself honored, he said, to be given such a vital job in this dangerous and critical defense of his old friends, the Cuban people. It would be the highlight of his remaining days and would redeem the sacrifice he and other loyal Soviet socialists had made on behalf of their Cuban comrades. He was prepared, he assured them, to add any additional sacrifices required—including being confined to the cramped headquarters of this patriotic group—to carry out this crucial task in the defense of his friends the Cubans.

There he sat, with Tony as his minder, in the gloom of the unlit clubhouse awaiting the return of the recovery squad.

The Bravo team meanwhile relocated the hiding place just off the Bejucal road used by Manny and Tony on their previous scouting expedition and ditched the truck with its nose pointed outward for a quick escape. The low-hanging palm leaves on the surrounding trees, augmented by loose leaves piled on the hood, completely concealed the old vehicle. Each man carried a break-in tool over his shoulder and had a small, high-intensity miner's light strapped on his black stocking cap. They all wore black, lightweight trousers and shirts and had blackened their faces. They proceeded the quarter mile up the road at ten-yard intervals until the gates of the military post were in sight. They crossed the road and collected twenty yards into the brush. They had gone over the drawings of the place repeatedly and knew with some precision how to proceed. They were close enough now so that every movement was carried out with hand signals. Manny led and Pete brought up the rear. The eastern side fence of the long rectangular installation was to their right as they proceeded down it, keeping a distance of about thirty yards, until they came to the south-eastern corner of the post. They squatted down in the thick brush and reviewed the next move, entry into the base. Pete the athlete went first. He held down the top wire of the fence and strong-armed the others over the top. Soft Orlando was last and worst, ripping trousers and drawing blood. Upon returning to Miami, he would need a tetanus shot, big time.

They were inside. Manny took the lead again and hand-signaled them around the last barracks building. It was dark and seemed likely to be an administration building. Looking north up the double row of buildings divided by the central road, there were random lights in some of the buildings, with the greatest concentration of light and activity near the front gate 200 to 250 yards northward. They moved quickly in a low crouch to the raised long dome of the bunker some fifty feet away. As before, when Manny and Tony were almost caught, the central door on the west side stood partly ajar. Clearly nothing of value was believed to be inside. It was unguarded and largely abandoned, the temporary tomb of long-forgotten armaments, relics of an ancient quarrel.

One by one the men entered. Joe was left to watch, only his head and shoulders peering around the door, while the others took the dozen steps down and inside. Once they were all inside, Manny turned on his head-lamp and waved the men to follow him to the north end of the hundred-foot-long bunker. They proceeded along the long west-wall corridor, off which were the series of storage rooms in which the warheads had been kept. They came to the north wall and huddled.

Unfolding the thin, cracked, hand-drawn map provided to Victor Isaacs by his father, Manny said in a low voice, "Now look. You see if you shift this map around so that the top points north—like this—there is a small space, about the size of one of these rooms, where he put the X. But there is nothing here. Which means that they were put in the last room of the original bunker, and then the son of a bitch sealed it off so that everybody would think this"—he smacked the concrete wall with the flat of his hand—"was the original end wall." They all hunched over the map, one or two other lights now on, to study the paper and consider Manny's theory. "The only way to really find out, before we break in, is to pace off the outside dimensions of the bunker . . . here it says a hundred feet . . . and then pace off the inside corridor. I'll bet the inside is about four to six feet shorter."

Johnny said, "We can't pace it off. They might see us." He was noted for stating the obvious.

"Of course," Manny said. "So, we have to crack this wall."

Pete waved them all back. They retreated ten or twelve feet. He took a chisel out of a utility pocket on the side of his black combat pants and held a sledgehammer by the throat. He began to drive the chisel into the wall with strokes of the hammerhead as easily as putting a nail into a wall. Manny said, "Shhhh!" He eased the stroke a bit, but the noise of metal on metal echoed up and down the bunker. Joe put his head down below and said, "Shhhh!" Pete brought out a thick handkerchief and wrapped it around the head of the chisel. He pounded again, the noise somewhat muffled. At first the chisel bounced off the wall without a dent. After about two dozen strokes, however, he penetrated the wall, chips of plaster flaked away, and an interior core of porous material was revealed. The men quickly gathered around.

Pete said, "It's cinder block. We can be in there in half an hour, an hour. We can have the whole wall down in less than two hours."

"But it'll make a racket. Right?" Johnny said.

Pete rolled his eyes. "It'll make a racket. We can soften it somewhat. Close the outside door. Muffle the hammers. But somebody nearby would feel some vibrations."

Joe stuck his head down again and hissed, "There's movement up at the gate. Looks like jeep headlights."

Manny looked at his watch. "Probably the regular patrol. The one that almost caught us last time. Get Joe down here. They may come down this road."

Orlando headed for the door and almost ran into Joe coming down. "Turn off the lights," he said urgently. "They're headed this way."

The place was immediately dark. Manny hissed, "Grab the tools, in case we have to break out of here fast." He and Pete were carrying the nine-millimeters, for emergencies. This could be one. Manny said, "If we have to go fast, remember to scatter and then get back to the truck. If the truck is gone when you get there, lie low until morning, and then hitch back to town." He didn't explain how to account for the minstrel makeup.

They now heard the rattling jeep engine and could see headlights approaching through the half-open door. Thank God they had not closed it. The jeep passed by and went the final thirty yards to the end of the road. It backed and turned, the engine roaring, a rookie on the clutch. The vehicle paused momentarily outside the bunker, and a flashlight swept through the doorway. Then the light and the jeep moved on up the road, through the gate, and out onto the town road to make its rounds. Manny and Pete returned the nines to their respective shoulder holsters.

Manny switched on his headlamp. "Let's go. We know what we have to do and how to do it. I'm sure there's a chamber in there and I'm sure the device is there. We'll come back late tomorrow night and we'll crack it. On the way out, let's see if we can get the truck down the next field. If so, that'll help a lot getting the gizmo out of here."

Pete leading the way again, the five men made their way back to and over the fence. Dogs now barked in the distance. Orlando required a boost from behind by Manny. Then they were over and into the adjoining field. They went due east almost fifty yards, and on Manny's command spread out across a ten-yard span. They walked north through the cane growth, which reached up to their shoulders. The growth was uneven. Excess moisture and subsurface rocks had left bare spots in the field. It was possible to bring the truck at least part of the way into the field. They were back at the truck and ready to roll when lights came over a slight rise. It was the patrol jeep returning. Manny waved the others back into the roadside foliage and noted the time. It had taken about a half hour for half the patrol to be completed. The jeep proceeded past the gate, and after a couple of minutes, the men cleared the truck, loaded up, and headed back to Havana.

At approximately the time they arrived at the clubhouse, McLemore was returning to his hotel after a stroll with Trinidad along the Malecón. She had rendezvoused after a briefing she had attended at the Ministry of the Interior involving late reports on intensified airport and marina security, tourist surveillance, local revolutionary vigilante committee reports, and, to her dismay, fragmentary intelligence from Miami regarding her sister's death. He noticed immediately her somber tone.

"How did it go?" he asked, taking her hand.

She walked a ways before talking. "It is difficult. Because of Juanita, and my mother, who is destroyed by this. But also because we cannot find the Bravo members in Miami, and there are no reports of them down here. They cannot simply have disappeared—all six, maybe more." She shook her dark hair. "I have a very bad feeling. I feel they are already here. If they are intelligent enough to penetrate our extra security, they are surely intelligent enough to carry out some terrible scheme. I feel we must find out something in the next day or two, or some people will die. I know it." She spoke with a clairvoyance that left little doubt.

He put an arm around her waist as he walked on the sea side, trying to protect her from the mist of the crashing waves. "We are as smart as they are. We'll stop them."

She suddenly remembered. "Lazaro said he would get the drawing from the Bejucal post tomorrow afternoon. They have been found in a military archive outside of town. They will be delivered tomorrow. I will call and you can meet us at the Ministry."

McLemore had a strange thought. "What is the name of Señor Suarez's boss?"

She looked at him, puzzled. "It is Colonel Nuñez. Why do you wish to know?"

"Nuñez," he said. His smile was bitter. "I have to make a strange request. Please do not tell anyone—especially Nuñez—about my interest in Bejucal. For the time being, I'd like to keep this among you, Lazaro, and me."

Before kissing him good night, she looked into his eyes and said, "Do not worry. Lazaro and I, we do not trust Nuñez either."

She quickly caught a late bus back to Vedado and McLemore returned to the Santa Isabel. He was walking diagonally across the darkened Plaza de Armas when a voice said, "Professor McLemore, it is a pleasure to have you back." The low, hollow voice resonated distinctively.

"If you hadn't found me by tonight, I was coming to look for you tomorrow," he responded. He looked around and saw the spectral figure of John Prescott sitting on a bench beneath a giant dark tree. He joined him on the bench.

They shook hands and exchanged greetings. Prescott said, "Have you found what you have been looking for?"

"Not yet," McLemore replied quickly, "but I'm getting close. I need to find one other thing first. Then I'll be home."

"Home," Prescott said quietly, "that's what we're all looking for. Strange it should be so hard to find, isn't it."

McLemore said, "There is going to be some kind of disaster here, unless I can find what I'm looking for. A bunch of crazy Cuban exiles are on their way here—may actually be here—to do something really mad on New Year's Day. There's some kind of a plot—a big one. I may have stumbled onto a key, maybe *the* key. Problem is, I don't know who to trust—on their side or ours. I guess it comes down to this: I feel a lot more need to help these people here than I do the people my father used to work for." He turned on the bench to face Prescott in the dark. He spoke lowly and quickly. "The CIA, the ones who sent my father down here, now claims it simply wants to help avoid a disaster that may have its roots in the U.S. It's like they're concerned about a public relations problem. But I'll tell you something. Down deep I wonder whether some of them, some of the hard-liners, might not actually like to see this government destroyed, even if it costs several hundred thousand lives. Small price to pay to get rid of Castro and communism in the Western Hemisphere . . . one fell swoop. A big thorn out of our side. And we sort through the rubble and put our guys in power. Right back where we were in the 1950s. And the Cuban people will be worse off than they even are today."

"You've fallen in love," Prescott said.

"What?"

"In love. With Cuba. Happened to me too when I first came down. Fell in love. It was a problem. I had taken the vows. And Cuba is a woman."

McLemore was stunned. Prescott had looked inside his heart. "Yes," he said. "I have fallen in love. And Cuba is a woman. Her name is Trinidad."

"I know," Prescott said. "I've seen her . . . know who she is. She works at the Ministry of Foreign Affairs, but she really is Cuban intelligence."

McLemore was stunned again. "You've seen her? How do you know where she works?"

"I've seen her with you. Several times. She fell in love with you right away. You could tell by how angry she used to get. It's a Cuban thing. The first thing that happens when they fall in love is they get angry. Pretty Latin, don't you think?"

Despite himself, McLemore laughed. "You're a priest, father. You're not supposed to know these things."

"I was a man before I was a priest. And when I became a priest, I didn't quit being a man."

"What do I do?" McLemore said. "I don't mean about her. I mean about this . . . crisis. I think I've got some information that's important. The CIA expects me to give it to them. I could go see Ramsay tomorrow and tell him what I think. But he's a loose cannon. God knows what he might do. If he is connected with some cabal to overthrow Castro, he might just sit on it and let the catastrophe occur. The more I think about it, the more I think all the Cold War chickens are coming home to roost in a few days." The men were silent as Prescott thought. Then McLemore said, "I don't want anything to happen to this woman. She has become the only country I have."

McLemore thought he could see Prescott's long white head bobbing up and down in the darkness. Then the old priest said, "People adopt a faith, even a political faith, out of hope and out of desperation. Cuba never had a chance at justice or freedom. Its present fate was sealed by centuries of plunder, occupation, domination, greed, corruption, and neglect. Its history is a tribute to the worst in man and, on a few occasions, the best in man. It has produced villains and heroes, cutthroats and martyrs. Fidel Castro is a rebuke to the United States. We helped produce him by our neglect. We permitted the conditions to exist that were almost guaranteed to bring him about. We're punishing the Cuban people for a condition we helped create. Who gave us the right to tell people what they can believe or who they can follow? Castro said, 'The emperor has no clothes—and he's an ugly naked bastard, besides.' "

"You really think we're that bad?" McLemore asked.

Prescott said, "Not bad, just foolish. What we've done, what we are doing down here, is nothing but folly. And, take it from an old fellow, folly is the one thing that the human race will never run short of. Someday some Shakespeare is going to come along and write the damnedest tragedy . . . or maybe comedy . . . about all this. All it takes is perspective, and we ran out of that a long time ago."

"It's a little late for perspective right now," McLemore said. "For the first time in my life I have to actually do something."

"You'll do the right thing," Prescott said, putting a hand on his shoulder. "You're going to do the right thing . . . just like your father did. There is no doubt you're going to save that woman. And when you do, I want to go with you when you put your father to rest."

■ ■ ■

On Christmas Eve, 1962, Colonel L. S. Isakov stood with a clipboard outside the door of the bunker at the Cuban military base at Bejucal. His deputy, Lieutenant Colonel D. D. Dankevich, was positioned at the Mariel port receiving the trucks his superior was loading at Bejucal. Special lorries, designed to transport Soviet nuclear warheads, had been ordered, and the last was prepared to depart. Four Soviet privates remained behind as Isakov pounded on the hood of the lorry, saluted, and waved it toward the front gate with a straight pointing arm.

Isakov waited five minutes until the base was clear and all was quiet. He signaled to one of the men who stood by awaiting orders on the top steps of the bunker. "Let's go," he said simply.

The private went up the road to a motor pool and presently drove back with a small covered truck. Silently the four men, operating under prearranged instructions, unloaded the cinder blocks and dry mortar mixture. They carried the blocks down to the north end of the bunker where a line had been drawn on the concrete floor from the end of the partial wall separating the last storage room to the west wall. Two of the men set up a small wooden box and poured dry mortar powder and water into the box. Although they worked quickly, the lack of air in the bunker and the thick humidity required them to surface for air every ten minutes.

A six-inch-wide strip of mortar was laid on the floor along the line, and the first row of blocks went down. Mortar was placed on that row and then another row of blocks went down. This process was repeated efficiently several more times, and the wall came almost to eye height.

Isakov peered inside. Two medium-size metal frames sat on the floor of the room. Their contents had been carefully wrapped in two separate thick plastic covers, which in turn were sealed with hot irons, fusing the plastic. The crates were raised from the floor by underlying concrete blocks and in turn were wrapped in heavy tarpaulins tied tightly at the top. The room had been swept and scrubbed almost surgically clean. A thick layer of extra plaster was placed on the floor, ceiling, and walls. Finally, a thick layer of special absorbent mixture had been placed on the floor.

Satisfied with what he saw, Isakov waved for the wall to be finished to the top. He and the men then sat outside the bunker for two hours, drinking cervezas Isakov had one of the men bring from the town, and waiting for the mortar to set up. They talked about their imminent return to the Soviet Union and their hometowns and families. After several beers, one or two of the younger men talked about the girlfriends they would marry. They seemed homesick and anxious to return. Inwardly, Isakov seethed.

As the light in the west began to fade, Isakov waved the men back into the bunker. Two of the men mixed more mortar and two spread it thickly on the cinder blocks now forming the new northern bunker wall. Care had been taken in the daylight to mix a little dust with the mortar to blend it with the older walls built months earlier and now aged. Soon they were finished, and Isakov inspected the work closely. He asked one of the men with a pointing trowel to touch up a spot here, rough up a patch there, add a bit in the corner. He inspected it again. It was near perfect. The bunker was now just under six feet shorter on the inside than it was on the outside. Except the outside was covered with three feet of earth and growing foliage. And the bunker was now empty inside. Someone would have to do very careful calculations to notice that the last storage space had been totally and completely sealed.

In exchange for their discretion and as a reward for their hard work, Colonel Isakov had promised the men a night on the town on him. They cleaned up all the tools and waste mortar, scuffed a little dust on the bunker floor, left the door slightly ajar, and loaded the truck. Isakov drove the truck with two privates beside him in the cab and two in the back bed.

Roughly a mile down the road to Bejucal, Isakov drove the truck off the road and into some thick trees. Had to take a leak bad, he said, complaining with a laugh. All that Cuban beer. More to come. Empty the plumbing for the party to come. The men piled out to join him. The colonel led them back into the trees well away from the road. As they lined up, backs to the road, one of them noticed the freshly dug, very deep trench nearby almost at the same time he heard the safety catch released on the special-issue officer's pistol behind him.

He began to turn toward the peculiar sound as the first bullet entered his brain. Three other bullets, equally well placed, followed quickly. Isakov stripped the identification tags from each of the men and, one by one, rolled them into the trench. Once they were neatly piled in the trench, troubled looks disturbing their young faces, Isakov retrieved a trenching tool from the back of the truck and filled in the remaining three feet of the trench. He scattered the loose earth and covered the tomb with loose palm leaves and dead foliage. Then, placing the identification tags in his shirt pocket, he got in the truck and drove to Mariel.

"Damned enlisted men headed for town as fast as they could after we loaded the last lorry," he said to Dankevich when he arrived. Dankevich handed him a clipboard with the total of Luna warheads tabulated from the lorries as they had been unloaded during the afternoon. Dockside cranes had gently settled each of the containers in the military freighter's hold. Tomorrow it would raise steam for the Soviet Union, the last of the nuclear munitions to leave Cuba, perhaps forever.

Isakov slapped Dankevich on the back. "Come on, Dankevich, let's have a drink. Maybe a dinner. Maybe a señorita—you know, to celebrate the great Soviet victory in Cuba."

Dankevich held him up momentarily. "Colonel, we've still got the same problem we had in October. Look at the inventory. We're shipping back ninety-eight Lunas."

"Right, Dankevich, that's what they sent us. Remember? Ninety-eight. Exactly ninety-eight. Remember, we went over this, you blockhead. Ninety-eight. You got the piece of paper saying they shipped ninety-eight, our dim-witted dummy colleagues in the Defense Ministry." He smacked the clipboard. "Here it says—your own count—we send back ninety-eight. Sounds right to me, Dankevich." He signed his name at the bottom of the page—L. S. Isakov. He put his nose very close to his deputy's nose and said in a very low, very ominous voice, "Sounds right to you, too, doesn't it, Dankevich?"

The deputy nodded and clambered into the battered truck, resigned to ask no questions. He did not intend to lose his life over two disappeared Luna warheads. They were the Cubans' problem now—wherever they were.

Puzzled, Dankevich noticed Isakov's brief return to dockside and his underhand toss of several metal objects into the water.

Must be coins, he thought. For good luck.

■ ■ ■

33 McLemore met Suarez and Trinidad at the Morro Castle on the twenty-seventh of December, the evening following his meeting with Prescott.

"Señor McLemore," Suarez explained, "we are taking a very dangerous step here. We are operating outside our chain of command. Colonel Nuñez is my superior and in charge of overall security for the celebration. We have told him we are dealing with you as an agent for us. But we have not told him of the links you are providing with your intelligence services. He would assume you were an agent for the CIA and, therefore, manipulating us. There are many additional reasons for our decisions. Needless to say, if . . . when . . . he discovers our cooperation, it will go very badly for both of us."

McLemore said, "I understand . . . at least partly. You must decide how best to proceed. But I don't want Trin . . . I don't want either one of you to get in trouble."

Suarez waved his hand away, as if to say, We will deal with this later. He handed McLemore a fragile piece of folded paper. "Here we have found what you requested—the plan for the Bejucal barracks. And you will see," he said as he helped McLemore unfold it, "here is the drawing of the weapons bunker you visited in September."

The three of them were leaning against an interior wall of the seventeenth-century fortress that guarded the entrance to Havana harbor. The ghosts of pirate ships, slavers, and the U.S.S. *Maine* swept back and forth below them. They studied the layout by the eerie rays of a floodlight that illuminated the great stone wall above them. McLemore pointed to the dotted rectangular outline stretching north and south at the south end of the military base. "Here's the bunker. Here's where the Soviets kept the nuclear warheads for the missiles. According to the documents in the Foreign Ministry and Defense Ministry, they were under the command of a Soviet colonel named L. S. Isakov. Now I am going to tell you a story."

They strolled across the courtyard of the fortress toward the seaside wall looking almost directly down on the harbor entrance. McLemore continued, "The documents show that in early October 1962, the Soviet missile forces shipped a hundred nuclear warheads for tactical—battlefield—use.

The long-range missiles were for strikes on the North American continent. The tactical were for battlefield use against an invading force. They could be fired twenty-five or thirty miles or dropped from bombers and had much smaller warheads. A 'small' nuclear warhead can still kill a lot of people, especially if they are crowded close together. At the end of December, the Soviets shipped all the missiles and, theoretically, all the warheads out. But the curious thing is that the documents in your files, which are inventories of incoming and outgoing Soviet weapons, show that ninety-eight warheads were shipped out."

Suarez and Trinidad looked at each other. "Now there are three possibilities," McLemore said. "One is that the count of the incoming warheads was wrong, and only ninety-eight came in. Another is that the count of the outgoing warheads was wrong and a hundred went back out." He paused and looked across the harbor to the spectacular lights of Havana. "The third is that two warheads—for the Lunas—were left behind."

"Left behind, where?" Trinidad said, dumbfounded. "That was ... thirty ... almost thirty-six years ago. Where can you leave two nuclear warheads—even small ones—on an island this size for that long and not have someone find them?"

"It wasn't almost thirty-six years ago. It was *exactly* thirty-six years ago. The Russian freighter with the warheads weighed anchor from Mariel on December 27, 1962!"

"My God!" Trinidad said.

"And I believe I know where the two extra warheads are," McLemore said.

"Where?" Suarez and Trinidad shouted together.

McLemore said, "First let me tell you how I know ... or at least how I think I know. Last week outside Washington I was 'introduced' to the Russian who negotiated the weapons sale with the Bravo group."

Trinidad looked at him wide-eyed.

"I got him drunk. No, the fact is, we got drunk together. I told him I was a professor researching the missile crisis period in Cuba ... that my father had been down here. Mostly true stuff—although I spiced it up a bit. Got his confidence. When he was really drunk, I led him toward the warheads ... and suggested strongly that I knew something about them. He got really cute and said I didn't know nearly as much as I thought I knew—that he knew the secret of the warheads."

Suarez said urgently, "What is the secret? Where are they? And how would this man know so many years later?"

"The last question is the next most important one," McLemore said. "The Russian calls himself 'Victor Isaacs.' That's the name he has adopted in the U.S. That's what his new passport says, 'Victor Isaacs.' In fact, he was born forty-two years ago in Ekaterinburg with the name Viktor Leonidovich Isakov. He is the son of the late Soviet colonel Leonid Sestanovich Isakov. The man who kept the warheads. Here. In 1962."

"My God!" Trinidad said again. Her face was pale. She looked aghast at Suarez. A picture was beginning to form in both minds simultaneously. "This Isaacs-Isakov has sold nuclear weapons to these killers—these terrorists?"

"I don't know for sure what they're planning to do or how. But I do think I know where the warheads are." McLemore unfolded the plan for the Bejucal military base and pointed out the outline of the buried bunker. "I think the warheads are right here."

Trinidad shook her head in disbelief. "It cannot be. We were there—three months ago. It was empty. Like a tomb. There was nothing there."

As they walked up an ancient flight of stone steps trod by lookouts and warriors for almost four centuries, McLemore shook his head. "I'm not sure. I think the warheads are there. And I have an idea how they were hidden." He looked at Suarez. "Can we go down there tomorrow? Take some digging equipment?"

Suarez said immediately, "Of course. Tomorrow is the twenty-eighth. We only have four days. So we must go early. We'll pick you up at your hotel at nine . . . no, eight o'clock."

McLemore said, "Any sign of Bravo? Has anyone seen them here . . . or up there?"

Suarez shook his head no. "We cannot find a clue of them." Though no one was around, he moved closer to McLemore and lowered his voice. "Quite frankly, given what we know of their connection with the Russian, their probable responsibility for Juanita's death, and their possible plan for terrorist activity at the celebration, we are assuming they are already here . . . in Cuba. We have some pictures Juanita took of them at a distance. They are not clear, but we have tried to improve them. They are right now being circulated all over the island to our local revolutionary committees. By tomorrow, everyone will have their pictures."

"If I am right," McLemore said, "both about the warheads and about their location, and if that's what Isakov sold them, that's where they'll go . . . to Bejucal . . . immediately."

"Tomorrow," Suarez said, "eight o'clock."

Even as the three people walked along the darkened parapet of the Morro, five members of Bravo were returning to Bejucal in their canvas-covered truck. Once again, Tony had been left with old Dankevich. The two men were going to have dinner in a small, dim *paladar* in the Cerro section and then return to the clubhouse to await their companions' return. For the others, they knew exactly what each one needed to do. They came around the base from the south, passing through the town of Bejucal and approaching the military installation from the east. They found the hiding place for the truck and concealed it for the time being with foliage. They would wait for the quarter moon to recede and the midnight watch to make its rounds, then move on the bunker.

Though the men had been resting, they took time to doze. They would not be back to Havana until 2 A.M. at least, and even that hour presumed no trouble with their recapture mission. They would particularly have to drive slowly in the early hours of return to avoid arousing the interest of patrolling policemen. Manny kept the watch, and when the security patrol passed shortly after midnight and passed into the main gate of the base, he said, "Let's go." Pete drove the truck onto the road, down a hundred feet toward the base, then backed it into the cane field. There had been only slight rain. The field was soft but firm. Two of the men walked behind the truck with flashlights dimmed and held at ankle level to guide Pete backward. They moved very slowly to decrease noise and feel their way down the field. Looking to his left, Manny paced off the distance until they had gone two hundred or more yards. Then he directed Pete to back toward the fence. Approximately 50 feet from the fence, Manny signaled Pete to stop the truck and cut the engine. They were now 150 to 200 feet from the bunker with only a barbed fence and thick cane between them and their target. The only way to detect the truck now was by helicopter.

Once again dressed in black and with faces blackened, the five men repeated their crossing of the fence and low crawl to the bunker beyond. This was now familiar territory, and they had rehearsed their movements repeatedly in countless run-throughs at the clubhouse. They had come to think of themselves as special forces in their own private army. This time they left Orlando, the most physically challenged of the group, as the watch at the door and proceeded immediately down the long corridor to the north end of the bunker. Before leaving the previous night, they had swept up the plaster and cinder block fragments from their exploratory excavation into the wall and poured them back into the small cavity.

Now, with Joe holding the sharpened chisel and the sledgehammer muffled by a thick pad, Pete scored the outline of a five-by-four-foot opening in the wall. Pete drank often from a canteen. In the close, almost airless confines of the bunker, he was soon drenched with sweat. He stepped back, and Joe took up a pick, deepening the outline of the opening with vigorous, full-arm swings. He was soon perspiring as freely as Pete. Now rested, Pete took up the sledge again and began to smash the inside of the oblong outlined on the wall. Within minutes he had broken a small hole through the wall, then widened it to the size of a human head, then made it wider and wider. He stepped outside for air, and Joe took up the project. He lacked Pete's strength but was able to make visible progress. Manny periodically checked his watch. A half an hour had passed. Weakened on the perimeter and with the mortar made fragile by age, the blocks gave way. Now the great barrier was the stifling air, thick with the dust of the four-decade-old plaster now being pulverized and atomized by the hammer blows and by the powerful damp smell emanating from the widening hole in the long-sealed room. In the eerie light of two headlamps, Manny's and Johnny's, the interior atmosphere became surreal, almost submarine.

Orlando's head appeared and he waved. "Shhhh!"

The two headlamps went off and everyone froze. They could hear the crunch of tires in the distance. Orlando pulled the blast door partly closed behind him after trying to wave some of the dust away. Thank God they had thought to bring oil for the ancient rusted hinges. Its normal shrieking complaint was dampened. They silently prayed that visible powder was not drifting upward from the doorway.

They waited an eternity. The slowly creeping tires seemed to have stopped. The vehicle, presumably a periodic interior patrol, had stopped somewhere very near. Manny, Pete, and Joe fingered the nines strapped to their sides. They heard low voices. Two men—how many more were with them?—were having a conversation. Orlando held up a hand for total silence as he strained to hear.

One of the soldiers said, "Alvaro swore he heard something like pounding down here. You hear anything?"

"Hell, no. He's dreaming. 'Pounding'? What kind of pounding?"

"Pounding! That's all he said. Check it out."

"You know the old story the colonel tells about the four dead Russians buried in that tomb? Probably just trying to get out. Whad'ya think?"

"Go check."

"Go check? Go check. You go check!"

"I'm not going to go check. Fuck it! No pounding. No goddamn ghosts. No way. Let's go. Next time, we let Alvaro check. Dead Russians give me the creeps."

Orlando listened as the jeep turned, reversed, and slowly moved away. None of the men had a doubt that, if more pounding was heard up the way, the place would quickly be swarming with sleepy Cuban soldiers. After the door was opened slightly and a little fresh air came in, Pete waited five minutes and began on the remaining half of the opening. Before doing so, however, Manny pushed his way up to the hole, turned on his headlamp, stuck his head in the hole with a handkerchief across his nose, and surveyed the inside. In the eerie interior, which had not seen light for almost four decades, Manny saw two squat, bulky objects wrapped in tarpaulin and tied at the top like chocolate kisses. He was exhilarated and chilled at the same time. If one of those things suddenly decided to blow up, there wouldn't be anything larger than an atom left of any of them. As if they were archaeologists uncovering a pharaoh's tomb, the others quickly gazed in. The Russian had told the truth after all. Manny was almost glad the wise guys hadn't killed him.

Pete swung the hammer. The others grabbed the loosened blocks and pulled them out. The process was repeated time and time again. Manny checked. It was 1:15 A.M. They had been in the bunker an hour. Time was running out. He circled his hand in a speed-up gesture. Hammer, carry. Hammer, carry. Now the scored hole was open—four by five feet. Pete and Manny went inside. If this thing doesn't like to be moved, Manny thought, Good-bye!

They felt a metal framework inside the heavy tarpaulin and pushed it and the blocks underneath it toward the opening. Good, Manny thought. Four men can carry this thing. The hole had to be widened. Hammer, carry. Hammer, carry. Another fifteen or twenty minutes passed until the hole was large enough for four men to come inside, lift the package up, sit it on the opened wall, then lift it to the outside corridor with two men on the inside and two in the corridor. Having done this, Joe went to check with Orlando. The two men could see lights up near the gate. All the barracks were dark, soldiers sleeping. But the night watch was still awake and active. Slowly the four men moved the heavy object some forty feet down the corridor, then rested at the bottom of the steps. Struggling, they carried it up the twelve steps to the top. Just as they were emerging, Jim caught a toe on the top step and lunged forward. They all lost their balances and toppled over. The crated object dropped a foot or two to the ground, and involuntarily, the men buried their heads in their arms and curled up like large fetuses. Then they heard Manny laugh softly. "Son of a bitch! Lot a good that would do. This thing goes, you can just kiss your ass good-bye."

They set out for the fence. And after stopping every twenty feet for rest, they got there. On their way in, Pete had left large wire cutters at a fence post. After a search he found them at the same time as Orlando caught up with them, all the other tools cradled in his arms. Holding his breath, Pete cut the wires, top to bottom. Clip. Clip. Clip. Clip. Clip. Clip. The wire sprang back, and they carried the treasure through the new opening. No sirens sounded. Whatever alert had originally been connected to the perimeter fence had been turned off or abandoned. After three more sit-downs, they got the bulky cargo to the back of the truck, set it on the back gate, and two men jumped into the truck and helped guide it in. It was pushed all the way up to the front, and after the tools were stored, the back tarp curtain was dropped.

The men then started back for the second package. They crossed to and through the fence and, hunched over, made for the bunker. They got within a dozen feet of the door when suddenly lights came on at the main gate area 250 yards to the north. The lights of two vehicles came on and swung toward the south end of the base where the men stood frozen. As one, the men bolted for the truck. They ran flat out. Orlando stumbled and sprawled. Pete scooped him up under a huge arm and practically carried him. They got to the truck and, as fast as they could, Manny and Orlando put cane worker clothes over the light black garments soaked with sweat and the others piled in the back with the pistols, prepared to deal swift death if they were challenged.

Manny started the truck and headed north through the cane field as

the two jeeps sped south down the central road between the rows of
barracks. The jeeps now moving astern, Manny speeded up and got to
the road as fast as he could. The ever-present farm dogs down the road
set up a howl as he wheeled out onto the road and turned left toward
the post main gate. To retrace their route back through the town would
consume time and give the guards a greater chance to intercept them, so
he took a gamble that all the night watch had gone in the two jeeps
headed toward the bunker. He picked up speed as he passed the gate
and headed toward the Havana road a mile or two away. He got to the
main road and turned right toward Havana. Now he would have to
maintain speed to put distance between them and the guards, but not go
so fast as to invite attention from night police patrols. Done properly,
they would merely appear to be farmers carrying a load of produce in for
the dawn market. Periodically checking the rearview mirror, Manny
went over several rises and had begun to merge with the thin night traffic when he saw headlights approaching fast behind him. He slowed a
bit, put on a battered straw hat, and hunched over the wheel. Over his
shoulder he shouted, "Here they come." He heard safety catches released
on three pistols simultaneously.

Around his left in the passing lane, a military jeep with a blue light
and three heavily armed soldiers pulled even, peered into the cab intensely
for a quarter mile, then dramatically increased speed for the city. After
they had passed from sight, Manny and Orlando breathed, then said to
the back, "It's okay. They went on." The catches clicked back on.

The truck slowly made its way into the city and into the Cerro district.
Driving carefully down the back streets of the district, the truck backed
into its narrow parking area, tailgate twenty feet from the back door of
the shabby clubhouse building. They sat for minutes, catching their breath
and waiting for any light sleepers in the neighborhood to resume uncon-
sciousness. Presently they unloaded and moved the bulky package to the
rear of the truck and then quickly into the rear entrance of the building.
It barely cleared the door. But there it now was. Sitting in the small
kitchen, taking up much of the room.

The tarpaulin was carefully removed and carried out to the truck. The
men now saw a rusted metal frame. Inside the frame was a shapeless object
wrapped securely in plastic. One of the men got a knife and carefully slit
the bottom of the plastic enough so that it could be slid off the object but
replaced when it had to be moved to its final destination. They now saw

a two-kiloton Luna missile warhead—an instrument of technological genius quite capable of atomizing close to a million people gathered in the
close proximity of the Plaza de la Revolución four short days away. The
whizbang.

34

The black car carrying Suarez and Trinidad appeared at the
Santa Isabel a few minutes before eight in the morning. It was
the twenty-eighth of December. From his breakfast table near
the front window of the hotel, McLemore saw the car make its wide sweep
around the plaza in front. He drank the last drops of his third cup of coffee
and quickly joined them.

The car picked up speed as it passed on the city side of the harbor
entrance across from the Morro Castle where the three had been the night
before. It continued through the tunnel leading onto the main highway
out of town and toward Bejucal. Suarez put a portable blue light on the
dashboard and the car started to dart around and through slower traffic in
its path. Suarez clearly wanted to get to Bejucal.

They swept southward at high speed and largely in silence. McLemore
had slept little. About two in the morning, the profound reality that Bravo
was moving faster than they were wrapped his mind with its tentacles.

The car screeched around corners and cut off competing vehicles. They
were soon pounding south on the more or less open road. The driver
leaned on the horn to little effect. Oxcarts and bicycles occupied the
passing lane as they saw fit. Still, weaving in and out, they sped on. Within
forty minutes they were near enough to the main gate on the side road
from the town to see a cluster of vehicles and people grouped in excited
knots. There was a great deal of anxious hustle and official bustle. Most
of the people were uniformed and quickly looked up as they saw the official
black car with the revolving blue light.

A senior military official, probably a general judging by the brass, approached the driver side door. He peered in and Suarez held up his identification. The general saluted and spoke at length in rapid-fire Spanish.

Trinidad interpreted. "He says that there was a break-in sometime in the night. The only damage seems to be in the old bunker the Soviets used in the crisis time." She looked at McLemore with dismay.

Suarez fired off a series of orders. Military vehicles moved quickly out of the way. People scattered, and the black car leaped down the long straight lane heading to the south end of the base, where several cars and jeeps and another cluster of perhaps a dozen uniformed personnel were gathered. The car had not yet come to a complete stop when Suarez was out one door, holding up his identification, and McLemore was out the other door right behind him. Another senior officer saluted and waved them toward the bunker. They grabbed available flashlights and dove down the steps. McLemore felt a powerful sense of déjà vu. It was like one of those bad-struggle dreams.

They shined the lights to the right and saw fifty feet away the south end of the wall, intact. They turned to the left and their lights revealed a burglar's dream. Piles of fractured concrete blocks, mortar, and plaster were strewn about. A great hole gaped in the end wall giving onto a small, dark chamber. Thick plaster dust still hung in the air, apparently stirred up by inspectors coming and going.

Over his shoulder he heard the military officer, probably the base commander, ask Suarez a question in Spanish. Behind him, he could hear Trinidad quickly say something to Suarez. Suarez said a few words to the officer, and they all moved toward the violated tomb. Their lights as they approached gradually revealed half of the chamber empty and the other half occupied by a large tarpaulin-covered object approximately four feet square. McLemore started to say, There you see Luna warhead number ninety-nine, when Suarez held a finger to his lips. They studied the debris for a few minutes looking for any clues left behind by the break-in team. Suarez waved them all out.

Suarez spoke quietly, forcefully, and rapidly to the officer who responded by nodding, saluting, and ordering his jeep driver to return him swiftly to the main gate. Trinidad said, "Lazaro has ordered this area completely sealed off. He has ordered a team from the Interior Ministry specially trained in dangerous substances to be called. They alone will handle the object inside. And he has ordered the military not to speak to anyone about this. We must not let anyone know what was in there. There will be great panic. Once we have a look, we will tell the military that it was an old bomb—a regular bomb—that the Soviets left behind and that some drunken Russians have returned to claim it as some kind of patriotic souvenir. That story will hold for two or three days . . . maybe long enough for us to find the Bravo group and the . . . *thing* . . . they clearly now have in their possession."

Suarez and McLemore returned to the bunker once more for a more thorough look. Then Suarez ordered a young officer to have his men sift through all the dust and debris for any small objects or clues they might find. The order given, the young officer pointed the way out of the bunker and then eastward toward the violated perimeter fence. They traced the footsteps of a number of men in the damp earth. Some footprints were deep, suggesting the carrying of a heavy object. They examined the cleanly severed wires. The officer explained that electrification of the fence had been discontinued years ago to save energy. Besides, the old bunker held nothing. They followed the tracks out into the adjoining cane field and, fifty feet on, found the tire tracks. It had been a large vehicle from the depths of the tracks. The officer explained that the tracks went straight northward to the road passing in front of the base, then turned westward toward the Havana highway. Since the early hours, when they discovered the break-in, they had traced and retraced this entire area and had found nothing. Whoever had carried out this operation, the officer surmised, had planned it very well. He just couldn't understand why they would go to so much trouble for an antique bomb. It had to be worthless.

This conversation carried Suarez, Trinidad, and McLemore back to their car. Passing the gate, Suarez had emphasized to the general in command that the entire area was to remain sealed, except for the bomb disposal experts, until further orders.

On the return trip, Suarez and Trinidad discussed all that had to be done in the next seventy-two hours. As soon as the hazardous materials team returned the remaining warhead to their disposal site and uncovered it, they would know immediately that they had a nuclear weapon, albeit an early-generation one, on their hands. That information would spread with the speed of light through the Cuban security network. Half the city of Havana and most of the people in the surrounding countryside would be rounded up like cattle and jailed. There would be mass confusion, even chaos. Every predictable step Nuñez took would make the job of locating

Bravo that much more complicated and likewise make Bravo's mission easier. Bravo members would swim through the confusion like fish in water. Under urging from Trinidad, Suarez agreed to try to convince Nuñez to pretend nothing had happened, to confine the information on a "need to know" basis, and to give the Bravo group the impression that they were undetected. It would make them bolder and more likely to operate openly, she argued.

Trinidad interpreted this plan for McLemore, who readily agreed. He had been thinking. As they approached Havana, he said, "Let's go see Ramsay."

Trinidad and Suarez looked at him as they would a madman.

"Here's why," he continued. "We need him for two reasons. First, he might convince Washington to send all its files on the members of this group, including clearer pictures. You need to circulate those fast. Second, it is unreasonable to believe that any member of this Bravo group understands nuclear warheads, particularly old Russian ones. They have to be able to detonate this antique, so Isakov must have guaranteed to supply some kind of technician—somebody from Russia who knows these weapons. This thing is almost forty years old. It's unstable, and God knows what the wiring is like after all these years. It has to be tuned up before it can be used, and they have to figure out some way to make it go off."

Suarez nodded, grasping the idea. "But I don't understand how Ramsay can help with that matter."

"I'll tell you how he can help," McLemore said grimly. "He can haul Isakov down here and nail his ass . . . sorry, Trinidad . . . to the wall."

As they sped into Havana, blue light flashing, Suarez ordered the driver to proceed as quickly as possible to the U.S. Interest office on the Malecón. At the entry gate, Suarez showed his identification and McLemore waved his passport. They told the guard they were there to see Mr. Ramsay. He called security, waited, then waved them in. By the time they reached the door, the beaming red face of Ramsay was there to greet them.

"What an unexpected pleasure, Professor. And I see you've brought your Cuban friends. What an honor. What an unexpected honor. Señor Suarez. Señora Santiago." His ironic jocularity suggested a comrades-in-arms relationship. "Well, Professor, are we here to discuss defection, or what is our agenda? As you might expect, some of our people in Washington are very disappointed that you left your last dinner party up there so . . . shall we say . . . unexpectedly. Come to apologize?"

"Our agenda, Mr. Ramsay, is to find a room where we can talk," McLemore said. His tone and pale color were all that Ramsay needed to convince himself something was up. He led them through security and into an elevator that took them to an upper floor where they entered the "bubble" that had been the forum for McLemore's first serious discussion with the agent.

The door secure, McLemore said, "Last night at the Cuban military installation at Bejucal, the old bunker used by the Soviets during the missile crisis in 1962 to store nuclear warheads, was broken into—most probably by some element of a group we all know by the name of Bravo—sometimes Bravo 99, Bravo ultra, or some variation. We need your help, Mr. Ramsay."

" 'We,' Professor?"

"The Cuban government needs your help. Señor Suarez is prepared to make a formal request. We—they—need all the information—including pictures—that you, the U.S. government, the CIA, the FBI, have on the members of this Bravo group. And one Victor Isaacs, aka Viktor Isakov, has to be located and hauled down here as fast as possible."

Ramsay held up a square hand the size of a stop sign. "Professor McLemore, please. You have before you a humble immigration officer who—"

"Cut the crap, Ramsay. This is serious. Everybody in this city—particularly all of us here— knows who and what you are. We don't have time for this horseshit play-acting."

Ramsay managed, in his maddening way, to look at once both offended and angry. "Releasing U.S. government records on U.S. citizens to the intelligence services of other countries—especially, with all due respect to Señor Suarez, to a country with which we do not presently have diplomatic relations—is virtually impossible. And as to our old friend Comrade Isakov, Professor, you were the last person I know to have seen him. Why don't you just call him up and invite him to join us. I'm sure you two left on the best of terms."

Trinidad briefly feared that McLemore would lunge across the table at Ramsay. Instead he reached for a side table where a telephone—a telephone that he was sure had to be linked to a secure line—rested. He put the phone on the table and shoved the handset at Ramsay. "Call up Worthy."

Ramsay studied him briefly, then spoke softly into the phone. He put the receiver down and they waited. The room was totally silent. Trinidad spent the three minutes wondering who was angrier—Ramsay or Mc-

Lemore. Then the phone rang and Ramsay answered. He handed the handset to McLemore. "Here's your man," he said.

"Mr. Worthy?" McLemore said. "I am here in the Interest office in Havana with your colleague Mr. Ramsay and two officials of Cuban intelligence." He listened for a moment, then said, "Yes, I understand. It was rather abrupt and I believe I can explain. Based on suspicions I had formed in my work down here, I got Isakov to confirm the nature of the weapons he sold to Bravo. The information was urgent enough that I had to get it to responsible officials here as quickly as possible. Frankly, I feared—rightly or wrongly—that our own bureaucracy might delay that effort. I shared that information—both the nature of the weapons and their location—with the Cuban security officials here with me. These are weapons that were left here following the Cuban missile crisis. They have been here that long. Isakov sold them to Bravo. The Bravo group is already inside Cuba. Bravo didn't have to bring the weapons in. They were already here. We went out first thing this morning to secure the weapons. Bravo beat us to it. One of these weapons was already gone. This call is to ask your cooperation in providing the information you and the Bureau have on the Bravo group—especially anything that will aid in identification. And second, we need Isakov—Victor Isaacs—down here as fast as you can bring him."

McLemore's narration was interrupted by Worthy. McLemore listened for a moment, then said, "Because to make this weapon operable will require highly skilled Russian expertise, and only Isakov knows who might do that. It has to be part of the deal."

McLemore listened for a moment again, then said, "You get whatever authorization you can, Mr. Worthy, as fast as you can. But get Isakov and your files on a plane down here as quickly as you can."

He listened again. "I'll tell you why. Bravo has taken possession of a Soviet nuclear warhead and they're going to blow it up in downtown Havana in four days."

Ramsay's face sagged. He looked genuinely shocked for the first time since McLemore had met him. McLemore handed him the phone and said, "Make the arrangements. Give Señor Suarez the identification number and arrival time of the Agency plane, and he'll make necessary arrangements at the airport." McLemore stood up, leaned across the table at Ramsay, and quietly said, "Do it. Now."

Ramsay talked to Worthy for several minutes as the three visitors gathered by the door. He joined them shortly. "Our people have to round up

Isakov. The Bureau is still on him, so it shouldn't be too tough. Worthy will round up the files, grab Isakov, and could be down here later today or—latest—early tomorrow morning." He exchanged direct telephone numbers with Suarez. "I'll call you as soon as I have a landing time." He seemed to be in shock. He turned to McLemore and said, "Nuclear warhead? Are you sure?"

McLemore nodded. "The Soviets brought in more than they took out. A madman took it upon himself to stock up for some private war of his own. Our friends in Miami, shopping for a way to make a political statement, struck gold . . . or, in this case, plutonium."

The three people moved to the door. Ramsay grabbed McLemore's arm and whispered in his ear, "Should I get my family out of Cuba?"

McLemore let the Cubans go ahead, then turned and whispered back, "If it were me, I'd send them down the coast to Pinar del Río." He started to leave, then turned again and said, "But what about the rest of the Interest office—and, for that matter, what about the rest of Havana? If you send your family, you have to tell the others here. If you empty out the Interest office, word will be around this city in twenty-four hours. They'll assume the long-awaited invasion is coming, and there will be uncontrollable panic. That's the last thing we need." He smiled grimly and gave Ramsay a pat on the back. "But, hey pal, it's your call. I just know you'll do the right thing."

35 The object of Dmitri Dmitrovich Dankevich's attention sat on a jury-rigged table made of the frame in which it had been found with several short, thick planks placed across it. Dankevich sat on a creaky straight-backed chair that placed him roughly at eye level with the beauty. He touched it here and there, as if marveling at its well-being and high degree of preservation. Blueprints spread on an adjoining chair, Dankevich had studied the technological wizard for an hour or two, tweaking it here, tapping it there. Finally, he began to remove a plate by taking out screws machine-tooled to the precision of the world's finest watches. The normally casual Pete, the only Bravo member left to chaperon Dankevich, gave early evidence of a nervous breakdown. Dankevich had assured him and the others repeatedly that nuclear warheads were without temperament, that it took an exquisite calibration of electrical impulses to bring them to life. Pete did not appear to believe a word the old man said. He perspired copiously in the closed-up flat.

From the farthest corner of the flat, Pete stared mesmerized at the device they had labored so hard to find and control. Its appearance provided no outward evidence that it could do what Dankevich assured him it could do—that is, kill hundreds of thousands of people in a closely packed square. It was no more than three feet high and less than that in width. It was shaped to fit in the nose cone of a modest-size rocket. It seemed to weigh no more than 250 or 300 pounds. Pete could bench-press that easily. But four men teamed up when moving it. They did not want to test how high it might bounce.

Dankevich knew well how it worked. It was only the second generation or so of Soviet nuclear technology. It was your basic warhead—exquisitely molded fissionable material surrounded by equally carefully shaped high explosives that were linked to a multipoint detonation system controlled by a permissive action link. Simple. From the way the warhead had been preserved, not much could have changed with the fissionable materials or the shaped high explosives in the past four decades. So Dankevich had three jobs. First, to make sure the timing circuits were intact. Second, to verify the permissive action link codes. And third, to wire the timing device to the timing circuits, which controlled the permissive action link.

Dankevich studied the wiring diagrams on the weapon's blueprint. To a layman it looked like spaghetti. But the refresher course he had given himself before leaving Moscow and the discussions he organized with some aging former colleagues in the rocket forces had served him well. Young Isakov's friends had obtained for him the permissive action link codes. He was proud of the way his mind had grasped it all again so quickly. It was like returning to his thirties. So new these devices were then. So exciting to learn their character and intricate design. It was as intellectually challenging as world-class chess. To have retained this clandestine knowledge provided its own unique pride. It was like a secret brotherhood.

In the old days he had asked some question about using these devices. Killing innocent people. His unit commander had lectured on this issue. First, it was a deterrent. To have these weapons meant the United States would not attack the Soviet Union. And, second, it was the United States itself that had been the only country ever to use this weapon. And it had killed many civilian people. Not to worry. It didn't matter. *Nichevo.* Since Colonel Isakov's son had contacted him, Dankevich had suppressed speculation as to what this weapon would be used for. He had tried not to ask or to think about it. Then his new friends, Manny and Tony, had explained when they met that they were there to help the Cuban people repel an invasion. His old boss Isakov would be proud. Now Isakov's demented secret—keeping the two extra Luna warheads there—made a kind of sense. What a genius. But what a crazy one he had been.

Manny's explanation had made sense to Dankevich. He didn't understand politics anyway. And even in the old days, he hadn't even tried to understand Cuban politics. So complicated. So angry. So dramatic. The Cuban military people he had dealt with had been likable. But their politics was well beyond his linear engineering mind. Tony was probably right. It would take something very dramatic—like this Luna—to protect these Cubans.

With a handheld magnifying glass he had brought with him, he painstakingly and methodically inspected each electrical connection. He tested every fastener and screw, occasionally tightening a connection half a turn. When he had to use both hands, he had Pete hold the glass for him while he worked. He didn't like to do it because Pete was sweating so much, and Dankevich feared his sweat might drip on the device. He worked his way around the warhead one panel at a time. Not a wire had to be replaced. Here and there a plastic coating had shredded or cracked with age. Once or twice he covered these cracks with a special quick-drying liquid plastic. But, all in all, he had to salute Soviet technology. This thing was like a time machine, preserved as if in a bell jar.

The work was tedious and precise. It could not be rushed. After several hours, he put his tools down, stood up, and stretched. He needed to walk and to eat. His muscles were very tight, and he was very hungry. They heard the truck returning. Manny and Tony came in and Dankevich briefed them on his efforts.

"So it's in good shape?" Manny asked. "We got a good deal from Vic?"

Yes, Dankevich assured them, functionally as good as new. "Now connection to timer. I do tomorrow. Is not need before then, I think?"

"How long does it take to attach . . . the timer?" Tony asked.

Dankevich waved them over to the machine. They approached reluctantly and gingerly. "Is not radioactive," he said. "Will not make hair fall out or strange-looking babies," he chuckled. "Look. See this one and this one, here. These are key ones, main ones. These attach here to timer." He held up a complex-looking box with various colored wires sprouting in different directions and something that had what looked like a sophisticated alarm clock face on one side. "Is timer." He held it close to the warhead, and the two men involuntarily leaned back. Dankevich chuckled, enjoying their ignorant fear. "This one attach here. This one here. Then two go here," he said, gesturing to a different panel. "Then we set time and"—dusting his hands dramatically—"ready to roll."

Manny said, "Mr. Dinkowitch, how long does all that take?"

Dankevich shrugged, looking at his watch. "For attach and checking all, one . . . no, two hours, maybe. Then—" Again he dusted his hands.

"How long can the timer be set for?" Tony asked. "We brought two of these with us. Both the same. One backup. We bought special twenty-four-hour timers."

Dankevich shrugged. "Is okay. You want machine to take away three days more. Take in afternoon. Set timer for next day. Sometime before twenty-four hours. Then . . . it work. Simple thing."

Tony looked at Manny and Pete. "That's the program. Sounds good. Just like we planned." They nodded, and Tony said, "Let's make Mr. Dankevich some dinner. He's worked hard today."

They brought in some provisions from the truck. More rice and beans. Some bottles of *cerveza* and two bottles of rum. And some freshly caught fish they found at dockside. The men gathered around the makeshift workbench and its precious cargo and lifted the whole apparatus slowly and carefully into a corner. They concealed it with a blanket that made the whole thing look like a bulky, covered parrot cage.

■ ■ ■

The old man, some organs eaten by nicotine, others by alcohol, and perhaps some by ambient radiation into the bargain, looked at his son standing at the end of his bed. Though only in his late sixties, retired Colonel Leonid Isakov looked twenty years older, the legacy of a lifetime of hazardous living. They both knew what they were doing there. One was crying and the other was dying. Despite a lifetime of abuse, Viktor was overcome by the notion of his father's death. No more ducking the ashtrays or the curses. But also no more Papa. Between groans and hacking coughs, the old man gestured to his son. Come closer.

Viktor, the only son, would now receive his father's dying testament.

"Now listen, you little bastard," the old man snarled, "take care of your mother. She sure as hell can't possibly take care of herself." He groaned in his agony. Viktor nodded, more in terror than in agreement.

"I don't think there's a chance in hell you'll make anything out of yourself. You sure haven't up to now." He interrupted himself with a racking cough. "I've had to look after you and her all your lives . . . and it looks like I'm going to have to continue to."

Viktor nodded again and said, "Papa, I'll do my best. I'll try."

The dying man waved his hand downward. He had heard it all before and didn't believe a word of it. "Listen, for a change. I've told you about my time in Cuba . . . in '62. Well, I'm going to tell you a secret. A very big secret." He motioned Viktor even closer. The stench almost overcame him. "I am going to give you the biggest present any father ever gave his son."

To Viktor's shock and dismay, the croaking old corpse displayed a wicked grin. It was both frightening and surreal. "Give me that box." He motioned to a Cuban cigar box, frayed and battered with age. Viktor had known from his boyhood that this contained the old man's treasures, his most valuable possessions in the world. Once, many years ago, thinking his father gone for the afternoon, he had tried to peek into the box. He had been caught and thrashed for a week. His hands shook as he passed it to his father.

Hands also shaking violently, Leonid Isakov pushed the frail lid up and dumped some papers on the bed. They were fragile, cracked and split at the folds. He motioned for Viktor to unfold them. One looked like a handmade map and the other an incredibly complex diagram or blueprint. The wicked grin, revealing yellow, vulpine teeth, appeared again. "Here is my gift to you, Viktor, my son, my heir, my no-goodnik. It's a bomb." He began to laugh like a maniac, coughing, spluttering, and wheezing. "It's a goddamn atomic bomb." More agonizing laughter.

Viktor stood transfixed. *What in the hell is he talking about?* he thought. *He is completely mad. Whatever else these funny-looking old papers are, they are not a bomb.* The only response he could manage was "A bomb?"

Apoplectic, his father shouted, "Yes, a bomb, you dummy! Can't you see? It's a bomb—an atomic bomb. Right there." He pointed with a quaking finger. "A bomb!"

To resist his strong impulse to suffocate the old man and put them both out of their misery, Viktor started to turn away. But the old man's clawlike hand grabbed his shirt and his tenacious death grasp almost tore the sleeve away. "Look," Leonid said, "this is a military base in Cuba. In a town close to Havana. Its called Bay-you-call. Here," he said, pointing to a rectangular outline, "this is a storage bunker . . . where we kept our warheads. See that mark?" he said, punching the paper. "That's where two warheads are. Lunas. Two kiloton. Make a hell of a bang. Kill a lot of people. Understand? I left them there . . . twenty-three years ago. I left them there . . . for you! It's my gift, you ninny!"

Through a surreal haze, Viktor began to form an idea. Maybe the old man was willing his future. Maybe there was something here. Ever the trader, the only game he had an instinct for, Viktor suddenly saw a future of wealth, of excitement, of purpose. Owning two nuclear warheads was the start of a career, a career in business. This was, after all, the dawn of the age of glasnost and perestroika. Walls and curtains were falling. People were saying they would soon fall for good. With no Cold War, no U.S.-Soviet confrontation, think of the demand for Soviet weapons and military hardware. He would get there first. He would be the man to see if you wanted a tank, or a plane . . . or a warhead. Possibilities were endless. He would be an entrepreneur. He would make deals. He would be a capitalist. He would be . . . rich!

Through his delirious haze, he heard the spectral voice. "Get out of here, you idiot!" He started to leave, but the old man said, "No, I mean get out of the Soviet Union. Gorbachev and his asshole crowd are going to ruin this place for good. It's been going to hell since that dummy Khrushchev anyway. Get out of here. Get a green card in the States. Set up shop over there. Use my old friends and set up a network. Sell everything you can get your hands on. Most of all," he said, waving the flimsy papers, "sell these. Dankevich is the key. Remember that. But listen. They are each worth at least a million U.S. If you take less, I swear I will come back and haunt you forever." A gigantic cough heaved him up and halfway out of bed. He fell sideways, and

Viktor gently put the wiry, bony body back on its pillow, convinced he was finally and truly dead. He waited a moment, then began to gather up and fold the two papers.

The corpse uttered a terrifying cackle. "Fuck the bastards." Then he was dead.

■ ■ ■

 In the late afternoon of the twenty-ninth of December, Lazaro Suarez finally got a call from Sam Ramsay. McLemore and Trinidad were in Suarez's office, trying to work out how to convince Isakov to talk. Given the circumstances of their last meeting, McLemore tried to explain why he was probably not the person to undertake that task.

The phone rang. Suarez waved at them to be quiet. It was Ramsay. Suarez wrote on a pad, expressed thanks, and hung up.

"The U.S. plane is arriving early tomorrow morning—about seven o'clock—from Washington. Ramsay says they have Isakov," he reported.

Trinidad asked, "What if there is a Russian technician here? What if we get his name? It still doesn't help us find him or the Bravos."

"At least we'll have his description and can add it to the others we're looking for," Suarez said. "He must be part of the plot, so he'll probably go with them when they deposit this weapon."

Trinidad said, "Have you told Colonel Nuñez yet . . . about the warhead?"

Suarez said, "No. He will have me shot probably when he finds out. But it's now in our secure bomb disposal building, and I've instructed the men not to open it up. I explained that it might contain radiation or leftover chemical agents. That we had to bring experts from Russia to disarm it. That will hold them awhile. They're all scared of the thing anyway."

Trinidad turned to McLemore. "Where do you think they'll put this . . . thing?"

"Do you have any doubt?" McLemore said. "As close to the Plaza as they can."

Suarez said, "Maybe. Maybe not. Thinking that is what we will expect, they might try another location. They can't even be sure we've discovered the break-in. They have to assume it, but they can't know for sure. The whole city—maybe even the whole country—is a target."

McLemore reached for Suarez's phone and said, "Give me Ramsay's number, if you don't mind." He dialed, then listened. "Red, it's Mac. Can you cable Washington and get the dimensions, yield, and as much technical data as you can on a Soviet 'Luna' warhead. If this thing's out and about—as it seems to be—we need to know what we're looking for. Is it bigger than a bread box?—that sort of thing. How much space is required to hide it, and so forth. Leave the information with Suarez if I'm not here. Thanks."

While this discussion was going on, across town in Cerro the shabby curtains of the clubhouse parted and Dmitri Dankevich peered out. He had a bad case of cabin fever, and he had to stretch his constricted old muscles. Manny and Tony had taken the truck. Johnny, Joe, and Orlando had gone for a walk, unbeknownst to him, to reconnoiter the Plaza for the third time, to check and recheck ingress and egress, surrounding buildings, and hiding places. A few minutes before, Pete had said, "I can't take this place anymore. Stay where you are. I'll be back . . . soon." Truth be known, he had seen a *señorita* pass by through the break in the curtains and wanted to check her out.

Why not? Dankevich thought. These young men won't mind if I have a little walk and some air. Very carefully, he slipped out the back door, down a narrow alley that the truck used, then out onto the narrow street and even narrower sidewalk. It was a brilliant day. Clean fresh air and a slight breeze. Warm sun made him feel like a new man already. It brought back those wonderful days in '62, when it was not too hot and the breeze came in from the west. He circled three or four blocks, carefully noting his course, then started to return to the clubhouse. Across the street he noticed some elderly men sitting at a table drinking coffee. The aroma reached him and took him back thirty-six years. His boss, Isakov, had liked the rum and the ladies. He had liked the coffee most of all. He walked across the street as the men watched him approach. Reaching back across the decades to retrieve his very limited Spanish vocabulary, he said, *"Café, por favor?"*

One of the men waved him to a chair and said, *"Habla usted español?"*

Dankevich smiled shyly and shook his head no.

The man shouted something into the house and then asked, "European?"

Dankevich shook his head and then, before thinking, said, "Russki."

Eyebrows shot up. Some Russians, older ones from the missile days, had come back. But it was still a rare thing. Among the older Cubans there was still lingering ill will from the military withdrawal half a lifetime ago. A few rich young Russians came to the beaches. But this was not a rich young Russian.

One of the older men, a distinguished-looking man with white hair, said, "Do you speak English at all?"

A matronly Cuban woman delivered a cup of coffee. Dankevich offered some pesos, which he had obtained at the cambio in the hotel. One of the men said with a smile, *"Nyet, nyet."* They all laughed.

Dankevich said, "Only little. One, two words maybe."

The English-speaking man asked, "Your first trip to Cuba?"

Dankevich had heard accented English, British English, and American English. This sounded very much like American English. "Nyet . . . no, sorry. I was here many years ago."

The white-haired man translated for the other two. Then he said, "During the crisis time?"

"*Da* . . . yes," Dankevich said. "Many years ago. Since then, not back till now."

"It is pretty much the same," the kindly man said. "Don't you think?"

"I think so," Dankevich offered hesitantly. "But I not here long, yet. Not see much, yet. Maybe soon." He drank the delicious coffee, grateful for the taste and the many fond memories it carried with it.

"Are you staying long?" the English-speaker asked.

Dankevich shook his head no. "Not so long. Little time. Look around. See old places." He liked the man he was talking with, the American. Maybe, when his job was done, he could have a dinner with him, learn a few more American phrases. "You live here . . . this area?" he asked.

The white-haired man said, "Yes, and you are also in this area?"

Dankevich nodded, then finished the coffee. He was suddenly afraid that his bosses would come back and discover him gone, and that maybe he had already said more than he should. He stood up, reached for the pesos again, and was again waved off. He bowed and said, *"Dasvedanya . . . buenas noches."*

The men watched him go. They looked at one another and quietly commented on the oddity of an elderly Russian in their neighborhood.

McLemore had insisted, out of Suarez's hearing, that Trinidad join him for dinner. He urgently needed to see her and talk with her. He had an agenda. They met at nine in the small front dining room at the Santa Isabel. Now that McLemore had become associated with at least an element of Cuban intelligence, Trinidad was less concerned about being seen with him in public. At least Lazaro might be somewhat less concerned now about McLemore's possibly trying to recruit her. McLemore had not eaten since early morning, and Trinidad not even then. Despite that, she picked at the dinner as McLemore wolfed his down.

He said, "I have a request—I'd make it a demand, if I had a right to— and I'll make it as strongly as I can. On Thursday"—which was New Year's Eve—"I want you to take your mother and leave Havana. Go west, go someplace in Pinar del Río. I'll get a car and you can drive down the peninsula. I insist that you do it."

She studied her plate, thinking of her mother, her father, her sister, then looked into his eyes. "You know I cannot do this. It is cowardly. It is unfair to all the others. Simply because I know this awful secret, I cannot take advantage of that and leave my whole city behind. If so many of my countrymen—my brothers and sisters—are killed, then I should not live. It would not be right."

"This is not for you," he said. "This is for me. It is my selfish request. I will not have you die. You are the first person I have cared about in . . . in many years. I am not going to let this happen to you. You have become too important to me. You are what I believe in now."

She placed her hand on his. The waitress, surely in the same business as she was, took note. "You are so kind . . . so very kind. You must know that I have come to feel much as you do. You are the one who must go. This is not your country. These are not your people. You have already helped this country so much. We would probably have found out about these terrorists without you. But we would not have known the exact danger or from where it came without you. Because of you, we still have a chance. We can still save ourselves."

McLemore looked out into the ancient Plaza, then back at her. "Let's be honest. If these people are clever . . . or even if they are just lucky . . . they can do this crazy thing. They can kill many, many people." The fierceness in his eyes and his voice almost frightened Trinidad. She had never seen him quite this way. He seemed almost beside himself. "I will not let them kill you."

"You cannot force me to go, as grateful as I truly am for your concern," she said. "It has also been a long time since anyone cared in such a way for me." She touched his hand again. "It is why I was as I was to you when we met. It wasn't just that you were a Yanqui. It was also that I did not much like men—any men. Now that has changed. Because of you, I feel like a human being . . . a real person . . . once again a caring woman. You have helped me get back my humanity." She smiled, tears in her eyes. "I can only thank you for that. . . ." Her voice broke and she turned away.

They did not talk for a while. The dishes were taken away, the observant waitress noticing the clasped hands. Neither of them particularly cared now. They knew something she did not: They could all be dead in three days.

37 After dinner McLemore walked Trinidad back to her flat in the Vedado section, then returned to the hotel. Along the way they discussed the steps being taken to find the Bravo unit. Juanita's pictures of its individual members, taken clandestinely in Miami weeks before, had been circulated throughout the Cuban intelligence network, including the local Committees for the Defense of the Revolution, or

CDRs, and the national security structure. When the U.S. files arrived—in the morning, they hoped—any additional pictures and information would also be circulated through the same networks. If they got Isakov to talk about the Russian connection, they might also have another target upon which to focus.

That same night Suarez was briefing Nuñez and other senior security officials on the Bravo group, the kind of weapon they had, and McLemore's unprecedented step of involving U.S. intelligence. This information would go to *el Commandante* immediately, and a decision would be made whether the anniversary celebration would go forward as planned. Trinidad expressed concern for Lazaro. He would be harshly criticized and possibly demoted or even fired. Nuñez would demand to know—in very angry language—why he had been kept in the dark for almost a full day after the warhead was found missing.

McLemore told Trinidad of Ramsay's dilemma—should he or should he not move his family. She reflected that now the Cuban leadership was in the same boat. If they called off the celebration, Bravo could still plant its weapon in or near the center of Havana and do enormous damage. Castro and the key leadership could not leave Havana without seeming cowardly and callous toward their fellow citizens. They could evacuate the city, but immense damage would still be done to buildings and infrastructure, and there would be chaos and panic. Besides, the government was not prepared to feed, clothe, and house close to two million Cubans roaming the countryside. And, in that case, Bravo could simply decide to put the warhead in Santa Clara, Santiago de Cuba, or any one of several other cities.

Trinidad observed, finally, that the whole country was hostage to Bravo, that the only solution was to find them before they struck. The discussion of other cities reminded McLemore of a fact he had not until then recognized. Guantánamo naval base was on the eastern tip of Cuba. Roughly five thousand U.S. military forces were there in conformity with a hundred-year-old treaty. He knew very little about radiation and nuclear fallout, but he had to surmise that the Luna warhead was "dirty," that it had the potential to carry deadly radiation and contaminants at least as far as the end of the island. In case Worthy, or someone else in Washington, hadn't thought about it, he intended to remind them in the morning. The United States had a genuine national interest, in addition to avoiding the opprobrium associated with U.S. citizens carrying out the worst terrorist act in human history.

As they parted, Trinidad and McLemore embraced for tense moments. He did not want to let her go. She had become, for him, the only history, the only cause, he cared about.

This new truth, one that he had come to realize only gradually, occupied his mind as he stood across from the Santa Isabel in the shadow of the thick old trees, waiting for the voice. It was close to midnight, and Suarez would pick him up in six hours to go to the airport to meet Worthy and Viktor Isakov. Prescott materialized in the shadows—McLemore had given up wondering how—and they sat down.

"Given all you've done for me," McLemore said, "I'm obliged to tell you a dirty little secret. The gang I mentioned to you . . . down from Miami . . . is planning to blow this city up in a couple of days. You probably ought to take the occasion to visit some friends as far away as possible."

"Why would they do a thing like that?" Prescott asked.

"Father, you know the human heart better than I do. It's a desperately complex place."

"Indeed," the old man said mournfully, "especially when its intricacies are turned to politics."

McLemore lowered his voice to a whisper. "They have an old Soviet warhead, left over from the missile crisis. They got into the country and snatched it, and we assume they're planning to blow it up, and as much of the Cuban leadership as they can, in a couple of days—at the celebration."

Prescott was silent. Then he said, "How can a small group of Cuban Americans know how to explode a warhead meant for a missile?"

McLemore was dumbstruck at his immense practicality. "We think—I guess by now you've guessed that I'm working with the authorities here—we think they have obtained the services of a Russian technician, probably some kind of military expert from the old days. The warhead is close to forty years old, so whoever this person is must be up in years."

"My age," Prescott said.

His thoughts having drifted to where Trinidad slept, McLemore said abstractly, "Yeah, something like that. We've given out pictures of this group, the Bravo group, to the local vigilante committees, and we should know more in the morning—some information from the States—about the Russian—or Russians—who's helping them."

"I would like to keep in touch with you," Prescott said. "Where can I find you tomorrow?"

Thinking he meant to find out the latest information, McLemore said, "Here at the hotel tomorrow night. Leave a message or meet me here. Most of the day I'll be at the Interest office or maybe Trinidad's office in the Interior Ministry. But unless something dramatic happens, I'll be back here tomorrow night."

Suddenly preoccupied, the old man nodded, bid McLemore good night, and promised to meet him the following evening.

As Prescott walked back to the Cerro district in the early hours, he could not know the drama occurring only a few streets away from his small flat. Dankevich slumped in his rickety straight-backed chair next to the warhead as Manny continued to berate him.

"You pull that trick again, and I'll strangle you with my own hands. What in God's name were you thinking about? Somebody gets suspicious, follows you back here, we're all in jail for the rest of our lives—if we're lucky. Better chance we'd be sliced up with tiny little razor blades and permitted to bleed to death over a couple of days. Think about that. That what you want?" The other men stood around taking turns harassing and threatening the old man.

He hung his head like a miserable schoolboy. "I need walking," he said during a pause in the barrage, "I need some nice air."

"You'll get walking. You'll get air. Three days, you get all the walking, all the air you can stand. Now you sleep," Tony, the good cop, said. "Now you sleep. In the morning you hook up this timer. Then your job is done. Understand?"

Dankevich nodded, still miserable. He didn't like to be treated like a captive. If this is capitalism, no wonder we didn't like it, he muttered grumpily to himself. And, just before he fell into a troubled sleep, a sudden question occurred to him: If Manny and Tony and their friends were there to help the Cubans stop a Yanqui invasion, why were they hiding out in this shabby place? Why weren't they working at a secure Cuban military base? Most of all, why were they afraid of being discovered?

Later, as the men bedded down, rotating nights on the two cots and the rest on the floor, a tall, lean white-haired figure passed by outside like a specter. In the late afternoon, Prescott had watched as the nice old Russian man had left his table of local coffee drinkers and headed in this direction. Prescott had a sense that he was somewhere close by. He also had a sense that the Russian was the man McLemore was looking for. It occurred to him that, after all, he might be of some service.

38 The twin-engine executive jet, unmarked except for a small U.S. flag and identification number on the tail, came into José Martí International Airport, ten kilometers outside Havana, landing fast, then followed the escort vehicle to a small, private VIP terminal. Even before the engines were shut down, the door popped open and the stairs automatically descended. A greeting party including Sam Ramsay, Lazaro Suarez, Trinidad, and McLemore moved toward the stairs as two men descended. McLemore was the only one who knew them both. One was Mr. Worthy and the other Viktor Isakov. Under the circumstances, McLemore hung back to let Ramsay make the introductions. Isakov refused to look at or shake hands with anyone except McLemore. At McLemore, he gazed with raw hatred.

They loaded into two cars, Worthy, Isakov, and Ramsay in an Interest office van, and the others in Suarez's Ministry car. With Suarez in the lead and his blue light flashing on the dash, they sped toward Havana and, by prearrangement, to the Interest office. Nuñez's insistence that the meeting be held at the Interior Ministry had been rebuffed by Ramsay on orders from Washington, and the delegation had been limited to those in Suarez's car. Nuñez and senior Ministry officials were apoplectic.

Once in the "bubble," Mr. Worthy led off. "Señor Suarez, I am turning over to you files relating to the identity of members of a group that calls itself Bravo or Bravo 99. You will notice that the Federal Bureau of Investigation has edited these files, obviously to protect our sources and methods. Perhaps most valuable to you are some fairly clear photographs of the half-dozen key leaders of the group who are most probably the ones who have penetrated your borders." He pushed two or three thin manila folders across the conference table to Suarez, who nodded thanks. "In this regard I must tell you that, since these pictures were taken, members of this group more or less disappeared or went to ground, and they may well have altered their appearances with new facial hair, hair dyes, skin coloring, or whatever. Therefore, these pictures were reliable only up until six or eight weeks ago, when we first placed these individuals under surveillance. In fact"—he smiled ruefully, acknowledging the well-known but little-discussed Cuban network in south Florida—"you may well have more current information than we have."

"Mr. Worthy," Suarez said, "we are most grateful for the cooperation your presence here represents. We acknowledge that it is without precedent, at least where we are concerned, and my government takes it as a gesture of very good will by your country."

Face redder than usual, Ramsay interjected, "I wouldn't go too far with that." But Worthy gestured him into silence.

Worthy continued, "Regarding the files, I must add one condition. As far as we are concerned, this meeting and this exchange of information never occurred. After the fact, and especially if you are successful at averting disas—ah—trouble, we will deny that we ever participated in this affair."

Suarez nodded acceptingly and obediently. "We have no reason to convert your cooperation regarding this critical threat to political advantage. You have my word that none of those with whom I am associated will ever publicly acknowledge our mutual efforts here. I will even be so bold as to suggest that our president, Commandante Castro, will personally and privately express the official thanks of our country and our people after our efforts, please God, succeed."

"Let's worry about the protocol later," Mr. Worthy said. Turning to Isakov, he continued, "I have with me Mr. Victor Isaacs, a citizen of the United States whose original Russian name was Viktor Leonidovich Isakov. Mr. Isaacs is cooperating with us, I think it is safe to say, reluctantly." Isakov was a study in dark brown funk. "He acknowledges that he is in the business of selling Russian armaments and that he negotiated for the sale of certain weapons to individuals"—he retrieved the files containing the pictures from Suarez—"identified as members of the Bravo group. I now ask you, Mr. Isaacs, if these are the two men with whom you arranged the sale." He separated out Manny's and Tony's pictures and showed them to Isakov. This was a formality, a repeat of a lengthy interrogation conducted the previous day after the Agency had picked him up from the Bureau. Isakov nodded his head, miserably, in the affirmative. "We take that for a yes. These negotiations took place in September and October, and we gather from what you told us yesterday that Bravo has possibly taken possession of the hardware here yesterday morning."

Ramsay and Suarez both nodded.

"Now, Mr. Isaacs," Worthy continued, "we have brought you here to ask you one question. You have already been informed that your dealings with the Bravo group were conducted without the appropriate licenses from the U.S. Bureau of Alcohol, Tobacco, and Firearms and amounts to a violation of about three dozen U.S. laws. Since you are a United States citizen, and therefore protected by certain constitutional guarantees, you will be permitted to retain legal counsel upon our return to the United States. Your counsel will inform you that you do not have to answer this question and that, if you do answer this question, it can be used against you in court. However, Mr. Isaacs, we have a very serious situation on our hands here. If you cooperate, my Agency will be willing to cooperate with your counsel to seek a resolution of your considerable legal difficulties in a manner that may preserve your citizenship and even keep you out of jail. If not, Mr. Isaacs, I can promise you that the full weight of the government of the United States of America will come down on your head like a ton of shit and we will find a jail cell for you that will make the gulag look like a Four Seasons Hotel."

Isakov blanched.

Ramsay said, "And, Mr. Isaacs, that is the best you can hope for. It is not out of the question that Mr. Worthy here might forget you when he takes off for the United States. In that case, Mr. Suarez has a boss, a certain Colonel Nuñez, who is widely believed throughout this country to be the meanest Cuban alive. We'll let him have you for a couple of days . . . say, until late morning Thursday . . . then we'll tie you to a stake somewhere near the center of the Plaza de la Revolución and let you enjoy firsthand the celebration of the fortieth anniversary of the glorious Cuban revolution."

By now Viktor was extremely pale and looking for a pen to sign any confession placed in front of him. He looked right and left for food or drink or, mostly, a men's room. Ramsay grabbed his arm and escorted him down the hall. As they went out the door, Ramsay turned and said, "He seems to want to think it over."

They returned and Mr. Worthy said, "Mr. Isaacs, you have sold a nuclear weapon to a group of men who know little or nothing about nuclear weapons—particularly rather old ones. Did you or did you not also negotiate an arrangement whereby someone knowledgeable about these weapons would be available to try to make them functional?"

Isakov nodded his heavy jowls up and down.

"Now we will expect you to tell us everything there is to know about this individual," Mr. Worthy said as he sat back and folded his arms.

Isakov's words spilled out like a flood. "Dankevich, his name. Dmitri Dmitrivich. Former Soviet army lieutenant colonel in the Strategic Rocket Forces. Deputy of my father. Now he is"—he thought momentarily—"seventy-four, seventy-five years old. Nuclear engineering specialist with warheads. Lives in Moscow. He comes here, to Cuba, maybe four—five—days ago under Russian passport. His name. You can check. He goes to Victoria Hotel, waits one day, Manny and Tony come get him. He fixes bomb. That's all. Is all I know."

"Why is he doing it?" McLemore asked. "Are you paying him?"

Isakov said, "Not me—them. Maybe ten thousand. A lot of money for him. He leaves to his family."

"Does he know how they will use this weapon?" McLemore asked.

Isakov shrugged.

"Do you know how they will use this weapon?" McLemore asked.

"How do you say, 'No ask, no tell'?" Isakov seemed pleased with his cleverness.

Ramsay looked ready to eviscerate him, with a dull knife.

Suarez said, "Tell us what he—Dankevich—looks like."

Isakov described his father's former subordinate, whom he remembered from his boyhood days. His father had continued to browbeat his colleague well into their retirement years and Viktor had witnessed much of it when they would get together. They all took careful notes, asking questions in as minute detail as possible—color of eyes, warts, dots, crooked fingers. They had exhausted all possible identification marks when Isakov smiled, "My father. He is throwing cognac bottle one time. Dankevich not see him. Stand up and bottle hit him right here." He pointed to his eyebrow. "Make little scar splitting eyebrow."

McLemore said, "Will they send him back when he is finished? What will happen to him?"

Isakov smiled again, almost as if to himself. "I think they kill him."

 While Dankevich had been arming the warhead the day before, Manny and Tony found the maintenance shops for the Havana city government. Located in a series of small buildings in the warehouse district, these buildings housed the workers who kept the municipality's facilities running. In one of the shops Manny said they wanted to report a stuck elevator at the National Hotel, and they were sent two buildings down. Behind the building where they had been sent, they saw men coming and going in ones and twos. The men all wore a standard coverall with a small cloth identification badge above the left pocket, and they drove trucks with distinctive city markings that were kept in an unguarded motor pool. At the end of the day, they noticed the men hung the coveralls on hooks in an uncovered outdoor shed. The coveralls were so worn and dirty there was little chance they would be stolen.

About the time Isakov was under interrogation at the U.S. Interest office on the morning of the thirtieth, Manny drove Orlando and Pete to the maintenance shop. Orlando knew the elevator business, and Pete was along for the heavy lifting. Joe, the electronics expert, stayed as Dankevich's assistant in attaching the timer, and Tony stayed as Dankevich's friend. Johnny rode with Manny to help "liberate" a vehicle. Manny dropped the three men off and arranged to meet them at a prearranged pickup spot three hours later.

They waited fifty yards away from the back of the shops and the motor pool until there was no activity and then went into a planned drill. Johnny went to the motor pool and quickly hot-wired one of the battered, ancient trucks in the back row. He drove it forward as Orlando and Pete picked up three coveralls from the open shed. They jumped in beside Johnny and headed toward the Plaza. Orlando had brought a weathered case full of tools his father had originally used in starting up his elevator business. A few blocks away, in a sleepy neighborhood, they pulled the truck over and put on the coveralls. Because he had grown up in the most Spanish-speaking household and, therefore, spoke in the most authentic Cuban idiom, Orlando drove and the other two sat in the cab with him. They approached the Plaza from the Avenida Carlos de Céspedes on the north-west side of the Plaza, then turned left briefly onto Paseo and then quickly right to the guardhouse protecting the approach to the Martí tower and the Palacio de la Revolución that housed the Central Committee of the Cuban Communist Party and the senior government leadership—includ-ing *el Jefe*. If the project was to fail, it would be in the next two or three minutes, and the passengers in the truck and most probably their Bravo colleagues would never see the United States or the light of day again.

The tension in the truck cab was palpable as Orlando spoke in his soft, lilting Spanish to the stern military guards. He said his boss sent him to check out the elevator, especially the motor, to make sure it was in good shape for the coming celebration. Somebody had called from the Central Committee, probably some bureaucrat. Said that *el Commandante* might want to take some distinguished foreign visitors to the top to see the city. Demanded that the elevator be checked. One of the three military guards went around to the back of the truck, looked in, then jumped in and fumbled through the tool case. He jumped back out and looked under the truck. Orlando showed them the papers registering the truck to the City of Havana motor pool. The corporal of the guard wanted to know how long it would take. Orlando said no more than half an hour—an hour tops—that is, unless they found a problem. The guard looked at the men closely, and they all silently thanked the clever Manny for telling them to scrape some grease from the truck bed to pack under their fingernails and smudge on their faces. The corporal motioned one of his men to go with them. Pete got in the back and the guard sat in front for the one-hundred-yard drive to the tower.

The guard showed them around to the back of the tower and let them in the utility entrance. Again the men silently thanked Manny for making them visit the Martí museum and case the ground floor in the process. The chief of maintenance showed them the electrical master panel and the fuses controlling the elevator. They then rode to the top and back down. Orlando suggested to the chief that the motor was making a strange sound. They listened, Orlando repeatedly pointing out the creak, click, or catch, and the chief agreed that he could hear it. He showed them to the master elevator motor, and Orlando went to work with his wrenches. He started and stopped the motor, speeded up and slowed down its calibration mechanisms, tested its lubrication and hydraulic fluids. While Pete distracted the chief and Johnny shielded his movements, he slightly loosened one of the principal electrical contacts. He started and stopped the motor, and it sounded distinctly irregular. At the same time, he reached in his coverall and pulled out a small plastic motor oil container and poured it on the floor.

Orlando summoned the maintenance chief over, showed him the oil, and demonstrated the irregular heartbeat of the motor. While he explained that the motor would probably hold up during the ceremonies, the chief saw his life flash before him. The only vision he could muster was *el Commandante* and a couple of world leaders stuck for hours at the top of the tower while the whole world watched or, worst of all, all of them splattered on the floor of an elevator carriage that had just free-fallen 142 meters. He insisted that Orlando and his crew fix the machine immediately. Orlando shook his head and said it was impossible. This motor was doomed to get worse. He showed the chief the registration plate on the motor: 1979. The only thing that had kept this motor alive was the fact that it had been used so seldom in recent years. "But," Orlando said, "we have some luck." Back at the shop he was sure there was a backup motor ordered from the manufacturer a few years ago and kept in storage ever since.

Orlando took him aside and said confidently, "Tell you what. We'll bring the other motor back tomorrow, late morning, jerk this old one out, put the new one in, all in less time than it would take to fix this one." He hit it a resounding whack with a wrench. "We'll get this old one out of here and no one will know that you had a defective motor in here. No one." Orlando was doing him a favor. He was saving his life. The only thing Orlando needed to meet his deadline was for the chief to get them through the guards tomorrow with no trouble. He thought the chief might kiss his hand. The chief promised all the preparations would be made and that no one would interfere with Orlando's work. *"Hasta mañana,"* Orlando said.

They had the truck and coveralls back at the shop well before closing time. No one noticed three guys coming back from a hard day, parking their truck, and dropping their coveralls. They were only fifteen minutes late for their rendezvous with Manny, who laughed with delight and relief at the canniness of his protégé Orlando.

As they pulled their rented truck into the parking spot behind the flat, Tony was returning through the front door with Dankevich. With Joe's help, Dankevich had attached the timer to the warhead. With Joe watching, he had traced and retraced the electrical circuits, explaining the flow of the impulses and the workings of the device—a high-energy explosion driven inward, an implosion created by the sophisticated electrical triggering circuits, causing the fissionable nuclear material to create the critical mass necessary for a nuclear "incident." Really very simple, he explained.

The atmosphere in the clubhouse was increasingly tense. Months of planning and waiting, days of implementation, hours of nuclear stress. Finally, worried that his charge might crack, Tony had taken him for a walk in the neighborhood. He gave Dankevich more traditional Caribbean clothing, and they strolled out into the late-afternoon stillness. If neighbors tried to engage them, Tony waved and muttered a greeting and moved on quickly. They were returning after a half-hour tour of ten or twelve square blocks when they passed a lone figure on the opposite sidewalk. It was the kindly English-speaking man Dankevich had met the previous morning over coffee. They nodded—and Prescott knew he had found his man.

Tony observed the exchange, but since the men did not speak, he made little of it. Prescott saw him take Dankevich's arm as if he were under arrest and steer him down the next side street. Prescott reversed course, staying comfortably back, and watched them turn another corner, to the right, a block away. He walked as fast as he could and arrived at the corner just as the two men entered an unremarkable doorway almost at the end of the block. He waited a few minutes and then walked slowly down the street. He knew the neighborhood and the street well. He had, after all, lived here almost forty years. He came to the corner and walked back down the block one more time. As casually as he could, he went around the block, noting the truck in the back parking area. Back on the narrow street running in front of the row of decrepit houses, Prescott saw a familiar old tree on a corner of the block beyond the cross streets and sat down with his back against the trunk.

He was not aware that his movements had been seen by Tony who, after depositing Dankevich safely back in the clubhouse, had returned to the single, curtained front window to see if anyone had been following them. Sure enough, there came the lanky old man, looking more American than Cuban, strolling down the sidewalk, slightly hunched with years, looking across the street at their house. Periodically, Tony checked the window while the others prepared yet another rice and beans dinner. Thank God they had more bottles of rum. He could hardly wait for the steak, the pizza, the hamburgers of home. Then, peering down the block from the corner of the window, he saw the thin old man sitting down propped up against a tree. They were being staked out!

Tony whispered to Manny, who came to the window and spotted the same man. He said to Dankevich, "Did you make friends with anyone since you've been here, in this place?"

Dankevich shook his head no.

"Who is this?" he asked, dragging the Russian to the window.

Dankevich shrugged. "I see him across street when walking day before," he lied. Manny's grip on his arm communicated seriousness.

"Do you know him?" Manny hissed. "Did you talk to him?"

Dankevich again shook his head. "Don't know him."

My God, Manny thought. We're so close. We can't let some old fool screw this up. He called Pete and Johnny. He showed them the old figure and instructed them to strike up an acquaintance and bring him inside as quickly as they could. This thing was getting much too complicated.

Within minutes, the front door opened and Father John Prescott found himself face-to-face with the members of Bravo 99.

40 That night, less than forty-eight hours before the anniversary celebration, McLemore sat in the open courtyard bar of the Santa Isabel hotel. He was on his third *mojito* and still no Prescott. Never before, in the three months since their friendship began, had Prescott promised to meet and then not appeared. He wondered if the years had simply overtaken the friend who had become his mentor and touchstone. During his two residencies at the Santa Isabel, he had become so accustomed to the chirping, singing birds in the large wicker cage in the corner of the courtyard that he seldom noticed them. When he did, it was their unself-conscious beauty that struck him. But tonight, while he waited, concerned for his ancient friend, concerned most of all for the woman he had come to love, he listened to their singing. Under the influence of the rum, he thought their music sounded sad and wistful. Bright, beautiful creatures of nature should not be caged.

Periodically he walked around the Plaza, listening for the now familiar resonant voice, as distinctive as a vintage wine or Trinidad's fleeting kiss. It was now well past even Prescott's late hours, and he was nowhere to be seen.

This day, December 30, 1998, had been one of the worst of McLemore's life. After seeing Mr. Worthy and Viktor Isakov off at the airport, he had stayed with Trinidad in Suarez's office. It had become the command post for the search for Bravo 99. Havana and surrounding communities had been divided into sectors, and security teams, equipped with Cuban and FBI pictures of the Bravo group, had searched district by district well into the evening and were even now searching block by block and would, if time permitted, begin to go door-to-door. The CDRs were provided pictures and descriptions and were encouraged to canvass their neighborhoods. Anytime Suarez had to report to Nuñez and other officials, Trinidad and McLemore made themselves scarce in small conference rooms or in her office. Nuñez had been briefed on the role McLemore had played in obtaining information from U.S. intelligence, but he refused to believe—especially after learning the identity of McLemore's father—that the Yanqui was not some sort of agent for the U.S. Nuñez made it clear he wanted nothing to do with McLemore. And, remembering Prescott's story about his father's last days, McLemore thought such a confrontation might, in any case, turn violent right away.

But the hours of the day, the minutes of the hours, and the seconds of each minute, ticked away with no Bravo and no Dmitri Dankevich. McLemore had seldom known such frustration, such helplessness. Somewhere within reasonable distance there were at least six men with a nuclear warhead planning to detonate it somewhere near a million people—and no one seemed capable of stopping them. His friend and mentor had disappeared. The woman he loved refused to save herself. Nearby the birds sang their sad chirping songs lamenting ages of folly.

After meeting all day with his top officials, Trinidad told McLemore as he walked her home, Castro decided he could not stop the celebration. It was too important. It was too symbolic. It must go on. The revolution had survived crisis after crisis. The revolution would survive this crisis. The terrorists must be found.

So now there was no turning back. By tomorrow morning people from all across Cuba would start pouring toward the capital. They would come for the Thursday festivities, and many would stay on for a long weekend in the big city. That is, if there still was a city.

McLemore looked up as Sam Ramsay sat down. The wily waiter, Ramsay's old friend, brought two more *mojitos*, unasked. He smirked at the red-faced Yanqui. Dummy, McLemore thought, you're not high enough up the ladder to know how close you are to getting your nice hairdo blown off.

"What's up?" McLemore asked.

Ramsay shrugged. "Feelin' lonesome. Thought you might have some news."

"You should be with your family, not with me," McLemore said. "Or have you got them out of town?"

"My family's in the States," Ramsay said, sipping his drink. "What's left of it. Wife got tired of the spook life. Husband out on the town, meeting and greeting every night. Doing what else, God knows. Too much for her."

McLemore said, "What was all that horseshit about should you get your family out of town?"

"Just that. Horseshit. Wanted to see how serious you thought this thing might get." He lifted his glass. "Here's to you. You gave me the right answer."

McLemore lifted his glass in return. "So, what are *you* going to do? No need for you to stick around. If I were you, I'd find a reason to check out a potential new source down around Cabo de San Antonio."

Ramsay laughed. That was the Cuban equivalent of Tierra del Fuego. "I think the best I could do is Guantánamo . . . wait with the troops."

"What are our geniuses in Washington going to do about Guantánamo?" McLemore asked.

Ramsay said, "Last I heard, they were sending some innocent-looking troopships around from the south. Get ready to load the troops up as fast as they can if the balloon goes up."

"Anybody know how long it takes the dirty stuff to drift down there if the bad guys win?" McLemore asked, suddenly feeling the rum and the stress.

"Oh, I'm sure some smart guys up at Langley are working on that right now." Ramsay seemed uncommonly reflective. "What about you? You should start thinking about shipping out, you know. Can't see any reason for you to hang around. You've messed this up about as much as you can, don't you think?"

McLemore said, "Thought I'd stick around for a couple more days. See how it all turns out. Compared to this, you can't imagine how boring teaching can be. I haven't had so much fun since I learned about sex."

"Speaking of that subject," Ramsay said, waving for yet more drinks, "your decision to stay for the fireworks, that wouldn't have to do with a certain female Cuban intelligence officer, would it?"

"I'm tempted to say it's none of your business," McLemore said, "but since we've become such pals over the months, I'll answer your question. Yes. It does have something to do with her."

"True love," Ramsay sighed. "My God. I never thought it would happen to my old pal Mac." The birds sang wistfully in the background. "I watched her this morning. I watched her watching you. You got a problem on your hands, pal. She's managed to set aside her Marxist-Leninism to fall for a . . . what? What exactly would you call yourself, Mac?"

"I'm a member of the people's party. Simple ideology. Live and let live. Give the other guy a hand when he needs it. Help old ladies. Protect nature. Be kind to children. That particularly. Be very kind to children. That about sums it up."

Ramsay said, "Sounds more like a church to me. Maybe you're a member of the people's church."

"Beats politics," McLemore said.

"I'll drink to that," Ramsay said, clinking glasses.

By now McLemore was feeling very drunk. The waiter was closing down the bar. It was almost two in the morning. "Good-bye, Red. Don't know when our paths may cross. But here's to you. You can be a royal pain in the ass. But, down deep, carefully hidden, there's a good guy trying to get out. I hope he makes it. And . . . I hope you make it."

Ramsay understood his meaning.

They shook hands and, on his way toward the door, Ramsay turned and said, "It's been a swell ride, Mac. I do hope to see you around. Most of all, take care of that *señorita*."

McLemore waited a few minutes for Ramsay to leave and the bar to close down. The waiter packed up and left. McLemore made one more pass through the darkened Plaza, the oldest spot in one of the oldest cities in the Western Hemisphere. No Prescott. In two days would there be an ancient city?

McLemore came back into the hotel, waved good night to the night clerk, then started through the courtyard for the stairs to his room. The birds sang him on his way. He stopped to listen. Then he turned back to the corner of the courtyard. He came to the cage, and the birds became silent. He and the birds studied one another solemnly. Then he opened the cage. He said, "Go on. Go on. Leave here. Leave this cage. Fly away." He stepped back. One bird came to the open door, perched, then with a shrill whistle to the others, flew into the night. His mate followed him. McLemore shook the cage gently. Another pair, one by one, flew away. "Leave now. Go south. Go west. Get away." Two others flew. "Leave now. Go. Fly away now." One after the other, two others fled, leaving a single pair behind in the back of the cage. "Go away," McLemore pleaded. "You're free now. You can go. No more cages. Go." They hung in the back. McLemore begged them, "Go sing. Please go sing. Get away from here." Still the birds hung back.

In the darkness of the early hours of the morning of New Year's Eve in the open courtyard, McLemore broke into tears, holding the wicker cage in his arms with the two frightened birds huddled inside.

41 Prescott watched various members of the Bravo group dress, drink coffee, and talk quietly among themselves. His hands and feet remained tied from the previous evening. He had spent more than twelve hours curled in a fetal position on the bare floor in the corner of an ordinary-size room now crammed with eight men. The old Russian man, his own age, had been treated only slightly better; he had been given a threadbare blanket in which to wrap himself. Though he had played the dumb *campesino* during his intense, sometimes brutal, interrogation by the man they called Manny, from all that McLemore had told him Prescott knew this to be the elusive—and deadly—Bravo group. More important, he knew the blanket-covered object in the corner to be the ugliest invention of the mind of man. Indeed, throughout the long, sleepless night, Prescott had hallucinated the face, shape, and evil intent of Satan beneath the blanket, grinning, gesturing vulgarly, and beckoning him to join the last great orgy knowable by man. Prescott reflected that a lifetime of asceticism now served him well.

In the opposite corner of the room, the old Russian, whom the men seemed to refer to as "Dank" something, like "Dank-witch," stirred, sat up, and asked politely in broken English for coffee. Although no one seemed to pay attention, the one they called Tony presently helped him up and into one of the three aged chairs, then gave him coffee in a cracked cup. Occasionally, one or two of the men went in and out a back door, apparently carrying things to the truck Prescott had seen in back while reconnoitering the clubhouse the previous day. Once or twice Prescott made out muttered references in conversations carried out in the tiny kitchen to "the old man." He didn't know whether they meant him or the Russian. In any case, he did not expect to leave this place alive. Throughout the night, he took the occasion to seek forgiveness for his sins, to express thanks for his many blessings, and to commend his soul to God. He also said a prayer for McLemore and the Cuban woman whom he loved.

At midmorning the blanket was lifted from the mechanical Satan. For Prescott, it was even uglier than his vivid dreams. The Russian sat down before it as though to worship a technological golden calf. Through partially closed eyes, Prescott watched the other old man undertake to attach something that looked like a very sophisticated, large electrical alarm clock to it. One man they called Johnny handed him tools and held a magnifying glass. The work was tedious. It seemed to take a great effort, as if he were repairing a very delicate clock, and the room had remained silent as the work proceeded.

After what seemed to Prescott to be at least two hours, the Russian, "Dank-witch," pointed out the clock mechanism to Johnny as the others collected behind them. In halting English, he explained how the outside edge of the clock's dial was to be turned clockwise until the arrow pointed at the number "23." Then an adjoining dial had to be clicked around until an arrow pointed at "timer." Then, finally, a switch had to be thrown. When it was, the underside of the switch would show red. The device was then armed and would become "operational" exactly twenty-three hours later. So that, if they wanted it to activate at noon the following day, these steps had to be taken at exactly 1 P.M. that afternoon.

The man called Joe asked the Russian several technical questions concerning circuits, volts, and impulse timing. Then, satisfied, Joe cloaked the Satan again in its shabby robe. One man opened the back door, and four of the men, two on each side, gently lifted the device back into its metal frame and then out the back way, Prescott presumed, into the truck. Although the men spoke softly, he could occasionally hear words like "boat," "truck," and, once or twice, "tower" and "elevator."

Four of the men prepared to leave. There was a discussion among the six near the back door. It seemed to be about returning to this place later that afternoon. There was something about "tools" and "boat." Presently, five men left, and the truck could be heard starting and moving away. The one called Tony, who seemed to care about the old Russian, stayed behind.

He said, "My partners have to take care of some things . . . some business. They've got to deliver that 'whizbang' . . . that thing . . . ah, to the, ah . . . to the Cuban military. You know, to fight against the invasion, like we told you. When they come back, we'll make some dinner for you. I'm going to stay here with the two of you . . . most of the time. . . . We're going down to Pinar del Río tomorrow morning. Maybe we can take you to find some of those old Cuban friends of yours down there. How would that be with you?"

Dankevich nodded and softly said, "Okay." Prescott was wondering why younger people always shouted at older people.

When the truck pulled up in back, Manny came in, talked quietly with Tony, then brought some rough hemp rope. "Mr. Dankewitz, we don't like to do this. But things are too dangerous for you to be out in the neighborhood again. Too many bad people out there these days . . . sticking their nose in, like this old-timer." As he tied Dankevich's hands to a water pipe in the corner, he said, "We really don't like doing this. But it is to protect you from all those CIA guys, like this old fella here. He snoops around, this old American here. Picks something up, sells it to the local CIA agents. 'Found a Russian nuclear arms expert down here.' They pay him, come looking for you, probably torture you, then shoot you." He stepped back and said, "Can't let that happen. You're our partner. We got to protect you." Tony put a glass of water on the floor next to him, then stepped outside with Manny, not explaining how Dankevich was to reach the water.

The two tied-up elderly men, one Russian, one American, were silent, confused, uncertain when their captors might suddenly reappear. Presently, Prescott said, "I don't mean to frighten you. But I believe these men are not your friends. I believe they mean to do you harm."

Dankevich snorted, shaking his bound hands. "Even me—a stupid old man—now understand this," he said.

"Do you understand their plan?" Prescott asked.

Dankevich said, "Americans prepare to invade. Luna is used to stop them."

Prescott shook his head. "There is no American invasion. The Luna will be used to kill a lot of Cuban people—tomorrow. During a big Cuban celebration."

Dankevich looked away momentarily. Then he said, "Do you believe in God?"

Prescott was stunned. "Yes. I do. One time, I was even a priest."

Dankevich nodded. "I know you are good man. Maybe even holy man." He was thinking. "I tell you sins. I . . . how you say? . . . confess to you."

Prescott watched with amazement as the old Russian struggled to his knees and bowed his head.

A mile away, Manny dropped the four men behind the maintenance shops and waited while Pete got the coveralls from the shed, Joe hot-wired a truck from the motor pool, Orlando clamored aboard with his tool case, and they all pulled away. Two blocks away the two trucks pulled up back-to-back behind a vacant warehouse. This being New Year's Eve, few people were working, and the entire district seemed abandoned as Cubans prepared to celebrate the New Year and the revolution. Very carefully the men moved their awkward, delicate cargo into the maintenance truck. Manny waved good-bye as they pulled away, then continued on his journey to deliver their break-in tools and other gear to the boat to simplify their getaway in the morning.

The four men, now in official maintenance gear, proceeded with the warhead back to the entrance to the Martí monument on the Revolutionary Plaza. Orlando drove, as before, with Pete beside him and the others in the back with the tools and the shrouded warhead. At the security checkpoint, Orlando showed the truck registration and explained they were returning at the urgent request of the monument's chief of maintenance and the Central Committee's planning office for tomorrow's activities. They had a new replacement motor for the tower elevator.

Dutifully, one guard checked under the truck and the other clamored into the back. Joe and Johnny lifted the covering back from the warhead, and in the dim space, it seemed to the guard to look like what an elevator motor should look like. His commander ordered him down quickly, explaining that orders had come from tower maintenance that morning authorizing their access and making it a high priority. They were waved through and proceeded to the utility door at the back of the monument. Hours before, special security teams had swept the entire Plaza and searched every square inch of the tower monument. The ground floor Martí museum was now closed to the public and sealed shut. Double guards were now posted at all entrances. As the men unloaded the metal-crated "motor," the maintenance chief met them and escorted them past the guards. Once the device was positioned next to the existing motor, Orlando secured his battered tools from the truck.

While Orlando, Pete, and Johnny went to work on the old motor, Joe engaged the chief in a long discussion about the history and construction of the tower. Proud of his prize, the chief described it in detail like a tour guide. Outside, work was nearing completion on the large VIP stand and speakers' platform. Virtually every official of consequence in the Cuban government, as well as representatives and observers from most Latin American countries, would be there. Voices testing the complex sound system boomed across the vast Plaza. Clusters of crowd marshals dotted the space as they were given assignments. An atmosphere of intense energy and mounting excitement pervaded the entire area.

Inside, Orlando and his helpers were involved in an intense effort to make an old motor look like a new one. First, he reattached the "faulty" electrical connections he had loosened the previous day. Then he mopped up his rigged oil "leak." He added new engine oil and hydraulic fluids. Wire brushes dislodged decades of gunk. Grease-dissolving solvents were applied to remove residues, then special detergents polished the motor, its connections, belts, and hoses until all looked virtually brand-new. The task was simplified by the fact that the motor was housed in a dimly lit space. As the others completed this task, Orlando lowered the elevator carriage to the basement, then, triggering the ground-floor entrance doors to remain open, he gradually raised the elevator carriage until its roof was level with the floor.

Orlando signaled Joe through the outside door. Joe asked the chief if he could get his amigos something cold to drink. The chief set out for the Palace of the Revolution building a hundred yards away. The four men then gingerly lifted the warhead from its metal frame and removed the plastic shroud that had contained it for forty years. Sweating from stress and fear, they gently carried the device through the elevator doors and set it gently on the roof of the elevator carriage. Its weight and cylindrical base stabilized it for any rides up and down.

The men quickly put all their tools, rags, solvents, and brushes into the truck and lifted the metal frame into the truck bed and covered it with the plastic and the old blanket. Orlando started the elevator motor and ran the carriage up to ground level just as the chief returned. The chief passed around cold *cervezas* as a means of thanking the men for their special effort on his behalf on New Year's Eve. "*Año Nuevo*," he toasted, and they all drank. Orlando took the chief inside and activated the elevator motor. It looked and sounded absolutely new. To the dismay of the other Bravos, Orlando took the chief into the elevator, closed the door, and ran the carriage up to the top. They stood in shock until the carriage returned and the two men stepped off. Orlando had been careful to punch floor twenty-one, one short of the top observation level, and then return quickly.

As the chief walked the men to their truck, Orlando excused himself to return for a missing wrench. Once inside, he again ran the carriage down between floors, triggered the doors open, and looked at his watch. It was a few minutes past one in the afternoon. He found the timer, turned its outside dial until the arrow pointed at "23," turned the second dial's arrow to "timer," and then, crossing himself and momentarily closing his eyes, he threw the switch until its base was on red. He crossed himself again, then ran the elevator to the twenty-first floor and shut it off.

Outside he cautioned the chief not to let anyone use the elevator until the big shots wanted it after the ceremonies. Gesturing at the bulky covered object in the darkened truck enclosure, he said, "Don't worry. We'll get rid of this broken-down piece of junk and no one will ever know it was left in here much too long." To his repeated expressions of gratitude, they drove away.

Atop the Jose Martí monument, a two-kiloton Soviet nuclear warhead was armed. It would detonate at twelve noon on New Year's Day, 1999.

42 As darkness descended on Havana on New Year's Eve, 1998, the city was coming to life. Relatives in from the countryside and towns across Cuba expected a festive meal that night with their city cousins. Flats and houses would be even more crowded than usual. But space for sleeping would be less a problem than it might be otherwise. For many, sleep was the least important thing on their minds. Tomorrow was a double holiday; it was not only New Year's Day but also the fortieth anniversary of the revolution. It was also Friday. Thus, it was a long holiday weekend. Mundane field labor could be put aside for three full days. Tonight, the celebration would begin.

For a small group of Cubans, however, the holiday had become a nightmare from hell. The vortex of the nightmare was Lazaro Suarez's office and adjoining conference room on the fifth floor of the Ministry of the Interior situated across the street from the Plaza de la Revolución. These two rooms were the command post for the national search for six members of Bravo 99 and an aging Russian nuclear weapons expert called Dankevich. Reports from units of secret police, a network of intelligence sources, military intelligence units, local CDRs, all came to the multiple phones now manned in Suarez's two-room office suite. Tips and rumors were sifted, sorted, and assigned priorities for investigation. The confusion was compounded by the constant cackling and cracking of a series of two-way communications systems carried by various intelligence officers. Regularly, Suarez was called away to account to Colonel Nuñez and the minister for his continuing failure, and twice he had been called with his superior to the Palacio de la Revolución to report to *el Commandante* himself. Out his window even now he could see small clusters of people camping out on the Plaza, staking out choice locations close to the speakers' platform at the base of the José Martí monument now glistening in its cluster of surrounding floodlights like a giant missile awaiting its launch command.

And a dozen feet from its top, a clock had already ticked off more than eight hours of its twenty-three-hour life.

A mile or so away on the seawall along the Malecón very near the mouth of the Havana harbor a group of a dozen young people laughed, sang, and danced to the music of a cheap boom box placed on the wall. The boys wore T-shirts and jeans, the girls skintight pants and halter tops that left lean midriffs bare. Along the picturesque corniche, they were but one of thousands of such clusters, remarkable only for this fact: one of their number was burdened with a terrible secret. He had become a partner of a group of gangsters—possibly even terrorist gangsters.

Since late that morning when the old man who was the boss of the local CDR had shown him the pictures, Osvaldo Sanchez's thoughts had been troubled. Why else would the Cuban government have activated its entire national jungle-drum network to find his two "Mexican" partners, Juan and Jorge, and apparently several others? Who *were* these guys, and what had they done? The local vigilante didn't know. All he knew was that *los jefes grandes* considered it *muy importante*. Sitting glumly among his generation of *Habaneros y Habaneras*, vigorously shaking their booties, the only thing Osvaldo knew was that he was in a shitload of trouble. His choices were few. He could step up and admit he had illegally rented out his place to a bunch of Mafioso up to God knows what, in which case he got to donate his services to the state for the next couple of *zafras*, or he could keep his mouth shut and hope those phony "Mexican" bastards Juan and Jorge did their dirty deeds—probably dope or smuggling, or both— and disappeared. If he didn't fess up, and he was caught harboring those bad boys, then the very best he could hope for was that they would give him some rope and let him hang himself.

As Osvaldo applied his limited mental energies to this project through-out the evening, he could not know that he did not have all the time in the world, that, indeed, the clock of his fate was clicking down with de-mented insistence.

Down the corridor from Suarez's madhouse of an office, McLemore tried one last time to get Trinidad to take her mother and leave, even for just one day.

"Listen to me," he whispered urgently. His eyes were fierce. "Get out of here. Leave. Now. Go get your mother and get as far away as you can. Do you understand?"

She seemed at once moved and determined. "Do not demand this. I cannot. My mother will not go in any case. She is no coward. And she gave birth to no cowards." Her wide eyes blazed back at him. "We remain here in this city with our friends and our family."

He gripped her shoulders so tightly that it hurt her, as if he might physically remove her.

Her mouth tight, she whispered back. "I could not live with myself afterward—whatever happens. Don't *you* understand? Just because I have secret knowledge, I cannot use that to save myself." Then she moved forward until her face and body were almost touching his. "Even though I now love you and want to be with you, I cannot leave my city. My fate is here . . . and"—she touched his lips—"my fate I hope will always be with you."

Their command post was now overrun with caffeine and/or rum-fueled security agents. McLemore took her hand and they walked out of the Ministry. He wanted her to walk with him to Cerro to look for Prescott.

"I'm afraid the old boy may be sick—maybe a heart attack," he said, once they were out in the clear night. Tomorrow was to be a brilliant day, helping swell the crowd to historic proportions.

They walked hand in hand silently. Then she said, "I tried to get him to go for a routine examination at the hospital while you were gone. He wouldn't. He said children needed the attention more." Then she said, "I did buy him food, with the money you left. But I heard later that he gave it away to some people in the neighborhood who are even older than he is."

McLemore chuckled quietly, unsurprised. As they walked, people flocked past them, headed in the opposite direction, to the city center for the all-night celebration.

Trinidad said, "You are the one who must leave. You do not have a responsibility to stay."

McLemore put his arm around her waist. It was remarkable how well they fit together, he thought. "You sound like Ramsay now. We had the same conversation last night . . . rather, early this morning. You know me well enough by now to know how much I enjoy doing things I don't have to . . . and vice versa."

"Then you won't go?" she asked.

McLemore said, "No."

She snuggled closer to him as they entered the Cerro district. After a few blocks they came to Prescott's tiny flat. Its single window was dark. Its door, as usual, was unlocked. Nothing to lose. Prescott's guidepost for almost forty years. McLemore turned on the single pathetic light. No sign. No clue. There were a few battered books in Spanish. One was *Don Quixote*. It had been well thumbed. By the cot was the Bible, in Spanish, equally well read. McLemore glanced at the passage marked on the open page. Trinidad read, "I was naked and you clothed me. I was hungry and you fed me." She turned away.

They closed the door behind them. Out on the street, they stopped people passing by. Trinidad asked them if they had seen the old gringo. "Padre?" they asked. Not for a day or two. Not like him. He was usually around, helping out. They canvassed a dozen blocks in the surrounding area. The only clue came from an elderly man who knew him well and who had shared coffee with him, as usual, one, maybe two, days ago. He seemed healthy, the man said.

As they were leaving, the man shouted something in Spanish. Trinidad stopped, turned back, and asked him what he had said. She translated: "Probably looking for that old Russian that was out walking around that day. Said he was staying around here." The man circled a hand in the air.

McLemore said, "My God." They looked at each other in the dark. "He found Dankevich. Bravo caught him. They're holding him."

Trinidad put a hand on his arm. "Or they may have killed him."

McLemore said, "They're somewhere around here."

"Or they've taken off—escaped," she said. She questioned the old man. He knew nothing more.

McLemore said, "They haven't taken off. They haven't finished yet. They're still around here. Somewhere."

They discussed calling in the elite security forces, sealing off the Cerro district, breaking down doors.

She said, "It's a big district. It would take most of the night."

"They would hear the commotion and break out, one by one. Unless we got one of them . . . and made him talk . . . we wouldn't find the warhead." McLemore was suddenly aware of the irony of this reverse replay of his father's capture—in this very neighborhood. Then he added, "And if they haven't done so already, they'd kill Prescott on their way out the door." He thought a moment, then said, "If they let the old Russian go out for coffee, they wouldn't have let him go far. I have to believe Dankevich and the Bravos are hiding out somewhere near where we are."

They walked up and down street after street, looking in doorways and windows, looking for anything unusual—groups of men, clothes slightly different, suspicious or furtive behavior, any old man fitting the description Isakov had given of his father's old subordinate. Except for the higher-than-usual level of social energy, the humble streets and buildings all seemed the same. Doors were mainly open. People were chatting animatedly. Life was more outdoors than indoors. Few flats or houses were dark. A few blocks from where they had met the man who had last seen Prescott and the old Russian, they noted one particularly shabby building that showed no life, had only a dim internal light, and displayed the rare closed door. Trinidad seriously considered knocking on the door, then decided it might be an intrusion. Occupants probably gone to the celebration in the center.

The couple continued on their amateur detective rounds until well after midnight. Trinidad noted the address of the man who had seen Prescott and Dankevich and the general boundaries of this area of the Cerro district.

Inside the building the couple had noted, eight men were preparing for sleep, though some would never achieve it. For them, a week of hard floors, thin blankets, tedious meals, crowded conditions, mounting tension, and historic purpose made sleep impossible. Manny, Joe, Pete, and Johnny spent most of the evening playing poker. It occupied the time but did not substitute for fresh air, good food, space, or movement. In one corner Dankevich huddled under a blanket on the hard floor. He had said, and eaten, very little all evening. He responded to questions with single-syllable answers. Across the room his American opposite number periodically changed from lying on one side to lying on the other. The bones of his thin frame had rubbed his skin raw where they pressed against the bare floor. He had refused food also and now gave few signs of life. From time to time, Dankevich wondered if he were dead. The others seemed not to care. The men knew they must now be the subjects of an intense search. Their various disguises—Joe's and Pete's light hair darkened, different styles of beards and mustaches on five of them, Tony's mustache shaved off—had served for a number of days but would not be good for much longer. In any case, before the neighborhood awoke in the morning, they would clean out the place, load up the truck, and head out of town for the boat hidden in the Bahía de la Mulata cove while the rest of the city poured into the center for the celebration. If all went well, they would be out to sea and part of the way back to Cancún when the balloon went up. Their alibi? They had all been fishing for the holidays well off the Mexican coast. Hadn't heard anything. Didn't know anything.

It was becoming quickly apparent to the two old men, each in his own way, that they would be, at best, abandoned and, at worst, killed. Indeed, they had to be killed. Presuming they might survive the collateral blast of the warhead one and a half or two miles away, they could identify the culprits to whatever authority might survive. The only question was, Who or what would be the authority? Rather than trying to think this through, Prescott's mind was on more eternal things. For himself, Dankevich knew that the concussion of the explosion would undoubtedly bring the fragile roof of this hovel down on their heads. They would be crushed by the falling building. But careful terrorists, and these men had taken considerable care, would not take a chance on blast damage they could not fully appreciate.

Dankevich now considered himself to be a complete fool for falling for a crazy story about helping the Cubans repel an invasion so that he could have money to buy a dacha. This realization made him ashamed of himself. He considered it the most bitter irony that the instrument of his final humiliation was the son of the man who had humiliated him throughout his military career. While across the room Prescott continued to say his prayers for those he cared for, Dankevich was generating a scheme to get revenge on these murderers and to reclaim once again his own dignity.

At this same hour Osvaldo Sanchez's sometime friend, Ernesto, was looking at some pictures being shown to his group by a Cuban security police officer. "There is a reward," an officer said.

Ernesto remembered something Osvaldo had told him ten days ago when he moved into Ernesto's place. "I'll pay some rent. I am going to make some money. I'm renting my place in Cerro to some guys—they say they're Mexicans—who plan to run a black market electronics scam of some kind. They're paying me for my place as their headquarters and for an old truck I got for them."

Ernesto really didn't have room for Osvaldo, but he did have room for the ten dollars U.S. that Osvaldo promised each month the guys had his place. But Osvaldo was a punk and Ernesto was sick of him. Besides, Cuban security was offering ten thousand pesos. Ernesto made a fast decision. He would turn. He described Osvaldo——tall, skinny, chain-smoker, always after the girls—and he described the deal, so much of it as he knew.

"Where's Osvaldo?" the agents urgently demanded.

"My guess is, he's somewhere right here on the Malecón where we are," Ernesto told them. With a security officer on each side, Ernesto set off southward down the Malecón, looking for Osvaldo. It was a more complex task than it might seem. At one in the morning on New Year's Day, there were between ten and twenty thousand young Cubans engaged in an all-night party along the two-mile seawall.

While this manhunt was under way, McLemore and Trinidad were returning from their search of Cerro. The question was: Returning to where? McLemore assumed he would take Trinidad to her flat. But she kept guiding him into turns in the more easterly direction of his hotel. As before, they walked arm in arm and talked little.

At one point she stopped and pressed herself against him. "I would not change my life," she said.

Holding her, he said, "Nor would I . . . now."

When they arrived at the Santa Isabel she walked with him through the small lobby past the night clerk's desk, out into the darkened outdoor courtyard where the two beautiful birds remained, songless, in their cage, and up the stairs to his room. They said nothing to each other when they entered. He knew she was violating every command given by her superiors against unauthorized intimacy with a foreigner, especially with a Yanqui. But now, what did it matter? Still silent, they both undressed, lay down in the bed, entered each other's arms, and quickly fell asleep.

Shortly after 5 A.M., McLemore's phone rang. Lazaro Suarez quietly said, "Please come to my office as quickly as you can. If you know how to find Trinidad, bring her also. Quickly." McLemore, still half-asleep, understood that Suarez knew where Trinidad was. "If you can find Señor Ramsay, get him here as well." That was all. Trinidad was immediately awake. They dressed, ran outside, commandeered the passing car of a drunken reveler, and showing her security identification, Trinidad ordered the driver to the Interior Ministry as quickly as he could go. Terrified, the driver careened across predawn Havana like a maniac.

They raced up the steps of the building and then, unwilling to wait for the somnambulant elevator, up the interior stairway to Suarez's fifth-floor office. It was a mess. Cigarettes spilled out of ashtrays and onto the floor. Coffee cups and bottles were all over the place. It was still jammed, but now with sleepwalking security officials victimized by fatigue. The only new addition was a rumpled young man slouched in a chair at the far end of the table in the conference room. He looked as if he might have been pounded with a telephone directory for an hour or so. As he reached for a phone to call Ramsay, McLemore smiled and stifled a laugh. Trinidad looked as if she had just got out of bed. As she looked at him, he made a hair-smoothing gesture. She blushed and bolted for the ladies' room.

Suarez was returning momentarily from yet another briefing of el Commandante across the Plaza at the Palacio de la Revolución. McLemore dialed the number on a crumpled piece of paper Ramsay had given him. It was his home number. After two rings, Ramsay answered. He sounded wide awake. Probably years of spook training, McLemore thought. McLemore said, "Suarez wants you down here at the Interior Ministry as fast as you can. Didn't say why, but it must be important or he wouldn't have the enemy in the holy of holies. Make it fast. Fifth floor. You'll be cleared in." He hadn't identified himself. He hadn't had to.

Within fifteen minutes, Suarez was back. He met Ramsay at the door and escorted him up. The three men sat in Suarez's private office with the door closed. "An hour ago," Suarez began, "our people brought in the young man in the next room who had been identified during the night by a friend of his who claims this young man, one Osvaldo Sanchez, rented out his small building in the Cerro district nearby to two men he met several weeks ago. The men claimed to be Mexican, spoke fluent Spanish, and discussed with Sanchez here the possibility of organizing a black market network for small electronic devices—radios and so forth. Given the timing of things, there is a chance these men may be part of the so-called Bravo operation. So far, we have not persuaded young Señor Sanchez to talk to us."

McLemore said, "Trinidad and I went down to Cerro last night looking for my friend Father Prescott. He has disappeared. One of his neighbors claims that he and Prescott encountered an elderly Russian man two days ago. Because I had told Prescott about our 'problem,' at least in general terms, I think he figured out the Russian was part of the plot, followed him, and Bravo captured or killed him. The main thing is, the Russian was wandering around the Cerro district. If this guy—Sanchez—is from Cerro, then I think we're in business." He looked at his watch—6 A.M.

Ramsay said, "Let's go talk to him."

In the next room, the young man held his head and asked for coffee. One of his guards cuffed him hard in the side of the head, almost knocking him out of his chair. Suarez called him down and ordered the guards out of the room. The three men pulled up chairs surrounding the young man.

Suarez said, "We want only two things. We want you to identify these pictures. Are these the men you dealt with? And, if so, we need to know the address of your house." The young man shook his head, and Suarez said, "I promise you, we will not hurt you if you tell us. We will not send you to jail."

The young man began to cry. He shook with sobs. Ramsay waved the others away and pointed to himself. As the other two retreated into Suarez's office, McLemore heard him speaking in Spanish and very softly. He was amazed at both facts. They listened inside Suarez's door as he whispered a translation. "He is saying, 'I am an important man from the United States. These men we want are big criminals in the United States. My government will be very happy if you help us catch them. In fact, if you help us catch them, my government will invite you to be our guest in the United States." Ramsay moved his chair closer and whispered into the young man's ear. The young man quit crying. He looked up, amazed.

326 ■ John Blackthorn

They heard him ask, *"Es verdad?"* Ramsay smiled and said, *"Es verdad!"* Then the young man smiled. Ramsay stuck out his hand and the young man gingerly shook hands with him. *"Es verdad?"* the young man asked again. Ramsay nodded his red face up and down.

Ramsay motioned for the others to come in. "Osvaldo wants to help us," he said.

Osvaldo looked at Suarez and said, pointing at the pictures, "These two, 'Juan' and 'Jorge,' are the ones I let use my house. I found a truck for them. They said they were salesmen from Mexico. I am sorry. I know I should not have."

With great intensity Suarez said, "Tell us your address. Where is your house?"

Osvaldo gave a street and number. Suarez in the lead, the three men burst out of the room leaving the stunned Osvaldo alone. Suarez had two black cars waiting outside the main entrance of the Ministry. He spoke to one of the security officers milling around the entrance, ordering reinforcements to seal off a two-block area around the address Osvaldo had given them. The three men loaded into the first car, and leaving instructions for Trinidad to follow in the second car but wait well back, Suarez ordered him to an intersection a block away from Osvaldo's house. Without lights or siren, the car sped southeastward toward the Cerro district as the sun began to light the sky. Suarez took the driver's pistol and gave it to McLemore, and he got one from the glove compartment for Ramsay.

Moments before, five members of the Bravo team had loaded and then piled into the truck, Pete in front with an assault weapon, Manny behind the wheel, and Joe, Johnny, and Orlando in the back with the remaining gear and the rest of the weapons, especially the other assault rifle and the two powerful shotguns, at the ready. All the men had their nine-millimeter pistols. Tony was the last to leave. He knelt down beside the slumped Dankevich who said, "Before you kill me, please take letter . . . for my daughter." He handed Tony a crudely folded piece of paper on which he had been writing within the last hour. "Please, please, promise you will mail to her. Here"—he gestured to some writing on the back—"here is her place of living." Tony put the paper in a shirt pocket. He said, "Mr. Dankevich, I'm sorry for all this. I didn't want this to turn out this way. You understand? We shouldn't be doing things this way." He looked over his shoulder at the thick truck exhaust boiling up outside the back door.

He said, "Lay down now, you know, like you're dead. Manny told me to kill you. But I can't. So pretend. Okay?" He started to leave, then he turned back. "I think that old man is already dead. I'm sorry. I hope you don't get killed when that whizbang goes off." Then he was out the door, and the truck could be heard pulling away.

The room was silent for an eternity. Dankevich was listening to see if the truck might return. He assumed, due to Prescott's silence, that the old fellow had died during the night. He had not been fed or given water for almost two days. Dankevich hated the men who had tricked him, men who would callously let an old man die like a dog, and a priestly man at that. He had never felt so ashamed in his life. He had only one hope left to redeem his soul.

Suarez looked at Ramsay in the backseat and asked, "In case it is a trick I might use in future investigations, do you mind if I ask what you said to that young man after we left the room?"

Ramsay laughed. "That was the easy part. I told him if he cooperated, we'd give him a trip to Disney World."

The car pulled to a halt at the intersection, remaining out of sight behind a house. The three men got out quietly. Suarez ordered Ramsay to go behind the building to cut off anyone escaping out the back. He and McLemore kept close to the buildings adjoining Osvaldo's house as they moved toward its door. The place was silent and dark. McLemore crouched down and slid past the door. They were positioned on each side. On Suarez's signal, they both jumped in front of the door and gave a powerful kick. The flimsy door opened with a crash. Crouched down on each side of the open door, the men cautiously peered in. The flat was empty.

They stood up and walked in. The men had fled. A quick glance suggested they had left only two piles of blankets and rags in the corners. Then, as light began to enter the room, one of the piles of cloth groaned. Just then Ramsay kicked in the back door, pistol leveled. The men raced to the groaning pile of rags and found a half-dead old Russian paralyzed with fright. Quickly they cut his bonds, and the old man gestured to the other pile. McLemore knelt down and found the frame of his friend Prescott. There was no movement. Behind them the front door filled with the faces and bodies of Cuban security forces. Trinidad pushed through them. She knelt down with McLemore. She put her head to the old priest's bony chest. "He's still alive," she said, "barely." She shouted in Spanish. Within minutes, an ambulance pulled up in front, and McLemore carefully carried the old warrior for justice outside. At McLemore's request, Trinidad went with him. Once he was on the stretcher in the ambulance, it sped off for the nearest hospital.

"Maybe thirty . . . forty minutes ago," Dankevich was saying as he sipped some water. "They have boat somewhere on coast. Six of them. Have truck, old truck." Which coast? they asked. "Not certain for me, which coast. They come from Mexico, as I know." Suarez stood up and issued a series of orders to try to look for any old trucks leaving the city, or already out of the city, probably headed into Pinar del Río by now. Security officers dashed away. The men helped old Dankevich to his feet. He groaned in agony. His old bones and muscles were too cramped for him to walk, so Ramsay and McLemore, one on each side, helped him outside. He sat in a chair they brought out. All the while, they asked him questions, anything that might lead to the location of the warhead. Ramsay said, "Colonel Dankevich." He spoke very slowly. "When is the warhead going to go off?"

"It is set by timer for twelve hours . . . noon."

Automatically, everyone checked watches. Minutes over four hours.

Ramsay said, "Colonel Dankevich, what does it look like?" Again he spoke very slowly, giving the old man a chance to understand. "The warhead. The Luna." He gestured height and width with his hands. "How big? What color?"

Dankevich wearily leaned forward from the chair, his ancient bones almost audibly creaking. "Is like . . ." He held his hand just over three feet off the ground. "And like . . ." He held his hands between two and three feet apart. He took pen and paper from Suarez's shirt pocket. He wrote a number in large, slightly wavy figures: 150. "This many kilos." About 300 pounds.

McLemore, Suarez, and Ramsay were suddenly shocked to see the old Russian smile mysteriously. Then he said, "You must look for these men— coming back. I think they come back." He nodded his head up and down. "I give them message. They come back."

43 Manny kept one eye on the rearview mirror. Pete watched the opposite one. If they were challenged, it would be in the next thirty minutes. The truck coughed and chugged down the old road through the Pinar del Río province. The trip would take another ninety minutes, and the sun was well up on New Year's Day. Manny remembered and shouted to those in the back, "Happpppppy New Year!" The men responded less vigorously. They would be at the boat by ten. It would take only a few minutes to load up and cast off. They would be at sea close to two hours when the whizbang went off. They would have a great vantage point to see the fireball.

Crammed between Manny and Pete in the front seat, Tony muttered a wry chuckle. "I'll tell you something, that old Dinkowitz is . . . was . . . really something." Manny looked at him quizzically. "You know, before I . . . you know . . . anyway, he gave me a letter for his daughter. It was really tough. He made me promise I would mail it."

"You sure as hell can't mail it, Tony," Manny said. "May have some names in it. She'll set off a howl about her old man. Get everybody after us. Can't do it."

Tony pulled the crumpled letter from his shirt pocket. Manny said, "You can't read it. It'll be in Russian anyway."

Tony unfolded the paper and studied it. "The hell it is. It's in some kind of English, I think. It's hard to read." Then he said excitedly, "Hey, here's my name. Hey, it's a letter to me."

Manny said, "What? A letter . . . to you? That makes no sense. What does it say?"

Tony read, " 'Toni. My fren. For water an tings, spasebo.' Must be thanks or something like that. 'Sory. I play trik for you. You nize for me. Sory.' What trick?" Tony said. " 'Switz on Luna ozzer way. Rong way. Som trik for yu. Sory. Switz ozzer way. Dasvedanya. By-by. DDD.' "

Manny slammed on the brakes so hard the men in the back tumbled forward into a cursing, shouting heap. Pete's head banged the windshield.

"What? What is he saying? What in the goddamn hell is he saying?" Manny was screaming even before the truck came to a halt.

Tony was tempted to laugh at the irony. The old man had tricked them after all. He had gotten even with them. What a joke. A million Cubans just got a reprieve. Three heads stuck through the curtain. "He told us to throw the switch the wrong way. He shut the timer off. Not on. He had us shut the timer OFF!" Tony started laughing. "He made us shut the timer OFF!"

The men were now out of the truck, Tony doubled up with apoplectic laughter. Manny got his pistol out and Tony shut up, afraid he might be killed. Through his furious rage, Manny became a madman. Through gritted teeth, he hissed, "Get back in the truck. All of you back in the truck." The men looked at him dumbfounded. "Get back in the truck. We're going back. We're throwing the switch back. Nothing has changed." He looked at his watch. "Nine-fifteen. We'll be back at the Plaza by . . . ten o'clock, ten-fifteen. Nothing has changed. Back in the truck."

Tony said, "Manny . . . ? We got to get out of here. We can't go back. It's crazy."

Manny waved his pistol. "Everybody back in the truck. We'll go to the shops, trade trucks, put on the coveralls. Just checking the elevator. We throw the switch. Back in the truck and we're down here by zero hour. Nothing has changed. Let's go."

Tony said, "Hey, I gotta take a leak." He hurried a dozen yards into the trees, away from traffic moving into town. The men waited.

"Goddammit," Manny shrieked. He ran into the trees. The men heard shots fired. Manny came running out. "The coward. Back in the truck. All of you. The goddamn coward took off. Let the Cubans get him. I hope they roast his cowardly ass—very slowly. Back in the truck." He waved the pistol. Wide-eyed, the men obeyed. Except for Orlando, who shook his head no. Manny said, "Orlando, get your flabby ass in here beside me where I can watch you. We need you for the elevator. You are not taking off after that coward Tony. Get in here." Manny kept the gun in his lap, ready to shoot. Orlando got in the cab between Manny and Pete. Joe and Johnny got in the back. Manny spun the old truck around in the roadside gravel, barely missing two old buses transporting people into the celebration, then roared back toward Havana at as great a speed as the worn engine could make.

Back at the Interior Ministry, Suarez had hot food and coffee brought to Dankevich as they continued to grill him. He gave detailed descriptions of each of the men, the clothes they wore, eye colors, skin tones, the beards, mustaches, shapes, sizes, most of all the personalities. "Manny is boss," he said with conviction. "Big man"—he widened his hands for the shoulders—"black eyes, also black hair." He waved his hand gently over his head. "Now, also black"—pointing at his lip—"how do you say?"

"Mustache?" Ramsay asked.

"Da, da. I think *moos-toche*. Then, *very* big one. Peet. *Very* big. Also, very big lifting." He flexed his thin old arms in a parody of a muscle man. "One is engineer . . . like me," he said proudly, pointing to himself. "He know wiring things. All electric things. Switching. Timing. He is Zho. Very smart one. One is also Zhanny. For truck things." He gripped an imaginary wheel and drove an imaginary truck until the men around him nodded understanding. Several were making notes. "My friend, Tony. He has . . . how you say? . . ." He rubbed his face all over.

Suarez said, "Beard? Hair on face?"

Dankevich nodded happily. "Nicest one is Tony. My friend, Tony. He give me *café*. He is helping Manny." He counted on his fingers to five, then after a moment said, "Ah, also one is Ahr-land-ah." He held his hand at Suarez height, but made a round stomach motion and blew out his cheeks. A chubby one, then.

"What did he do?" Ramsay asked urgently. "The round one"—patting his ample middle—"what was he doing?"

Dankevich's old face wrinkled. He was not sure. "They took him to . . ." He knew it was a lift, but he could not remember the word the men had used. Something about "elevator." He could not remember the word. He tried to do a floor-to-ceiling motion with his hand.

"Stairs? Ladder?" McLemore asked, making climbing motions.

Dankevich shook his head no. He stood up from the chair and walked to the far wall. He mimed pushing an imaginary button on the wall. He waited. Then he showed with his hands a door parting. Then the old man pretended to step forward. He turned around, pressed another imaginary button and showed with his hands a door coming together. All the men in the room stared at him transfixed. Then he pointed up.

"Elevator!" they shouted in unison.

McLemore grabbed Ramsay's sleeve. "They've put the goddamn thing on an elevator!"

Suarez issued orders like a fiend. Within minutes, teams of security patrols were inspecting elevators all over the city, starting in buildings surrounding the Plaza, then working outward in concentric circles. Hundreds if not thousands of people were involved. They looked in, under, and above. Everywhere around an elevator they could think of. They had been given Dankevich's description of the Luna warhead. So they had an idea what they were looking for. Suarez, Ramsay, and McLemore looked at their watches every three minutes.

Traffic coming into the city was thick. Buses and trucks loaded to the brim and overflowing. Caught in this moving tide, the Bravo truck crept forward at barely fifteen miles an hour. Manny stared furiously at his watch. Quarter past ten. He cursed and beat the steering wheel. To the other members of Bravo, he had now become a complete madman. The others wanted out but were afraid he would shoot them. It would be at least ten-thirty before they got to the maintenance shops and changed clothes and trucks. It would be close to eleven before they got to the Plaza. Manny pulled around a line of vehicles, his horn squawking. Curses went back and forth from vehicle to vehicle. He was drawing attention. Not what they needed right now.

It was minutes after ten-thirty when they came to the shops in the warehouse district. Their truck was steaming, overheated, and possibly out of water and oil. If they tried to take it back down to the boat, it would throw rods and burn up. They would keep the maintenance truck. To their shock, the shop for elevator maintenance was alive with activity. It was a holiday! What in God's name was this? Men were rushing in, grabbing coveralls, and piling into trucks that quickly sped off. The five Bravos, two looking through the forward curtain from the truck bed, stared from half a block away with amazement. Manny said, "Let's go. Whatever's going on, we're part of it. We got no time to waste."

Dutifully, while Manny ditched the truck next to one of the shops, the men piled out and headed for the shed with the coveralls. As before, Joe went directly to one of the remaining trucks, popped the hood, did the wires, and got it running. They all jumped in the truck and headed out, pulling on the dirty coveralls as they went. As they paused beside their abandoned vehicle, Pete jumped in and tossed the assault rifles and shotguns to the others. They each stuck their nines in their coverall pockets. When they bolted from the truck pool, several men from the shop came running and saw them transfer their weapons. They then dashed back and called Havana police.

Manny headed for the Plaza as fast as he could. Traffic was terrible and getting worse. It would be impossible to get through the mob to the main entrance to the tower. They would have to park and walk at least two blocks. Maybe more. The long guns would be a problem. On orders from Manny, the men wrapped the rifles and shotguns, now fully loaded, in rags thrown in the back of the truck. Before abandoning the old truck at the shops, they had all filled their pockets with extra ammunition. The streets were full of people. Despite repeated horn honking, no one paid attention. Within one more block they would have to leave the truck and walk. They were still almost three blocks away. Manny looked at his watch. It was almost eleven. They had to hurry—in the tower, throw the switch, and out—unless they wanted to go up as part of the general dust.

As they struggled from the truck, trying to keep the wrapped weapons from showing, and into the surging mob they could hear great cheers from the hundreds of thousands of people already on the Plaza. They could see an endless tide of humanity covering the Plaza's sloping hillsides and cresting forward to join and swell it. Almost directly across the Plaza from them they could see the detested outline of the features of Che Guevara decorating the Ministry of the Interior and overlooking the entire scene.

Somewhere near the top of Che's signature beret, Lazaro Suarez, Red Ramsay, and McLemore looked back at them, wondering whether in the next hour this scene and these million souls would even exist.

There had been no warhead found in any elevator within a widening circumference of the Plaza. Repeatedly they had demanded that old Dankevich think of any other phrase, any clue, any word the men had said that might identify the elevator. They had not overlooked the tallest and most obvious elevator in town, that in the Martí tower directly in front of them. But they had been reassured, in response to repeated inquiries, that the tower had been sealed off for days, with armed guards round the clock outside. In fact, less than an hour earlier, the chief of maintenance of the tower had heard the discussion among the security officers near the reviewing stand about the citywide search for a bomb on an elevator. He had been fortunate enough to get a new motor for his elevator before the big shots decided to use it. What a catastrophe that might have been otherwise. He made a note to call the repair guys to say thanks next week, when things quieted down. He went inside to look at the motor one more time before *el Jefe* and all the dignitaries showed up. It was eleven-fifteen. They would come over from the Palacio in another fifteen minutes for sure. Then there would be some noise and some excitement.

The motor looked beautiful. Shiny. New. Hummed like a sewing machine. He wiped it with a pocket cloth. What a beauty. Squatting down, he flicked a tiny spot of grease from the manufacturer's plate. New machine. Take *el Jefe* and his guests up and down for another twenty years. That was enough for him. He retired in three. Squinting, he looked at the date. Let's see how recently this baby was made . . . 1979. Same as the old one. But the guy who replaced it had said this one came in just a few years ago. The chief scratched his head, then sat down on the floor, his back to the motor. If they brought in a new motor and they hadn't replaced the old one, where was the new motor? If they hadn't replaced the old motor, why had they pretended that they had? He suddenly had a chill. Maybe those guys weren't from city maintenance. Maybe that wasn't a new motor they brought in. Had he actually seen it? No.

He whispered, *"Madre de Dios."*

He walked outside and ran into an important-looking man with a pin on his shirt collar and a two-way radio. He started to say something to him when a huge roar began at the front of the Plaza near them and swept backward like a concussion. The big shots were coming down—Fidel in the lead. The man shook his head and started to walk away. The chief ran after him and shouted. The man couldn't hear. He shouted again. The man finally heard him say, ". . . bomb . . ." He stopped, turned, and made him shout in his ear once more. "Get the bomb squad. I think what you're looking for is in my tower."

He turned back to the utility entrance to the tower and saw five men wearing the familiar maintenance coveralls and carrying wrapped-up tools thirty feet away. He suddenly recognized one of them as the elevator motor man. He dashed for the open utility door. But the larger of the men beat him by a foot and shoved him inside as the others followed.

Across the Plaza, Suarez's phone rang. He couldn't hear. The noise immediately below him ricocheted off the Ministry building like thunderous waves. He shouted, "What?" He listened. Then he hung up the phone. He turned to Ramsay and McLemore and said, "We've found the warhead." He pointed out the window. "It's over there, in the Martí tower."

44 As Suarez, Ramsay, and McLemore dashed down the steps of the Interior Ministry, Suarez ordered half a dozen heavily armed security guards to follow. In the 350 yards from the Ministry door to the tower were a quarter of a million people as tightly packed as they could be and surging forward to see their leaders. Suarez swiftly calculated that surging straight ahead required half an hour. He motioned left and, with three guards blocking in front, they started a long, looping end run around the bulk of the crowd. If they were lucky, they could get to the tower in ten to fifteen minutes. As they alternated dashing and pushing, Suarez yelled into a two-way radio he had grabbed on the way out the door, "Seal off the tower! Seal off the tower! Don't let anyone in! Do not let anyone in!" In the deafening noise, he could not tell if his order had been received.

Inside the tower, Pete had the maintenance chief against the wall with a gun at his head. Orlando activated the elevator motor. Manny stood by with an assault rifle in one hand and his pistol in the other. Joe and Johnny each had the pump shotguns and stood guard on either side of the door. Against the deafening noise outside the door, Johnny shouted to Orlando to be careful, that Dankevich might have secretly wired some other fail-safe switches to the warhead. Orlando lowered the elevator carriage very slowly, praying that the warhead had not become unstable in the last twenty-four hours. Above the elevator door, the floor numbers clicked down with exquisite lethargy. To fifteen, then to twelve, then to nine, then to six. Orlando slowed it down even more as it approached the ground floor. Seconds passed between floors.

Outside, Suarez led the others crashing through the crowd almost to the halfway point round the perimeter. He looked at his watch. It was 11:45. They plunged on, now knocking protesting Cubans to the ground in their rush. Ramsay was now in the lead, imposing his bulky frame with a vengeance against the mass of humanity.

*　　*　　*

The elevator came to the ground floor. Slowly Orlando lowered it to the basement. He triggered open the elevator doors, then gradually brought the roof of the carriage back up to ground level. The men peered in. There it sat. Manny looked at his watch. "For God's sake, Orlando. Reverse the switch, and let's get out of here!" he shouted. They had only fifteen minutes to escape the radius of the blast. They all sweated profusely. Orlando very carefully reached for the switch. The timer clock showed virtually no space between the sweep hand and zero. Just as he started to throw the switch, there was a crash against the door outside. Men were shouting and hitting the door with metal objects.

They were gun butts. Suarez, Ramsay, McLemore, and the Cuban guards had just arrived and were banging for the maintenance chief to let them in. A few yards away, dignitaries were being introduced to deafening roars from the crowd. The crowd noise blocked out the banging as it continued and intensified. Suddenly it stopped.

"Get ready," Manny shouted, "the fuckers are coming in!"

A hail of gunfire ripped the door lock away and instantaneously feet kicked the metal door inward. Joe let loose with a shotgun blast, sawing a guard in two at the waist. They heard shouts. "They're already in there! They're in there!" As Johnny stepped forward to kick the door shut, Ramsay dropped him with a single pistol shot.

Pete shouted, "Watch out for grenades!" as he shot the maintenance chief in the head and stooped to pick up Johnny's shotgun.

The door swung inward again and Manny fired burst after burst from the assault rifle. One of the Cuban guards put the barrel of an AK-47 around the door frame and swept the maintenance room. The Bravo team hit the floor, but not before a single round found poor Orlando's forehead. He slumped forward over the warhead. Manny fired back, even while wondering whether Orlando threw the switch. It was 11:55. Leave the switch alone, he thought. If we can get out of here and into this crowd, we'll still be alive. We'll have another chance. Fuck this bomb. Joe was fumbling on the floor for the other assault rifle that Orlando had carried in when Ramsay looked around the doorway and shot him dead.

Now the Cuban guards were pouring fire into the partially opened doorway. Pete started to the other side of the doorway, firing the pump shotgun as he went and, screaming, was cut down like a tree. Manny fired the assault rifle until he ran out of ammunition. He fired two shots from the nine through the doorway, then made a dash for the double glass doors across the ground-floor museum lobby.

Thinking them all dead, McLemore stepped through the shattered doorway and saw the fleeing figure. Prescott will not approve, he thought, as he raised his pistol and put a single bullet through the man's spine and out through his heart.

Ramsay almost knocked him down as he leaped for the warhead. With one hand he tossed Orlando's body out of the way. He saw the timer on zero, the second dial on "timer," and threw the switch, as Dankevich had instructed, into the black.

Outside, the crowd that—except for the terrified few close by—had totally drowned out the furious gun battle, let out a thunderous roar as *el Commandante*, the man who brought the revolution to Havana exactly forty years ago, was introduced.

Ramsay said something to McLemore and Suarez. They couldn't hear a thing. He shouted again, and then a third time. They both heard him say, "I guess this means I have to take Dankevich to Disney World, too."

EPILOGUE

January 1999

Father John Prescott was released from the hospital—*el Commandante's* own hospital, as it turned out—at the end of the first full week in January. Given his ordeal and his age, he was surprisingly spry, and he was very eager to return to his neighborhood. He had preliminary government approval to turn Osvaldo's shabby flat into a neighborhood clinic, and he wanted to get on with it.

Despite the revolution's success at making Cuban medical care among the best in Latin America, the four-decade trade embargo had seriously eroded Cuban access to modern medicine and equipment. Because there were some medicines the old priest needed that the Cubans did not have, McLemore called in his friend Sam Ramsay who, with his government, was more than happy to help. The required medication had been on the next flight from Montréal to Havana.

Prescott had an opportunity to thank Ramsay personally when McLemore and Trinidad took him to dinner at Julia's *paladar* on the night of his release. McLemore's helper Carlos made sure Julia understood the importance of her guest, the old priest who had helped save the city. Julia turned all three of her tables over to the party. Trinidad brought her mother. Carlos brought his parents. Suarez and his timid, ailing wife came. Suarez's boss Colonel Nuñez was a casualty, in more ways than one, of the shoot-out at the tower ten days before. Hearing the shooting from his coveted position on the VIP platform where he had assigned himself to protect *el Commandante*, Nuñez had shattered his leg badly trying to jump from the stand and had subsequently been retired. In recognition of his role in the tower incident, minimized in the Cuban press as the apprehension of some foreign troublemakers, Suarez's promotion to the position of deputy director of the State Security Department had thereafter been quickly approved.

Ramsay excused himself from attending the dinner on the grounds of pressing business. McLemore understood the awkwardness of his presence at such an occasion. Wanting to meet the famous priest, however, Ramsay welcomed the alternative invitation to stop by, as if by chance, early in the evening for a *mojito*—or two.

Ramsay worked the room like a gregarious frat president, then pulled up a chair close to the old priest. Prescott said, "Your friend, Mr. Mc-Lemore, claims that you are not such a bad fellow, just in a . . . an unusual . . . line of work. But I thank you for the medicine. It probably saved my life."

"Not at all, Father . . . sorry . . . Mr. Prescott," Ramsay said. "Mac's not a bad fellow himself. He just needs to figure out what he wants to do when he grows up. By the way, I spoke to some important friends of mine in Washington. They wanted me to give you this." He handed Prescott an official-looking envelope. Prescott opened the envelope. It was a new U.S. passport. Ramsay shook hands with Prescott and said, "Welcome home."

"Thanks, Mr. Ramsay," Prescott said. "I don't quite know what to say. I guess I am home. I guess this is where God has wanted me to be all this time. If you and your friends don't mind, I may use this to go see my sister in Salinas one more time. She is all the family I have up there now, and she is getting well up in years. But the rest of my family is here. I'll come back and I'll try to do my best to lend a hand down here."

Ramsay shook hands all around and stood to go. Prescott took his arm and asked him to lean down. "I have one more favor to ask. Please tell your folks in Washington to do what they can to make friends with these people again. They are decent and good people. And you can begin by sending some of that medicine you got for me down here for these children. They need it and they deserve it."

Ramsay patted his hand and said, "I'll see what I can do. And," he said, looking at McLemore, "I mean it."

Several evenings later, Trinidad and McLemore drove one of the Ministry's black cars to Cerro and collected Father Prescott at his tiny flat. He had a small, wrapped package that he asked be put in the trunk of the car. They drove past the docks of south *Habana vieja,* farther south around the harbor through the colorful independent community of Regla, whose point projected northward into the harbor, up the road winding above the tiny harborside village of Casablanca, directly across the harbor from the docks of the old city, through whose precincts still ran the electric railway built many decades before by the Hershey chocolate concern, and then on through the suburban town of Cojímar some ten kilometers to the east of Havana.

Trinidad drove, and McLemore sat in the back, giving the front seat to Prescott with his long, storklike legs. McLemore watched Trinidad's dark brown hair sway back and forth across her shoulders as she occasionally turned to converse with the old man in Spanish. He sighed. It was clear he was going to have to learn the language, and he had barely slipped past the language exams for his doctorate. But, he smiled to himself happily, this time he would have a much more provocative teacher, and she knew some very private beaches for his lessons. From time to time, Trinidad looked back at him, her wide smile flashing and her deep brown eyes warm. For the first time since they had met four months before, she looked relaxed and happy. He marveled at her transformation from stern escort of September to passionate beloved of January. He supposed that he himself had changed during a period that now seemed to encompass a lifetime. He had found a real purpose for the first time in his life. Given the extraordinary events over the past few weeks, centered upon the entombed Lunas, he should have little trouble finding a publisher for that dramatic history, the last chapter of an even greater drama almost exactly four decades before. He would stay in Cuba to write the book. If necessary, he was sure Ramsay and Mr. Worthy could help with that. The project should take at least six months, probably a year if he was lucky. And by then, who knows, maybe some sanity would return between his country and Cuba. In any case, he was now on his way to negotiate the final provision of his separate peace.

Shortly after the revolution, the government had set up a small secret prison east of Cojímar for high-level *batistianas* and, thereafter, during the missile crisis, had used the facility for suspected spies and agents of foreign powers. Thus it was here Jack McLemore had been taken over thirty-six years before, after his capture in John Prescott's flat. Trinidad had checked Ministry records, including Colonel Nuñez's private files, and found that after several days of interrogation, McLemore's father had been killed and buried in a small, unmarked plot outside the prison courtyard on a bluff overlooking the ocean. Since those times, the prison had been abandoned, and ironically, its facilities were used now as a neighborhood school.

Using the old documents Trinidad brought with her, the three people walked almost a hundred yards east of the former prison to an area covered with wildflowers and natural foliage. This, she pointed out, had to be the place. Prescott unwrapped the parcel he had brought with him. It was a small cross made of native wood. One of his old friends, a woodcarver, had etched into its crosspiece: *John McLemore*, and under that, *1924–1962*.

McLemore went back to the car and got a tire iron with a chiseled end. With it he dug a small hole in the loose earth near a particularly beautiful tall flower. Prescott handed him the cross, and he pressed it firmly into the ground. On his knees, McLemore pressed earth around the base of the cross. With Trinidad's help, he piled small stones around the cross to help hold it, and then he placed next to it a small cluster of fresh flowers Trinidad had brought with her. Finished, he started to rise, but then saw that Prescott had, with considerable effort, joined him.

The old priest was silent for a moment, then he said, "Let's have an end to war. Let's find a way to respect each other. Let's find what's good, and not what's bad, about our neighbors. Let's find a politics that's not about power but that's about human life. Most of all, let's have a kindly society, one that lets people be free and one that helps people—old people, young people, hurt people—who can't help themselves. Let's worship our children . . . God's greatest blessing." Then, after a silent moment, he said, "God bless Jack McLemore. God bless us all."

McLemore and Trinidad helped Prescott to his feet, and one on each side of him, the three people started back to write an uncertain new chapter.

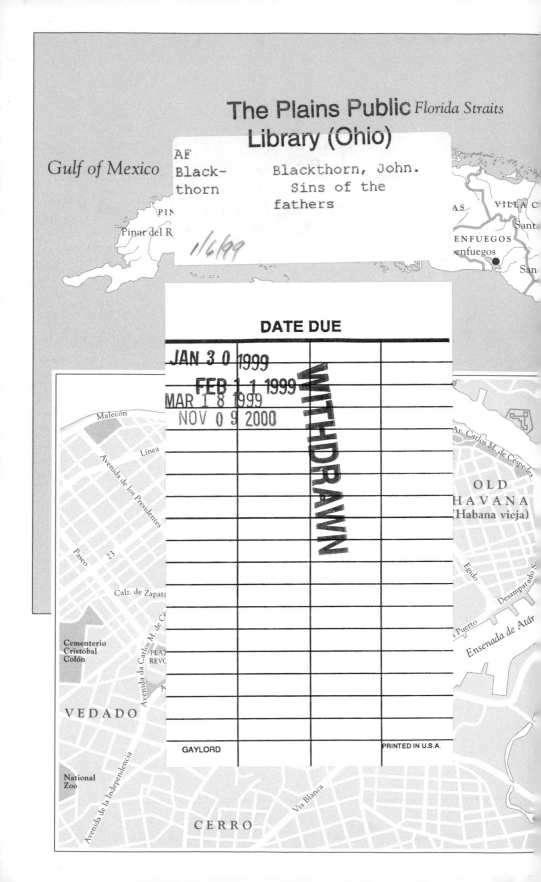